SERPENT'S BLOOD

BOOK SIX OF THE SNAKESBLOOD SAGA

BETH ALVAREZ

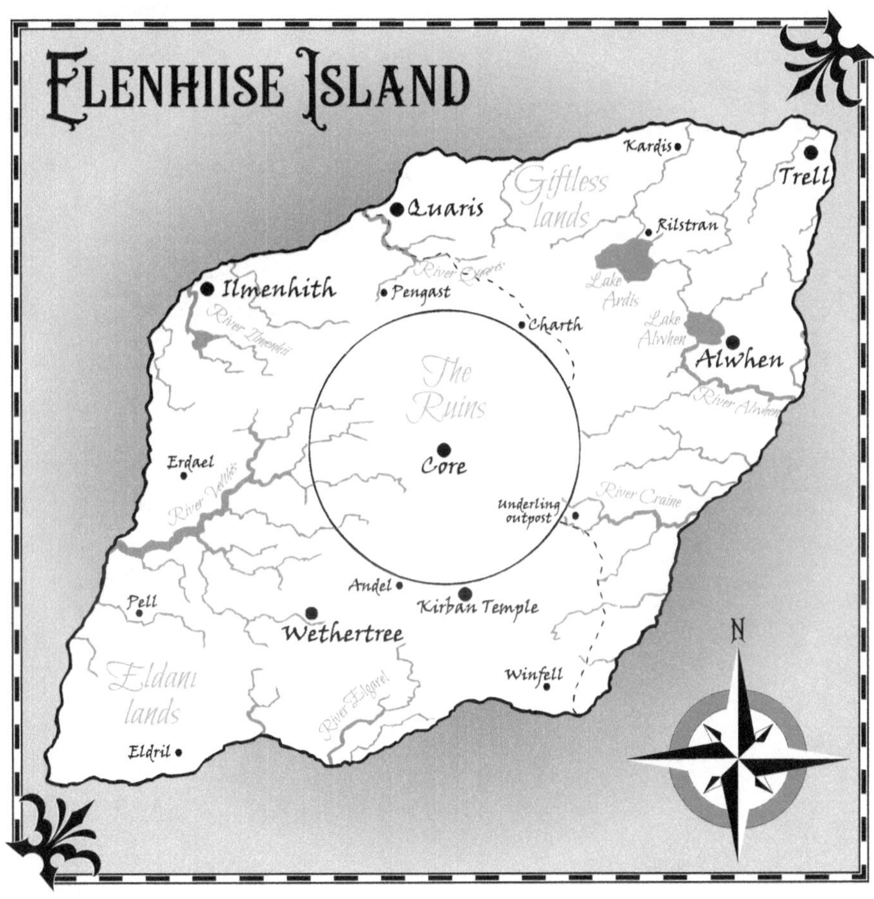

Elenhiise Island
Giftless lands
Kardis
Trell
Quaris
Rilstran
River Quaris
Ilmenhith
Pengast
Lake Ardis
River Ilmenhii
Charth
Lake Alwhen
The Ruins
Alwhen
River Alwhen
Erdael
Core
River Velthis
River Craine
Underling outpost
Andel
Kirban Temple
Pell
Wethertree
Eldani lands
River Elgarei
Winfell
Eldril
N

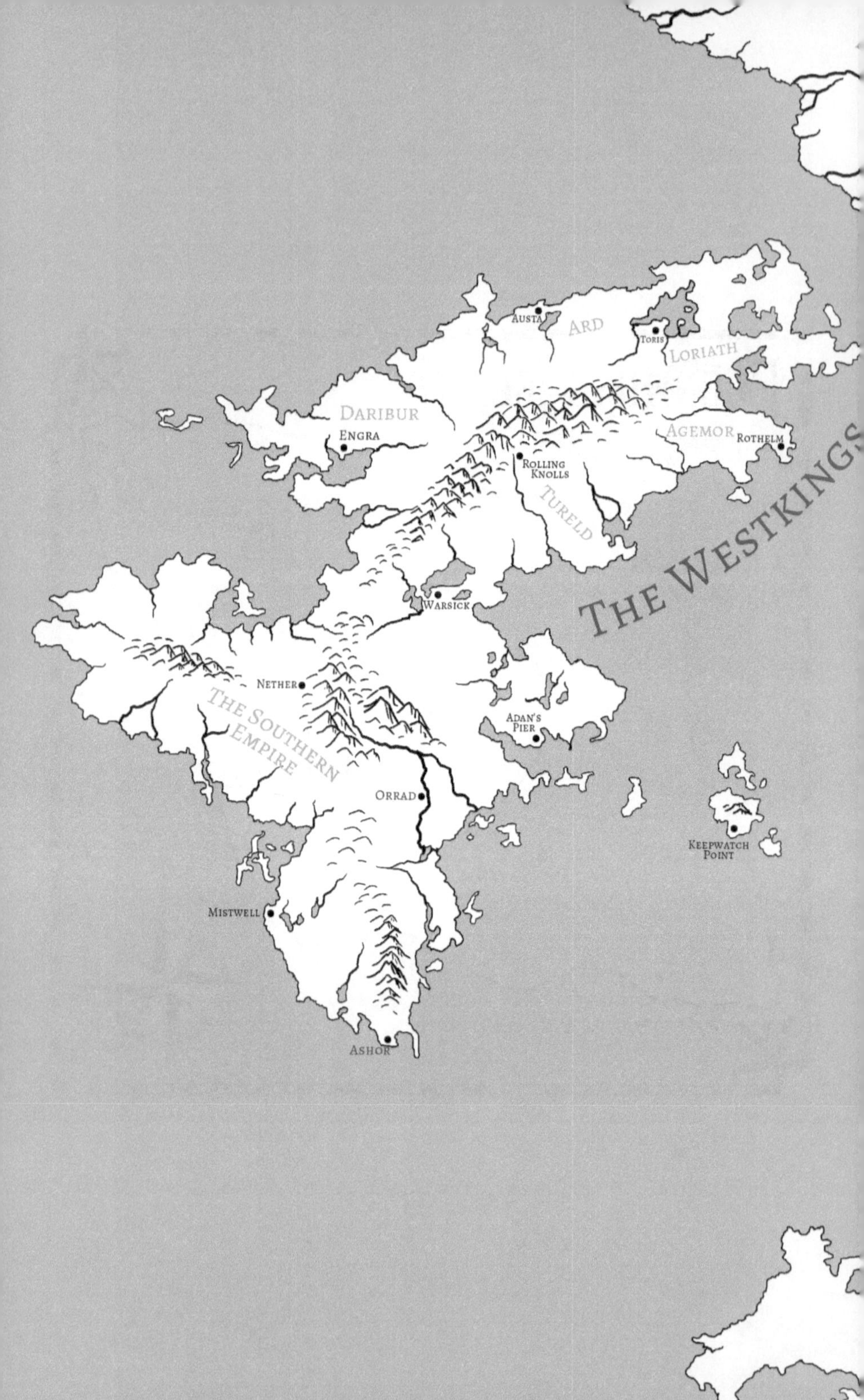

AUSTA
ARD
TORIS
LORIATH
DARIBUR
ENGRA
AGEMOR
ROTHELM
ROLLING KNOLLS
TURELD
THE WESTKINGS
WARSICK
NETHER
ADAN'S PIER
THE SOUTHERN EMPIRE
ORRAD
KEEPWATCH POINT
MISTWELL
ASHOR

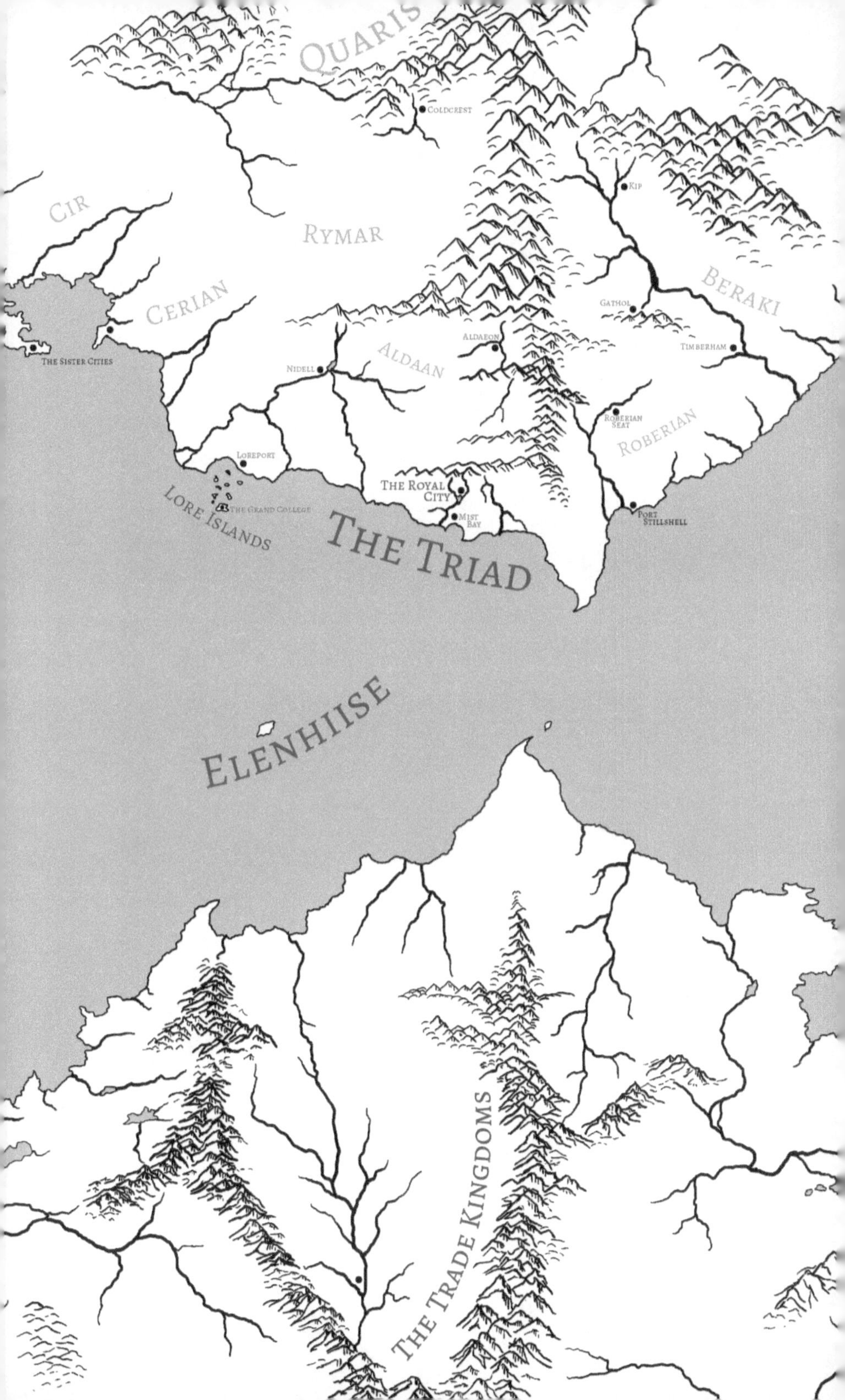

QUARIS
CIR
RYMAR
CERIAN
COLDCREST
KIP
BERAKI
GATHOL
THE SISTER CITIES
ALDAEON
TIMBERHAM
NIDELL
ALDAAN
ROBERIAN
SEAT
LOREPORT
ROBERIAN
THE GRAND COLLEGE
THE ROYAL
CITY
LORE ISLANDS
MIST
BAY
PORT
STILLSHELL
THE TRIAD
ELÉNHIISE
THE TRADE KINGDOMS

CONTENTS

A MEETING OF MAGES

In all the years Elenhiise had been allied with the Triad, Firal had never spent more than a handful of minutes with King Vicamros. They had always communicated primarily through dignitaries and messengers. Few circumstances had been important enough to demand they meet. To walk into his palace and demand asylum seemed arrogant, despite the strength of their political bond.

Firal smoothed the front of her dress and examined herself in the mirror again. The green gown was simple, but it fit well enough. There wouldn't be time to find anything better before they met with Vicamros, so it would have to do. She tucked stray ebony curls behind her pointed ears one last time and turned away. She didn't want to think about why there was such an assortment of women's clothing in the manor.

Truthfully, Firal did not want to be in the manor, herself. It had been more intimidating than welcoming when they'd arrived that morning, seeking refuge. That was before she knew who the estate belonged to.

After the harrowing days behind them, she hadn't expected Rune would want to protect her. She still wasn't certain why he had. Instinct, she thought, though the fact he had rescued every mage in the throne room and not only her indicated some conscious effort went into it.

Still, he could have taken them anywhere and it would have been more comfortable than dumping them into his private home.

The room she occupied was as finely furnished as the rest of the house, decorated in pale blues and greens that didn't suit Rune's personality at all. There was time to enjoy the comfort of the chairs and plush bed before her meeting with Vicamros had to take place, but she was too restless to sit.

Instead she folded her discarded gown and left it on the foot of the bed, then emptied the dirty water from the washbasin into the wooden pail beside the washstand. She considered tossing the water out the window, but she didn't see any way to open the pretty diamond-paned glass, so she carried the pail with her into the hall instead. It was small, menial, but Firal had grown desperate for distractions in the wake of everything that had unfolded that morning.

Ordin Straes, her Captain of the Guard, waited outside. He fell in step behind her without a word. She pretended not to notice, studying her surroundings as they walked.

She hadn't seen any serving staff, or any sign of a staff's existence. Now that she looked closer, tangled cobwebs hid in the corners, and the fine decorations sported a light coating of dust.

Aside from Ordin, Firal didn't encounter anyone else on the way down to the main floor, though she heard the mages in the parlor murmuring as they prepared for departure. Everyone had agreed it was best that they meet with the Triad's Archmage before Firal met with King Vicamros, but she almost wished she could go with them. It would be easier to face the foreign Archmage than to appear before an ally and explain how she'd lost her kingdom in the span of a heartbeat.

She paused at the front door and stepped outside to empty the pail. Her eyes drifted down the quiet lane as she set it aside to dry. She'd fetch it later. Or perhaps she'd forget and it would sit there collecting dust, like the treasures in the hallways.

"You may take a rest, Captain." Firal tried to sound as coolly dismissive as she had in the past, like a queen ought to when giving an order to her subject. Instead her voice cracked and Ordin looked at her in concern.

"Are you certain, Majesty?"

She nodded. "You may sit in the parlor, if you wish. I will be in the kitchen."

"If you're hungry, I can—"

Firal raised a hand to silence him. "If I have need of you, I will let you know."

Ordin frowned, but nodded and let her continue through the parlor alone.

The soft, rhythmic clack of a knife led her to the kitchen on the south end of the house.

Rhyllyn stood at the counter, humming to himself as he chopped vegetables. He worked alone. What with the lack of servants, she hadn't expected anything else.

Only a few hours before, the youth's existence had been shocking. Firal refused to blame herself for her assumptions, though. His olive-scaled hands and snake-slitted eyes gave him a strong enough resemblance to Rune that anyone would assume them related by more than the taint in their magic.

Mindful to walk a little louder, Firal joined him. "Can I help you?"

The boy blinked at her, surprised. "You're a guest. You don't have to do anything."

She tried to smile. "What if I want to?"

He hesitated, then returned her smile and offered his knife by the handle. When she took it, he retrieved another for himself from the knife block an arm's reach away.

Firal hadn't done more than set foot in a kitchen since her coronation. The knife felt awkward in her hand, but she was grateful to have something to distract her. She took pains to ensure the slices she cut were uniform, biting her lower lip as she worked. It was a blissful distraction.

Rhyllyn watched her as he took another carrot from the basket beside him. He finished cutting it before she'd done more than a quarter of her own carrot. "So, you're a queen, huh?"

She laughed weakly. "It shows, doesn't it? I can't even cut vegetables anymore."

He flushed. "Oh, no, I didn't mean—"

"No, it's all right. It's been a while since I've done anything like this, that's all." She chopped slowly, mindful not to catch her fingers. "It's been a long time since I did anything for myself, really. I wanted to, when I was first crowned. I was used to being self-sufficient. I didn't like people doing anything for me."

Rhyllyn nodded. "I understand. I felt the same way right after I changed. It was hard, learning to use my hands all over again, but I didn't like people babying me, either."

Firal glanced at his four-fingered hands. They certainly didn't trouble him now. He was deft with his fingers, unhindered by his claws. "He said they made you, but I assumed it was something more like the way they made him. Rune, I mean." She ducked her head. "So you weren't born that way?"

"No. I used to be human, actually." He flashed her a grin. His blue eyes sparkled with an unexpected mirth. "I was young when they took me. I don't remember much of it, just the before and after. Alira says it's better that I don't."

She pursed her lips to keep from frowning. "Doesn't it bother you?"

"What?"

"Being... changed." Firal tried not to shiver at the word. Until Envesi had appeared before her, she hadn't believed it possible. Now she stood beside proof for the second time in a single day.

"Oh, that." Rhyllyn laughed and went back to chopping. "No. Actually, being changed into whatever I am is the best thing that ever happened to me."

Her knife cracked against the wooden cutting board as if in

exclamation. "How can you say that?" The words escaped before she could stop them. She cringed when he looked at her, but he only seemed amused.

"Well, I know it seems odd to you. I know Rune's never been happy with himself. That's why he was always traveling, looking for the Alda'anan after they disappeared. Hoping they could fix him. But for me, changing was a gift. For one, I'm a mage now. I don't think the magic was strong enough in me to develop on its own, but now it has. The college and embassies are like a second home, and I've learned so much."

"Are you a mageling?" she asked. If he were, she couldn't imagine him being allowed to stray so far from an embassy.

"Well, not exactly. They teach me other things. I can read now, and write, and play a dozen instruments because the college bards will teach me. But all that aside, there were still benefits. After all, I'm somebody now." He shifted, and his grin turned sheepish. "I lived on the streets before I changed. Not an orphan, but my uncle abandoned me, so there was little difference. I probably would have frozen to death that winter. Instead, I became what I am and received a new family. And when his brother is the famous Champion of the Royal City Arena, it's easy for a strange boy to find friends."

She tried to focus on her work instead of staring at him. It was strange; to a boy with nothing, his condition was a blessing. But for Rune, a man with everything, it had always been a curse. "Arena?" she repeated at last.

Rhyllyn put his knife aside and scooped cut vegetables into a pot to clear their workspace for more. "You haven't heard of it? I'm sorry, I thought with the alliance and everything..." He trailed off and shook his head. "The Arena is where they take criminals for execution. Nobles face them in armed combat. It's a battle to the death, but since most prisoners have never so much as touched a sword, there's usually not much of a fight."

Her stomach turned. It was not her place to judge the justice of other countries, but such a practice was nothing short of barbaric. "He participates in that?"

"Well, no, not anymore. We don't go often, usually only when council is called, and then only to see the other councilors. He hasn't fought in a long time. Not since I've been old enough to watch, anyway. I wish I could have seen him fight. I hear he was amazing." Admiration filled his voice.

Firal tried to hide her disgust. "I suppose he must have been, to gain a title like that."

The boy beamed. "To this day, he's still the only prisoner to have won and been granted pardon."

Unexpected relief flooded over her, followed by burning embarrassment. She'd not even considered he could have been anything other than one of the nobles participating in the slaughter.

"Anyway," Rhyllyn went on, "it's not like there aren't challenges. It's harder to do some things with claws, I guess, though I find workarounds. I think the most difficult part is that I didn't grow up like everyone else."

That, at least, Firal understood. It had never been her struggle, but her dearest friend came from a family where not all children were Gifted. With how magic prolonged the life of its wielder, she'd often wondered how Kytenia would cope with the passing of her Giftless siblings. "The Eldani grow slowly from birth," she said slowly. "I suppose if your magic wasn't strong enough to manifest on its own, you didn't experience that."

"Nope. I was just like every other kid. And for a while, it stayed that way, but as I got older, it just sort of ground to a halt." He paused to inspect a potato. The dark spot on one end made him crinkle his nose. He sliced it off. "That part was hard, I won't lie. All my friends got to grow up, and I didn't. I mean, I obviously didn't stay a child, but I definitely haven't made much progress compared to them. And let me tell you, having your voice breaking during singing lessons for eight years isn't much fun."

She snorted a laugh.

Evidently, that was what he'd hoped for, because he flashed her a grin. "Anyhow, I didn't mean to take over the whole conversation. I'm sorry. You wanted to talk about something, right? I find it hard to imagine a queen would want to chop vegetables otherwise."

"I think I just want a distraction." She reached past him to take a turnip from the basket. "I've not had the most pleasant day." The understatement was so great it made her want to cry.

He grew solemn. "I understand. I wasn't trying to listen to you and Rune, but—"

"Yes, Ordin already told me." Firal stifled a sigh. "We do not always fight, by the way. There are occasionally times we agree on things. Or there were, anyway. These days, we seem to be like oil and water."

Rhyllyn snorted. "You're not oil and water. You're more like those chemicals the scholars keep. The ones that explode when you mix them."

Firal cringed.

"There you are." Kytenia appeared in the doorway, her hands on her hips. She looked more the part of Archmage than she had after their arrival. What she now wore must have been one of Alira's robes, stark white and an acceptable fit, though the sleeves were a little short. "We need you. We're about to leave."

Firal put down her knife and wiped her hands on a rag. "Excuse me, Rhyllyn."

"Both of you," Kytenia said.

Firal raised a brow.

Rhyllyn cleaned his hands as well, unsurprised. He covered the pot of vegetables and followed Firal and Kytenia to the doorway. The three of them returned to the parlor where the other mages waited.

"We've decided it best to be clear and forthcoming with Arrick about the situation," Alira said the moment they stepped in.

Finding Alira in Rune's home had been another shock, perhaps worse than Rhyllyn's presence. The Master mage had been an exile and a villain, as far as Firal was concerned. But Rune and his companions seemed to trust her, and the mages who had come from Elenhiise seemed to have accepted her after relatively little conversation. Who was Firal to disagree? She was a queen without a kingdom.

With that sullen thought in mind, she seated herself on one of the couches. Rhyllyn stayed beside the door.

"I'm not sure what King Vicamros will say," Kytenia said. Across the room, Rikka and Temar, two more of Firal's most trusted Master mages, made room for her to sit. Kytenia sank to the couch between them without a second look. "However, I do think taking action is within our jurisdiction as mages, regardless of which crowns we serve. We will begin an effort to summon mages to assist our cause immediately. Hopefully Arrick will be cooperative, though I wouldn't be surprised if he wishes to wait for permission from Vicamros. He tends to tread carefully."

"If all goes according to plan," Alira said as if their speech were already well-rehearsed, "they will begin gathering forces in the Grand College. Assuming they can get any of our mages out of Ilmenhith."

"Don't try if it seems too risky," Firal said. "Don't forget we sent Envesi to the college. She can reach us there as easily as if we were still on Elenhiise."

Kytenia nodded. "We will exercise caution. In the meantime, we will also begin closing the permanent Gates, starting with the one in the palace, though I am not certain how quickly that can be done." She grimaced, an expression mirrored by the other women. Opening the Gates had taken days. Closing them might take just as long. "As soon as we're able, we'll send someone to join you in the Royal City. I doubt it will be me, but perhaps Temar or Rikka."

Firal's eyes flicked toward Anaide, who sat on her own,

huddled in one of the chairs. The Master of Water was the only one of the Elenhiise mages who had not seemed to recover from the morning's events. She was also the only mage who still seemed unwilling to accept Alira's presence.

Kytenia followed Firal's gaze. "Anaide will stay with me, of course. I will need her expert assistance in organizing our mages."

"Of course," Firal said, as if the explanation made perfect sense. Truthfully, she was relieved she wouldn't have to worry about the woman. She had her hands full enough already.

"What if she's already in the college?" Rune asked from the doorway. He reminded Firal of a grumpy house cat, the way he prowled the halls and lurked just outside of conversations. She glowered in his direction, but he stared back, unfazed. The frigid intensity in his snakelike eyes still gave her chills.

"She won't be," Alira said.

"What makes you so sure?" Rune challenged. "She's taken an entire nation today, and it's barely noon."

"You handed her that nation by bringing its queen here." A note of warning colored Alira's words.

Firal averted her eyes. A faint flicker of anger stirred in her chest, but it paled in comparison to her guilt. Running had been a mistake. Not that she'd seen another way forward.

"Furthermore," Alira continued, "I have worked with Envesi before. You have not. She will take her time planning her next move. Her entire life has been a sequence of carefully planned actions."

Firal scowled, reminded of her conversation with the former Archmage only hours before. No matter how they were related, she could never view the scheming woman as her mother. Even Firal's existence was plotted and planned, nothing more than a means to an end.

Someone else appeared at the door. It seemed everyone was invited. Not that Firal was likely to complain about Garam's inclusion; she offered the old man a smile and he returned it in kind, though his eyes were pinched with weariness.

"Alira makes a valid point," Garam said as he clasped Rune's shoulder with one brown hand. "Not everyone is as rash as you."

Rune's expression darkened.

"In any event," Kytenia said, "we're ready to go. Rhyllyn, I understand you'll be opening a Gate for us?"

The boy squirmed. "Not exactly."

"Please remember that he is still a child," Alira said. "At his age, half of you weren't yet in a gray mageling's robes. Though Rhyllyn is powerful, he lacks the developed skill to manage such feats. He's more of a..."

"A conduit," Rune finished. "Rhyllyn?"

Rhyllyn grew still. Firal felt the air ripple with power as he extended his energy, like a hand seeking another to hold. No one in the room dared grasp it. The boy's power was raw chaos, a tumult of energy that put an unnerved look on the face of every mage present.

Every mage but one.

From the doorway, Rune responded. He seized the offered tendril of energy and tied the two of them together. The narrow stream of magic that flowed between them grew to a raging current. Power sizzled in the air, making Firal's hair stand on end. She shuddered, but dared not look away. The magic itself was invisible, but their reactions were not.

Rune closed his eyes and, for a moment, looked at peace. Her heart wrenched. It was the first time since they'd been reunited that he didn't seem miserable. But it was fleeting, and his expression returned to the scowl she knew so well the moment he opened his eyes.

Power burned inside him now. The subtle glow that was ever present in his violet eyes flared to brilliant luminescence. He drew his hands together overhead and traced an opening with his claws. Light crackled and burned in midair as trails of magic followed his gesture. It shot across from one pillar of light to the other, spiderwebbing through the empty space, piecing together an image of the Grand College's courtyard in Lore.

Everyone but Alira stared in amazement. She only smiled at Rhyllyn, rather like a proud mother.

Rune stepped back as the wavering image solidified. "Go," he ordered.

Rikka and Temar jumped to their feet. Kytenia rose slowly, waiting for the others to collect a cowering Anaide from behind a wing-backed chair. Asula and Kella seized the woman, one on either side, and escorted her to the Gate.

Kytenia slid past them to embrace Firal. "We'll contact you as soon as we are able."

Firal rose to meet her and swallowed hard. She squeezed her friend even as a cold knot of fear tightened around her heart. Even the college was no longer guaranteed to escape Envesi's grasp. "Be safe."

The mages filed through the Gate unceremoniously. Only Kytenia looked back after she stepped through. She nodded, though she couldn't have seen them from the other side of the Gate. Rune released the flows that held it open and relinquished his ties to Rhyllyn. The image of the college fell apart, and the fragments dissolved into glittering motes that soon dissipated into nothing.

Rune sighed and seemed to deflate as the power left him. The light all but disappeared from his eyes and Garam offered an arm for support. He did not seem offended when Rune ignored it.

"Your relay abilities are excellent now." Alira said, smoothing Rhyllyn's hair like one might pet a cat.

"Yes," Firal mused, giving Rune a frown. "A remarkable skill."

Rune's eyes narrowed. "Don't think you're going to involve him in this."

"I can help," Rhyllyn said.

Rune raised a finger. "This isn't your fight. This has nothing to do with you."

"But I can help you!" the boy insisted.

"Rune—" Alira started, but cut herself short when he fired her a vicious glare.

"I said no. He is not to be involved. Period."

Firal clutched her skirts. "If he can feed you power, then we already have everything we need to end this now. You came to Elenhiise acting like there was nothing we could do to help you face Envesi—"

"Rhyllyn can't do that," Rune interrupted. "Are none of you capable of thinking straight anymore? For me to do anything, we have to link. Rhyllyn doesn't yet have the control to link with me and do things on his own at the same time, which means it's one of us or the other. Drawing through him slows me down because he's inexperienced, and what happens if the flows are cut? She can do that now. She'd render me powerless, and he certainly can't face her alone."

"But—" Firal started.

"And what happens if she captures him too?" Rune went on. "The only reason we even stand a chance is because if your daughter was born with this kind of power, she's a free mage without corruption." His hands twitched with the word. He curled his claws into his fists. "The taint in Envesi's magic will keep her from being able to use the girl as a conduit like I can with Rhyllyn. But if I can draw through Rhyllyn, so can she."

"*Your* daughter," Garam corrected gruffly.

Rune scoffed. "How can you call her that? I don't even know her name!"

"Lumia," Firal said.

Rune's head snapped back around.

Firal couldn't bring herself to meet his eyes.

"What?" His voice was tight, strained.

"Her name is Lumia." Her hands tightened in her skirts. The tension was all that kept her from shaking. "A name given to unify a broken people as an act of goodwill. The name of a woman who played an important role in shaping your life."

All the anger drained from him. His shoulders sagged, his face slack with disbelief.

"He has a daughter?" Rhyllyn asked, barely above a whisper.

Firal raised her chin and swallowed hard. "Does that make it more real to you? Is that what you need to make you care?"

Rune shut his eyes and exhaled. "Rhyllyn helps open Gates," he said, as if Firal hadn't spoken at all. "Nothing more."

The boy's brow furrowed, but he bowed his head and did not speak.

"The lot of you make me real hesitant to go back to the Royal City and leave you unattended." Garam walked with a stiff gait, one hand pressed to his lower back. Through most of the day, he hadn't shown his age. Now that they were settled, Firal noted the man's discomfort. She pitied him, but there was little she could do. Healing could not repair the natural wear of an aging body. She had often tried to find ways to ease Nondar's aches and pains, before the old Master had passed, but it made no difference.

"I'll look after them," Alira said. "It's only an evening, in any case. If all goes well, we'll be settled in the guest quarters of the Spiral Palace for bed."

Garam grunted in displeasure. "We'll see. I'm so stiff it may take me until tomorrow morning to walk to the palace."

"We can Gate you to the palace instead of your estate," Rhyllyn suggested.

The older man shook his head. "No, no. The estate is a safer choice. Are you ready?"

Again the air around them hummed with invisible power as Rune and Rhyllyn connected. Rune nodded, his brows knit with concentration as he traced another portal in the air. This time, the air split to reveal the courtyard of a tall and narrow stone building with walls to either side. A horse whinnied and snorted, Firal assumed in response to the feeling of power in the air on the other end. Animals were strange like that; most Masters agreed they could sense magic, but not all beasts were fond of it.

Sighing in relief, Garam inched toward the Gate. "With luck, I'll have a team of mages bring me back before nightfall. If I'm not back by tomorrow, you should probably storm the palace on your own. Be good while I'm gone."

"Good luck," Rune said.

Garam waved a hand in dismissal, then trudged through the portal and toward the house. Rune let the Gate drop and released his ties to Rhyllyn again.

"Well," Alira said cheerily. "Now things are right back to normal, aren't they? Just the three of us and a woman your brother has no business dallying with."

Firal gasped. A fiery heat of anger and embarrassment bloomed in her face.

"Thank you, Alira." Rune gave her a nasty look. "That's exactly what I need." He turned to leave.

"Where are you going?" Rhyllyn asked.

"To change into something proper for a trip to the Royal City. Send up food when it's done." Rune paused in the doorway. "I suggest you bring it yourself, Rhyllyn, since I can't guarantee anything nice will come from Alira speaking to me again."

Alira shrugged, indifferent. "Do you need help in the kitchen?"

Rhyllyn swallowed and glanced nervously toward Firal. "No. I think I'm okay. Why don't you go up to your room and rest before we travel, Alira?"

"Very well." The mage nodded stiffly and made for the stairs.

Once Alira was gone, Rhyllyn offered a polite cough. "She doesn't mean any offense to you. He just doesn't... I mean..."

"No," Firal said, raising a hand. "I think I've heard enough to understand. How he chooses to live his life is no business of mine, anyway." The words came with a twinge of guilt. She knew it was none of her business, but it still bothered her. Yet she had been angry when Rune refused to aid her, ignored the frustration in him that betrayed the same conflicting emotions she experienced now. Life had moved on. They should have, too.

Rhyllyn opened his mouth to speak but seemed to think better of it. He turned back toward the hall to the kitchen. "If you want to go upstairs and rest as well...?"

"Certainly not." She hurried after him. "It's been ages since I was allowed to get my hands dirty, and I have to say I'm enjoying it."

He grinned and led the way. "In that case, I have something you might enjoy more. How are you at kneading bread?"

Despite her troubles, Firal laughed.

For as long as Archmage Arrick Ortath could remember, magelings had run all the errands around the college. To open his door and find a white-robed Master waiting on the other side instead signaled nothing good.

Worse was the news of who waited for him in a private room. He would have thought it bad enough for the Archmage of Elenhiise to call on him again so soon after they'd brought a message for the king, but that she'd already been escorted to somewhere they could speak in private meant something of great importance.

In his experience, things of great importance were rarely good.

He tried not to hurry, though the lump of dread in his stomach told him to run. When he arrived at the small classroom and the Masters at the door let him in, the grim expressions on the six faces that greeted him were enough to tell him he was right. Bad news awaited.

"Thank you for meeting with us, Archmage Arrick." Kytenia and the other five mages—more Elenhiise mages than had ever been present for one meeting—had a disheveled look about them, as if harried and hastily put back together.

"I would say it a pleasure, Archmage Kytenia, but something tells me it's no pleasure at all." He closed the door and spun a ward over the room before another word could be spoken. She nodded in approval, which made the lump in his stomach grow cold.

Kytenia motioned for him to join her at the table. The other mages took places behind their chairs. She had arranged their seats so that the two of them would be at the opposing heads of the table, as was befitting their rank, with her mages arranged down the side. They were to be spectators to the meeting, rather than included in it. Even worse.

He strode forward and sat down.

"I must thank you for your assistance following our previous meeting," she began, sinking into her chair with a sigh. The other mages followed suit. "If not for your excellence in fulfilling King Vahnil's request, I fear we would not be present to speak with you now."

Arrick leaned forward over the table. "I beg your pardon?"

"No other mage would have been strong enough to Gate us out of the throne room this morning. It seems we have a powerful enemy, and I suspect she will be your enemy soon." Kytenia laced her fingers together and rested her hands against the table's edge. "I fear our predecessors have set us up for failure. Do you have records of the mages who were exiled from Elenhiise and taken in by the Grand College?"

"Exiled?" He glanced between them. The sense of trouble grew. "There are records of transfer, but no mages have ever been admitted on the basis of exile."

Kytenia frowned at her companions.

"Corruption runs deep," Anaide murmured. "It always has."

"Would it be possible for us to look at your records?" Kytenia asked. "I don't mean to impose. I would like you to be a part of it, of course. I simply think it would be beneficial to both of us to see what manner of information is present."

"Oh, certainly." Arrick tried not to sound too eager. He knew Eyrion had been a questionable leader, but if the previous headmaster of the Grand College had hidden something as dramatic as mages in exile—and allowed them free access to the college and its resources—Arrick wanted to know. He had little reason to mistrust the mages from Elenhiise. Besides, considering how many thousands of mages inhabited the island, keeping on their good side was important.

The Grand College had fewer and fewer students to admit every year. He suspected that, in time, the college would be swallowed by Kirban Temple. It was knowledge that made him sad, but he accepted it. As Archmage, it was important he consider the future, and part of being a good Archmage was sacrificing his own desires or interests for the better of the people in his charge. Sometimes he wondered if the future held mages at all.

"Thank you." Kytenia rubbed her brow and straightened. "There is time for that later, though. This cannot wait. For now, I'll speak as if your college is unfamiliar with the woman responsible for our trouble. As you know, the queen's daughter was kidnapped some days ago."

"Efforts to retrieve the girl are still in progress?" Arrick asked.

Kytenia nodded. "None of our attempts have been successful. We know our temple's first Archmage is responsible, but that's where the trouble begins. Were she just any mage, we would have rescued the child and likely put the woman to death."

He paled. "You would execute a mage? But the Gift is so rare now, I..." He trailed off and swallowed hard.

"At this point, I feel we have no choice. It's not a decision I make lightly, Arrick." Kytenia grew more solemn, more regal. "She was exiled for treason, on top of crimes against nature.

Archmage Eyrion Tolmarni accepted her and two of her colleagues found guilty of treason against the crown of Elenhiise. He offered to rehabilitate them."

Arrick's eyes narrowed. "Are you sure of this?"

"I was in the courtyard when the Masters of Kirban opened the Gate through which they were exiled," Kytenia replied.

"Of course, of course. I do not doubt you, I merely wish to be sure of the details." He found himself worrying his hands. Instead of trying to still them, he moved them beneath the table. "So one was your previous Archmage. Who were the others?"

"A Master named Melora, and one named Alira."

The second name gave him pause. Surely it was a coincidence.

Kytenia went on. "Alira has since redeemed herself and found a home and title in the Triad. She has proven a great asset to us since our arrival this morning. Melora, as I understand it, is dead. But they are not important. The fact of the matter is that Envesi, our former Archmage, has taken King Vahnil prisoner. Just yesterday, she laid siege to the temple and took control of it. She leads an army of mages, though where they came from, I'm not sure. Today, she attacked our queen in the throne room in an attempt to seize power. We escaped with our queen, but in doing so, forfeited the island."

Arrick's stomach lurched. He knew it. News from a Master was nothing good at all. "Where is your queen?"

"Safe, for the moment. She is in the company of Rune Kaim-Ennen, who rescued us this morning."

Glancing at the mages seated alongside the table, Arrick made himself breathe deep and exhale slowly. "It seems no matter what we do, mages keep becoming involved in wars."

"That's the nature of power, it seems." Kytenia smiled with sorrow in her eyes. "Unfortunately, the problem doesn't stop there. There were a number of mages present when Envesi arrived at the palace. Under normal circumstances, we could have stopped her. But circumstances are anything but normal.

I'm sure at this point, you are aware of Rune's physical condition?"

"As well as his brother's." Arrick frowned and rubbed his chin. "It's been a topic of research for the college for a long time, but we've made no headway in unraveling the corruption in his Gift. Never mind the seal the Aldaanan mages placed on it."

"Envesi is the one responsible for creating that corruption." She shook her head, troubled. "In exchange for the taint, they have power that, as I am learning, rivals the Aldaanan mages. It seems the corruption has spread to her."

Arrick swore.

"We had hoped having Rune with us would mitigate the imbalance in power, but..." She shrugged.

"The seal on his power eliminated that option." Arrick wiped his face with both hands and let his shoulders slump.

Kytenia leaned forward, her face pleading. "If you know anything that might help us overcome this challenge..."

He resisted the urge to laugh. Before Arrick took the title of Archmage, Eyrion sent a legion of mages up against the Aldaanan, foolishly thinking he could wipe them out. Instead, the army had been devastated by less than a handful of opposing mages. Only one of them had wielded the sort of power they claimed Envesi now had. The college was just as helpless as the rest of them.

"Knowing what I do, I'm afraid your island is as good as lost."

Kytenia closed her eyes and swallowed the news with only a slight pained expression.

Arrick pitied her. There was little else he could do. "If we had the benefit of the mages of Aldaan at our backs, perhaps things would be different, but they've been gone for some time. Mages at the other colleges are beginning to think they no longer exist."

"And we won't have time to look." She pursed her lips and drummed her fingertips atop the table.

"If I may be so bold," Arrick began, sparing a glance for the other mages, "might I question why this woman wishes to have control of the island?" Revenge was the obvious reason, given their history, but if she'd ventured onto the mainland—where mages were few and her power would be more readily recognized—why return to the heart of her troubles?

Kytenia let her eyes flick to the other mages as well. "I suspect she wishes to use it as a base of operations. We were able to question one of her supporters, but only briefly. She fears the extinction of magic, but..." Her mouth worked without producing words and she squeezed her eyes closed. A moment passed before she forced herself to go on. "Lumia—Firal's daughter—was born with free magic. Free of corruption, Gifted as I'm told the Aldaanan are. We believe Envesi means to spread the corruption to others in hopes their children, too, will be born as free mages."

A revolutionary concept. One that elevated the status of mages and ensured their survival, as well. Arrick's heart leaped at the idea, then plunged to the pit of his stomach. The ideals the Aldaanan upheld, particularly the belief mages should not bear unlimited power, were controversial. That they favored the extinction of magic had led to the last civil war in the Triad. He wasn't foolish enough to agree with their stance in public, but there was a grain of wisdom in it. The Aldaanan were level-headed, aged and disciplined. Having a new wave of young mages with free magic, combined with a lack of such elders to guide them in its use, could be disastrous.

Yet trying to stop the existence of free magic might as well have been a step against magic itself. They needed the mingling of blood, free mages to restore the strength in lines too far separated from the Aldaanan ancestors who had passed on their Gifts to begin with.

Startled, Arrick shook himself. "How can the queen's daughter be born a free mage? That would require—"

"A free mage as a parent," Kytenia interrupted with a nod. "Yes."

He turned that over in his head for a time and his eyes narrowed to slits. "Perhaps I ought to view your records as well, Archmage Kytenia."

"Of course," she said coolly, her face as calm and unmoving as if carved from marble. "But for now, we need to arrange a sitting with King Vicamros."

"Of course," Arrick repeated, absently mopping his brow and making a note to never answer his door for a Master again.

2

ALLIES

WHEN THE EVENING'S INSECTS BEGAN TO SING AND THE SUN FELL below the trees surrounding the manor, the hum of power in the air announced the opening of a Gate outside.

Firal and Rhyllyn had consumed the evening meal in peace, though there was little conversation to be had. Ordin had deemed the meal safe without needing to test her food, a compliment Rhyllyn took to heart. Alira avoided them all, but her sour attitude dampened what might have otherwise been a pleasant evening.

"She's anxious about the meeting," Rhyllyn said, assuring Firal it was nothing else.

Truthfully, Firal didn't mind the quiet. Rhyllyn left her alone after the meal and she wandered the library and offices on the sprawling main floor of the house with Ordin trailing behind her, until the tingling sensation of the Gate spurred her to the front door.

Rhyllyn descended the stairs alone, his brother nowhere in sight. Alira came from the parlor.

"It's Garam," Rhyllyn said before he reached the floor.

Firal paused halfway across the foyer. "How can you tell?"

He regarded her with a quizzical frown. "I could see out the window on my way down."

She flushed and opened the door.

Lord Kaith stood before the manor, watching as a half-dozen white-robed mages stepped from thin air and formed a semicircle around him. Firal had grown so used to seeing anchored Gates that it was strange to see the other end of a free-standing one.

"I was beginning to think you wouldn't return." Alira slipped past Firal to meet them and murmured greetings to the mages. One stepped forward to embrace her. Friends from the capital city, it seemed.

"Gaining an audience with the king on such short notice isn't easy." Once again, Garam walked with a cane. He leaned on it more now, his other hand against his lower back. "I expected the lot of you would be ready to go when I arrived. We'll need to be quick."

Alira took his arm to aid him to the door. "It won't take us long to prepare, I assure you. Rhyllyn, where is your brother?"

The boy shuffled his feet as he held open the door. "He's still upstairs. I didn't take him anything to eat. I hoped he would come down."

"Well, one of you is going to have to go up and tell him to put on a shirt," Garam said.

Alira snorted.

Rhyllyn offered a nervous laugh. "I'll go get him."

As Firal stepped aside so Garam could come indoors, she turned so the mages couldn't see her face. After the unexpected reunion with Alira, she didn't want any more surprises. "Will it be a formal meeting of council, Lord Kaith?"

"Not all the councilors will be present, but that may work in our favor. We were selected for the council due to our differences, after all." Garam paused in the doorway and jerked his head toward the house.

The mages hurried forward and filed in one at a time. They

were all women, which wasn't uncommon, but they wore such empty expressions that it gave Firal a chill. Were they bored, or were college-trained mages really so different from those in the temple?

She gave them a wide berth, slipped in just ahead of Rhyllyn, and lingered beside the boy while the visitors made themselves comfortable in the parlor. "Should I come with you to fetch your brother?"

"It won't take long for him to get dressed." He smiled, evidently trying his best to appear reassuring.

Firal took a small measure of comfort. He was a pleasant youth. Though they'd spent little more than an afternoon together, she already felt a sense of fondness for him.

Rhyllyn bounded up the stairs and disappeared.

Alira emerged from the parlor and went up after him, more sedately, but she turned at the top of the staircase. "Sit with our guests, would you? I'll just be a moment. I need to fetch my good slippers."

"Make it fast," Rune growled from above. He appeared behind Alira and waved her out of the way. He'd changed his blue and silver clothing for black. The color suited him better, and it matched his expression, besides. He'd put aside the crown he'd worn when they arrived, too, which Firal appreciated. Where he'd gotten it or what inspired him to wear it, she didn't know, but it had been an uncomfortable reminder of the life he'd had before.

And by all rights, Elenhiise should have been his.

His sharp violet eyes turned toward her and Firal dropped her gaze. If she'd thought he'd seemed cold before, the icy emptiness in that stare made his previous behavior friendly by comparison.

Garam gave the couches a wistful glance before he turned back to the foyer. His mages sat down without him, awaiting further command. "Vicamros provided mages to take us directly into the council chamber."

Rune scoffed, stalked down the stairs, and pivoted to face the man the moment his foot touched the floor. "What, does he think I don't remember what it looks like?"

"It's been several months since you were in the city for a council meeting," Garam said. "Besides that, the city doesn't know you're still alive. He's just being cautious. Seems he's had his hands full the past few days. He doesn't want to risk anything else going wrong."

Firal twitched, but forced herself to remain quiet. She doubted anything that could have happened to Vicamros would be worse than the ordeal she faced.

Without a word, Rhyllyn positioned himself beside her. His presence came with a sense of peace, a gentle energy of reassurance. She felt a hint of guilt for her initial assumptions about him. He was so calm and pleasant, cheerful and tranquil. Nothing at all like the man who'd taken him as a brother.

"His concern is unnecessary." Rune adjusted the cuff of his sleeve, then sighed and rested a hand on the hilt of his sword. The sheath it resided in now was plainer than the one he'd lost in Ilmenhith's throne room, which made the twisted black hilt look out of place at his hip, for all that it matched his attire. "But since they're here, we might as well let them work. Rhyllyn, make sure the doors are locked. And get your money."

The boy's face lit up. "Am I going with you?"

"Not into the council meeting, but I'm sure you'll want to shop if we're going to be in the Royal City."

Rhyllyn was up the stairs in the blink of an eye.

"You think we'll be back soon enough for his groceries to keep?" Garam asked.

Rune shrugged. "We can hope."

THERE WAS a difference between the Gates bound mages used and the ones Rune and Rhyllyn opened. Firal didn't realize it until she passed through the portal Garam's escort opened to the council chamber in the Triad's Royal City. She gasped and shuddered as the electric tingle coursed through her.

The sensation was different. The same wild power created both sizzling Gates, energy that didn't want to be tamed. Normally, it took half a dozen experienced Masters or more to make it obey.

But Rune's Gates were powerful—more powerful than those she was used to, truthfully—and with his, there was an order to the way the magic flowed. It still sparked and crackled when he opened one, but once open, it was steady, seamless. She would have preferred to travel through one of his.

Now that she thought of it, when Kytenia had looked back after stepping through one of his Gates, it had seemed as if she'd met Rune's eyes. If it were any normal Gate, she would have emerged as if from thin air on the other side. There would have been nothing to see. Yet as far as Firal understood, having a Gate that worked two ways required energy anchoring it on both sides. How could he possibly manipulate power in another location to achieve something like that? She shivered and tried not to think of it. She'd thought she understood him, once. Now she couldn't believe how wrong she'd been.

Despite the three decades they'd spent as allies, Firal had never visited the Royal City. When they'd needed to speak face to face, which was a rare event to begin with, she and Vicamros had always met in the Grand College or Kirban Temple. Though recognized as parts of their respective kingdoms, the mages were a faction unto themselves and the schools proved the closest thing to neutral meeting ground the two rulers could manage.

Firal doubted Vicamros gave other allies such dignities, but she held a unique position. Elenhiise was small enough to seem insignificant, but the island's location had always led trade to thrive. It had provided a point halfway across the sea for merchants from north and south to meet until the permanent Gates were established. That the Triad was linked to Elenhiise by the mages provided an advantage like no other. After the Gates were built, there was no need for merchants to travel from Elenhiise to the north. The seas to the south were filled with ships, and everything passed through Elenhiise and its Gates to their sole ally—the Triad. Merchants, on the other hand, held alliances only to fat purses. The loss of her kingdom's support could easily spell doom for the Triad.

Ordin positioned himself beside Firal once he was through the Gate, a quiet reminder that she wouldn't find a moment alone. He'd been kind to give her more space at the manor, but hiding around the next corner meant he was still always there. The Spiral Palace would prove no different.

She'd heard stories about the Spiral Palace and why it had been given that name. From the council chamber they stepped into, she could only imagine what the place actually looked like. The room bore no windows. It was so empty as to seem sterile, hosting only a round table with chairs around it. A throne stood opposite the doorway, which the Gate emptied through, but it wasn't as ornate or grand as she might have expected. Instead it was barely bigger than the chairs around the table, its polished wood only gilded for accent. The three banners of the Triad hung from the walls—blue for Lore on the left, gold for Aldaan on the right, and the green that represented Roberian behind the throne.

Otherwise, the council chamber stood empty.

The rest of the group filed through the Gate without ceremony. Garam paced halfway around the table, his cane clicking in the silence.

"I shall notify His Majesty of your arrival," one of the white-robed mages said as she bowed and turned toward the door.

Alira cleared her throat. "If you are going that way, please escort Rhyllyn out of the palace. He will be back to attend us before it is too late, so please ensure he will have an escort upon his return."

"The sun had just set when we left. How late are the markets here open?" Firal asked in a murmur.

"We're pretty far west of my estate," Rune said. "I expect the sun is still up here, if barely."

"His favorite merchant will stay late for him, besides," Alira added. "Go on, boy. He'll only stay if you catch him, after all."

Rhyllyn flushed and spat hasty goodbyes on his way after the Master mage.

The other five Masters arranged themselves like guards beside the door, as stoic as any soldiers on duty Firal had ever seen.

Alira made her way to the table and pulled out a chair that seemed random, but Firal assumed it was where she was used to sitting. "Before the king arrives, do we know what we want to say?"

"I figured we'd let Firal do the talking." Rune caught the leg of a chair with his foot and dragged it back from the table. "It's her problem, after all."

Indignation made color rise in her cheeks and Firal opened her mouth, but Garam spoke before she could.

"That's a kind way to speak of your child," the old man growled. He gripped his cane with one hand and the back of his chair with the other, his knuckles pale.

Rune's eyes darkened. "I was talking about the island." He dropped into his chair, ignoring the glowers he got from the other councilors.

"It wouldn't be a problem if you hadn't brought me here," Firal snapped.

Garam grunted. "The alternative wasn't any better. It's fairly clear she didn't mean to let you live."

The mages shuffled away from the door to let someone in. Firal turned, expecting the king. She was surprised to see another familiar face instead. "Archmage Arrick."

The Archmage smiled, somewhat nervously, and nodded in greeting. "Your Majesty. Councilors."

Alira leaned forward, her brow furrowed. "Where are Archmage Kytenia and the others?"

"At the college, sorting through records. They were looking for something in particular." He gave her a thoughtful look, as if contemplating her existence. Then he shook his head and hurried to his place at the table. "My presence was requested."

"As was mine," added an old fellow from the doorway. He looked familiar and had the air of a mage about him, though his curly hair and his lengthy beard were the yellowed white of age, not that which came with magic. He wore fine robes and a peculiar close-fitting cap, and Firal was certain she had seen him before.

Rune rose as quickly as he'd sat.

"Ah!" The man opened his arms wide. A grin split his face and the light of joy filled his eyes. "Brant's mercy, you're alive!"

"For the moment," Rune said. For an instant, there was a hint of mirth in his voice. He crossed the room and embraced the man. It struck Firal as odd that all his friends were elderly, but then again, she and Rune were mages. They didn't age like other people, and it seemed he'd been a part of this world for a long time.

Booted footsteps echoed in the hallway outside and everyone turned to face the soldiers that filed into the council chamber. They parted the crowd for the king.

Vicamros II bore little resemblance to his father, but Firal thought it grew as he aged. He was a fine looking man, less severe than most, with gentle eyes and a stern set to his jaw that always struck her as forced.

She'd had few dealings with him directly and had worked more with his father, who had established their alliance. The man who stood before her had ruled for the better part of the time since the treaty was signed, but it seemed there was always something that kept them apart.

She had been invited to his coronation several decades prior, but hadn't attended, as Lumia had been ill. Instead she'd sent the finest rubies ever pulled from the mines in Core, including a number of fine asteriated stones—serpent's tears, as the island knew them—and received a kind letter of thanks, but communication after had always been scarce. She sometimes wondered if it hadn't started their relationship off on the wrong foot.

"So it's true," Vicamros said as he stopped in the doorway. He looked past Firal with the shine of emotion filling his blue eyes.

Rune straightened, released the old councilor, and turned toward the king. He lowered his eyes, pressed a hand to his heart and bowed with more deference than Firal ever would have expected.

Vicamros closed the distance between them and clapped him on the shoulder.

Rune returned the gesture. "I'll tell you the whole story another time."

The king chuckled, though his eyes remained pinched. "That much of a story?"

Grimacing, Rune said nothing.

Vicamros nodded and let him go. He turned to face Firal and his expression grew cool, the practiced neutrality of a leader. "Welcome to my palace, Firal of Elenhiise. Would that you were visiting under happier circumstances."

She made herself smile. "Politics are rarely happy circumstances."

"True enough," he agreed, motioning for her to select a seat. He rounded the table to take his place at the throne while the councilors drew back their chairs.

Three of the mages slid into the hallway without needing instruction. The guards positioned themselves around the room as another pair stepped out and closed the door. No one else would be joining them, then. Firal chose her seat and sank into it as Vicamros settled into his. The rest of the councilors sat.

"As I am sure you've heard by now," Firal began, lacing her hands together to keep them from trembling, "Ilmenhith has fallen. I seek asylum in the Triad."

"Asylum is granted," Vicamros said as if it were a given.

"Thank you." She straightened in her chair. "This morning I was attacked in my throne room by a mage who has freed herself from the bonds of affinity and warped her physical form. My people are in danger, but from here, I cannot act without assistance."

"What makes you think they are in danger?"

She blinked at the question.

Vicamros raised a brow and continued. "A kingdom is useless without its inhabitants. An empty country isn't worth ruling. Keeping the people beneath her happy and healthy is in her best interest. Why would she put them in danger?"

Alira cleared her throat. "If I may, Majesty?"

He granted permission with a wave of his fingers.

"We have no reason to believe she is of sound mind." Alira cast a sidewise glance at Arrick. "She once led Kirban Temple. Despite leading it, she tried to destroy it."

"Worse still," Arrick added, catching the cue, "we have reason to believe she was involved in the movement that began the Aldaanan war and ended with the downfall of Eyrion Tolmarni."

"You are familiar with her?" Vicamros asked.

"I served penance as a mageling in the college alongside her." Alira bowed her head. "I served under her once, before I had reason to believe she was mad. I thought she had the temple's best interest at heart, but I know now I was mistaken."

The corners of the king's mouth twitched, but he didn't allow himself to frown.

"She was exiled from Elenhiise for treason," Firal said. "She ignited a war that nearly destroyed us, all for self-serving reasons."

Vicamros regarded her evenly. "Which were?"

She hesitated. "She wished to seize power—"

"You wish to seize power," he interrupted. "Right now, she has it."

"It's completely different," Firal protested. "Elenhiise is mine by right!"

Rune turned away.

The old man in the blue robes coughed. "May I speak, Majesties?"

Vicamros opened his palm in invitation. "Of course, Councilor Parthanus. I wouldn't have requested your presence only to have you remain silent."

The councilor rose halfway, his hands on the table. "I am aware of these issues, somewhat. The old blood runs in my family, as you know. Relatives of mine were sent to Elenhiise centuries ago to aid the founding of the temple. The woman they speak of—Envesi—was never well liked by my family, even those who remained beneath her in the temple. They spoke of a conniving woman with dangerous methods. One letter I received from a cousin spoke of atrocities of magic, though he was unable to say more. If this truly is the same woman, then the temple mages very well may be at risk. Without them, we have only the permanent Gates. Trade would be throttled."

Vicamros leaned back in his throne and drummed his fingertips against the table.

"The temple is within her jurisdiction now," Garam said quietly. "We don't have to like it, but it's the truth."

"If I am to be candid," the king began, still tapping his index finger on the tabletop, "I should let you know I've already spoken to an emissary of this woman. Lord Kaith had already told me of your situation, so I was surprised, but the woman was pleasant. She expressed a desire to keep connections between the Triad and the island, taking the mantle of allies without altering any terms."

Firal glanced at the councilors present. Aside from Rune, they all appeared troubled. His head was down, his eyes closed and his face solemn.

"What did you tell them?" she asked.

The king shrugged. "That I appreciated their consideration

and would ensure our trade agreements remained healthy, for the benefit of both our kingdoms."

She felt a chill and tried not to shudder. "You were a sworn ally to me."

"And I cannot do anything that will hurt the Triad," Vicamros said.

"Is trade really so important to you?" she asked.

He hesitated, glancing toward Rune. He still sat unmoving, not looking. Vicamros's shoulders sank and he exhaled. "Important enough that I sent a friend to his death on your behalf." There was ice in his gaze when he looked at her. Bitterness, as if accusing her of stealing from him.

Her stomach tied itself in knots.

"We can't remove her from power without an army," Alira murmured.

"And I can't act against the Triad's lifeblood on the basis it's been conquered," Vicamros said. "Ours is a business arrangement. First and foremost. If they have no reason to eliminate that agreement, there is no reason for me to raise a finger against them. Better for my people if I don't."

"And if they strike against the college?" Arrick clearly worried about just that. He wrung his hands and didn't bother trying to hide them beneath the table.

Vicamros didn't bat an eye. "Then we address the issue when that happens."

The Archmage sighed. "The college—"

"The college answers to the crown," Garam cut him short. "You can't act without the king's permission. After your predecessor's war, I'd think you'd know a thing or two about following orders."

"The college will wait for direction," Vicamros said. "Unless the island acts against us, we cannot risk a mistake."

Firal's heart sank and though she struggled to stay composed, tears pricked her eyes. She tried to understand his position. If the situation were reversed, she too would hesitate to raise a finger. But it wasn't just the crown at stake. It was her family, her friends, everything she'd ever known.

"I am sorry," Vicamros added, softer. "My hands are tied."

"In the meantime, I imagine we'll need to call a meeting of council to discuss the drafting of another trade treaty." Councilor Parthanus stroked his beard. "She can't simply take up the agreement without signing something, herself."

"In time, yes," the king agreed.

So simply as that, everything went on without her. Firal squeezed her eyes closed.

Wood barked as a chair's legs dragged across the floor. Her eyes snapped open again.

Rune was halfway across the room before Vicamros spoke.

"I have not dismissed council."

As if he hadn't heard, Rune stalked out without a word.

Firal turned, expecting the king to be angry. Instead the man looked startled, dazed, and glanced to his councilors as if unsure what happened.

"He can't possibly want us to strike them," Councilor Parthanus said, almost as surprised as the king.

Garam frowned. "Forgive him, Majesty. His life has been... difficult... since we departed from the Triad."

"Of course," Vicamros murmured, bemused. He sank against the back of his throne. He wet his lips with the tip of his tongue and exhaled before he returned his attention to Firal. "I am sure it has been a difficult day for you, as well. I am sorry I can offer you nothing more than hospitality, but you are free to make yourself at home in the Spiral Palace. Or anywhere else in the Triad you choose."

For now, she thought bitterly. After how easily as he'd turned Rune over to her, how could she expect he'd do anything less if Envesi asked for her to be returned to Elenhiise?

"Thank you," she made herself say, adding as an afterthought, "Majesty."

After all, she was no longer a queen.

"I am sure you are ready to retire." Vicamros beckoned one of the Masters closer. "One of my mages will see you to your quarters."

The woman bowed and crossed to Firal's side.

Firal pushed herself up. "Of course. Thank you for meeting with me."

Ordin followed her to the door, as silent as ever.

The resplendence of the palace was a blur before her eyes. The mage droned on about their surroundings as they walked, giving directions and sharing history, but Firal didn't hear more than snippets. Her thoughts hummed too loud, whirling pools of dismay that spun hard enough to make her sick.

Her husband was gone. Her child, her kingdom. How could she save them when she couldn't even set foot on the island in safety? She'd only dealt with the Archmage directly twice, but the tales of the woman's disposition were legendary even before this new rise to power. The only way Envesi would let Firal back into Ilmenhith was if she crawled in on her belly, begging for it. And even then, that promised nothing for reuniting her family.

As the mage opened the door to a private suite, she turned to Firal, seeking approval. Tending a guest was below most Master mages, but this woman knew Firal had been a queen and powerful ally. Perhaps that warranted some measure of respect, even now.

"Thank you," Firal managed with an incline of her head. "You've been very helpful."

The mage smiled, dipped in a curtsy and backed away to let Firal explore the suite in privacy.

It hosted a sitting room with a small cot for a guard, reminding her Ordin still walked at her heels. A wide door at the far end of the room led to a separate bedchamber, no doubt. At least she could have that space to herself.

"Give me peace," she said to the captain as he closed the door. She never looked to see if he nodded or bowed. She paced across the front room and shut herself in the bedroom before gravitating to the glass doors that opened onto a private balcony.

The Royal City spread for miles, the rooftops a blur through the tears that brimmed against her dark lashes. Firal sank to the stone balcony and hugged her skirts to her knees. She gulped for air as her control unraveled, and all the emotion she'd held back for days bubbled to the surface and spilled over.

Crimson lit the sky as the sun set. It stained the clouds pink as the sun fell below the horizon and dusk swallowed the city.

The wash of shadow felt like the death of all hope. Tears emptied her of pain and helplessness, leaving nothing but despair. Firal knew what was left in her power, but it crushed her to think of submitting herself to that woman. Had it been anyone else, she wouldn't have given it a second thought. To save her family, she'd do anything. But this was her mother. The one person she should have been able to count on, instead of the first person to use and discard her.

Quiet footsteps made her sniffle and rub her nose. She hadn't heard the door open, but over her crying, she couldn't have heard anything. With the way she'd blubbered through sunset and dusk, it was a wonder Ordin hadn't come to check on her sooner.

Except it wasn't Ordin who joined her. She blinked tears away, as if they were responsible for tricking her eyes.

Green-scaled feet stopped beside her and shifted a moment before Rune eased himself to the floor. He didn't look at her, his eyes trained on something in the distance, though she couldn't imagine he saw anything clearly in the dark. Despite his lack of power, his eyes still held some of the otherworldly glow she remembered. The soft violet luminescence was more evident in the shadow of night.

Without looking, he offered a handkerchief.

Firal stared for a long moment before she took it and forced herself to turn away. She sniffled and scrubbed tears from her cheeks with the cloth.

His presence was strangely comforting. He just sat there, gazing at the lights of the city without expecting anything from her. She sniffed and dried her eyes again, then offered the handkerchief back to him.

He took her hand instead.

Her heart jumped into her throat and she swallowed hard to put it back where it belonged. He didn't say anything, just twined his fingers with hers and gently squeezed.

Color rose into her cheeks and she turned away. "Now I know how you feel. Losing everything that was important to you."

"At least you can go back," he murmured. There was no bitterness in his words, just resignation.

"And face that woman." She snuffled, wiped her nose with the kerchief and crumpled the cloth in her hand.

He squeezed her fingers. "Don't give up."

She fell quiet and watched the city. There were enough lights that the stars overhead were almost invisible, but the city lights flickered and winked the same way.

"Will you fight for them?" he asked quietly.

She snorted her annoyance. "Why? Hoping to learn by example?"

His hand twitched in her grasp and she quashed her heart's first response. She refused to feel guilty. She'd felt enough already.

"I know I'm a coward. You don't have to tell me." His claws rasped against her skin, tracing absent shapes.

The evenness of his response startled her. She couldn't think of any way to give her words teeth so she let it be, falling short of scathing and instead reminding herself how different he'd become.

He studied their linked hands for a while, then turned his attention to the city beyond the balustrade. "The first year was a nightmare. What money I had didn't go far. I didn't know the language, so I couldn't communicate. Couldn't barter. I had to hide what I was so I wouldn't be hunted." His claws grew still against her skin as a troubled look grew on his face.

"Foraging was hard. I didn't know the plants. Didn't know how to hunt anything but rabbits and other small game. Turns out they're harder to hunt when they aren't trapped inside the walls of the ruins. Things were better when I made it to the Royal City. For a little while." His mouth twisted with a wry smile. "Until Garam's men arrested me for thieving."

Firal wrung the handkerchief, working it into a ball in the palm of her hand. "Rhyllyn told me about the Arena."

He grimaced. "It was nowhere near what he made it sound like, I'm sure. It was sheer luck that got me out alive. Turns out I wasn't very good at fighting, either."

She didn't reply.

Sighing, Rune let go of her hand and raked clawed fingers through his shaggy dark hair. "I always thought I'd be able to go back. I didn't know how. Everything I did was just to survive, scrape through another day, piece together more of an idea how I'd make it home. Then the war ended and the alliance with Elenhiise was established. I thought that was my chance. I stayed by that Gate all day, waiting for you to reply to that letter. When it closed, I..." He trailed off and turned away.

Her brow furrowed and she shook her head. "What Gate?"

Puzzled, he frowned. "The one in Lore. When the Triad's councilors went to negotiate trade of food and the establishment of a formal alliance."

She remembered that day as clear as anything. How could she forget? It had been her first victory, the famine solved, her people saved, peace established between Ilmenhith and Core. But a letter? She stared at him blankly.

He searched her face, understanding slowly dawning in his expression. His shoulders sank. "You didn't get it."

What was she supposed to say? She swallowed.

Disbelief mingled with disappointment in his eyes. "All these years—I—" He couldn't finish.

She couldn't blame him. All these years, she'd thought he'd abandoned her. She'd forced herself to accept it and move on, letting her hurt fuel her desire for a new and better life. Knowing that he'd tried to contact her, that he'd been so close... Her heart ached anew and she lifted the handkerchief to her chin, sure she'd need it. But her tears were exhausted, and though her eyes burned, she was too weary to cry anymore.

He buried his face in his palms and exhaled heavily. Slowly, he wiped his face and lifted his head to stare at the horizon again. In a moment, everything had changed. All the seething anger she'd sensed in him seeped away, leaving an air of deep and bitter regret burdened with deeper disappointment.

She said nothing. No words she had could have given him peace.

"I sent it with Redoram," he murmured after a time. His head hung between his shoulders, his elbows resting atop his knees. He was deflated, defeated. "I told him to make sure it got to you. I asked him later if he'd remembered it needed to be delivered. He said yes, then never mentioned it again. I thought..."

"That your answer came in silence," she said softly.

He let out a single humorless laugh.

"I thought the same thing, you know. I kept hoping for contact. I..." She forced a smile. "I tried to open a Gate to you, but it failed. Then you never responded to my Calling, and I... well, I gave up."

A faint crinkle formed between his brows. "Calling?"

She searched his eyes, but his uncertainty seemed genuine. Something inside her ached, and a strange tightness took her throat. Hadn't he felt it? That he might not, that the magic-based summons might not work over a great distance, had never crossed her mind. She swallowed hard.

"I tried twice," she said. "After so many months of silence, I was no longer sure you lived."

That line between his eyebrows only grew deeper.

He hadn't felt it. He hadn't known. All that time, he'd felt as abandoned as she had.

This time she reached for him, and laid her hand on his shoulder in an attempt to offer comfort. Her fingertips brushed something beneath the thin fabric of his shirt and her heart jumped in concern. Before he could stop her, she jerked up his shirt and exposed the delicate lacework of crisscrossing scars that decorated his sun-kissed skin. Her stomach lurched.

"Your back," she choked.

He shrugged away from her touch and pulled his shirt back down. "Neither one of us is so perfect as we used to be."

"Why didn't you tell me?" Thinking of the pain he must have endured made her ill. What sort of person could do that to another? She pressed her lips together. No, she knew. Someone like Envesi wouldn't bat an eye.

"What difference would it make?" He shifted, adjusting the way his shirt rested on his shoulders.

She touched his arm, concerned.

"I don't like the way it feels," he murmured. "The fabric on the scars. I notice it sometimes. It's a reminder of all my failures, everything that led to them." He met her eyes, then turned away with a shrug. "Better not to think of them at all."

Another time, she might have scolded him for his self-deprecating words. But there was a sincerity in the way he spoke and the way he sat, baring his thoughts and feelings.

She'd been unfair. As much as she'd struggled, things had been no easier for him. And while she'd thought him changed, she began to see traces of the person she knew. Still there, but buried beneath his struggles and locked out of sight, leaving only anger to swim on the surface. The man beside her was hardened, jaded, but those were new facets cut into him by time. A wrong cut could break a man, just like any flawed stone. But in a gem worth keeping, sometimes a cut that first looked wrong proved vital for exposing its brilliance.

Firal didn't know why he'd come to see her. Caught up in her own emotions, she hadn't thought to ask. He'd said nothing, offering quiet support and then baring his soul just when she needed that most. At heart, it seemed he was no different than she remembered. And—uncomfortably, she realized as she looked at him in the dark—that momentary connection made forgotten feelings stir in her chest.

Yet the quiet moment of companionship seemed contrary to all their interactions in recent days. He'd done nothing but needle at her, provoke her to anger. She couldn't fathom why he'd want to offer comfort now. He was a mystery, it seemed. As always.

She forced herself to turn away, swallowed hard and tried to make herself focus on pressing matters. Now that she'd settled, perhaps she'd be able to think clearly. But no ideas came, leaving her as useless as ever. She fiddled with the hem of her skirt. Why *did* he have so many dresses at the manor? She grimaced and tried to banish the thought. Why did it matter? His life was his own.

"So what now?" she asked quietly.

"I spoke with Garam before coming to see you." He rubbed the back of his neck, then smoothed his hair. "We go to the Grand College in the morning. We'll meet up with Kytenia's group instead of trying to bring them here. Arrick leaves at sunrise to get things ready for our arrival. The Triad's alliance with the island remaining intact gives us a few advantages. For one, the college mages will still be welcome in the temple and Ilmenhith. Vicamros forbade Arrick from letting his mages get involved, but if anyone chooses to flee the island, the college can pass along information on where they might go. If people can get through the Gates, we'll be able to escort them out of the Triad."

"Where would they go?"

He hesitated, then bowed his head. "We'll figure that out. Right now, their safety is more important. And if we get that started, we can get important information out of the college mages who visit Elenhiise. As well as any from refugees they're able to bring over. If Envesi is going to have control of Ilmenhith, she's going to need to stay in or near the palace. That means keeping high-profile captives nearby."

Which meant someone might see Vahn or Lumia. Firal exhaled and smiled weakly. It wasn't ideal, but it was good news. "Who all is going?"

"Alira and Rhyllyn will be staying here, in the Royal City. I doubt he'll be happy about me leaving again so soon, but it's safer if we keep him away from where he might be discovered. The college mages likely wouldn't think to mention his existence, but who knows how many temple mages will be coming and going from the college while the agreements for the renewed alliance are drawn. Other than that, just Garam."

"He seems very invested in all of this," she mused.

"Getting bored in his old age, I suppose." Rune shifted to get up. "In any case, you'll want to rest. We'll Gate to the college, but it'll be another big day of politics, and today's been rough on everyone."

Firal caught his sleeve. "Rune?"

He froze.

"Thank you."

His eyes flickered. Colors other than the familiar, soothing violet danced in their depths. Then he pulled away. "Get some rest."

As she watched him stalk through the doors and disappear into the suite, she lifted her hands to rub her arms.

She still held the handkerchief.

Unfolding it from its crumpled ball, she drew her fingers over the neat edges. It was unadorned, plain ivory fabric. It smelled of him, faintly; a sweet sort of musk that brought back dozens of memories in a moment. She held it to her face and closed her eyes.

After so many years, how could he give her butterflies again?

AN OBSTACLE TO PROGRESS

"THERE'S BEEN A... COMPLICATION." ENVESI'S LIPS PRESSED TO A thin line as she spoke, the closest to a frown she'd allow herself to come.

Ennil's eyes narrowed. He'd been caught off guard when he answered her summons and found her perched on the throne, but he'd regained composure quickly. She doubted the statement surprised him, but he gave her a calculating look. A shrewd man; one of many reasons she'd always found him a useful contact to keep. He clearly assumed the worst, but said nothing. Instead, he motioned for her to continue.

"I believe your son's wife is safe," Envesi said. "But, as near as I can tell, she's been removed from the island." In truth, it was a relief. It had not been her intention to harm the girl. She couldn't recall ever losing control of her temper. With the changes to her power, things were different. She felt the stirrings of chaos sometimes, strong emotions spurred to new heights by the constant connection to power she now had. It was an interesting finding, if unexpected. Perhaps this explained Lomithrandel's seemingly constant anger. She'd always had the impression he was perpetually on the verge of losing control.

She feared the same outcome, but she was stronger. There was no way she'd let those raw feelings get the better of her again.

"By whom?" Ennil didn't sound concerned, but the pinched look at the corners of his eyes gave him away.

"The father of her child."

"And this just happens to end with you on the throne?" Skepticism oozed from his words.

Envesi shrugged. This was where she had to tread carefully. Ennil stood no chance against her. He could never be a physical threat, but he was more than just useful. If not for her connection to him, she never would have made it back to the island. He'd helped reunite her with her loyal followers, granting the power she needed for her mission. His keen mind for politics made him a precious asset for her success. As long as she had his family's backing, the island would come to accept her work. Even with the shadow of murky reputation she'd left behind.

"It's called a seat of power, but it changes occupants so easily. Like a child's game of circling chairs." Envesi stood, beckoned him and motioned toward the empty throne with an open palm.

He stared at it, contemplating. Then he stepped onto the dais and sank into the throne. His hands hovered over the arms for a moment before they settled. He lifted his chin and gazed out across the empty hall before him.

"It could be yours," she murmured. "You already know I don't wish to rule. I require resources the crown can provide, but I have no time to devote to watching over a country. My work, as always, comes first."

Ennil drummed his fingers against the arm rests, his lips pursed. He shook his head and stood. "It belongs to my son. He is the only legacy I have."

"And that legacy will grow, Lord Tanrys." She chuckled. "So long as his woman is safe."

"A wife can be replaced," he said dryly. "She hasn't proven herself useful in that regard." The disgust in his tone made it clear he didn't believe they'd tried for children. He thought the marriage a sham and always had.

Envesi didn't care whether it was or not, but she understood his concern. "I suppose that's true. You've already taken measures to ensure the throne would pass to him first, haven't you?" In fact, she could think of several women who would make adequate replacements as queen.

Grunting his displeasure, Ennil stepped down from the dais. "We'll have to bring him back to the capital. With Vahn and the girl back in the city, things will settle. How fortunate for us that Kifel's boy left behind such a reputation."

Envesi did not reply. She'd last heard whispers of Lomithrandel when she'd been exiled. He was to be executed then. She'd always assumed they'd gone through with it after her departure. As result, she'd washed her hands of that loss some time ago.

Encountering him here had been an amusing surprise.

Milking information from the palace serving staff hadn't been hard. There was a girl full of apparent knowledge who spilled everything with little coercion.

According to hearsay, he'd been living on the mainland since her exile began. There was even some tale about his remarkable status in the Triad's Royal City, something about a title of Champion and a position on the king's council. It was ironic they would land in the same place, but it seemed his rise to glory started well after she'd escaped the Triad and begun to worm her way back into the island. She assumed she would have heard of it otherwise. A man like him was hard to miss.

"What are you thinking?" Ennil asked.

Just like the man to know when something weighed on her mind. His attentiveness was one of the many things she liked about his nature. "We will settle Vahnil in Ilmenhith before nightfall," she said. "Make him and the girl comfortable. Then make it known that I have entered negotiations to be welcomed by the temple, and do what you can to make it clear the throne backs my goals." With fortune, that would distract Vahnil long enough to keep him from leading a crusade to save his wife.

Lomithrandel was an interesting piece to have back on the table, and Envesi wasn't ready to let him be taken so easily.

THE PEACEFUL STILLNESS after the Gate closed left Arrick sighing in relief. He prided himself on having the trust of King Vicamros. Earning it had been no small feat, given the war his predecessor had waged against the rest of the Triad. But trust meant expectations. He didn't object to the orders the king gave him, but he already knew the college would be scrutinized until things settled.

That was just what he needed. Year after year, the college shrank. Its reputation gave mages a bad name, and though he'd spent his tenure as Archmage trying to repair the Triad's perception of the school, he often wondered if his efforts had any effect.

For a time, the alliance with Kirban Temple had elevated the status of college mages. Regardless of the stigma the college had in the north, temple-trained mages were revered on the island and at least appreciated in the south.

But if the temple had been conquered by a lunatic, as their young Archmage implied, Arrick didn't know how long the association would be a benefit. He didn't mean to question his king, but Vicamros was far more calm about the situation than Arrick thought he should be.

Especially if this woman had fueled the war in which the king had earned his stripes.

A mageling in lavender robes popped around the corner before he'd had a chance to right himself. "Archmage Ortath, there's a visiting mage here to see you."

Arrick could have groaned. Another visitor was the last thing he wanted to deal with. He still needed to meet with Kytenia and her mages to go over their findings in the college records. "Where?"

"Waiting in the auditorium, Archmage. Shall I tell her you're coming?"

"Yes, yes." He smoothed his short crop of white hair and followed the mageling into the hallway. "Go ahead, I'm coming."

The mageling dipped in a curtsy and scurried on ahead.

Few visitors *needed* the Archmage, but ego meant every visiting Master inevitably demanded an audience with him. He couldn't risk the college seeming unfriendly, so he obliged them as often as he could. Of course, he also tried to escape and shrug them off onto other college Masters as often as possible. This time, at least his need to speak with Kytenia offered a valid excuse.

Arrick hurried to the auditorium, rehearsing his greeting and quick escape in his head.

The moment he stepped into the auditorium, the words fled.

"Archmage Ortath, I assume?" The sense of the woman's power overwhelmed him before she even looked his way. She smiled, though the expression was strained and never touched her frigid, snake-slitted eyes.

"Yes," he said slowly, his gaze traveling from the stern black ink that rimmed her eyes down to the glittering claws on her white-scaled toes. Dread knotted his stomach. Willpower was all that kept him on his feet. "I was told you requested my presence."

She swept her white skirts to the sides in a grand gesture. The silken fabric shimmered as it fell back into place. A display of wealth; in the college, mage robes—even white ones—were made of spun cotton or wool. "I did. I am Archmage Envesi, founder and leader of Kirban Temple. I've come to speak to you regarding the future of the college and your connection to the temple."

"Mages throughout the world have been allies for centuries,

regardless of location." He chose his words cautiously, hoping he sounded as cordial as he tried to be. "Our relationship is not unique, is it?"

"No." Envesi smiled, though it was with smug satisfaction. "In fact, I've come to ensure it isn't. I understand the Grand College faces reduced enrollment numbers."

"As do many schools of magic across Ithilear," Arrick agreed, letting his disappointment show. "From my conversations with your..." He hesitated. Would she have recognized Kirban's other leaders? "With your temple's interim Archmage, I understand even Kirban has been affected."

She spread her clawed hands in a gesture of indifference. "To an extent, though it will be remedied. As I'm sure you know, the blood of mages flows strong on Elenhiise. It was the reason I chose the island as my headquarters in the first place."

An interesting piece of information, that. Arrick cocked his head to the side, curious. "I knew of the island's abundance of mages, but I didn't realize you'd chosen it."

"After a fashion." Envesi paced to the bottom row of the auditorium's seating. "I initially planned to work from the Grand College, as I was trained here. My arranged marriage to Kifelethelas of Elenhiise was a minor inconvenience, but I was presented with the option of returning to the mainland. The number of mages on Elenhiise swayed my opinion. Will you sit?"

He cast a worried glance around the auditorium. It was open at all hours between lectures. Crossing through the auditorium even provided a shortcut through the college's primary building. Both Masters and magelings in colored robes filtered through, sometimes in small, chattering groups.

Envesi sat as if she didn't notice.

"Wouldn't you prefer to speak somewhere in private?" Arrick suggested.

The woman chuckled. "I appreciate the offer, but one of my mages suggested the time for secrecy was past. I believe she may be right. If more of us were consciously united in our work, we would have made considerably more progress. Let them hear. I understand the decomposition of magic is more commonly known in the Triad."

"Known, but not frequently discussed." He took a seat nearby, leaving more than an arm's length between them. "Regarding that issue, the Grand College has held a unique position. We've done our best to continue to preserve our knowledge, if we cannot preserve our abilities. The Aldaanan mages opposed us every step of the way."

"Disappointing," she murmured. "I did not expect otherwise, but if they wish their Gift to expire with them, it is a wish that can be granted. They are no longer necessary."

Arrick studied her for a time, allowing himself to feel her power while he observed her white scales. "You've become a free mage, haven't you?"

This time, the smile that wreathed itself on her face was pure pleasure. "I am. An imperfect solution, obviously." She extended a hand and flexed it. Like Rune, the Royal City's Champion, she had only four fingers. Unlike him, there was a caution in the way she moved. She was too conscious of her claws, like a noblewoman with enameled fingernails. But she did not appear to be offended by the way he studied her.

He licked his lips and wondered how many questions he'd be allowed. "I sense the wildness in your Gift. I have interacted with the Aldaanan mages in the past and none of them bore it. There was an order to their power. The mutations to your body —they result from your new power?"

"A corruption," she confirmed, drawing her hand to her chest and studying it herself. "I've been unable to eliminate it thus far, but only one generation needs to suffer. The offspring of a corrupted free mage appear to be normal."

"Offspring?" Arrick's brows climbed his forehead. Memory of his meeting with Kytenia regarding the queen's stolen daughter flitted to the forefront of his mind. *A free mage for a parent*, Kytenia had said. He hadn't made the connection before, hadn't had time to give it thought. Before now, he'd never noticed the Arena Champion spoke the Old Aldaanan tongue with the same accent as the island mages.

"Only one exists, so far as I know. I have studied the girl and her Gift is pure. I would learn more if I could link power with the child, but her power rejects mine, due to the corruption." Envesi resisted a frown, but her brow still puckered in a way that portrayed a great deal of struggle.

"And such a rejection would have to be due to the corruption," Arrick mused. "A bound mage can link with a mage of Aldaan, but to do so would surely mean death."

"Without proper safeguards," she agreed.

The auditorium fell quiet for a time, only the distant murmurs of magelings walking through the upper tier to keep it from utter silence.

Arrick's skin prickled with discomfort. At last, he cleared his throat. "A curious situation. But what does it have to do with my college?"

Envesi blinked in surprise. "Why, I wish to assist with the college's efforts to preserve magic. I am unbound and more shall be. There are risks, of course. Some may not survive the change. But I am sure some among your mages will be willing to make the sacrifice so their children may be free."

He paled. "I couldn't ask that of them."

"You would be surprised who is willing to lay their life on the line for a cause." Again she smiled, sweet and genuine, though even that warmth couldn't melt the ice in her slitted eyes. "Of course, if you are concerned, you are free to experience the change yourself. You are older, but you will find there's a certain vitality that comes with freedom. You could sire many new mages yet."

Pure revulsion made his stomach heave. "I couldn't."

Her icy gaze hardened. "Then you will find some who shall."

Arrick bristled. "You have no authority over me, Archmage of Kirban. King Vicamros alone can tell me what I will do."

Anger twisted her smooth face and shadows of color moved through her eyes. "Mages will be freed or the college will fall."

"If Vicamros wishes the college to fall, then so be it."

She fought her agitation. "I'm not sure you understand, Archmage Ortath. I shall explain one more time. I am not here to negotiate. If you refuse to cooperate, I shall have to consider you an obstacle to progress."

"Then you may consider me whatever you please, and the alliance between the college and temple shall no longer exist."

Envesi regarded him thoughtfully for a time and rested her hands in her lap. "Very well."

Energy hummed in the air. Arrick's hair stood on end as something plucked at him, sending a wave of discomfort through his limbs. He jerked to his feet and the air closed around him, trapping him in place.

"I'd heard good things about you, Arrick. I had hoped we could work together." She stared at him, her eyes so empty he thought her soulless.

Again the power in the air picked at him, and his discomfort was replaced with searing pain. His eyes widened as he realized what she was doing. Singling out a thread of his energy, preparing to pull it out of the weave of his very being.

"You're mad!" Arrick choked before the pain gagged him. The world before his eyes darkened and grew hazy as the thread began to come loose.

"Certainly not," Envesi protested. "Insanity is thinking any of us would survive without magic to serve us. But no matter. If you will not do what is best for your mages, I will simply have to do it for you. Goodbye, Arrick. The college shall answer to me now."

He drew a breath to curse her, but as she tore his energy free and his being unraveled, all he could do was scream.

4

GENTLE EDUCATION

THE AIR IN THE AUDITORIUM WAS STILL, YET PREGNANT WITH energy. Traces of every element buzzed in Shymin's senses, but none so strongly as the power of life. As a mage with a healing affinity, it was the only power she could touch directly.

She'd often wondered why her affinity was referred to as healing when it was better described as an affinity to life. Healing was the best use of a connection to the life force of all growing things, but it gave her other abilities, too. It let her drink in power and extend her own energy. It could accelerate the growth of living things, such as plants and animals. She'd long suspected she could accelerate the growth of people, too, but such arts were forbidden—as was the power to manipulate the body by coaxing only certain parts to grow.

Shortly after the corrupted Archmage contacted her, Shymin had asked to attempt use of that forbidden craft, hoping to heal the deformities that came with the taint in Envesi's magic. The woman had obliged, but appeared unsurprised when the corruption was unyielding. Whatever patches of scales Shymin managed to return to flesh had succumbed again to the foul energies entrenched in the Archmage's body only moments later.

She avoided the woman now, giving Envesi a wide berth as

she paced around the auditorium. The sensation of life in the room would be the first to fade. It weighed heavy in the air only because of Arrick Ortath's unmaking. With that knowledge firm in her mind, Shymin's skin crawled when she moved too close to the place the man had been when it happened.

"It may have been excessive," Shymin said at last. Her heart thumped against her ribs and she avoided looking at Envesi, afraid her fear would show through. She'd always been awed by the woman, but this was different. The Archmage had grown unpredictable and her temper was poor.

But the Archmage also expected her to be truthful, and Shymin wasn't certain she had it in her to lie when she already felt the cold grip of fear. She'd been spared because she was useful. What if she, like Arrick, outlived her usefulness?

"He was an obstacle." Envesi waved a hand in dismissal. "The college will serve us better now that it is under my control."

"Opposition isn't always a sign of an enemy. Many can be corrected with gentle education." Shymin hoped she sounded confident. Her opinion was not popular among Envesi's followers, a group that had begun calling itself *Giftkeepers*. She thought the need for a name was silly, but she wouldn't ruffle more feathers than necessary. It was hard enough that the Giftkeepers saw her sister as an opponent. Shymin didn't think Kytenia was wrong in her choice to stand against them; she was merely misguided, like so many others.

"I appreciate your gentle heart, girl. But we do not have time to educate all of them." Envesi chuckled softly. "I will have to send a battalion of mages to act as reinforcements here. I will not have the time to manage the college myself. Not yet."

Shymin paused mid-stride. "You aren't staying here?" Why seize control if she didn't mean to use it?

"I must return to Ilmenhith. I have to secure my standing there before I can expand my reach." The Archmage stood and dusted off her white dress. "We have so little time. There are so many other schools I must attend."

Worrying her hands, Shymin breathed deep and willed her stomach to settle. "I don't understand, Archmage. Why did you call me here, if you will be returning to Ilmenhith so soon?"

"Why, to educate the opposition." Envesi blinked at her. "Is that not what you just suggested? I may not agree, but I will give you a chance to try, if you desire. The rest of the college council will need to be handled."

Shymin's stomach dropped to her knees and she regretted that she had not taken a seat when the Archmage invited her to make herself comfortable. "But they're all above me in station!"

The Archmage looked offended at the suggestion. "Certainly not. You are a Master of affinity and part of Kirban Temple's council. You answer to your Archmage and your ruler, no one else. I would not expect you to educate King Vahnil, but these people are your peers, dear child. Less than that, if I am leaving the college in your hands."

Now Shymin swayed on her feet. Uncaring of how it looked, she staggered to the lowest tier of seating and climbed onto the bench. Her, in charge of the Grand College of Lore!

"I am honored by your trust." Her heart tried to choke her. She wished it was for joy at the recognition. Instead, fear clenched her chest and made her limbs grow cold. Acting as leader of the Grand College made her second only to the Archmage herself. There was no greater honor. No greater chance for failure.

"I could choose no one else." Envesi rose as if to replace her in pacing the auditorium.

Instead of avoiding the place Arrick had been unmade, the Archmage gravitated to it, tilted her head back and breathed deep, as if savoring the remnants of energy. The world would reclaim them soon, pulling each element back into harmony.

It was different from when a person died, though Shymin couldn't put a finger on how. Not for the first time, she wondered what came after death, and how death by being unmade differed. Even mages had no answers for that question.

"You will be given a short time frame, not because I lack faith in your capability, but because we cannot stretch ourselves too thin." Envesi strode toward the lectern in the center of the auditorium stage. "I will expect daily reports on your progress. If you cannot convince the remaining members of the college council to support our cause, we shall have to replace them."

Shouts rose from an adjacent hallway and Shymin turned toward it, sensing a swell of approaching power. Mages, strong ones, and lots of them.

"Ah." The Archmage turned to face the hallway as well. A coy smile danced on her lips, a cold sparkle in her serpentine eyes. "There they are now. Let's introduce them to their new leader, shall we?"

***

MAIDSERVANTS POKED and prodded at Firal until she was ready to scream. Her own staff at home were fussy enough, but they paled in comparison to these girls. They stuffed her in a corset and tightened it until she could scarcely breathe, then swathed her in the layered style of dresses popular in the Royal City. She pined for her own wardrobe, with its cool colors, light fabrics and flowing fit. Worse was pining for her own maids while not knowing if they still lived.

Firal tried to take comfort in what Vicamros had said, but the memory of his words fell short. An empty kingdom was worthless, but she couldn't think her people safe when the woman who surely now sat on her throne had tried to kill her own daughter. Firal could only pray Vahn and Lulu remained useful enough to stay safe.

Ordin regarded her with some amusement when she finally stepped from her private bedchamber and joined him in the suite's sitting room. From the way he gawked at her, she had to look as foolish as she felt.

The gown they'd stuffed her in was a tawny brown-green silk, layered over a high-collared ivory brocade undergown and more petticoats than she could stand to look at. Large puffs of fabric protruded from slits in the sleeve both at shoulder and elbow, leaving her to expect the sleeves would have hung to her knees otherwise. The bodice laced up the front with wide brown ribbons, distracting from the way her corset crushed her bosom and left her torso near shapeless. A wrinkle in her shift beneath the boning pinched when she moved, and the voluminous gathers in the skirt made her hips feel twice as wide. The fabric was so heavy she felt like she waddled, rather than walked, which set her hair to swaying atop her head.

Her black curls were so thick she often wore them down, as it took half a dozen hands to work them into any semblance of order. She'd had that many and more this morning. The maids teased her locks into an absurd swell that bulged from the sides of her head and then pulled it into a fat topknot of a bun, which was netted with pearls and secured with countless pins that dug into her scalp.

Having observed her exhibit of the mainland's peculiar fashion sense, Ordin cleared his throat and turned toward the door. "If we're to stay in the Royal City for an extended period of time, perhaps we can plan a trip to a dressmaker."

Firal glared daggers at his back.

"A message arrived a short while ago. We're to meet the local court mages for a Gate to the Grand College. Archmage Arrick should be prepared for our arrival by now." The captain peered into the hallway. If there were any guards on the other side of the door, he gave no indication.

"I haven't even had breakfast yet," Firal grumbled.

"Forgive me, my lady, but it looks as if they've laced you so tight you wouldn't be able to swallow a grape." Ordin pushed the door wide, revealing the armored men waiting in the hall.

"I'm sure the college mages will be happy to provide you with a meal."

She studied him from the corner of her eye as she passed. It was the first time he'd called her that. Until now, he'd always referred to her with a title befitting a queen. Did he fail to see her as a leader now? Or did he simply avoid calling her anything that might remind her of their predicament?

Ordin positioned himself beside her while the group of guards moved ahead. Alira and Rune were to accompany her to the Grand College, though what she was to accomplish there, she wasn't certain. There was little to be done aside from giving Kytenia and the others orders to keep their heads down while spiriting refugee mages out of the temple, but she supposed they'd expect her to make it a formal command.

Garam would be somewhere on the southern continent by now, or at least she assumed; he didn't have to wait for anyone else to prepare, and she didn't expect he'd have to wait while half a dozen maids stuffed him into an ugly dress.

Her company moved upward from the guest quarters, guiding her to the mage quarters higher in the Spiral Palace. She began to understand the name. The whole place twisted inside, most of it connected by the long hallway that ran around the building with rooms to either side. There were stairs for shortcuts, but the hallway bore a gentle slope that carried them through each floor eventually.

Alira waited outside the Gating parlor. She smiled when she saw Firal, though the expression was stiff and formal. The woman had been friendly enough, but there was a shortness to her manner that made Firal think Alira wasn't comfortable in her presence. Was it because Firal had been the queen to exile her, or was it something else?

Firal smiled politely in return. "Is Rune here?"

"Inside. Arguing with the mages." Alira chuckled and smoothed her robes as her eyes traveled over Firal's dress. She didn't say anything about it, but one of her fine white eyebrows quirked upward.

Firal pretended not to notice. "Whatever for? Is everything all right?"

"Oh, yes." Alira spread her hands and shrugged. "They are having a small disagreement over whether or not he should be present. I am a member of the college, so it's obviously best that I attend, and the mages from Elenhiise answer to you. It seems the Royal City mages decided that means it is a formal meeting for mage business. He is not a part of the college or temple, so what right does he have to attend?"

The guards fanned out to let Firal join the mage. She frowned at the closed door. "Is there always this much red tape involved with college business?"

"Of course." Alira hid her mouth behind her fingertips, though her eyes crinkled at the corners, betraying her amusement. "It's only gotten worse beneath Arrick. He's a good Archmage and the college has performed well beneath him, but he's always been fond of ceremony."

The hushed voices in the Gating parlor went silent. The door opened a moment later and a white-robed woman appeared from behind it.

"Forgive the delay," the woman said. "We have reached a conclusion. The Gate will be opened now."

"What sort of conclusion?" Alira asked.

The Master mage cringed. "Though not recognized by the Grand College, King Vicamros II does favor him with the title of mage. The word of the king supersedes the word of the Archmage."

"I could have told you as much half an hour ago." Alira rolled her eyes and picked up her skirts.

Firal started to follow.

"Wait!" A familiar voice echoed up the sloping hall and sent a chill down her spine.

Alira frowned and leaned back from the doorway to see who it was.

A small entourage of guards lagged behind a lone figure in white, the skirts of her robes hiked halfway to her knees to let her run.

Kytenia was supposed to be in the Grand College, sitting with the college council for the meeting Firal was about to attend. Not running through the Spiral Palace to meet them.

"What in the world?" Firal started toward her friend, but halted when Ordin put an arm in front of her. She shot him an acid glare, but he wasn't looking. His eyes were trained on the soldiers behind the Archmage, his hand on the hilt of his sword.

She followed his gaze and her hands tightened in her skirts. The men wore the blue of Lore, rather than the three colored stripes of the Triad. Firal hadn't even noticed.

Alira stepped from the Gating parlor, followed by Rune and a pair of disgruntled Masters.

"Kytenia, what is the meaning of this?" Firal thrust past Ordin to meet her friend and take Kytenia's hands in hers.

"It's Arrick," the Archmage gasped, leaning into Firal.

Rune slipped around the guards to join them. He offered an arm for support when it looked as if Kytenia could no longer stand. "What about him?"

The Archmage lifted her head and leveled her eyes with his. "He's dead."

"It could be taken as an act of war." King Vicamros paced behind his throne at the far end of the table. His face was calm but he moved like an animal, muscles tightly wound and ready to strike.

The predatory nature of that movement reminded Firal of Rune. She suspected the king's pacing was one of the reasons Rune stayed still, leaning against the wall to the side of the room with his arms crossed. She thought they'd clash if they tried to stalk like that at the same time.

"It wouldn't make sense." Councilor Parthanus—the old man in the dark blue robes and odd hat—had joined them again, but the council meeting was smaller than ever.

The only council members present were Councilor Parthanus, Alira, and Rune. Kytenia was there, as was Ordin, but she was the messenger and he was only there because he refused to leave Firal alone. Firal wasn't certain why she was there. Perhaps only because she'd been the one Kytenia sought first.

Councilor Parthanus stroked his white beard with three fingers, gazing thoughtfully at nothing. "She expressed interest in preserving our alliance. Why would she rescind that offer only a day later?"

The king grunted in displeasure. "I cannot afford to lose that alliance."

"You cannot afford to ignore her actions, either," Rune said. Whatever warmth Firal had seen in him the night before was gone. The man's moods always had changed like quicksilver. His tongue was sharp today. "The temple, Ilmenhith, the college, how long until she's after the Royal City as well?"

"The Royal City is protected by the barrier," Vicamros protested. "The moment she's in the city, she'll be helpless."

"She wasn't helpless against Medreal," Firal murmured.

Vicamros and Councilor Parthanus both looked at her.

She winced and bowed her head.

"Ilmenhith's stewardess was Alda'anan." Rune lowered his voice. "When magic won't suffice, a dagger certainly will."

"The Alda'anan are pacifists," Councilor Parthanus put in. "They always have been. We can't be surprised to find another one killed. If the question is whether or not this Envesi could threaten King Vicamros, I find it unlikely. Guards aside, he's an accomplished swordsman on his own. You of all people should know that." His bushy white brows rose.

Scowling, Rune turned away.

"Even if she did come close enough to challenge me, my death would only result in the council taking control of the Royal City until my son comes of age," Vicamros said. "The three provinces of the Triad have always been self-governing. They would not feel my loss, and she couldn't possibly kill the whole council."

Firal cleared her throat. "This barrier you mentioned. It prevents use of magic?" She'd had no reason to use her Gift since her arrival. That she might be unable to had never crossed her mind.

"It was why I had to run up the palace to find you," Kytenia said. "The throne room was the only part of the palace I remembered well enough to Gate into, and once I was there I couldn't grasp power to try again."

"Some mages are given access stones that allow them to bypass the barrier." Vicamros scratched his beard and resumed pacing. "We'd have the upper hand against anyone who tried to stand against us."

Rune snorted softly. "Assuming she can't figure out how to get an access stone."

"How common are they?" Firal asked.

Alira shrugged. "Not common. Only the Alda'anan were capable of making them, and each stone has to be tuned to its wearer. We can tune them ourselves, but I doubt she'd know how to do it, even if she found one to take."

Kytenia frowned and stared at the table. "What's stopping her from making her own? If free mages can do it, why not her?"

That brought the room to silence.

Firal squirmed in her seat, clasped her hands in her lap and worried her lower lip.

Every moment only seemed to put them one step farther back. For a single night, she'd thought the Grand College might offer a key to reclaiming her throne and rescuing her family. How foolish she'd been to think it would be so easy.

"The clash will happen here, Vicamros," Rune said. His words fell like a weight. "We both know it."

The king squeezed his eyes closed and stood still beneath the three colored banners that represented his empire. "I must consider my people. You keep pushing me to act and I know I can't sit and do nothing, but how can I strike against a force of mages when it puts my people at risk?"

"If the fight happens here, they'll be at risk anyway, Cam." Rune's voice softened, the nickname colored with years of companionship. "What choice do you really have?"

Vicamros swallowed thickly. His shoulders sagged.

Firal's skin rose in gooseflesh, prickling with the sensation of magic. Sizzling heat filled her senses and every mage in the room looked up. Though invisible from this side, there was no mistaking the location of the Gate.

Vicamros lifted his head and did not look surprised when a dark-skinned woman stepped from thin air, her white robes swirling around her ankles.

"How dare you meet without waiting for me!" Fury burned in the woman's mage-blue eyes. Dozens of tiny, snow-white braids tumbled when she shook her head.

Two men followed; Garam, and an unfamiliar man who was likewise dressed in white Master's robes, his skin so dark it reminded Firal of a starless night.

The woman marched forward with a distinct waddle. Striking as though she was, with her high, wide cheekbones and perfectly full lips, Firal found her eyes drawn instead to the slim-fingered hand that rested on her protuberant stomach. "And after you sent my brother all that way to fetch me."

Garam appeared embarrassed. Alira merely looked amused.

Worst of all, Rune's eyes brightened, and the warmest smile Firal had seen since their reunion wreathed itself upon his face. Ice stabbed at her belly and her heart wrenched at the sweet sound of his voice as the woman's name passed his lips.

"Sera."

5

THE MAGES OF UMDAL

Sera's palm cracked against Rune's cheek like a thunderclap. The sheer force rattled his teeth in his skull. A moment passed before he felt the sting.

"How dare you speak to me, you filthy lizard!" Her eyes flashed, creating pools of cold fire amid the warm colors and soft contours of her face. She spun to look at Firal and Kytenia, the only people in the room who hadn't yet heard her story. Quite possibly, they were the only people in the Royal City who hadn't heard it by now.

She gestured toward him with an open hand. "I invited him to my son's naming day, and what arrives at my doorstep instead? A knife. A knife! For a newborn baby boy!"

Rune stepped back, rubbing his cheek. "I would have thought you'd be over that by now."

"I would have thought so too," the darker-skinned man behind her said with a chuckle. His teeth flashed pearl-white in his broad grin, brought out by the stark white of his robes and close-shorn hair. "Twenty years seems like it should have been long enough."

The men locked eyes and Rune nodded, a greeting Stal

returned. They'd never been friends, but they were grown men. They could be cordial, if nothing else.

"We'll have to hope he doesn't repeat it for this one," Vicamros said. His pale eyes flicked toward Sera's stomach. "How many is this, now?"

She drew herself up with pride and her hands skimmed her abdomen. "Seven. Another boy, I think, though Stal insists it is a girl."

"Five girls is more than enough to restore House Kaith to glory." Garam chanced a smile as he joined them, though the expression was fleeting. "We have news."

"As do we." Rune glanced at the sparse handful of people clustered around the table. Firal met his eye and lifted her chin. Her face was smooth, but it was that forced serenity she always put on when she was angry.

He raised a brow. In response, her shoulders hitched higher and she twisted away with a scowl. A surge of irritation made him grit his teeth. What had he done to make her mad this time?

"You first, then." Sera waddled to the table and murmured a sweet thank-you when Stal pulled back a chair for her.

Vicamros, too, finally sat, though he rested an elbow on the arm of his throne and planted his cheek against his fist.

Rune considered sitting too, but by the time Stal and Garam took their seats, there were no gaps where he could comfortably isolate himself. He kept Alira at arm's length as often as possible. If Firal was angry at him over something—Brant knew what it could be now—he wasn't going to chance sitting next to her, either. Instead he crossed his arms and made himself more comfortable with his back against the wall.

When no one spoke, Alira took it upon herself to break the silence. "Archmage Arrick Ortath is dead."

Both Stal and Sera's heads jerked up. She clapped one hand onto the tabletop. "I knew it. I knew that woman meant no good."

Rune wasn't the only one who twitched.

"What do you mean?" Vicamros leaned closer and shifted his elbow from the throne to the table. He seemed like he needed the support, wearied and worn after the worries laid before him.

Stal rested a hand atop his wife's and frowned. "We entertained a visitor last night. It would have been the small hours of the morning here. A woman who..." He paused and his ice-blue eyes drifted to Rune. "Her power was evident. We shall say that."

A muscle twitched involuntarily in Rune's jaw. He lifted one scaly hand to rub it.

"She insisted on speaking with me, wanting to discuss revolutions and changes to magic as we know it," Stal continued. "She wanted Umdal to declare themselves allies and join her cause."

"Stal had the presence of mind to send me away before the discussion began." Sera smiled coyly at the man. "Wise as ever. The woman was a zealot. I don't think I could have held my tongue."

Stal made a quiet sound of disapproval. "I told her I would consider it, but needed to speak to the Collective before I could make a decision, as all the houses of Umdal are self-governing. She said she intended to visit all the schools. I assumed the Grand College would be next, but I did not expect it would be so soon, or that she would escalate to violence if a response was not favorable."

Unable to resist, Rune shot Vicamros a vindicated smirk. "Imagine that."

The king frowned back at him.

"I asked her to give me a fortnight to gather the conclave and discuss the matter," Stal said. "It's unrealistic to think I can contact each member of the Collective in so little time, though I suspected she would object to any longer a wait."

"What is this Collective you speak of?" Firal asked. "Mages?"

"A conglomeration of them," Rune replied. She glowered at him. He took it as encouragement to speak. "Stal is Archmage of the Umdal Schools of Magecraft. There are fewer mages in the south than there are here or on Elenhiise. It's likely the Alda'anan never traveled that far."

"So being a mage in the southern kingdoms is a great honor." Sera smiled and straightened with pride. She'd been blessed to have a mage for a father. As her half-brother, Garam hadn't had that benefit. The two of them made a curious pair now, her white-haired and youthful-faced, and him grayed and grizzled with age. Garam had never been fond of magic. Now Rune wondered if some part of it had been born of jealousy.

"Since there are so few mages and the southern continent is so vast, Umdal splits its mages into small wandering groups that form the Collective," Rune went on. "They're more able to find and educate Gifted youths by keeping their Masters on the move. That way they can ensure there are no wild mages out there to cause trouble, even if the Gifted don't join the Collective."

Stal nodded. "Each group elects their own headmaster, and they operate by their own subset of rules. The headmasters answer to me. My position means I can make absolute decisions for them, but my respect for the leadership of their individual groups means I will not."

Kytenia seemed most interested in the explanation and leaned forward as they spoke. "You don't require your Gifted people to join the school? Why not?"

The question seemed to surprise the Umdal mages.

"Why would we?" Sera asked. "Our purpose is to ensure magic is wielded safely until it meets its end. Nothing more."

Firal and Kytenia shared worried glances.

"That's why this woman is such a danger to us." Stal stroked the short, frizzled hair on his head. "I don't know how much time I can buy. I had hoped to consult with Archmage Arrick, but if he has already fallen..."

Kytenia shook her head in disbelief and leaned in farther.

"I'm not sure I follow. She's a threat because you don't force mages to join you?"

Again the Umdal mages appeared surprised. Both hesitated to reply.

"They don't know about us," Rune said softly. The statement recaptured Firal's ire, her upper lip drawn with disgust. He squared his shoulders and rested a foot against the wall. Let her glower. She could speak to him later or she could sit and seethe. "They don't know about the Children."

"Why would they?" Vicamros mused. "Elenhiise is a trade ally above all else. They don't involve themselves in our politics, and I've made an effort to stay out of theirs." A hint of irony colored his words. Whether he liked it or not, the Triad had become ensnared in Elenhiian politics the moment Rune set foot on Roberian's shores.

Garam reclined in his chair with a sigh. "The Iron Children are responsible for a number of engineering feats in the Triad. From the aqueducts running through the Royal City to the steam engines they're laying rail for between here and Roberian's capital."

"Steam engines?" Kytenia repeated.

"They harness the power of rising steam to propel themselves." Sera grinned. "They're quite fast."

"They outpace a good horse and can keep going for as long as they have water and keep a fire burning." Rune smirked at the astounded looks on Firal and Kytenia's faces. "The only problem is figuring out how long that is, so we can set up waypoints for refueling. They keep getting stranded."

"It's a young invention," Alira said dismissively. "I expect they'll be quite useful once the scholars have had time to experiment with them."

"Remarkable." Firal shook her head, frustrated. "But what does this have to do with magic?"

"Why, everything." Redoram Parthanus chuckled. "Mages

are a dying breed. The Iron Children seek to replace them with machinery and research."

"Replace them?" Kytenia cried. "Mages can't be replaced!"

"Not completely," Vicamros agreed, "but there are advancements that will greatly reduce our dependency on them. Nothing will ever be so convenient as a Gate, but steam machines to power rail-carts and ships will increase travel speed beyond what horses could ever hope to achieve."

Firal snorted and crossed her arms. "Next you'll tell me you're working on machines that will fly."

Sera shrugged. "That isn't necessary. We have the gryphons for air relay. If needed, we can request their kind carry messages for us."

This time Sera was the one to receive Firal's glare. "I suppose you'll expect me to believe you have dragons and other folktales among you, too?"

Alira covered her mouth to hide her smile.

"No dragons," Redoram sighed and adjusted his odd velvet cap with both hands. "Alas, they've been extinct since the First War in Aldaan."

"At least on this side of Raeldan," Rune added with a smirk.

"I'm not sure I believe there is any land in the sea past the Chains of Raeldan," Garam muttered.

"I didn't believe there were any mages with powers like mine until I reached the Triad." Rune pushed himself off the wall and paced behind the throne to claim the empty chair just left of Vicamros. He wasn't arrogant enough to put himself at the king's right hand, regardless of whether Vicamros had asked him to take the place before. It put him next to Garam, but that seemed the safest choice.

He stared across the table without seeing Redoram or the Umdal mages on that side. "Either way, we've gotten off track. The point is if magic is fading, the best thing we can do is help it fade gracefully. We all know Envesi won't agree with that sentiment."

Stal nodded once, and his expression grew steely. "Even if Umdal's primary goal was preservation of our craft, I could never believe letting free mages run wild would be wise. We've seen firsthand what that sort of power can do."

Though the Umdal Archmage didn't look his way, Rune knew Stal was speaking to him. He tried not to resent Sera's marriage to Stal; she was free to marry who she pleased, but that had never been the objection. Out of everyone in the world, why had she chosen him? And while on a mission where Stal had tried to kill him?

"Surely not all of you embrace this philosophy," Kytenia said.

Most of those gathered shifted in silence.

"Certainly not." Alira was the only one who spoke. "As a mage of the Grand College, it would be ridiculous for me to join their movement. They are free to prepare all they like. I prefer to err on the side of preservation. Mages will be around for years to come."

"Unless Archmages causing wars becomes a regular occurrence." Sera rolled her eyes. Stal rubbed her shoulder with one hand to soothe her.

Perhaps that was what Firal needed. A gentle touch, some quiet reassurance she wasn't alone. Now that he thought about it, Rune wondered if that was the source of her anger. He had a strong friendship with House Kaith. Garam and Sera were as close to kin as if they'd been his own blood. Outside of Elenhiise, Firal had only Kytenia. And Ordin, though the captain remained stoic and silent by the door, detached from the conversation.

"It's true we seem to average one altercation every few decades," Redoram said, tapping his chin.

Sera scoffed. "Altercation is a mild word."

Rune studied Firal for a time, the argumentative words of the councilors faded to a dull droning in his ears.

She seemed miserable, the fine lines of worry on her brow growing ever deeper. Dark circles shaded the milky skin beneath her eyes. She reminded him of a wilting flower, desperate for relief but unable to find it on her own. He had tried to offer an olive branch—in the form of a handkerchief the night before—but perhaps she wasn't ready for a proper alliance. Perhaps he wasn't, either.

"We'd be better served by addressing one thing at a time." Rune didn't hear who he interrupted, but the edge in his voice brought everyone to silence. "We know now that Envesi means to control Umdal, in addition to Kirban and the Grand College. We can't let that happen. I think that's one thing we can agree on."

A few heads nodded. Vicamros and Garam just frowned.

"Then we'll come back to that," Rune said. "Don't forget why we ended up in this meeting to begin with. The girl needs to be found."

Firal's brows drew together, her lips pursed. Rune met her eye and, for a moment, his feelings felt as raw as if scoured by sand.

That was why Firal had demanded he help, wasn't it? An alliance. Not simply because of what he could do, but because of the desperation that came with the feeling of being isolated and alone, stripped of power and hungry for help. The feeling that just one person on your side, one person to trust, would turn the tide.

But he'd balked at the summons and contemned her begging. Perhaps her anger at him was more justified than he wanted to admit.

Vicamros twitched his head in agitation. "We've been over that issue and I've already said I won't be involved."

"Then I will," Rune said. "I ask to be released from your council, my liege, and to be excused from your armies. I will forfeit my land holdings if you so require."

Sera's mouth fell open, her shock mirrored by the councilors.

The king blinked at him in disbelief. His mouth opened and closed a half dozen times over before he managed a single word. "Why?"

"Because it's my fault." Rune curled his left hand into a fist and rubbed the namesake scar that marred the scales on its back. "The queen's daughter was taken because of her Gift."

"That has nothing to do with you," Vicamros protested.

"It has everything to do with me. She's a free mage, Cam." Rune's throat constricted and it was all he could do to keep his voice from cracking. "She is my child."

Disbelief clouded the king's face and he turned to Firal as if seeking verification.

Firal sat with her head bowed, the crimson flush of shame coloring her cheeks.

Rune's heart sank.

Vicamros gripped the gilded arms of his throne and stiffened. "Then... your wife..."

"Yes." Rune didn't know what else to say.

Slowly, Vicamros slouched back in his seat.

"What does that make you, then? The consort? Or the king?" Redoram regarded him thoughtfully, stroking the length of his white beard. So much like the first time they'd met, the old scholar sat trying to determine what, exactly, he was.

Rune hesitated, searching the faces of his friends and allies. Garam inclined his head in the slightest of nods. Redoram appeared pleased, as if he'd found the fit of another piece in a complex mechanical puzzle. Stal and Alira were indifferent, while Sera wore an amused smirk.

He didn't dare look at Firal or Kytenia.

"*Does* this make you royalty?" Vicamros asked.

"I suppose it did," Rune said at last, smiling mirthlessly. "Briefly."

Vicamros rubbed the side of his forefinger across his lips before he smoothed his tidy, graying beard. "You never cease to surprise me, my friend. Though I should have guessed you were an old hand at business and politics from our time on the battlefield alone."

The king drew a breath, rested his elbows on the table and

laced his fingers together. "But you are sworn to the crown and I will not relinquish that oath. I will not release you from your service."

Bubbling anger overshadowed the pang of despair that tore at Rune's heart. He shoved himself back from the table and rose. "You don't own me."

"Sit and wait for me to speak to you," Vicamros snapped back. The gleam of determination in the man's steel-blue eyes gave him pause.

Vicamros turned to Alira. "As a member of my council, you have special privilege over most college mages. Use it now. You are to act as my emissary to Roberian. Recall all mages to the Roberian embassy and then bring them to the Royal City. Every last one. Councilor Parthanus, you are to do the same with the embassy in Aldaan."

Redoram nodded. "Of course, Majesty."

Cowardice. Hiding beneath the barrier that kept the Royal City safe from mage assault, as if it alone could save them. The rest of the Triad would be on its own. Rune scoffed and spun away.

A hand snatched his sleeve. "You were not dismissed."

Rune jerked against the king's grasp, which tightened in response. Gritting his teeth against his swelling rage, he pulled harder. "You can't stop me from going after her."

"I didn't say I was." Vicamros stood.

"Then grant me my freedom!"

Vicamros hauled him closer. "I am king! In my council, you will—"

Rune backhanded him across the mouth and tore himself free.

Startled cries and curses echoed behind him. Chairs toppled as Garam and Alira leaped from their seats.

The guards beat them around the table, but not before Vicamros returned the blow.

Rune staggered backwards. Crimson light flared in his eyes as he touched the back of his hand to his bloodied lip.

The king raised a hand, stalling his guards. "You think fighting me will change anything? I'm not your enemy."

Rune wiped black blood from his mouth and spat at the floor. "If you won't let me go, then I'll fight my way out."

Vicamros leaned closer. "Stand down."

"You're in my way," Rune replied through clenched teeth.

The king struck first.

Pain burst in Rune's jaw, radiating through each of his teeth and making his vision blur. He shook his head to clear his vision and lunged at the king.

Strong arms intercepted him before his fists made contact, dragged him backwards and shoved him toward the floor. His claws squeaked uselessly against armor. The light in his eyes burned brighter as his anger grew.

A boot struck the back of his knee and the men wrenched his arms behind his back. Memories flashed through his head as they forced him to kneel. Vicamros loomed before him, ready to pass judgment.

"Stop!" Firal tripped over her own feet in her haste and caught a chair to right herself. "Don't harm him, please!" The sheer panic in her voice pulled at Rune's heart and for a moment, the color in his eyes faltered.

She put herself between them, though she wasn't so forward as to block the king's view. Vicamros stared past her skirts.

"I could have your head for what you've done." The king spoke as calmly as if he remarked on the weather.

"Spare him, I beg you," Firal pleaded. "He is a man of passion, he knows not what he does."

"A loose cannon, more like. He knows precisely what he does." Vicamros touched his mouth and checked his hand for blood. It came away clean. He dropped his hand to his side. "But no amount of passion will make me walk blindly into war. Each step I take will be planned." He cast Rune one shadowed glance before he went on as if nothing had happened. "Lord Kaith, I trust you will be able to help the military prepare to host the incoming mages?"

Garam stood close by, body tense. Even in old age, he was a man of action. Every inch of him showed tight control and preparation to fight. "Of course, Your Majesty."

"There will still be the issue of drawing mages out of Lore, if the Grand College is already outside our control." Vicamros returned to his throne and allowed Alira to inspect him for injuries.

Firal was so near, her skirts brushed Rune's face as she twisted to kneel before him. Though her shoulders relaxed, lines of anxiety still marked her face. And anxiety was all he saw. There was none of the hate she'd voiced. Not in her eyes or the distressed set of her mouth, and certainly not in the gentle way she touched his bleeding lip.

Bitterness swelled inside him. It was all too familiar, a scene that had played out in his head a thousand times or more. Him, forced to his knees before his ruler, waiting for his sentence to come.

Thirty years, he'd wondered what would have happened if she'd said the words that seemed to come so easily now.

Spare him.

So simple, yet powerful.

He wasn't foolish enough to think she said it now because she cared. She needed him, that was all. He was a tool too useful to lose.

Rune tore his gaze away and let his head drop. "You're years too late to save me."

Firal said nothing.

"Will Umdal be able to shield its own mages?" The king waved Alira away, evidently deciding a swollen lip wasn't worth healing.

"We may need refuge," Stal admitted. "The best way to

protect the Collective would be to track them down one at a time and send them to the Royal City."

Vicamros nodded. "Then that is what we'll do."

"And hide while the rest of the world crumbles beneath a mad free mage?" Rune's voice cracked and he clenched his teeth.

"And shelter my people to the best of my power, while organizing a retaliation against forces I cannot hope to match right now," the king replied. "Not that I have to justify myself to fools being restrained on the floor until I see fit to deal with them."

Garam made his way back to his seat, using the chairs for support as he circled the table. "I thought you couldn't risk a war?"

"Arrick's death and the threat to the Umdal mages changes things. It seems war will come for me, one way or another." Vicamros rubbed his eyes and sagged in his throne. "The best I can do is be prepared to meet it."

"Assuming we can gather our people, what else is there we can do?" Sera stroked her stomach with her fingertips. Now and then, she paused to untangle the mess of bracelets at her wrists. "I don't mean to validate the lizard's opinion, but we cannot hide behind the Royal City's walls forever."

Regardless of whether she intended it, Rune still felt a small twinge of validation. At least someone took him seriously. He flexed his shoulders, just enough to test the guards who still held him. Their grip tightened, ensuring he stayed against the floor. He changed the motion and merely shifted on his knees, keeping his head down.

"Be still," Firal whispered.

He'd been so focused on thoughts of leaving that he hadn't realized she still sat with him.

"Don't draw any more attention to yourself and perhaps he'll let you off easy." She leaned in and touched his face again, pretending to examine the injury. He wouldn't have objected to healing, but beneath the Royal City's barrier, it was unlikely to come.

Rune did not reply. His heart stirred with confliction. She sounded as if she was concerned, but was it because she worried for him? Or because she feared she might lose his assistance after he'd finally voiced his allegiance to her cause? He was still powerless, but he had determination. That alone was powerful in its own way.

Her fingertip slid beneath the split in his lip and her hand cradled his swollen jaw. Her cool skin offered some comfort, but her touch stirred violent emotions. Rune knew Vicamros well enough to be sure his life wasn't at risk. He'd be punished, surely, but Cam wasn't a king who ruled with fear. He was too creative for that. A prison term, perhaps, or another stint with the city guard. Even worse, there was the possibility Rune would be forced to sit on all the king's council meetings. He couldn't think of many punishments worse than that.

But no matter what the king had in store for him, it couldn't be worse than the torture of the gentle caress of Firal's hand on his face and the knowledge that—no matter how desperately he wanted it, no matter if he did somehow rescue their child and restore Firal to her throne—she would never be his again.

He pulled away from her touch and made himself focus on the conversation that had gone on without them. His anger dulled to a simmer and bitterness swelled in its wake.

"Having so many mages present does open possibilities for expansion of the barrier," Redoram said, "but encompassing the entire Triad would still be impossible. Even the Alda'anan couldn't do that."

Sera flicked her fingers in dismissal. "It doesn't have to be the whole Triad. Lore is a lost cause, and Aldaan might as well be uninhabited after we pull the mages from their posts. Even Aldaeon never recovered."

"Roberian is certainly large enough to host the whole of the Triad if it comes down to it." Alira tapped her fingernails on the edge of the table. Distracted as he was, Rune hadn't seen her sit down. "The mountain range makes Aldaeon more defensible, but Roberian is a good second. If anyone tries to break the barrier, they'll have to assault it from the east and south."

"But we cannot merely defend forever." Stal scrubbed a dark hand over his scalp. He'd done that half a dozen times already, a sure sign of stress. "How many mages would it take? How large a knot of power would have to be tied to rival someone like that?"

"Ten Masters from each major affinity," Kytenia supplied, quoting the exact request Rune had given. "At the very least. But they would need to be tied with a mage who knew what to do with that sort of power."

If she was trying to suggest Rune for the part, it came at a poor time.

Vicamros heaved a sigh and ground his fingers against his eyes. "We'll still have to start by collecting mages. Even the Grand College doesn't typically have fifty Masters in it at once. And we'll still have the college mages to contend with, for that matter. As well as the temple mages. She won't be alone."

"But we have two free mages." Sera smirked across the table. "They only have one."

"Rhyllyn lacks control," Alira protested. "He cannot be involved."

"With all due respect, Master Alira," Vicamros said, "I believe he is going to have to be."

Rune twitched at that and started to stand, then cursed beneath his breath when the guards shouldered him to the floor again.

The king turned his head as if suddenly reminded of his presence.

"Begin with the mages," Vicamros ordered, rising to his feet and donning the cold, impartial mask of an expression he wore when meting out punishment and discipline. "We'll develop our attack plan once our defenses are in place. Council is dismissed. If you will excuse me, I have another matter to attend."

Rune lifted his head and tried not to cringe when he saw the king unfasten his cloak and lay it over his throne. One by one, Vicamros removed the jeweled rings from his fingers. So. His punishment would be like that.

"Go," Rune whispered to Firal. "We'll speak later."

She hesitated, but inclined her head and followed the others as they filtered out of the room.

The guards released Rune's arms.

"Bind his claws, would you?" Vicamros cracked his knuckles with a grim smile. "If he wants to fight, it's going to be a fair one."

6

OLD FLAMES

FIRAL TOOK A HALF DOZEN STEPS FROM THE CLOSED DOOR BEFORE the angry voices erupted in the council chamber behind her, followed by the sound of fists against flesh.

She spun on her heel and started back, but a hand on her arm stopped her.

"Leave them." Sera grinned and tilted her pointed ear toward the door. "They'll be at it a while before things are settled."

"But Rune—" Firal started.

Sera waved a hand, then rested it on her bulging stomach. "The lizard will be fine. It's not the first time he and King Vicamros have used fists to establish dominance. They call it unscheduled sparring." She rolled her chilly blue eyes and started down the hall slowly.

Unsure what else to do, Firal followed.

"I didn't have a chance to introduce myself," Sera said. A cheery smile put a glow into her cheeks. Her dark skin had an undertone like burnished gold, which only heightened the contrast between her natural coloration and the shocking white hair and ice-blue eyes of a Master mage. She was a beautiful woman, and graceful despite the typical waddle of late pregnancy. "I am Sera Kaith, ruling matron of House Kaith, wife to Archmage Stal Kaith of the Umdal Collective and elder sister to Lord Garam Kaith, former Captain of the Royal City Guard."

"Sister?" Firal studied her from the corner of her eye. "Garam bears your surname."

Sera's fine brows climbed her forehead. "Of course he does. Things are done differently in the trade kingdoms in the south. One's surname is their house name. When you marry, you take the name of the more powerful house. I would be Sera Obane, but Stal was not yet Archmage when we married." She winked.

"Oh." Firal frowned and looked ahead. Sera's husband walked with Kytenia, chatting pleasantly, while Garam and Councilor Parthanus walked with their heads bowed close together for murmurs of business.

"And you?" Sera prompted gently.

Firal grimaced at her forgotten manners and cleared her throat. "My apologies, it's been a difficult week. I am Firal. I suppose I no longer have a title to go with it."

The other woman's eyes grew sharp. "I thought you might be, but I wasn't sure."

"I beg your pardon?" How would she have any idea who Firal was? The Umdal mages had come through a Gate directly into the council chamber. From the sound of things, Garam hadn't been with them long enough to share many of the events from the past few days.

Sera turned her head to inspect her with a shrewd eye. "From the description I heard, I expected a goddess. You're not quite what I had in mind, but I do see the appeal." The corners of her full mouth twisted upward and for a moment, Firal wasn't sure if she should be amused or offended.

Sera didn't give her time to decide. "In any case, it's nice to have a face for the name. Garam told us about your daughter. I'm truly sorry to hear it. I know if it were one of my children, I would go to the ends of the earth to get her back."

So Garam had spoken to her before Envesi's interruption. Firal made herself nod, but words were harder. A lump grew in her throat and threatened to choke her. "It's all happened so fast. It seems every time I find a new ally, things get worse."

"Well," Sera chuckled, "it sounds like you've got a few more on your side now."

Heat crept into Firal's cheeks. "I don't think King Vicamros will have much energy to spare for my daughter."

"You may be surprised. I suspect the amount of effort he puts into that matter will depend on who wins the fight."

"Who wins?" Firal blinked.

Sera shrugged. "Sometimes we're able to guess. Other times, we never know. It was the way Rune and Garam preferred to settle things, too."

Firal had a hard time envisioning Garam as young enough to participate in such things. "It sounds barbaric."

"I agree." Sera paused in the hallway, cradled her stomach and pursed her lips.

Firal recognized the discomfort of a child rearranging themselves and paused alongside her.

After a moment, Sera sighed and resumed walking. "For a long time I thought it meant some men just communicated better with their fists. As I've grown older, I've realized it's more about the chance to vent their frustrations. For some, it's easier to speak after they've had a chance to release some of that anger. And I'm sure you've noticed, but Rune has a terrible temper."

Unable to help herself, Firal laughed.

It wasn't humorous. That temper had caused more grief than most would ever know. If not for his temper, none of this would have happened. They'd still be together, nestled happily in a cavern-house inside Core, or maybe in a cottage in the village they'd carved out on the surface. They'd been married there, the ceremony performed by an officer, since the ruin-folk had no priests.

That village had burned before the temple mages put Firal on the throne. From what she'd pieced together in the aftermath, it was the belief she'd burned with it that led Rune to challenge her father, the man who raised him.

That temper was the reason Kifel died.

If she didn't laugh, she didn't know how she would cope.

"That is one way of putting it," Firal murmured.

Sera smiled knowingly, a distant look in her eyes. It was a response that made Firal wonder again what connection there was—or had been—between them. Sera was married. From the sound of things, she had been for a long time. But she and Rune shared an obvious comfort with one another, a deep familiarity that left Firal... unsettled. She didn't know what else to call it, but the cold queasiness in the pit of her stomach when she'd heard him say the mage's name returned now.

"Either way, you have more working in your favor than you may think," Sera said. "No matter who wins the fight, one of them is willing to stand beside you. Even if Vicamros does not come out on your side, you have that."

"I suppose I do." Firal sucked in a breath and willed herself to smile. "It's been a pleasure to meet you, but I think I'm going to return to my quarters. That meeting took a lot out of me, and I have to admit I've not been sleeping well." In truth, she didn't want to spend another moment at that woman's side, lest that queasy feeling get the best of her. She hadn't had a bite to eat before their tiny council met, but that wouldn't stop her stomach from trying to empty itself.

"I would imagine not." Sympathy shone in Sera's bright eyes. "Rest well, Lady Firal. Stal and I will return to Umdal this afternoon, but if there is anything we can do to help, Garam will be happy to help you reach us."

"Thank you," Firal said. "That's very kind."

Sera laid a hand on her arm. "From one mother to another. Any would do the same." Then she picked up the skirts of her white robe and waddled ahead to join her husband and brother in the knot of conversation farther up the hall.

Firal knew it was meant as comfort, but she couldn't help the way those words pierced her heart.

After all, her own mother had done this.

"Is that a dress?" Firal eyed the mass of black silk slung over Rune's arm.

She hadn't expected to see him until council met again. She'd half expected he'd wind up locked away for a while.

Instead he'd arrived at her rooms only a few hours after they parted ways, and if he'd suffered at the king's hand, he didn't show it. She suspected he'd been seen by a healer, since the bruises were near invisible, but traces of multiple splits in his lips lingered, as did a gash at the corner of his eyebrow.

She doubted the mages left any such marks on Vicamros.

Rune glanced down as if he'd forgotten he carried it. "Oh. Yes. I thought you might appreciate something a little less..." He eyed what she wore and offered the garment he carried. "Well, a little less."

She snorted. The sea of petticoats swirled around her ankles as she turned to take the dress. "It took five of them to get all these layers on me, I doubt I can get them off. But thank you."

It was certainly an improvement over the gown the maids had stuffed her in that morning. The black dress bore a simple bodice with laces in the back and a skirt only half so full as what she wore. The long, straight sleeves ended in pointed cuffs, sporting none of the ridiculous poofs and frills that appeared popular in the Triad. She was not fond of the color, but anything was better than the murky brown-green.

"Yes, this is much better. Thank you." She mustered a smile, folded the dress over her arm and shifted awkwardly.

Rune took a half step back. "Should I send up your maids?"

She flushed and ducked her head. "Oh, no. I've had quite enough of their gossip for one day." And she couldn't call for her friends, not in good conscience. They were mages and were busy, and an uncomfortable dress seemed a trifle compared to their troubles.

"I'm sure Captain Straes could help," he said. Had she not known he'd just been trading angry punches with his king, she might have thought it teasing. As it was, she didn't imagine he could feel that light-hearted after his outburst in the council chamber.

Firal offered a polite smile. "I wouldn't dream of asking Ordin to help me dress. I'll just have to try on my own. In a minute, that is. I'm sure you had something you wanted to talk about." She moved back, giving him room to join her in her private quarters.

The captain looked up at the sound of his name, though he frowned and lowered his gaze back to his book when Rune stepped inside. Ordin hadn't said anything after the display in the council chamber, but she could sense his disapproval just the same. She wasn't certain what he disapproved of, though she suspected it was more about Rune's misbehavior than anything to do with her. Even so, Firal felt a twinge of guilt as she let Rune in and closed the door behind him.

"I thought you'd want to hear what Vicamros said after you left." Rune lingered beside the door as she started across the room. He did not stir a step until she beckoned for him to follow.

"I'm surprised he said anything. It didn't seem like he intended to give you a stern talking-to." Firal doubted it would have worked if he had. She eyed Rune's injuries again. If Vicamros had something to say, did that mean Rune won? Or had the king? Rune was certainly in a better mood, though that could have been just from the fighting. She thought of what Sera said and frowned.

He snorted. "Kings always have something to say, in my experience."

"So they do," she agreed. "What did Vicamros tell you?"

Rune followed her through the room, his hands clasped

behind his back. "That there are terms to my position in council that must be fulfilled. He wants me to make an appearance in the public eye, now that I'm here. There will be a formal discussion of everything else during the evening meal, so you'll hear most of it from him. Stal and Sera have already gone back to the trade kingdoms to rally the Umdal mages. Alira's back in Roberian with Rhyllyn, but I think Redoram will still be here tonight."

"Redoram?" She raised one dark brow.

He touched his temple with one claw. "Sorry. Councilor Parthanus."

"A friend of yours?"

"More of a mentor, I'd say. He taught me the trade tongue while we were in prison. As well as giving me a handful of lessons in politics."

She hadn't noticed until then that they weren't speaking the trade tongue. His speech was so fluid and easy in both languages that when he'd greeted her in Old Aldaanan, the native language of Elenhiise, she'd responded in it without thought. "You keep interesting company."

"I always have."

Firal paced through her private bedchamber to peer out the glass doors and across the balcony. It was midafternoon; she'd have several hours to brace herself before she had to sit through another meeting. At least it sounded like this one wouldn't be so formal, if it was being held over dinner. "Will I be expected to contribute to the conversation tonight?"

Rune followed to the doors, his expression unreadable as he looked across the city. "Yes. Right now, Vicamros hasn't decided if we should wait for her to come to us, or if we should go to her. It's a choice between the element of surprise or having a solid defense. Neither is ideal. If you have other suggestions, I'm sure he'd be happy to hear them."

She appreciated that he didn't use Envesi's name. It was easier for her to think of the woman as some nameless opponent to be dealt with that way, rather than her mother and former Archmage. "So he's willing to let you go?"

"Willing might be a generous term." He rubbed the back of his neck. "But he was right about one thing. If I'm going, every step needs to be carefully planned out. I could be on Elenhiise in half an hour and it wouldn't do a blighted thing to help if I don't know what I'm doing."

So Vicamros had won the fight. Firal doubted Rune would have come to such senses on his own. "Why did you do that?" she asked softly. "Offer to give up your title and holdings to be able to go?"

Rune's apparent levity disappeared. "I thought that was what you wanted from me."

She couldn't make herself face him. "I wanted your help, not your surrender."

"Funny way of asking for it, considering you had me in chains."

"I had nothing to do with that." She trained her eyes on the bright splashes of green that marked tree-lined roadways between slate-roofed buildings. "I have no idea what was in the letter Vahn sent to Vicamros. If I'd known asking for your help was a possibility, I'd have penned a letter to you."

"Would you have told me the truth?" he asked. "Or would I have been left to assume it was Vahn's child I was meant to rescue?"

She hugged the black gown to her stomach. "Should it make a difference?"

Rune didn't reply.

Firal cleared her throat and raised the dress. "I should change. I'd rather wear something less ridiculous to dinner, so I suppose I should slip this on. If you'll excuse me, that is."

He gave a slight bow, wordlessly slipped out of her bedchamber and pulled the door almost closed.

She expected to hear pleasantries exchanged between him and the captain in the sitting room, but there was only silence.

Trying not to let it bother her, she worked free the laces of her bodice and tossed the black gown onto the bed.

Perhaps Ordin was displeased with her, and not Rune. She hadn't stopped to consider how he might view the situation. It was the second time Rune had come to her in her quarters, expecting to speak to her in private.

But Ordin knew Rune. Surely he knew him well enough to be sure speaking was all that would happen. Considering all she'd asked of Rune, it wasn't unreasonable for him to wish to speak with her away from prying eyes and ears.

Layer by layer, she wiggled out of the ugly brown dress and its multitude of petticoats. She worked her way down to the corset over her shift and allowed herself a small sigh of relief, knowing she'd be able to breathe properly again soon. Twisting her arms around her back, she found the tucked and tied laces and tugged. The ties came undone, but no matter how she pulled, the corset wouldn't loosen.

Now she'd gotten herself into a mess. Firal nibbled her lower lip, staring at the discarded clothing on the floor. She could sit in there all evening or break down and call for a maid. With her nearly undressed and Rune waiting in the parlor, she couldn't imagine what sort of gossip that would stir around the Spiral Palace. She certainly couldn't put all those layers back on by herself, which meant the only other option for assistance was one of the two men in the other room.

She stood considering the options for an unreasonable amount of time, until the circles working in her head were finally interrupted by a knock.

"My lady, is everything all right?" Ordin called through the door.

"Yes," she called back with a grimace. Two men. Neither was a good option, but at least one of them was unlikely to be shocked by the sight of her in her undergarments. "Would you send Rune to speak with me?"

A long silence, then the creak of the door's hinges.

Firal clasped her hands at her chest. The tips of her ears turned red when Rune stepped in and immediately turned away.

She lifted her chin and did her best to sound imperious. "Close the door, please. Come assist me. I can't seem to get these laces loose."

He stared at the floor and pushed the door until the latch clicked. "I'm surprised you'd want me to help with such a thing, considering how much you hate me."

She turned her back to him to expose the laces. "That's precisely why I want you to help me. No one could possibly expect I'd want anything else from you."

From the silence that answered, she assumed her words bit.

His claws clicked on the stone floor as he walked, but she would have felt his proximity without the sound to mark his location. Sealed or not, he still bore power. The signature was muddy and indistinct, giving the impression of a man with no trainable Gift rather than the wild force he'd once been. Even so, the sensation made her hair stand on end.

She expected a sharp tug, like the palace maids and her own maidservants in Ilmenhith used to loosen the strings fast. Instead there came a gradual easing of the pressure on her ribs, the laces unthreaded a bit at a time. After so many years, she'd forgotten how gentle he could be.

When the corset shifted freely around her middle, she waved him away and wiggled it off overhead. She glanced over her shoulder. Somehow, she'd expected he would watch. Instead, he stood with his back turned and studied the far wall with far more attention than it deserved.

Firal slid the black gown from the bed and drew it on, settled the cuffs at her wrists and breathed deep. "Tie me in, would you?"

Again, he joined her without a word. His claws had always given him trouble with small buttons, but he was nimble with laces. The fine tips of those talons let him poke stubborn lace ends through eyelets more easily than she could ever manage on her own.

The bodice of the dress pulled snug over her shift, but still gave her room to breathe. "It fits well," she murmured, surprised.

"I had your attendants compare things to the dress you wore from the manor. I'm not so good at guessing." He tied the laces and tucked in the ends.

"Really? Is that why there's such an assorted wardrobe in your home?" Sarcasm dripped from her tone. "So many discarded dresses from lovers you tried to fit by guess?"

Rune didn't rise to the bait. "A lot of guests come and go from my home. Some to see me, more for Rhyllyn. Garam's family visits frequently, as do the mages. After enough surprise visits, it starts to seem like a good idea to have plenty of clothing on hand. There's more than enough space to store it."

A sensible answer. Not that she'd expected he'd confess if anything had been left by lovers. She adjusted the neckline, which sat high enough to hide all but a sliver of her bosom. Not as modest as the ugly dress she'd been given that morning, but the comfort was a clear improvement.

A claw rasped against the back of her neck and she froze.

He didn't touch her again. Instead, he slowly pulled pins from the net of pearls over her hair. When it came free, he tossed the jeweled thing onto the pile of discarded petticoats on the floor.

One by one, pins followed it, letting down her hair. Raven curls cascaded around her shoulders and she heard him inhale.

Gripping her skirts in both hands, she whipped around to scold him. Instead, she found herself lost in his eyes.

After all the cold things Rune had said upon his arrival in Ilmenhith, she never expected to see such emotion in him again. Deep longing reflected in his violet eyes, shadowed with hurt and suppressed desire.

Ever so careful not to touch her skin, he coiled one of her

dark curls around his finger. Then his eyes fell from her face to his scaled hand and his expression hardened, the cold shield of ice erected again in his eyes.

He stepped away with a stiff bow. "Excuse me."

She let him go without a word, still clutching her skirts. After so many years, she finally began to understand the inexorable pull that kept him returning to her in their youth. But this time, instead of snaring him, it had its ties around *her* heart.

7

NEW STRATEGY

As a soldier, Vahn had often been the butt of jokes. He was too docile, too tender-hearted, too much like his mother. If his companions from the guard had been present now, they would have changed their minds.

Vahn was not a violent man, but tonight, he suspected he could be. Fury burned white-hot inside him. His fingers twitched with a painful desire to strike something or hurl something across the room, just to watch it shatter.

The only thing that kept him from lashing out was Lulu's presence in the office. He wasn't about to let the girl out of his sight, and he hadn't been able to bring himself to return to the chambers he'd shared with Firal. Instead he trained his attention on work to be done—or tried.

"You need to sit down." Ennil was stern, as always, but this time the command only made Vahn want to laugh.

He teetered on the verge of mad rage and his father wanted him to sit down? No. He needed to move, pace off the nervous energy, settle his racing mind enough to form a coherent plan. Right now, it was all he could do to keep from screaming.

His return to Ilmenhith was supposed to be triumphant. Shymin's message had been enough to make him cheer. An

95

alliance with Ilmenhith, she'd said. Envesi and Ennil waited in the palace, eager to welcome Vahn and his daughter back to the capital. It should have been his victory. He'd thought it would be.

Instead he arrived to find an empty throne and servants still cleaning broken glass from the floor.

"There's nothing you can do." Ennil's tone grew dangerously sharp.

Vahn almost wished the man would snap at him and give him a reason to break. Then he saw Lulu at the window, her dark curls bobbing as she bounced on her toes. He willed himself to stay calm, breathed deep and exhaled slowly as he tried to focus and think.

Kidnapped.

The answer had been impossible to deny after he'd seen the wreckage in the throne room.

It should have been easy to solve. He'd called for the mages, thinking to open a Gate directly to Firal. But the court mages were missing—including Temar—and those who could be found were dead.

Vahn shuddered at the thought of the white robes full of ash. He didn't know much about magic, not being Gifted himself, but he knew it took a great deal of power to do something like that. And it required the will to break the temple oath against taking another mage's life, besides.

He didn't want to think Ran capable of such atrocities, but he couldn't deny it had happened. Either he was wrong in his steadfast belief in his friend and the Ran he knew no longer existed, or someone else was responsible. Vahn only knew of one other mage with that much power.

She was supposed to be on his side.

Vahn made himself stop behind Lulu. He smoothed her wild curls and gazed out the window. "I know," he replied at last. Ennil had been waiting for him in the capital, but Envesi had gone before he returned.

He'd thought to seek help from the Grand College's mages, but the permanent Gate between the palace and the college had already been closed when he arrived. And the mages in Alwhen had only opened a Gate to send him home with his daughter; they hadn't come through. That meant there was no one to take him anywhere until mages from the temple could answer his call.

Strangely enough, the Ilmenhith chapter house had been empty, as well.

"A message can only travel so fast." Ennil shifted in his chair, watching.

In truth, Vahn was as weary as his father looked, but he couldn't make himself comfortable. Ennil always had a sense of control about him, as though he was always prepared and never surprised. Perhaps it came from so many years as Captain of the Guard and a member of Ilmenhith's council. Or maybe those ties to the council meant he never was surprised. He'd been useful as a part of Firal's cabinet because he had connections everywhere, which provided a constant trickle of information. It was possible Ennil knew things before they happened. In the case of Firal's apparent kidnapping, he'd had time to come to terms with what happened before Vahn ever left the palace in Alwhen. It lent him an air of confidence, while Vahn still felt like tearing out his hair.

"I know," Vahn said again. He rubbed his face with both hands, then raked his fingers through his hair. He didn't know what else to say. He'd sent messages to the temple and Alwhen both, informing the mages of the queen's disappearance. Mages would come from the temple within hours to answer his need, but he still had to decide what to do.

A month before, he would have said life was perfect. Now it seemed he was trying to build castles with dry sand, struggling to hold Elenhiise together while the grains slipped through his fingers and escaped.

Save Shymin, the Masters that headed the temple were missing, and she seemed to be elsewhere. Firal was missing. The court mages were missing. And if Vahn left to find them, Ilmenhith would be without a leader.

Vahn was not fond of his title. He'd never wanted to be king, but a promise had put him there and he took his responsibilities seriously.

Besides, leaving Ilmenhith meant leaving Lulu. If he had his way, she'd never leave his sight again.

As if hearing his thoughts, the girl spun to face him. She clung to his legs, wailed in fright and hid her face in his trousers.

"What is it?" He petted her curls and crouched beside her. The girl flung her arms around his neck, hugged him tight and trembled in distress.

"Seems the Archmage has returned." Ennil paced across the office to join them by the window. "The girl fears her."

"I can't say I blame her," Vahn muttered. He kissed Lulu's temple and sighed. He carried her to the chair behind Firal's desk, sat down and rocked the girl in his arms.

"She'll want to speak to you." Ennil frowned over his shoulder before his gaze swept back to the moonlit gardens beyond the windowpanes. "Shall I join you?"

Vahn gritted his teeth. What difference would it make? He didn't know how much he could get the Archmage to agree to. She wanted him in the palace, she'd made that much clear. And though they'd established a tenuous alliance, he knew he still walked a fine line. If he cooperated, Ilmenhith would still be theirs to rule. Life on Elenhiise could go on as it always had. But if rescuing Firal meant leaving Ilmenhith in hopes of finding her, what would happen to that agreement?

"I need to speak to Mother." Vahn pressed another kiss to Lulu's brow.

Ennil hesitated. "Vivenne? What—"

"Bring her." Vahn left no room for negotiation.

His father regarded him silently for a long time, then dipped in a respectful bow and crossed to the door.

Vahn allowed himself to exhale after the door was closed. Lulu wriggled against him and he hugged his daughter close.

He had to steel himself. He had no doubt Ennil was right, and that Envesi would be joining him any moment. That gave him precious little time to brace for what he'd have to do. It pained him. That pain grew worse with how Lulu held to him in desperate fear. The last thing he wanted to do was work with someone who frightened his child. He simply no longer saw other choices.

Too soon, Ennil returned with Vivenne at his heels.

"I will speak to her alone," Vahn said, willing his face to stay smooth and emotionless when his father's so clearly showed displeasure. But Ennil wouldn't defy him now, not after seeing the mood he was in.

The door closed again, this time leaving him alone with his mother.

She studied him the way a bird might watch a cat from the shelter of a tree, unable to decide if he was dangerous or not.

"Come," he called softly, nodding toward the chairs on the other side of the desk. "Sit."

Though she wrung her hands, she did as she was told.

Vahn pitied her, but he didn't have time to lend comfort. Lulu remained still against his shoulder, sniffling now and then, and gave no indication she sensed any mages nearby. He suspected that would be his only clue to Envesi's whereabouts.

"I will be brief," Vahn said, keeping his voice low. No mages meant no one to spy on them, but he had no doubt Ennil would be waiting with his ear pressed to the door in hopes they'd speak up.

Vivenne bowed her head and twiddled her fingers in her lap. "Why me?"

"You're the only one I can trust now." It hurt to admit, but until he found Firal and had the whole picture once and for all, how could he put faith in anyone? The only constant left was his mother, whose gentle goodness was as unyielding as stone.

Sobered, she met his gaze. Vahn had always been her child first and foremost. Now it was as if she saw him for his position for the first time. A king—her king—seeking audience for a grave matter in which she alone was worthy.

"I am no one," Vivenne said, a quaver in her voice. "I have no authority or power here, save what I gain through Ennil. How can I meet any of your needs?"

"This isn't a matter of politics. It's a matter of family and heart. For that, I can think of no one better." He smiled at her and his eyes slanted to the little girl nestled in the crook of his neck.

Vivenne's lips parted. Sympathy and understanding played across her face at the same time.

"I must take the matter of Firal's disappearance to Vicamros II of the Triad," Vahn said. "She is his ally. He will need to know. The Triad casts a wide net of influence. If she is seen somewhere, eventually, Vicamros will know."

He stood slowly, so the movement wouldn't frighten the girl. "If I am to meet him, it means leaving Elenhiise. With fortune, my absence will be brief. But taking Lumia with me might make Envesi think I'm trying to run."

His mother rose to intercept him and take Lulu from his arms. The girl settled into her familiar embrace, as accepting of Vivenne as her grandmother as she was accepting of him as father. She knew no better, but that the girl's love was genuine had always been a small comfort.

"Don't make Father's mistake and assume I'm working with her willingly. After all she's done to Firal, never mind what she's done to Elenhiise, I could never give the woman blind trust." Vahn stroked Lulu's back as he let go. "I'm not foolish. I am cooperating with Envesi because it's safer for our people. Safer for Lumia. Envesi's power can benefit us, but it means treading dangerous ground. I don't dare tread it with Lulu alongside me."

"And I am to protect her?" Vivenne choked. "I have no Gift, I cannot fight."

"Not protect her," Vahn said. "Love her. Until I return. Don't let her out of your sight. Don't deny the mages if they insist on poking and prodding, but stay present and aware. I don't want her to be alone or afraid ever again."

His mother drew a shuddering breath and kissed the child's silky black curls before she spoke again. "A trip to speak with Vicamros should not take long."

"Unless he already knows where Firal is." He lowered his voice until it was just above a whisper. "If it were just Firal, I might have believed them. If it were just Firal with Captain Straes having gone after her, I might have still believed. But Firal, the captain, all the court mages, Kytenia, and all the heads of affinities, save Shymin?"

Shadows of sorrow darkened Vivenne's eyes. She put a hand on the back of Lumia's head and rocked the girl. "Your father's always thought himself clever in the games he plays," she murmured. "He thinks I don't notice. I suspect he thinks me a fool. But he knows, Vahnil. I'm sure of it."

Vahn hesitated. "He knows what?"

She shrugged. "Everything. He makes it his business to know. If it happens on the island, he has ears to listen. If something's happened to Firal and the mages, he knows. Just like he knew..." she trailed off and her eyes flickered to Lumia.

"That she's Ran's," Vahn finished.

"Yes." Vivenne deflated. She moistened her lips with her tongue and turned away. "But I think I knew first, you know."

His heart sank. He'd fought so long to keep it secret. Was he really so transparent? "How?"

"Because you loved Kytenia so." Tears glittered on her eyelashes, but she smiled and dashed them away. "But you loved Ran more."

"He was a brother to me," Vahn agreed. "I would have died for him. And he for me. Which is why I don't believe for a moment that he's responsible for this."

"Just be careful, Vahn. I promise I'll do what I can, but it won't mean anything if you don't come back." Vivenne started to sit down, but Lulu cried out and buried her face in her neck.

Vahn frowned. "That's our sign. Take her to your room, Mother. She'll be more comfortable if she can sleep in bed beside you."

Vivenne turned after him as he started for the door. "Why, aren't you going to sleep?"

"If Envesi is here, it means I don't have to wait for mages from the temple to answer my call. The sooner I can act on this, the better." He was almost to the door when Ennil knocked and let himself in before Vahn had a chance to reply.

"The Archmage is here," Ennil said. His attention drifted to his wife and his eyes narrowed. "What have the two of you been on about?"

Vivenne huffed and hugged her grandchild close. "He was asking advice on rearing a child. Something you'd certainly know nothing about. I swear, Vahnil, when you were an infant, I did all the raising by myself. We couldn't afford a nursemaid then, and by the time he was promoted to Captain of the Guard, you were already three pents old. Three!"

Ennil rolled his eyes, his interest in their conversation dissipating. "Envesi wishes to speak to you, Vahn."

"Good." Vahn kissed the top of Lumia's head as his mother passed. He breathed deep to ease the aching pull of his heartstrings as she carried his daughter down the hall. "I wish to speak to her, as well."

He pushed past his father to cut toward the main corridor. Envesi wouldn't likely be familiar with the back ways. His best chance of intercepting her was to head for the throne room.

"She will likely be tired," Ennil warned. "Her temper may be short."

"And mine is already gone. I am not the one who has to mind my manners. Archmage or not, right now, I'm the only thing standing between her and open rebellion in Ilmenhith." Vahn held his head high. He'd never be comfortable as a leader, but he readily embraced his role as a protector. With Lulu secure and comforted in his mother's arms, Firal's safety was the only thing left on his mind.

Even without a Gift, he felt Envesi's presence before he saw her. It was like a pressure in the air, or the shadow of a cloud passing before the sun. Heavy, oppressive, like the still before a thunderstorm.

Vahn suppressed a shudder and reminded himself that he was king. No matter how powerful she was, if she wanted Elenhiise to go along with her plans in peace, she needed him.

"Why, King Vahnil." Envesi feigned surprise as she rounded the corner and found herself in his path. She swept her white skirts wide and curtsied, though only as deep as courtesy required. "I expected you would be in bed at this hour."

"Which is why you sent my father to fetch me?" His tone was as dry as his throat.

"It was why I sent a messenger to your father," she said. "I expected him to send a response if you were unavailable. I apologize if you were wakened on my behalf."

He waved a hand. "It doesn't matter. I would have spoken with you regardless. I sent a request for mages to Kirban by messenger pigeon, but I don't have time to wait for their response. I must speak to King Vicamros about my wife's disappearance."

Envesi smiled, though a tiny twitch at the corner of her eye betrayed her. "But it's the middle of the night. Surely you'd rather rest and meet your ally in daylight hours, when you're both awake and clear-headed."

"I would prefer not to leave Ilmenhith without its leader for more time than necessary. I will be needed here in the morning and I intend to be present to speak with my council." Vahn's fingers twitched with the urge to coil themselves around the hilt of his sword. This woman always woke his fighting instincts. He restrained himself.

Her cheerful expression cooled. "I'm afraid I cannot help you reach Vicamros directly. I've never been to the Royal City. The closest I can hope to take you is the Grand College in Lore."

No closer than the palace's permanent Gate would have taken him, had it not been closed because of this woman. Vahn could have cursed. "I suppose that will have to do. I'm sure the college mages will be able to help me reach the Royal City once I am there."

She regarded him for a moment too long, her face too still. There was something wrong in the Grand College, he was sure of it. Would accepting her offer of transport send him straight into a trap?

"Of course," Envesi said, her cool smile restored. "Shymin is there now, discussing things with the college council on the temple's behalf. Perhaps you can express your concern to her and she can assist you."

"I shall." He glanced over his shoulder, half expecting to see his father behind him. The hall was empty. "Will you open the Gate now?"

"Certainly. The Gating parlor is this way, is it not?" She inclined her head toward the parlor used by Firal's mages and led the way.

Vahn bit back an oath. She didn't need a doorway to anchor a Gate like other mages, but he didn't know why she might stall.

She moved with a fluid grace, her white skirts rippling behind her like water. "I trust Shymin will be able to assist you in returning to the island, as well. Until the permanent Gates to the mainland are restored, I believe that's the only option."

So she wanted information. Permanent Gates required Gate-stones on at least one side to hold them open. The stones had to be anchored in the archway that contained the portal. The stones they'd used had belonged to the temple, but they had been removed when the Gates were closed, and Vahn did not know where they might be. They were powerful artifacts, useful to any other mage, but why did Envesi want them? She had grown stronger than any stone.

"I'm afraid I'll have to leave those Gates to you and the court mages. I know nothing about their working, but I'm sure someone as powerful as you wouldn't need the stones to reopen the Gates." He put effort into the praise, wanting her to believe it. It was easier to learn things from people if they believed you liked and respected them.

Envesi sighed and flicked one clawed hand. "It simply can't be done without a Gate-stone. I can open Gates on my own, certainly, but I cannot hold them open forever. They do require concentration, even when you are powerful. I suppose a man without a Gift wouldn't know such things, though." She sounded almost pitying, rather than condescending.

"I appreciate your efforts to enlighten me. But why not simply make your own stones, if they're needed?" He followed her into the Gating parlor.

She chuckled and smoothed her skirts. "I appreciate your confidence in my abilities, boy, but no living mage can do that. Are you prepared?"

Choosing to ignore what she'd called him, Vahn nodded.

Hissing power filled the air, crackling and snapping as white light flooded the empty archway in the middle of the room. The image rippled like the surface of a pond after skipping rocks, then stabilized to reveal an image of the Grand College's auditorium.

"Merely ask for Shymin once you're through," Envesi said.

Steeling himself, Vahn strode through the portal.

No matter his lack of a Gift, the power still rolled through him with an electric tingle and made all his hair stand on end. It was rather like the pins and needles sensation of a limb that had fallen asleep, except they jabbed from head to toe and all the way down to his core. He shuddered once he was clear of it and rubbed the back of his neck and his arms as if to rid himself of the unpleasant feeling. He'd always wondered if what mages felt when passing through Gates was worse. Somehow, he'd never thought to ask what it felt like for anyone else.

Though the auditorium usually held any number of mages on their way to some other part of the college, whether day or night, it was curiously empty now. Vahn's footsteps echoed ominously as he walked. He'd been to Archmage Arrick's office a handful of times; perhaps he'd find the man there. Though Vahn considered Shymin a friend, he didn't mean to seek her. As far as he knew, she'd visited the college only a few times more than he. And if a mage needed to visit a place before they could open a Gate to it, he didn't see how she could help him reach the Royal City. Their mages had never ventured that far. No, he definitely needed a college mage.

Frowning at the emptiness, he turned the corner into the hallway and almost collided with a white-robed figure.

"Majesty!" Edagan gasped, just before he caught her shoulder and pinned her to the wall.

A GATHERING ARMY

"Where is Firal?" Vahn strained so hard not to shake the mage in his hands that veins bulged in his hands and arms.

Edagan jerked out of his grasp, her fingers twitching in a gesture he'd seen countless times before. Gestures weren't necessary for working magic, but many mages used them as a crutch, and they almost all used the same motions. That one meant she'd spun a ward around them to deaden the sounds of their voices.

"How did you escape?" Normally steadfast, the Master of Earth looked shaken.

"Answer my question!" Vahn growled through clenched teeth. His hand went for his sword before he could stop himself.

"I thought she was in Ilmenhith. I came hoping to send word to her—"

"Came from where?" His voice pitched low and dangerous.

Edagan drew back. "Core. When the temple was attacked, I fled into the ruins with my magelings. The last I'd heard, you'd been taken prisoner by Envesi, and—"

"I don't have time for the whole story," Vahn snapped. "Firal is gone. If you don't know where she is, I need to speak to Archmage Arrick."

"He's dead."

Vahn froze.

"I didn't believe the news myself. I thought I would find him, but I've just come from his office and I fear we have little time to escape before we're found." Edagan spun away and hurried down the hall. She did not go far before she stopped to look back at him, her brow furrowed. "Come."

Vahn glanced over his shoulder toward the auditorium. Arrick dead? But Envesi had just come from the Grand College. She'd met with him only that morning. Unless...

Understanding hit him like a wave. He shuddered and hurried after Edagan. "Firal's been—"

"Shh," Edagan hissed.

Vahn had thought the ward was still in place. He lowered his voice. "According to my father, she's been kidnapped. But the court mages disappeared, as well as Ordin Straes and all the temple's heads of affinity."

"That doesn't sound like a kidnapping to me," Edagan muttered. "More like a rescue party."

It wasn't comforting to hear his thoughts echoed. "I've been out of Ilmenhith so long, I thought you'd been part of it."

The mage shook her head and led him across the abandoned courtyard. The archway that held the permanent Gate to Ilmenhith's palace stood empty, the hollow frame eerie in the moonlight. Ahead, a permanent Gate to the shore remained.

Edagan led him through without another word.

From the shore, the Grand College was beautiful to behold. It soared from the top of the jointed basalt columns that rose from the sea, its spidery towers and buttresses illuminated by the glow of the stars beyond. Golden light in windows marked where mages must be, though they were few and far between. The permanent Gate from the college to the coast shone like a pinprick of light in the courtyard, lit by the dozens of buildings at their backs.

Vahn had been to the coastal city that served as the capital of

Lore, but not often, and he had never ventured far. He stared at the scene as if to commit it to memory.

"Come," Edagan said gruffly, laying a hand on his arm. "I will tell you what I can."

He wasn't sure he was ready to hear, but he followed.

She remained quiet as they wove through the city. Eventually, they reached a shabby-looking inn that bustled with life. Sailors and dock hands filled the front room, but they cleared a path for the mage in front of him and never gave her a second glance. They were used to mages, this close to the college, and it seemed that included their pushy and authoritative ways.

Instead of heading for the stairs to the lodgings as he expected, she took him to a room at the back of the inn. A private dining chamber, he expected. The moment she opened the door, he understood why.

Two Masters in dirty white stood among a sea of magelings in their colored robes. Every face turned their direction, the despair on the magelings' faces replaced with awe.

They knew their king.

Given the circumstances, Vahn didn't know if that was good or not.

"Balen," Edagan prompted gently.

The Master of Fire flicked his fingers in the same gesture of spinning a ward. With all the ears that waited outside the door, Vahn was grateful for the precaution.

"Now tell me what's happened," Edagan ordered, reminding him of a stern grandmother. He was compelled to oblige.

"I hardly know where to begin." Vahn sighed and raked his fingers through his blond hair. A mageling pulled a chair from somewhere and pushed it behind him. He sat without a thought. "So much has happened since I left Ilmenhith."

"Well, start at that point." Edagan shrugged. "Then I shall tell you what happened to us."

Vahn started with the problems he'd overlooked; the party his father had chosen and the path they took, which led them straight to where Shymin's party waited to capture them. He shared what he could of his time as a captive in Alwhen, though he left out Envesi's offer to aid him. Edagan and Balen knew of their struggles, but it was no business for magelings to overhear. He concluded with the tale of Firal's apparent kidnapping and Envesi's offer to transport him to the Grand College.

All the while, Edagan's frown grew deeper.

"I should have expected Shymin's involvement, given her history," the Master of Earth muttered. "Now what I've seen makes more sense.The girl being easy to control was a boon when she was younger, but I'd hoped she would outgrow it. Now I thank every one of the Lifetree's leaves her sister is Archmage. If anyone can manage her, it will be Kytenia."

"I don't think we'll solve much with the force we have here," Balen said softly, casting Vahn an apologetic look. "The magelings with us were all we were able to rescue from the temple when Envesi attacked us. As it is, it's a miracle we made our way down to Core. The permanent Gate there has not yet been closed."

"Core's Gate opens to a trade station just north of the city. We came thinking we could find shelter and reinforcements at the Grand College, but the place was in a frenzy." Edagan eased herself into another chair offered by a mageling. "I fear we've been here no more than a few hours, so you've caught us without a plan. Arrick was killed this morning and Shymin was put in his place as acting leader. We were able to slip out of the college in all the confusion. I returned with doubts as to the legitimacy of Arrick's death, but even if I hadn't heard the council, I felt his unmaking in the air."

Shudders rolled through the mages like a ripple.

"What reason did she have to kill Arrick?" Vahn glanced between the Masters, but Balen shook his head, so he focused on Edagan instead. "I thought the college was allied with the temple. If Envesi controls the temple, she'd control that alliance. Wouldn't she?"

"She's a madwoman," Edagan said. "What reason does she have for anything?"

"Which is precisely why I don't want to be gone too long." Vahn rubbed the back of his neck. Aside from her name, he didn't know Neve, the third Master with Edagan and Balen, but their presence meant he'd be able to return to Ilmenhith with ease once his consultation with Vicamros was over. Both Balen and Edagan were familiar with the Gating parlor in the palace.

But that left the question of how he was to reach the Royal City to begin with. He rubbed his temples, thinking of the maps he'd studied all afternoon. Riding could take weeks, assuming he could find a horse. He'd left so quickly he had nothing more than his sword, crown, and the few coins in his pockets he kept handy for tipping messengers. He could sell the crown come morning, but that wouldn't get him far.

"What is that?" Neve asked in a murmur.

Edagan and Balen swiveled to face the door. Without prompting, the magelings stood and organized themselves behind the Masters.

"Mages," Edagan said before Vahn could ask. "Coming closer."

"Do you think they're coming for us?" Balen asked.

The Master of Earth harrumphed. "Really, Balen, don't be daft. They wouldn't send such a small party to recover us. If anything, it's a messenger."

"A messenger from the college could be a problem." Vahn stood and stalked to the door. He drew his sword slowly, muting the sound with his left hand.

"Wait." Edagan raised a finger. "Something about them feels familiar."

The door creaked open and, seeing nearly two dozen mages behind Vahn with his sword drawn, Councilor Redoram Parthanus clapped a hand to the velvet biggin on his head. "Oh, goodness me."

RHYLLYN TUGGED his cravat a little tighter, tucked it into his vest, and wiggled the knot straight. Regardless of how fine his clothing was, there were still times he looked in the mirror and saw little more than a shabby urchin. The vibrant glow of his blue serpent's eyes helped detract from it, but his earliest memories were of life on the streets. No matter how long it had been, no matter how far he'd come, he still felt like an impostor whenever he dressed for court.

His vest was a rich burgundy and gold brocade, his shirt and cravat fine gold silk. Rhyllyn hadn't picked the colors himself, but Alira insisted they'd look good on him. Matters like clothing still seemed unimportant compared to having food on the table. That was one of the reasons he was fond of cooking, but he did acknowledge that appearing in front of the king in his stained apron and linen shirt simply wouldn't do.

"You're sure he wants to speak to me?" Rhyllyn asked. He cringed when Alira glowered.

"For the dozenth time, yes." She twirled her hand in the air as she paced. "Even if he hadn't requested you by name, Vicamros ordered every mage in Roberian be returned to the Royal City. That includes you."

Rhyllyn licked the palm of one olive-scaled hand and swiped it through the stubborn forelock of his mousy brown hair that refused to lay with the rest.

Vicamros was one of his dearest friends but as a rule, Rhyllyn wasn't involved in matters of the court. That was Rune's domain, and Rhyllyn was happy to leave it that way. The mages had inundated him with politics, as well as the logic and reason needed to deal with them, but he didn't have experience. Vicamros was king and Rune was... well, Rune. What Rhyllyn was expected to offer in a formal meeting of council, he had no idea.

"Are you ready yet?" Alira asked, exasperated.

"Yes, ma'am." Rhyllyn pulled on his deep burgundy overcoat, flicked dust from the velvet and straightened a cuff that had folded back on itself. The cuffs bore heavy gold embroidery that matched the shapes embroidered down the thigh of his charcoal gray breeches.

"Good. There's one more thing I need you to do before we go." She gave herself a once-over in the mirror, though she didn't preen. Rhyllyn had never seen her do more than glance at a mirror long enough to straighten the part of her white hair.

"What's that?" He padded across the floor, flinching at the click of his claws against the wood. Perhaps he ought to wear his leather spats. No one expected him or his brother to wear shoes in court—for obvious reasons—but with all the rest of him dressed up, it was odd to be barefoot.

"Your brother's access stone. He left it here when he went to the Royal City, he'll need it now. Fetch it?"

"Of course." Rhyllyn ducked past her, slipped out of his room and jogged to the narrow spiral staircase that led to the loft. He didn't visit Rune's quarters often, though they were never locked. His brother preferred privacy, and Rhyllyn preferred to respect it. But as primary housekeeper, he did know where everything was kept. That alone made him a better choice to retrieve anything, though the grief Rune would give Alira if he found out she'd been in his things was a close second.

The loft spanned the top of the entire manor house, though the less usable parts had been walled off. It was hot in the summer and chill in the winter, but Rune still preferred it over the finer rooms on the house's second floor.

Several large dormers let in plenty of light, and the glass-paned windows could be opened to let air flow through on summer days. Most of the windows had chairs tucked beneath them, but the large one on the back of the house hosted a wide seat beneath a wider window that stood as tall as a man. That was Rune's favorite spot, a fact betrayed by the stacks of books and scattered papers that surrounded it. A blanket spilled from the seat to pool on the floor. More often than not, Rhyllyn found his brother sleeping there instead of the wide and comfortable down-filled bed at the far end of the loft.

Rhyllyn crossed to the window, shook out the blanket and tossed it to one end of the window seat. The useful things were usually there. When Rune was home, his sword would be sheathed and propped against the wall and an assortment of keys, stones and jewelry ended up scattered across the floor. The odd collection of things the man kept made Rhyllyn wonder if his soul hadn't been meant for a crow.

He found the access stone atop one of the stacks of books, weighing down a piece of thin paper covered in lines of what could have been poetry, if any of it were ever finished. A crow or a bard, Rhyllyn thought, bouncing the stone in the palm of his hand.

Though he'd been promised an access stone of his own, Rhyllyn wasn't eager to own one. Even in carrying his brother's, he felt the weight of the responsibility that came with it. The stone itself was simple, a mottled piece of green and white jasper that had been polished to a reflective shine. Coils of silver wrapped both ends and connected it to a black leather strap, which was knotted at just the right length to be pulled on overhead. From what Rhyllyn understood, the stone had to touch the user's skin to take effect. He didn't know how it worked, but along with the burden of responsibility, the stone also gave him an incredible sense of power.

Enchanted objects were rare, something only the Alda'anan could make. Rhyllyn occasionally wondered if his free magic might give him the strength needed to create his own, but thoughts of what the Grand College would demand if he could prevented him from trying. He appreciated the college mages and everything they'd done for him, but he also enjoyed his freedom. In that, he and his brother were alike.

Perhaps that was why Rhyllyn so dreaded being called before the council. He would have done anything for Vicamros, even take a seat on the Royal City council if he was asked. But that didn't mean he had to like it, and it didn't mean he had to look forward to going. He would much rather stay home, baking bread and stealing off with some of those papers by the window so he could turn those poetic lines into songs.

He lingered for as long as he thought he could get away with, then sighed and returned downstairs. "Do I need to get anything else?"

Alira locked the front door. "No, I believe we're ready."

Rhyllyn stopped on the bottom step. "It's just the two of us?"

"Of course. Why?"

"We're not riding to the capital first?"

She snorted. "Don't be ridiculous, Rhyllyn. That would take hours."

"But Rune's not here," he protested. She couldn't possibly expect him to open a Gate alone.

Alira planted her hands on her hips and gave him a hard look. Evidently, that was exactly what she expected.

Crestfallen, he took the last step and cringed when his claws clacked against the parquet floor. He should have worn his spats. It was too late now; any retreat upstairs to get anything else would be seen as procrastination. He could cooperate now, or receive a tongue-lashing and some sort of punishment and then be forced to cooperate afterwards.

"You have to learn eventually." Her voice softened. "He was not much older than you when he discovered he could do it himself, you know."

"I know," Rhyllyn said, scuffing his clawed toes against the floor and stuffing the access stone into the pocket of his breeches. "But I'm not him."

Alira studied him a long while before she sighed and closed the distance between them. She rested her hands on his shoulders. They stood the same height now, or Rhyllyn was a shade taller, but he still saw her as a towering, imposing figure.

"A great deal will be asked of you, Rhyllyn. I advised against it, but at the end of the day, that's all I can do. The councilors are advisors, not rulers. We cannot defy the king's word."

"And I'm willing to help, but everyone seems to want more than I can give." Rhyllyn tried not to feel bitter. It had always been that way. From the moment he'd been taken from the streets and his magic unbound, he'd faced nothing but demands. It was one of the reasons he enjoyed Rune's company so much. Though their first meeting had required his brother to push him, he'd never asked much else. Occasional assistance opening Gates, yes, but Rune was the only one who could withstand the torrent of power Rhyllyn could access. And he never asked Rhyllyn to handle the opening, just to lend him the power to do it himself.

Alira wrapped him in a hug, then patted his cheek. "I cannot link with you to show you what to do, but I will explain it to the best of my ability. You've done it with your brother a hundred times at least. It shouldn't be a problem."

Rhyllyn lowered his gaze as she slipped past him and into the parlor to gather her things from the couch. Though a Gate on his own was a lot to ask, he wasn't worried about whether or not he'd be able to do it.

It was how much more useful he became with each new thing he learned that worried him.

"You'll want to use a doorway to anchor it, I suppose." Alira beckoned him into the parlor and indicated the doorway as he passed through it. "It will take practice for you to create a free-standing Gate. Even most practiced mages prefer to have the aid of a physical opening to give their power shape."

Rhyllyn tried not to groan. "Where are we going?"

She shrugged. "You'll need to think of a familiar place inside the Spiral Palace. You have to be able to picture it clearly and accurately to open a Gate to it. Where that place is will be up to you."

Turning his attention to the doorway, he tried to think. Rune spent more time in the palace. Most of his Gates opened to the throne room or council chamber, though some opened to the private quarters kept aside for his use during visits and council sessions. Rhyllyn didn't spend enough time in the palace to be afforded his own rooms. When he did stay, it was in either Rune's quarters or Alira's. Neither was a place he was intimately familiar with, as sleeping was all he did in either location.

"I think I know of somewhere," he said haltingly. "It's outdoors, though."

"It doesn't matter, so long as it gets us there." Alira paced to the doorway and traced the wooden frame with a fingertip. "This is where you'll focus first. Channel energy into the concept of a passage to another place. Will it to fit the door, both in physicality and in purpose. It is a door, a portal to another place, just like moving from one room to another."

She made it sound easy, but anything that required half a dozen mages or more couldn't be simple. Closing his eyes, Rhyllyn tried to tune himself to the energy in the air around him. It hummed in his senses and stirred when he opened himself to it.

Lessons with the college mages had always been difficult. They spoke of grasping power and forcing it to shape. When Rhyllyn tried to touch the flows of power that way, there was always a shock and backlash. He could force it, but it was exhausting. Instead he preferred the methods his brother taught him. Magic was warm, comforting, ever-present and ready to answer if he called.

It answered him now with a pleasant tingle that crawled over his skin like a static charge.

He'd asked Rune once, in the middle of one of their lessons, if the power they called 'magic' was alive. He hadn't received an answer. With the way it responded to him, questioning and able to obey directions, it was hard to imagine it could be anything other than sentient. But the idea of it being aware was unsettling in its own right. Rhyllyn knew too well that when something was unmade, its power was swallowed by the ebb and flow of reality nearby. Did all life end that way? Absorbed back into the world around it? Or was it only when the threads were pulled apart that the wild power preyed on its source?

Disturbed, Rhyllyn shuddered, and the energy fled from his touch.

"What's the matter?" Alira asked. Had she felt that, or was it only his imagination?

"Nothing," he lied. "It's just... complicated, that's all."

"It is a lot to work with all at once, but you'll manage. Try again." She pointed to the doorway again and her finger outlined the shape of the arch. "Call the power there, then we'll move on to the next step."

Rhyllyn stared at the highest point of the arched wood as he asked the power to return. It answered readily, collecting along the edges of the doorway and awaiting his command.

Despite the prickling sensation of the energy around him and the calm tones of Alira's voice issuing directions for each step, Rhyllyn found his thoughts drifting again.

Rune began life as a free mage. A child without parents, pulled by mages from the streams of energy that formed the world and given a broken body to inhabit.

If magic was alive and Rune was born of it, then what did that make him, really?

KEEPING APPEARANCES

FOR THE FIRST TIME SHYMIN COULD RECALL, SHE PITIED KYTENIA. The mountain of paperwork on her desk rivaled that which always decorated the Archmage's office, and the burden never seemed to grow any lighter. She rubbed her eyes, then grimaced and looked at the dark smudges left on her fingers. The eyemarks she'd earned as the Master of Healing were not necessary any longer; if anything, the role of Headmaster of the Grand College had been a substantial promotion, and abandoning the ways of Kirban Temple might have helped endear her to the councilors who remained.

Yet she couldn't bring herself to abandon something she'd worked hard to earn. Kirban was a part of her, and while Envesi had left her in charge of the Grand College, she'd said nothing about replacing her as Master of Healing. From that alone, she had assumed her position leading the college was meant to be temporary. Questioning Envesi's choices was never wise, and so Shymin had opted to accept the title of Archmage and Headmaster of the Grand College without abandoning her previous responsibilities.

Some of those responsibilities sat in the heap of meaningless busywork on her desk. Her shoulders heaved with her sigh.

Shymin pushed herself up from her desk and paced to the washbasin at the back of her temporary office. The remaining councilors were still working to empty the former headmaster's quarters and primary office so she could take over, though they had surrendered his paperwork with little fuss. Given the way Envesi had demanded it, any fuss might have ended with their unmaking. The thought of Arrick's demise left a foul taste in the back of Shymin's mouth, but she knew better than to oppose. One did not have to agree with a movement's leaders to see the value in their work. That had become a mantra, something she'd repeated to herself so often that it ran through her head without needing to be summoned, any time she faced a new difficulty spawned by the woman's short temper.

She filled the basin and scooped water into her hands. It was cool and pleasant, but did nothing to refresh her when she splashed it against her face. She sought her eyes with her fingertips and gently scrubbed away what remained of the eye-marks she'd smudged. Councilors came to her door at all hours of the day and night, since she'd taken the space as her living quarters as well. No matter how fatigued her work left her, she refused to be seen with the black ink that rimmed her eyes smudged across her cheeks, as if she'd been crying.

"They'd love that, wouldn't they?" she muttered to herself as she finished and patted her face dry. Remnants of ink clung to the roots of her eyelashes when she inspected herself in the mirror, but that didn't matter. She found the vial of ink and the delicate brush she used with it and returned to the mirror to paint her eyes once more. Purple smudges beneath her eyes betrayed her weariness, but she had no powder with which to hide them. Nor did she suppose she would try, if she had. To remain calm and put-together no matter her level of energy could only help her efforts to bring the college to heel.

As of yet, those efforts had pushed the limits of her capability.

The moment that grim thought crossed her mind, a firm

knock at the door demanded her attention. Shymin sighed and swept across the room to answer. The sour face that greeted her was the last one she'd wanted to see.

"Headmaster," Orneld murmured, as if the title itself hurt to speak. "A messenger bird just arrived with a reply from the councilors in the Royal City."

Shymin glanced toward the window of her office-turned-bedroom. The first soft light of morning colored the cloudless sky outside. "I did not expect anyone to be awake yet to receive it."

"Someone is always stationed in the dovecotes," the dour man said. "A mageling brought the message to me, instead of you." His mouth took an unpleasant twist.

She forced herself to smile. The councilors had not been the only ones to snub her leadership. Most of the magelings avoided her presence. This was not the first time one had refused to bring correspondence directly to her. Part of her tried to be reasonable; it had to be difficult to report to a new headmaster, especially someone whom nobody was familiar with. Yet part of her knew Envesi's manner of seizing power had to be at fault for the way all the magelings and low-ranking Masters looked at her. The woman had torn Arrick's very being apart and then put Shymin in his place. How was she supposed to overcome that sort of shadow?

"Well, I appreciate that you took the time to deliver it." She held out her hand and willed her smile to reach her eyes when he scowled and deposited the small roll of paper in her palm. It bore no seal and was not tied. That it curled loosely against her hand indicated he'd already read it. "When will the councilors arrive?"

"They won't," Orneld said.

Shymin blinked at him.

He nodded at the message. "You can read it for yourself, but it's terse and clear. The members of council stationed in the Royal City have been ordered to remain where they are. In fact, most mages in the Triad have been called to the Royal City. To insist they return for your meeting at this point would be to challenge the king. Vicamros is a bull-headed man. He won't take opposition lightly."

"I am certain he won't." She kept her shoulders square, though she felt crestfallen. A surprising number of councilors were stationed abroad. If they would not answer her summons, it did not bode well. Those in the college were not amiable toward her, but at least they were willing to work with her for the good of the college and its occupants. The councilors who were away from the college, however, posed a problem.

"Do you mean to challenge his authority?" Orneld arched a thick white brow at her, though his mouth pulled farther downward than she thought a man's face could. It was as if he went out of his way to appear miserable.

"Of course not. We are not enemies, after all." Shymin closed her hand around the message and tucked it into the pocket of her robes. She could worry about the contents of the message and the refusal of her request later, when she was alone. "I shall simply move forward in meeting with the councilors who can attend for now. Perhaps one of them will be able to carry transcripts of our meetings to those whose services the king requires."

Orneld snorted. "The king's mages are too deep in his pockets for your transcripts to make any difference."

She raised her brows and he seemed to remember himself, for his expression softened.

"Your eagerness to make peace between Kirban's new Archmage and the college is admirable," he added, "but you aren't likely to win anyone over. As long as that woman is Archmage, the college would prefer to cut ties than build stronger bridges."

"The councilors are welcome to feel that way, but perhaps they would be wise to recall that I speak for the college, now."

From the soft sound of disapproval he made in his throat, she knew he disagreed.

Shymin stifled the urge to sigh. "Thank you for this delivery. I need nothing else from you at this time, so you may return to your duties. I expect the former headmaster's office shall be prepared for me soon?"

"Of course," Orneld replied dryly. He did not bow or even so much as nod before he turned to depart.

As he left, at last, she let her shoulders fall. No matter her determination, her methods of gentle persuasion had yet to bear fruit, and the longer she worked to bring the college to order beneath her lead, the more she was convinced she'd been set up to fail.

"One thing at a time," she murmured to herself as she closed the door. Mages being called to the Royal City and held beyond her grasp, however, was something she'd have to grapple with soon.

Without thought, she rubbed her eyes.

"YOU KNOW, I can't recall ever thinking this before, but I wish Cam had scheduled some kind of event for me." Rune straightened his sleeve and gave the mirror beside him a fleeting glance before he tossed a towel over it. He never looked long anymore. Over the years, his reflection had grown more and more unfriendly.

Garam chuckled. "You know what they say. First time for everything."

"Which may be, but you have to agree a little direction would be nice."

"You'd have plenty of direction if you'd taken the time to read any of those papers I brought you yesterday," Garam said.

Rune fought the urge to roll his eyes. "You know I don't have time for that right now. I don't have time for *this* right now."

Considering everything that had happened across the past week, venturing out into the city for the sole purpose of being seen was one of the last things on his list of priorities. But Vicamros had made things clear; if he expected assistance befitting his station as councilor, he had to live up to the role. An uncomfortable amount of serving the Triad revolved around petty politics.

"And I didn't have the time to go get those reports for you, but I managed to fit it in, didn't I?" Garam leaned forward in his chair and rubbed his knee. His cane hung from the edge of the table, where the stacks of paper he'd brought still rested, untouched. He gave them a wistful look.

"You shouldn't have had access to those reports to begin with," Rune protested as he finished buttoning the cuff of his other sleeve. Tight-fitting cuffs and loose sleeves had always been common on Elenhiise, along with the high-collared coats he preferred, but they were unusual in the north. Given the nature of the day's expedition, he wanted to do anything he could to stand out. "You haven't been Captain of the Royal City Guard in how long?"

A wry smile twisted the old man's mouth. "Not long enough, according to my wife."

"She's right."

"I'll be sure to tell her you took her side. Again."

Rune couldn't resist a smirk. "Ready?"

"No, and I don't want to be part of this, but you aren't the only one with expectations heaped on you." Garam dragged himself from his chair with a sigh. "I collected those reports while I advised the guard on how best to defend the city. As a result, I have a loose understanding of most of them. I'll summarize while we walk."

"Why expect me to read all that, then?" Rune waved a clawed hand at the papers before he took his sword from his bed and cut toward the door. When he opened it, a pair of guards blinked at him. He scowled back.

One of the two guards had the sense to duck his head and

turn away. "Begging your pardon, Councilor. We were just on our way to deliver a message for Lord Kaith."

Garam grunted and hobbled to the doorway to join them. "Good timing. Or bad, depending on what the message is."

"A fight," the guard answered. "Just outside the academy. It was just reported a moment ago."

"A fight," Rune repeated, his brow furrowed.

Garam sighed. "Very well. First stop, the academy. Let's get going, shall we?"

Rune strapped his sword to his side and motioned for his companion to lead the way. The guards departed the moment they set foot in the hall, leaving the two of them to descend the Spiral Palace alone. As they walked, Garam rubbed the back of his neck and turned his eyes toward the ceiling. Scuffles around the city were hardly Garam's responsibility anymore, but from the way his eyes tightened at the corners, he still felt it was his burden to bear. Rune didn't envy his commitment.

"You think they came to you because they want me to do something about it?" Rune asked.

"That's as good a guess as any. For some reason, most people seem to think you listen to me." A hint of humor touched the older man's voice, but it was short lived. He went on. "But we were talking about the reports. From my understanding, everything started to fall apart after word got out you were to be found and delivered to the crown."

"That's a polite way of saying arrested and sent for execution," Rune said dryly. He harbored no grudges over the difficult choices Vicamros had been forced to make, but the fact those choices were so readily swept aside with vague pleasantries reminded him of everything he hated about his station.

Garam shrugged. "At least it's being said. You know the way the council operates."

Unimpressed, Rune grunted in response.

"When Vicamros gave the order, there was a definite change

in mood around the city. Groups at the palace gates protesting the decision, people refusing to attend the arena fights, a lot of anger. Brant knows why anyone likes you, but they do."

"Yourself included," Rune said.

The hard set of Garam's mouth indicated otherwise, but Rune still laughed.

The old man went on. "After that, relations with some groups became strained. The nobles were pleased, but you're more of a folk hero than I think any of us realized."

"People like the idea of a nobody being able to rise to glory. The problem with that assumption is I was never nobody."

"I don't think any of us realized how true that was until all this started." Garam gave his head a shake, a rueful smile on his lips. "You were made for great things."

The choice of words sent a cold chill of displeasure down Rune's spine and he fought back a shudder. He knew what Garam meant, but the nature of his own existence had only become more haunting after seeing what Envesi had done to herself.

Garam didn't seem to notice his discomfort. "The biggest issue has been with the Iron Children. After everything you did to sway the mages to start cooperating with them, the Children have decided you're indispensable."

"And that they resent their king for deciding no one is indispensable, I'm sure." The statement wasn't fair to Vicamros or the personal turmoil Rune was sure the king had struggled with, but he had difficulty caring after all he'd been through for the sake of preserving an alliance. After all he'd done to encourage it, it hadn't been a surprise that he'd be sacrificed to keep the accordance intact, but that didn't stop the situation from being unpleasant. Which was, perhaps, too nice a word. Ironic that he tried to smooth over his struggles in his own mind.

Garam nodded. "Which is why we're going to the academy. This isn't the first issue they've had."

Which did nothing to make Rune eager to carry out his

orders. He restrained a sigh as they emerged into the palace courtyard. Beside the gates, a carriage waited. "Are we riding? I would have thought a walk would be more effective, given the whole point of this outing is for me to be seen."

"You're welcome to walk. I am close to seventy and I'm tired." Garam slid his cane into the floor of the carriage and then climbed inside.

Though he would have preferred to walk, Rune followed.

The city outside the carriage windows looked no different to him as they rolled down the wide streets. He was content to watch in silence, and Garam offered no further information. Outside, the market was still thriving, people clustered together to gossip like they always did. None of the faces that caught his eye looked more glum than usual. To think he'd impacted everyday life in a city as big as the Triad's capital would have been arrogant. Rune would not profess humility, but his vanity was not that great.

"There," Garam said.

Rune turned his head to look out the narrow glass window on the other side of the carriage. He got little more than a glimpse of the crowd before the carriage turned and halted.

A moment later, the driver appeared at the door and the sound of people flooded the air. "That's as close as I can get with the horses. Not safe to take them much closer."

Garam clambered out of the carriage and took his cane from the floor. "Thank you. That's close enough."

With considerably more grace, Rune slipped out behind him and turned toward the roar.

Just in front of the academy, a teeming mass of people churned in the street. Angry voices echoed off tall buildings and cries of pain rang in his ears.

"Should have just planned an arena fight for you," Garam said.

"I think I'd prefer that. I could go for beating some pompous noble into the dirt." Rune rested a hand on the hilt of his sword and strode forward. His other hand went to his throat and he winced. He still didn't have his access stone. Magic would have made clearing the streets easier by miles.

Garam did not hurry to follow as he made for the crowd.

There were few combatants; people stood around the brawlers in loose rings, shouting and jeering or cheering them on. All of them blocked the academy's stairs. Guards shouted from the edges of the cluster, trying in vain to disperse the crowd. Above, a handful of scholars hovered near the academy's doors, their faces pinched with distress.

Rune shoved his way into the throng. People pushed back. He pushed harder and spilled into one of the empty circles where a pair of combatants threw fists. Someone spun as if to strike him, then froze, mouth agape.

"Clear out," Rune snarled. His hand tightened around the hilt of his sword.

The other fighter stopped and stared.

One of the scholars at the top of the stairs stood on tip-toe and pointed, his words lost in the noise, but the excitement on his face unmistakable.

"He said, clear out!" Garam roared from somewhere on the other side of the wall of people. The crowd parted like a curtain drawn back as the old man and a handful of guards pressed forward. Even aged and unarmed, Garam bore a commanding air, and Rune fell back to join him at the front of the new triangular formation.

"Hand off your weapon," Garam said, voice low. "I know you want to pummel someone, but now is not the time."

Rune's jaw tightened. He made himself release the hilt of his sword, then squared his shoulders and progressed toward the white stone stairway.

The crowd parted readily now. Rune raised his chin as he climbed the steps.

"So," one of the scholars exclaimed the moment he was

within earshot, a wide grin on her face. "The Arena Champion lives!"

"For the moment. Whether that's fortunate or problematic will strongly depend on how well these people listen." Rune shot a glare over his shoulder at the people below.

Garam issued orders to the guards that surrounded him. Most split off, though a pair remained close at his heels as he trailed up the stairs. "What's the meaning of all this?" he demanded.

The scholar who had spoken rubbed her hands together and retreated a step. "We don't know. There are always people out here, these days. As far as I know, someone only asked them to leave."

"They're leaving now." Rune lifted his voice and let his eyes wander across the crowd. "Is Redoram here?"

"We both know that if Councilor Parthanus were present, he would have been out here betting on fights," another scholar sneered.

"Councilor Parthanus has never made a bet in his life," Garam said. "The man's so moral, he makes me look shady. Get inside. All of you. More guards will be on the way to clean this up and it's going to be uglier before it gets better."

The scholars didn't take much convincing. They scuttled inside and let Garam's pair of guards replace them at the door. Once the group had entered, one of the less bookish-looking scholars hefted a wooden beam into brackets on the door to bar entry.

Rune spared the beam a glance. "Still have that, do we?"

A dark-haired woman emerged from a row of bookshelves nearby. "The Children have never been popular in the Royal City. It's half of why we try to stay focused in Roberian. Room for development aside." A twinkle lit her eyes. "It's good to see you, Lord Kaim-Ennen. It seems the city's nobility have been premature in celebrating your demise."

Garam snorted and pointed over his shoulder. For all that

he'd been stoic and commanding outside, he now leaned heavily on his cane. "Was that a celebration?"

"That wasn't all that unusual," the woman replied with a grin. "The Royal City has always found us to be an unpleasant addition to the Triad's educational opportunities. I don't believe I've had an opportunity to speak with you before, Lord Kaith. My name is Wilaena."

"A senior representative of the Iron Children," Rune added as she motioned for them to follow. The academy had little space to spare, crammed top to bottom with books, scrolls, and worktables surrounded by shelves and crates of strange parts. He ran one scaly hand over an unfamiliar metal oddity as he walked.

Wilaena stopped beside a wide table and drew out a chair. She gestured for Garam to sit. "Scuffles like those were common, shortly after the academy's founding, but days where Lord Kaim-Ennen is present always seem to be a little more peaceful."

"Not in my experience," Garam grumbled as he sank into the offered chair.

Rune chose not to respond. Instead, he leaned against the table and scanned the drawings spread out on its surface. "Is this another new iron horse?"

"Yes," Wilaena sighed. "Sooner or later, we'll come up with one that doesn't explode."

"You do realize statements like that are exactly why people have issues with your organization," Garam said.

She nodded. "We are aware. Not everyone can understand that even mechanical failures are a form of success. But I am sure designs are not what have brought the two of you here today."

"No," Rune agreed. He traced the outline of the smokestack with a claw. "We're here to be seen."

Wilaena tilted her head. "Seen, my lord?"

"King's orders. He wants people to know I'm not dead."

"Yet," Garam added.

Rune shot him a dark look, then reached for a stick of

graphite. "When I go, I'm taking someone with me." He drew a blank paper from somewhere on the table and began a new drawing. "I want to revisit the bathhouse idea for the Royal City. I think having a public installation that's less prone to explosion would help our reputation."

"A bathhouse? Now?" Wilaena rounded the table to watch as the diagram took shape. "If we start now, construction wouldn't finish until midwinter. No one wants to roam the city in freezing temperatures while wet."

"No, but we're more likely to get financing now. Vicamros didn't give me an assignment, so I'll make my own. If we have a rough idea of how big it needs to be, I can visit a few potential locations around the city and be seen making notes before I report to the mages this afternoon." Line by line, the idea took form. Halfway through, Rune paused. His memory of the baths in Core had grown hazy, he realized.

Garam leaned forward to watch, too. "Seeing you involved in another project would also probably aid the public's view of the Children."

"Especially one that would benefit the public in general," Wilaena said. "Very well. Let's try it."

Rune set his jaw and stared at the paper, though his eyes grew unfocused. Try as he might, he couldn't summon the layout of the water races in the boiler room to mind, and the harder he tried, the more he found himself distracted by a new, subtle understanding.

Somewhere along the line, Elenhiise had ceased to be his home.

GUARDIAN'S DUTY

A LIRA CLICKED HER TONGUE AND PLUCKED ANOTHER LEAF FROM HER hair. "I suppose that's what I get for letting you choose the location, isn't it?"

Abashed, Rhyllyn ducked his head. "Well I got us here, at least."

Never mind that it had taken hours. Between his inexperience and his nerves, he'd thought the Gate a lost cause. He appreciated Alira's patience through the ordeal, but they were both tired and cross now. Emerging in a leafy hollow on the back side of a bush hadn't helped her mood.

"Yes, at least we're here." She huffed and brushed dirt off her white robes. "How in the world would you know to put us behind a bush, anyway?"

Rhyllyn stifled a nervous laugh. "We used to sit there for privacy. To talk about things, before Vicamros took the crown." It had also been a preferred hiding place whenever he'd stolen treats from the palace kitchens during visits, but he wasn't going to admit to that.

Alira swept into the Spiral Palace and raised a hand to stop him before he stepped inside. "Brush yourself off. I won't have you appearing before the king covered in leaves and dust."

He doubted Vicamros would care, but he obliged her nonetheless.

They made the long trek up the tower in silence.

Rhyllyn was not a stranger to the palace. He'd seen most of it, in fact, but he'd never been to the council chamber while council was in session. Given the stories he'd heard, he imagined it as boring or frustrating. He'd been present when Vicamros held court before and that was dull enough. But he'd never been involved then. He'd only been a spectator.

"Here we are," Alira sighed. The sound of a heated argument filled the hallway even with the door closed. Ignoring the noise and the guards outside, she walked straight to the door and rapped firmly.

If anyone heard, they gave no indication. The voices carried on, as angry as ever. Alira let herself in anyway.

Politicians and members of the court crowded around the round table, every chair filled. For each person who sat, at least two more stood behind them. Among the angry voices and wild gesticulating, Vicamros sat with his elbows on the table and his fingers laced, listening to the fighting with mild interest.

When the king saw them at the door, his eyes brightened. "Ah. The guest of honor." He pushed himself up and the angry voices around him dwindled to silence. "Please, sit. I am sure someone would be happy to offer their seat."

Alira nudged Rhyllyn forward and his eyes widened when he met the king's gaze. For some reason, he'd assumed Vicamros was speaking to Alira.

"No, thank you," Rhyllyn managed, "I'd prefer to stand. If I may. Majesty." He winced inwardly as he tacked the title onto the end. No matter how friendly things were between them, Vicamros was king. In front of so many courtiers, it wouldn't do to forget that.

"Of course. If you change your mind, however..." The king's gaze slid to a nearby politician, who grew deathly still in his chair.

Rhyllyn forced a smile.

"This shan't take long," Vicamros promised. "I fear we don't have time to dally even if I wanted to. Rhyllyn Kaim-Ennen, I've summoned you to beg your assistance."

All of a sudden, a chair sounded like a good idea. "Me?" Rhyllyn pointed at himself with one claw and struggled not to gape.

Heads swiveled to face him. Dozens of courtiers studied him in silence.

"Under normal circumstances, I wouldn't consider involving you. But these are hardly normal circumstances." Vicamros sank back into his throne. "You have unique skills, and I have need of them. The barrier surrounding the Royal City that renders magic unreachable must be expanded. As the Aldaanan mages created it, my first choice to oversee expansion is one of them. However, as I'm sure you're aware, the Aldaanan are in short supply."

Rhyllyn paled. Prior to lunchtime, he couldn't open a Gate by himself. Now, an hour before supper, he was expected to manage the Royal City's mage-barrier? "I don't mean to question, my liege, but surely there are better choices for someone to oversee this. No matter my strength, Alira is a far more competent mage."

"Unfortunately, competence is not the only issue in this matter." Vicamros spread his hands placatingly. "I'm afraid whoever manages this task needs to be able to withstand movement of a great deal of energy. A free mage is our only choice."

"My brother, then," Rhyllyn said. "If he only has to move it, he shouldn't have any difficulty. He's considerably stronger than I am, in addition to being more skilled."

"Yes, he was my first thought." The king rubbed his eyes in weariness, then rubbed his beard in thought. "But he was unable to assist. The seal on his power caused conflict with the barrier. I asked Alira to retrieve your brother's access stone while she fetched you. If the barrier still reacts to the seal on Rune's Gift with the stone in his possession, I fear you may be our only remaining choice. And expanding the barrier is of utmost importance in keeping the Triad safe, as I'm sure you understand."

Rhyllyn shifted uneasily. His gaze drifted across the judgmental faces of the silent courtiers.

"Please, Rhyllyn." The steel in Vicamros's eyes softened. "I will not order you to do this if you think it a danger to your well-being. But I ask you, as a friend, to try."

Suppressing the urge to groan, Rhyllyn forced himself to look away. Had it been an order, he would have felt better. He could claim he had no way to object, giving his fears no way to take root. Instead Vicamros used their camaraderie to prod him to act and pretend to be happy about it, all while knowing refusal was no real possibility.

If this was the Triad's council, he prayed he never saw it gather again.

"As a man of my country, I could not possibly refuse it service," Rhyllyn said, doing his best to sound diplomatic.

His words appeared to please the nobles. Quiet murmurs of approval and appreciation rose from several places around the table. It seemed odd until Rhyllyn recalled his brother's disposition. No doubt when Rune was presented with the same request, his sharp tongue and self-importance would have caused a stir. Most knew him by his assumed surname; Kaim-Ennen. *Dream-Hunter*. But the council had another name they used for Rune: Ryol'orann. It was Old Aldaanan, scathing words Alira had been reluctant to teach him. *Snake-heart*.

"Your efforts will be compensated," Vicamros said. "I realize what I ask will be difficult, but you will have every mage possible to offer you support. Councilor Parthanus has already gone to Lore to begin collecting what mages can escape the Grand College."

"It may take weeks," Alira warned.

The king shook his head. "And we unfortunately cannot wait

that long. Rhyllyn's work will begin immediately. My court mages will assist him in beginning."

"I need to speak to my brother before I can begin." Rhyllyn clutched the access stone through his pocket. He wasn't certain how he was supposed to work with magic without a stone of his own, but there was still a slim chance he wouldn't have to. If the access stone let Rune manage the barrier on his own, Rhyllyn would have nothing to worry about. If it didn't, they'd still need to discuss what he'd tried and what had failed.

"He is with the mages. It would be best if you join him there. Once you've had a chance to speak, you are both welcome to join us in the formal dining hall. Alira may escort you, if you wish." Vicamros inclined his head, granting permission for them to go.

Though Vicamros said *welcome*, Rhyllyn knew it was not an invitation.

Rhyllyn bowed at the waist. "Thank you, Majesty. I shall see you at the evening meal."

Alira laid a hand on his shoulder and Rhyllyn followed her out.

As the door closed behind him, the voices resumed, but this time softer and more amiable.

Rhyllyn bowed his head.

"They put a great deal of confidence in your abilities," Alira noted softly.

And she hadn't tried to curb the enthusiasm. That stung more than the king's needling plea. She'd been so eager to discourage his involvement when he'd wanted to help. Now that he'd rather hide, she pushed him harder than ever before.

The sensation of Alira manipulating energy flows beside him startled him out of sulking. A ward enveloped them, tied to Alira's power so it drifted along with them as they walked.

"I shall tell you what I can." She stared straight ahead, her face solemn. "I am not happy you've been pulled into this, but I also understand we have reached desperate times. The Triad is now at war."

Rhyllyn gaped. His mouth never closed as she recounted the events of the day, leading up to her orders and his retrieval.

The ward remained up after she finished, a silent indicator she expected a response.

It took some time before he could speak. "But Alira, if she's taken the college, what about me?"

Alira blinked. "What about you? You'll be here in the Royal City, managing the barrier and helping the mages here in any way you can. They're already working on finding an access stone that can be attuned to you."

"That's not what I mean." He rubbed his arms against an uneasy chill. "She's looking for another free mage to link with. She'll be after Rune if she doesn't know about the seal, but what if she does? If she's taken the college, she'll know I'm still alive."

He'd been a child when the last war happened. Envesi and her mages had unbound his power. But she'd left when the wild magic warped his body, claiming the experiment a failure. She'd left Alira and another woman he barely recalled with orders to kill him. Instead, Alira had struck down the other mage and fled. Though Envesi would know by now that Alira had escaped, she was unlikely to expect Rhyllyn still lived.

Evidently, Alira hadn't considered that. She pursed her lips and her face slowly twisted into a frown. "Well, I imagine the Royal City is the best place for you to be. After all, if you're within the barrier, you're untouchable."

Untouchable by magic, at least. Disheartened, Rhyllyn turned away.

She released the ward and he remained quiet, trying to think of the task ahead of him instead of the conversation they'd just finished.

A cluster of white-robed mages stood outside the mage quarters when they arrived, though the group parted readily to let them through. Some gave Alira curt nods, while others regarded Rhyllyn with suspicion. Knowing most of the mages and having shared lessons with a number of them, Rhyllyn knew he wasn't the problem—it was what he was supposed to do they were suspicious of.

But whether they were worried over his capability or the issue of expanding the barrier to begin with, he didn't know. In the end, it didn't matter. He saw his brother sitting on the floor with a handful of mages surrounding him, and Rhyllyn pushed forward to join them.

One of the mages cradled Rune's head. Her energies prickled in Rhyllyn's senses as she explored for injury.

"Are you okay?" Rhyllyn asked as he knelt in front of his brother.

Aside from a trickle of black blood another mage wiped from beneath Rune's nose with a handkerchief, he didn't appear to be harmed. He waved the mages away, though he took the dirty handkerchief before he finished the motion. "The mage-barrier here is nothing like the one they had in Kirban when I was young. This one kicks hard when it doesn't like you."

Rhyllyn crossed his ankles and rested his hands on his knees. "What happened?"

Rune grunted softly, closing his eyes and shivering as the mage behind him finished her inspection and released his head. "I pushed."

"No, I mean the reaction." Rhyllyn glanced at the handkerchief and the mottled black blotches on its folds. "Was there a physical backlash, or was it all energy?"

"Both. Like you scuffing your feet on the rug and then touching me, times a thousand." Rune rubbed his forehead and released a slow, hissing breath.

"And it did that?" Rhyllyn motioned to the bloodied handkerchief.

"No, she did that." Rune glowered at a mage across the room, who bowed her head in guilt. He gingerly felt his nose. "We were linked, since I didn't have my stone. When the barrier's anchor threw me back, she went down with me. From the sound, I thought she broke it with her skull. Never mind what it felt like."

Rhyllyn mustered a smile. "Seems the mages gave you a clean bill of health."

"Nothing broken or bleeding anymore, at least." Rune pushed himself to his knees, paused, and cradled his head with a grimace. "This headache is something else, though. Help me up. I'll show you what I did."

Rhyllyn slid forward, put an arm around his brother's ribs, and helped him to his feet. Rune was plenty taller, making it easy for him to drape an arm over Rhyllyn's shoulders for support.

"You said the barrier has an anchor?" Rhyllyn had never thought about what actually held the barrier in place. It was just something that had always been there, steady and unchanging. It made sense for it to require an anchor, since permanent Gates did and the barrier appeared to be a permanent installation as well. He wasn't yet familiar with things like permanent energy loops and ensorceled objects. That it needed to be a physical anchor, not just a place the energy was put in an endless cycle, had never crossed his mind.

Rune found his feet after a few steps, pulled away from Rhyllyn and walked on his own. He still cradled his head with one hand, but he moved as if his strength had begun to return. "Alira said she'd have you bring the stone."

"Oh." Rhyllyn paused, dug it out of his pocket and turned it over in his hand. He hurried to catch up and offered it on one outstretched palm. "Here."

Rune took it without comment, though Rhyllyn felt the shift in the air as his brother drew power. Instead of fleeing, the energy flows homed in on the stone and allowed themselves to be snared.

As he pulled power into himself, Rune sighed in quiet relief. That was one of many things the Alda'anan mages had taught him; to use energy around him to replenish his own stores when weak. He'd tried to explain the process before, but Rhyllyn hadn't been able to do it on his own.

Such lessons often ended with everyone around him expressing frustration, but Rhyllyn didn't mind. As far as mages went, he was young. That he'd come as far as he had was a wonder on its own. The Alda'anan had taken Rune as a student weeks before Rhyllyn met him, meaning he'd had six whole pents to hone these skills. As far as Rhyllyn was concerned, feelings of jealousy or discouragement over his own inability to keep pace would be foolish.

Rune led him to the back of the mage quarters through a narrow doorway. Formal mage business was handled in the front room, but halls leading to their private offices branched from this private study. Couches in muted ivory tones sat atop matching rugs, all positioned around a sculpture in the center of the room.

A framework of silver rings, it moved of its own accord. Each ring rotated inside the next, moving at different speeds and, at times, shielding a large, polished orb of citrine. Light from the far windows struck it now and then, whenever the movement of the rings provided a clear path, and it glowed like golden fire in the center of the astrolabe.

Before they neared it, Rhyllyn felt its power. What it was doing, though, he couldn't tell. The energy around it was mighty but muddled. "Is that it?" With the ripple it caused in the flows around it, he didn't know what else it could be, but he couldn't help but ask.

"The legendary nullifying barrier of the Royal City," Rune said with a smirk. He moved ahead and dropped onto one of the couches beside it with a sigh. "Self-sustaining until the end of time. Or until someone jams up the rings, I suppose." He extended a foot toward the outermost ring, yielding a harsh sound of reprimand from a nearby mage.

Chuckling, he lowered his foot and flexed his clawed toes. "It likes me about as well as the mages here do."

"Self-sustaining?" Rhyllyn paced around it, studying the motion of the rings. "It's... it's feeding itself off the disruptions caused by the rings, right?"

"Precisely. One loop of power keeps the rings in motion. The movement generates enough energy that it feeds itself, but also feeds the stone. Which is what anchors the barrier." Rune shrugged. "Some of the court mages have concerns that if we extend the barrier to encompass a larger area like Vicamros has ordered, the rings won't be enough to sustain it."

Rhyllyn looked toward the windows, crestfallen. "Which is why they want me to stay here."

"I'm sorry." Rune leaned forward to rest his elbows on his knees. "But it's not a permanent solution. It only needs to be extended until the threat is eliminated. Then it can be restored to the original boundaries and the armillary will be enough to maintain it once again."

"Eyrion's War went on for months," Rhyllyn muttered. "How long will a war against a stronger mage last?"

Rune said nothing.

Smothering his frustration, Rhyllyn made himself sit. "All right. Show me what I have to do."

"Let me see if it'll allow me to move it, first," Rune said. "You may not have to do anything but help the mages here keep powering it."

Rhyllyn bit his tongue. He couldn't do anything without an access stone of his own, unless they expected him to bat at the rings with hands and feet to keep them moving at a brisk pace.

Rune slid the access stone on overhead, tucked it underneath his shirt, and settled it with the other necklace he always wore. Though Rhyllyn had never used one himself, he had a rough idea of how the stones worked. The barrier—a poor name for a complicated mechanism, really—reacted to the probing energy of mages and repelled the flows of magic from their grasp. No matter how a mage might try to reach the power, it slipped from their grasp, called by something greater.

That greater something was the stone inside the astrolabe, he assumed.

The access stones negated the barrier by counteracting its call. They attracted energy flows like a lodestone attracted iron. The nearby flows answered the access stones before they answered the astrolabe. By extension, a mage attuned to the stone attracted that power as well—so long as the access stone touched their skin, anyway.

Of course, Rhyllyn could only assume this served to limit the power a mage could wield within the city, as well. A mage like Rune or himself wouldn't be as hindered, since they were able to draw on and manipulate any power source, but mages bound by affinities could only reach so far before the astrolabe won out and the barrier pulled power from their fingertips. If there was another way to reach power within the barrier, he didn't know. He preferred not to find out.

"Go ahead," Rhyllyn said. "I'll watch. That way if I have to do anything, I'll already have an idea of how I'm supposed to touch it."

"Suit yourself." Rune slid off the couch and fixed his gaze on the glowing golden orb in the center of the astrolabe. He stopped just beside the swirling silver rings and studied their rotation the same way Rhyllyn had. It was that energy he touched first; the power generated by the gentle rotation that fed into the rest.

Rhyllyn closed his eyes and let himself feel the proceedings. What happened visually was unimportant. Magic wasn't visible, but shutting out that sense made it easier to envision what it might look like if it were. Gentle currents filled his mind's eye, flowing patterns like swirling water and soft zephyrs.

Each element felt different and he applied colors to them according to how the college mages represented them. Red for fire and blue for water. Soft, mellow greens for life and the white of pillowy clouds for air. Beneath them all was the gentle thrum of earth, reflected in the warm color of sand.

All the elements interacted in the stone, but air and

something else shone most brilliantly in his senses. Air made sense, with the movement of the rings shifting those flows around them, but what was the other one? Rhyllyn focused on it, his brow furrowing. It was something else, something the mages had never explained. Lacking an element, it created a low and steady buzz of pure power.

Even with an access stone, the flows resisted Rune's pull. The draw of the citrine orb was stronger, and the orb proved a jealous mistress. When Rune tried to seize a strand of power, it struggled to wrest it from his grasp. The fight went on for long moments between his brother and the mindless force the Alda'anan had set in motion, but after what seemed an eternity, Rune's nimble manipulation of the power pulled the thread of energy free.

It coiled around Rune like a snake, awaiting command, but alone it could do nothing. There were thousands of the same tendrils of energy swirling around the orb, and removal of the one revealed only the tiniest glimmer of something else. A knot of power inside the stone, the heart of the command the Alda'anan gave. It would have to be exposed fully to change its shape. If all went well, at this rate, the process could take hours.

"I see why they needed one of us to do it. A whole room full of bound mages wouldn't be able to contain that much power." Rhyllyn chanced a look at his brother.

Rune stared at the orb, though his attention was elsewhere. He didn't move, his face pinched with concentration. Despite his stillness, he spoke. "Even if they could, they'd need a whole legion to rearrange the energy anchored in that thing."

"How do you know what to do?" It made sense once he was watching it in action, but Rhyllyn never would have guessed there would be power layered on power. He might have figured it out if he'd had time to pry at the energy flows, but Rune hadn't been there long enough for that sort of study.

"That's the easy part. The Alda'anan left a book with instructions. The difficult part was getting the mages to hand it over." Rune's eye twitched and he stared harder at the gem sphere, correcting a pull that had almost gone wrong. "It explained everything, in case any adjustments ever had to be made. But it's written in Old Aldaanan, so you'd need me or one of them to translate it if you want to know the exact wording."

The more strands his brother seized, the more the shining core of the barrier anchored in the gemstone blazed in his senses. Rhyllyn shook his head. "Seeing this, I find it hard to believe one of the Alda'anan would be able to do this easily."

"They couldn't," Rune said. "The book called for a half-dozen free mages. I think we're a little short of that."

Alarmed, Rhyllyn jumped forward. "No wonder it threw you back! Let me—"

"Stand by and watch," his brother ordered through clenched teeth. "If I need your help, I'll ask for it. Until then, let me work."

Rhyllyn shrank back, though he didn't hide his displeasure. "You could at least let me hold some of that for you. It's not like I'm doing anything else."

Rune eyed him and hesitated so long Rhyllyn thought he might change his mind. Then he looked back to the armillary and resumed work. "Just watch. As long as you're not distracted, maybe you'll be able to figure out what I did wrong."

The work continued on for ages before the tipping point in power came. Half the astrolabe's energy still flowed to the orb, while the other half swirled around Rune. It was a sea of brilliance in Rhyllyn's senses, though still dwarfed by the gem's might. The power teetered between them in a delicate balance for a tense moment.

Then it snapped, the flows of energy separating from the orb rapidly as Rune became the greater pull.

Rhyllyn jerked upright as he felt the power tilt and everything shifted into better clarity. The knot of power bound to the sphere shone unhindered, displaying such intricacies as he'd never seen. Next to it was the blinding harmony of Rune's power and the flows he'd pulled free. He didn't hold them so much as control them. They coursed through his body, gravitating around a central point. A strange ball of tangled energies, so similar to the anchor in the orb.

Rhyllyn's stomach dropped. "Wait!"

The last threads of power swayed from the orb as Rune reached for the barrier's anchor and sought to change its orders.

The magic embedded in the orb sparked, resonating with the similar knot in Rune's energies. They pulsed quicker, and sizzling energy built between them like a static charge.

Then it burst.

Rhyllyn shoved between Rune and the astrolabe with one hand toward it. Pure, crackling power coursed through him, and every hair on his head stood on end. His other hand snapped upward to create a straight line from talon-tip to shoulder.

The heat stole the air from his lungs as the magic lanced through his body and shot from his fingertips to crash against the wall.

The whole tower shuddered with the explosion. The clatter of debris around them almost drowned out the way Rune cursed.

Shuddering, Rhyllyn fell to his knees.

His entire body tingled. His heart hammered off-rhythm and his pulse roared in his ears. A coppery taste filled his mouth and a hot, acrid scent burned in his nostrils. His stomach heaved, but he gulped against it, forcing himself to fill his lungs and release his breath slowly.

Rune grabbed his arm and Rhyllyn moved blindly, dizzy and dazed as his brother helped him onto one of the couches. He said something, but Rhyllyn couldn't hear.

It didn't matter. He grabbed Rune's hand, forgetting to breathe. "The seal on your power," he panted. "I know what it is!"

A CLEAN SLATE

SINCE HER GIRLHOOD IN THE GRAND COLLEGE, ENVESI HAD followed this path. More years than she wished to count had been invested in research and careful maneuvering, with painfully little to show for it.

She wanted nothing more than to scream.

"They are *my* mages," the Archmage snarled, unable to rein in her temper. She did a better job controlling her power than Lomithrandel ever had, but myriad colors of light flared over the magic-bleached ice blue of her eyes. "It may stand within his territory, but Vicamros does not control the Grand College. He has no right to move them anywhere!"

And to a city with no magic, at that! The man sought to cripple them for his own sake. She could think of no other explanation. Remove the mages, and it would remove anyone who could challenge his rule.

"I've done the best I can," Shymin insisted, though she cowered at the far end of the table. "The college council resists me. I lack your strength, so I cannot overwhelm them—"

"Then the college council shall be dealt with." Envesi twisted away to resume her pacing, unwilling to look at the girl. "I should have killed them all when I removed Arrick. Select a

Master from each major affinity in the temple and they will go with you to act as the new council of the Grand College. Issue orders for all the Triad's mages to return to the college and close those infernal Gates that lead to shore."

The girl bowed her head. "Yes, Archmage."

Envesi sniffed. "What are you waiting for, then? Go!"

Shymin jumped, then bowed her head and hurried out of the room.

When the door clicked shut, Envesi released a slow snarl of a breath.

She should have protested when Vahnil demanded he be taken to the college. The place was in an upheaval of her design; she should have guessed it was too soon. Now he'd be tangled up in mainland politics and who knew when he would return. She needed Vahnil, loath as she was to admit it. His presence made the Gifted girl-child more tolerable, and did the same for Envesi's time in Ilmenhith.

The city did not want her, for all she'd once been its queen. Envesi hadn't wanted the title, had believed it would hinder her efforts. Now she wondered if rejecting it had been a mistake. She wouldn't have needed the help of a Giftless wretch to walk freely in a city that should have been hers. No doubt she wouldn't have been loved as queen, but she would have been feared, and often that was more effective.

It didn't matter now, Envesi reminded herself as she opened a Gate. As Archmage over the entirety of the known world, she answered to no one.

Breathing deep as she stepped through the portal into the auditorium of the Grand College, Envesi rendered herself calm. She would not let them get the best of her. If the leaders of every school of magic in the world opposed her, it meant they had to be replaced.

Just as how if none would volunteer to have their magic unbound to ensure the survival of magic, she would have to select mages and make them willing.

Envesi took comfort in the thought of her work as she paced the halls of the Grand College, seeking the offices she knew the councilors would occupy.

They might think her a villain before all was said and done. Her name might live alongside curses on tongues and songs could be written of the horrors she caused.

It didn't matter. In the end, her name would live on in history books. Centuries from now, perhaps millennia, the world would sing her praise and see her for what she was.

A hero. A savior.

The one who saved their magic.

"THAT'S TWO MORE. At this rate, we'll hear from all of them in the span of a year." Stal buried his face in his hands and worried his coarse white brows with his dusky fingertips. "There's simply no better way to reach them. I don't know what else we can do."

Bracing both hands beneath her heavy stomach, Sera squirmed to the edge of her chair and stood. "The best we can. No one expects you to work miracles, my love." She waddled around the desk and kissed his temple. Her hands settled on his shoulders and she worked her thumbs into the tight muscles of his back.

Stal grunted, though his shoulders did relax. "Even with these responses, that's one tenth of the Collective. How can I speak for the whole when I haven't heard from half?"

She dug her fingers in harder and grinned when he jerked. "Simple. You say no, since you already know that's the only way we can answer."

He craned his neck to look at her over his shoulder. Sera smiled innocently in return.

Her husband wasn't often so dismal. She liked him for his even keel, found it a good contrast to her passion. Few things riled Stal, and even those that did were normally met with a calm face and cool head. But like most men, he had his weaknesses. No matter how steady he seemed, he was not impervious to fear.

"We've come this far, love." Again she kissed his temple, then rubbed her hands through the short crop of white hair that curled tightly against his scalp. "What's one more hurdle for the Archmage of the Umdal Collective and patron of House Kaith?"

Stal caught one of her hands and brought it to his mouth to press kisses between her knuckles. "You put a great deal of faith in me, wife."

"It hasn't led me wrong yet," she teased.

He stood and guided her back to her chair. It was a tall-backed thing with thick padding, one of few places she found any comfort so late in pregnancy. Her hand wandered over her stomach again as the child stirred.

They'd rebuilt her family's empire together, sparking alliances between several of the small trade kingdoms beneath House Kaith's banner. Their first daughter had ensured the family's survival, but every child had helped increase their standing. As mages, they were blessed in ways many weren't. Mages were no longer common in the trade kingdoms. Compared to their peers, Sera and Stal were still young and vital, able to bear many more heirs to help bring their home country back to prosperity. Sometimes she wondered if her rivals thought that was all her many children were—heirs, a means for power. Few were likely to believe she simply loved being surrounded by family.

"We still haven't discussed names." Sera sank back into the plush cushions with a smile.

"Really? I thought we had." Stal knelt beside her and rested his palms on her stomach. When the child kicked beneath his hands, he glowed. "I like Kasma."

She snorted. "And who says it's a girl?"

"We have five girls already and only one boy. I think we've already proven we're predisposed to matrons for House Kaith."

He grinned and shifted his hands to follow the baby's movement.

"The odds are always half and half. I think it's a boy."

Stal laughed aloud. "Fine, then. We can call him Garam, after your brother."

"Certainly not!" Sera protested, though she grinned. "I would never hang that sort of stoic shadow over my child."

They laughed together and their hands met. Their fingers twined as if by their own accord. Sera smiled, though the moment was bittersweet. They would have so few happy moments like these in the coming weeks.

"I like Eben," she murmured at last, tracing the shape of Stal's broad hand with her fingertips.

He caught her hand and kissed it again. "It's a fine name. Eben for a boy. Kasma for a girl."

"Perfect." She stroked his chin, savoring his warmth. Then something pricked at the edge of her awareness and the moment was over.

Stal turned his head, sensing the same thing.

"No." Her face crumpled. "Not so soon."

His gaze returned to her and for one brief, terrible moment, she saw the fear in his eyes.

"Sera," he sighed in the sweetest, most infuriatingly loving tone.

She pressed a finger to his lips. "No. We face this together."

Grasping her wrist, Stal wrestled her hand from his face. "Any other time, I would agree. But this is not just you, Sera." His free hand slid over her stomach in a slow, loving caress.

She could have strangled him for being right. "Come with me. We can send a missive to the rest of the Collective from anywhere in the world. It doesn't have to be here." Again she touched him, stroked his strong cheekbones and springy white curls.

"I am Archmage. I will not abandon my people in their

moment of need." The vivid blue of his eyes darkened to the color of cold steel.

"Even if it means abandoning your wife and child?" Sera regretted the words the moment they left her mouth, but he took them in stride. He was a good man. Far more level-headed than she deserved.

"It is not abandonment if I choose to stay behind so that you can go." Stal kissed her brow and pulled her to her feet. "Now, go. Hurry across to the chapter house before she sees you, or it will be too late."

She hugged him tight and lingered for as long as she thought she could, then stole one more kiss before she went.

She couldn't run, not in her condition, but Sera laced her hands together beneath her stomach and waddled out the study at as brisk of a pace as she could manage. Instead of making for the door, she cut a path through the service access hallways.

The narrow passages were numerous in her home, a relic from the days when House Kaith had been one of the ruling houses in the trade kingdoms. They could have reclaimed such a title, but she had no interest. Besides, it was best if high-ranking mages were kept separate from the political power of royals. As long as there was peace, she was content.

Her family had sought refuge in the Triad in her youth, when wars splintered the alliances between the many small trade territories. The ruling houses had tried to control the mages, withholding aid and healing from those who stood against them.

Sera's parents had cooperated for a time, until cooperation resulted in her father's death. Even then, her mother struggled nearly a decade more before she gave up the fight. After she remarried to a Giftless man, her family was more vulnerable than ever. Sera had been the first sent north, the trip disguised as a means to further her skills by enrolling in the Grand College.

For a second time in her life, it seemed the Triad would provide refuge.

A liveried servant encountered her in the hall near the back of the house, his face solemn in the feeble light of the candlestick he held. Sera met his eyes and nodded; he nodded in return. Then he swept away, soundless and graceful in the night.

A second servant met her at the back door, a drab cloak and a small basket of hastily-gathered personal effects hung on her arm. She pushed the basket into Sera's hands and draped the cloak around her shoulders, then kissed both her mistress's cheeks.

"The children?" Sera asked.

The maid lifted a finger to her lips. "They're being gathered, mistress. They'll scatter like leaves and be sent along from different locations. You go on first, mistress. I'm afraid you're the slowest."

Sera couldn't help but smile. She patted the girl's cheek and pulled up the cloak's hood, then slipped into the kitchen and crept out the back door.

Positions of power came with great danger. They'd rehearsed different flight patterns a hundred times, but never needed to use them. Sera hugged herself and her unborn child as she wove through the narrow alleys between grand mansions of orange plaster.

Umdal's chapter house wasn't far from her home, its windows aglow with inviting lantern light and its doors open to welcome the cool night breeze. Few mages called the chapter house home, but there were always enough members of the Collective coming and going to keep the place fully staffed.

She kept composed as she marched across the street and ignored the blur of white that stole through the front door of her house. How long would Stal be able to hold her off? He was a skilled diplomat, but if Envesi had returned so far before their agreed date, the time for diplomacy was past. There was no mistaking the sense of energy behind her. Sera had met many free mages before that woman, and they all felt the same. Wild and frightful. But there was something else in the self-proclaimed Archmage's presence, something Sera had only felt in two others. A sense of wrongness, of a Gift sullied by corrosive power.

In Rune and Rhyllyn, that foul tinge had never bothered her.

The mages in the chapter house greeted her with surprise. Some looked past her as if confused to see her alone.

"A Gate to the Spiral Palace," Sera ordered. "I carry an important message on behalf of the Archmage. He'll be along with instructions before long, I'm sure." That would eliminate any questions or suspicions. As Stal's wife, he trusted her with everything.

She stood tall and regal as the mages assembled to fulfill her demand, but her hold of that composure slipped as the first shards of reality fell away from the portal. Somewhere in the city behind her, she felt the numbing tingle of a power flare.

So soon after her departure, she assumed it was a ward. Erected far more forcefully than a ward required, but that was something Sera noticed when they'd last met with Envesi. She had no finesse with her new power, striking with a war hammer what might have been toppled with a twig. It gave Sera a new appreciation for the dexterity and skill of the two mages she hoped she'd find in the palace.

Speaking to Vicamros about Envesi's presence was important, but all Vicamros could do was offer her sanctuary in the Royal City.

The Gate before her stabilized and Sera made herself breathe. No matter what happened next, news would come from Umdal.

Gripping the access stone she always wore around her neck, Sera steeled herself and strode through the portal.

She arrived with her chin up and her bearing proud, but the acrid stench and choking dust in the air made her wrinkle her nose and gag.

"So sorry, Lady Kaith." A handful of Masters waited around the archway kept in the mage quarters for Gating. She assumed they were there to greet her, having felt the Gate open, until her eyes followed the dust to its source.

More mages clamored around the doorway to the sitting room where the mage-barrier was anchored. Most held cloths to their mouths and fanned away dust with their hands.

Sera pushed them aside to find the source of the mess. Her mouth dropped open when she saw the rubble and a hole in the wall as large as the Gate she'd just come through. Her eyes dropped to the pair on the couch beneath the gap and her surprise faded.

"You two can't be left alone for a second!" She squeezed between the mages and hurried across the room to catch Rhyllyn by the ear.

The boy yelped and twisted in his seat to lean closer to her.

"What in the world are you doing?" Sera demanded, shooting Rune a glare. She shouldn't have expected anyone else.

He glared back. "Attempting to have a conversation!"

"Expanding the mage-barrier to encompass as much of the Triad as possible," Rhyllyn answered at the same time. He pried her fingers apart with his claws and rubbed his ear as he escaped.

"Or trying to," Rune added. "But that doesn't matter right now. Rhyllyn, what you said—"

"What do you mean, it doesn't matter?" The boy looked downright offended. If not for what she'd just escaped, Sera might have been amused. For the moment, she couldn't feel much more than a nagging sense of worry that fluttered in her stomach.

Rune looked at her again and she expected another protest, but instead, his brow furrowed. He stood, then paused with his hands spread to aid his balance. When it didn't fail him, he moved closer. Concern painted his expression. "What are you doing here?"

"Envesi broke her word. She did not give us the promised time. Stal is with her, but I've come to warn Vicamros there may be a problem."

Before either of the free mages could speak, magic flooded

the adjacent room. Sera shivered at the sensation as another Gate opened.

Rune raised one clawed finger to indicate she should stay behind. He patted her shoulder as he went to investigate.

She wasn't about to wait. She waddled behind him to stand on tip-toe and peer over the heads of the Masters still at the door.

Sera didn't know what to expect, but the handful of magelings in dirty robes that poured through wasn't it.

"I come bearing an urgent message for King Vicamros," a Master in likewise dirty clothing said as she herded the magelings forward and the Gate closed at her heels. The magelings flocked around her like chicks under a mother hen.

"Vicamros is locked in council," Rune said, presenting himself in front of the woman. "I am Councilor Rune Kaim-Ennen, Champion of the Royal City Arena. I can deliver your message."

The woman looked at him and grew pale. Rune didn't seem to know her, but there was no mistaking the recognition in her eyes. She shrank back.

Sera heaved a sigh and worked her way through the mages again. "Vicamros is firm in his policies. We can escort you to the door of the council chamber, but you will not be admitted. Tell the councilor what must be said."

The Master's eyes never left Rune. "Queen Firal," she asked in a hoarse whisper. "She is alive?"

Rune's brows knit together and he gave the woman a closer inspection.

Sera examined her, too. The woman had the golden complexion common in Elenhiise natives. A messenger from Kirban, then?

"I thought Kirban Temple was under Envesi's control," Sera remarked, startling the woman out of silence.

"Y-yes," the mage stammered. "As is the Grand College. We fled Elenhiise and sought refuge in Lore, but arrived to find

Archmage Arrick Ortath deceased. We had hoped to petition the college council after organizing ourselves, but..."

"But?" Rune prompted.

The mage's eyes drifted back to lock with Sera's. "The council is dead."

Sera's heart skipped a beat. "All of them?"

"We left the college as soon as we heard about Archmage Arrick," the woman continued. "We stopped in the city to eat and, as I said, organize ourselves to petition the council. We were found by one of your king's councilors, Redoram Parthanus, and his mages. There was a bit of confusion. He mistook us for his party and came to join us. It worked out well enough in the end."

"At least we know Redoram's doing a good job of gathering mages in Lore," Sera murmured. "And your group sought the council?"

The Master shook her head. "Councilor Parthanus sent one of his Masters in hopes of arranging a meeting outside the college. The Master discovered the college in a frenzy. One of the councilors was unmade right in front of him."

Sera shuddered along with the other mages. Only Rune remained still, his face stony.

"He tried to flee," the mage added, "but there were mages from Elenhiise pulling down the permanent Gates that led from the college to the shore. Had Councilor Parthanus not sent a Master with a water affinity, he likely would not have returned to us. He pulled a wave up the side of the college and escaped into the water."

Rune shifted then, folding his arms across his chest and narrowing his eyes. "If only one of you saw, how do you know the council is dead and hasn't just turned traitor?"

The woman wiped her face with one hand and her shoulders slumped. "There was no mistaking that. The wrongness lingers in the air when something—someone—is taken apart. It clung to him as surely as the seaweed on his robes."

Rune gave Sera a sidewise glance. "Sounds like Stal was right in sending you here." He turned toward the door as if to go.

Sera couldn't deny that now. If the Masters heading the council of the Grand College had been killed, it was likely for the same reason as Arrick. They'd opposed Envesi's goals, refused her leadership.

There was no doubt Umdal was next on the list.

Her knees gave out and Sera sank to the floor, with a hand held to her mouth as if to trap the tears that desperately wished to escape. She was a warrior. A soldier in the Royal City's army until the day she married Stal, and a powerful representative of magic before that. Not some weepy housemaid given to emotional fits. But that only made the tears worse. They burned in her eyes and threatened to spill hot rivers over her eyelashes. Seeking comfort, or perhaps driven by the need to comfort someone else in troubled times, Sera wrapped her arms around herself and hugged her unborn child.

Reassurance came when Rune knelt beside her, gathered her into his arms and stroked her countless white braids with one rough-scaled hand. "Don't give up on him yet," he murmured against her ear. "If I couldn't kill him, I doubt she can."

Sera buried her face in his shoulder and allowed herself two lonely tears before she focused on her breath.

Their friendship was hard earned, forged through trial and violence in the years they'd served together. War was a horror, but if she was to face it, there were few others she'd want by her side.

A WAR BEGINS

HER POWER WAS LIKE A PULSE. STAL FLINCHED EVERY TIME IT throbbed in his senses. The world around him seemed to seethe in anticipation. He'd felt that sort of chaos before, though never on that level. If that was the sort of power Rune had when Sera had met him, Stal was grateful he'd never experienced it firsthand.

He placed his hands, palms flat, on the surface of his desk. As Archmage, he easily could have left his work at Umdal's formal headquarters, but he'd always studied best in his own home. Now he regretted the office he kept on the first floor. Had he been in the Archmage's quarters in the chapter house, he would have been surrounded by mages and perhaps he'd stand a chance.

The warm light of his home cast eerie shadows across Envesi's face as she appeared in the doorway. Her frigid eyes glowed bright enough to rival the lamps. It was her eyes that unsettled him most.

"I have grown impatient," Envesi said, though her voice was placid.

Stal straightened and met her stare. "You promised me time."

The woman waved a white-scaled hand in dismissal. "I

promised nothing. What time I gave you was a boon. My generosity, too, has worn thin." She lingered at the entrance as if ready to leave in an instant. "Where are they?"

"The Collective has not yet replied to me," Stal said. "I don't know where they are."

Her eyes narrowed.

"I understand your desire for speed, but I cannot make them move faster. Right now, I cannot even guarantee my messengers have reached anyone." He spread his hands in a placating gesture.

A flicker in her gaze gave him a chill. "Where have you sent your messengers?"

"I mean this respectfully, but I don't think you understand how the Collective works." A large map was mounted on the far wall. Stal motioned toward it. "There is a gold pin in our location. Ours is the only permanent chapter house on the southern continent."

Envesi stalked toward the map. "You do not include markers for temporary stations?"

"That's precisely what I mean. We don't have temporary stations. Our mages are vagrants. They might stay a few days in one location, but they are always on the move. That is the only way we can see to the needs of the trade kingdoms, and we've fought hard to regain the right to move between them." It wasn't that long ago that magic had been forbidden. Stal had been moved nearly to tears on the day the mage-truce was formed.

She did not seem to care. "Which directions did they go?"

"I could not tell you that, either," he said. "I was not present when they departed. They choose their own destinations."

"Archmage," Envesi said as she studied the map.

His brows drew together. "Pardon me?"

"My title." She turned toward him, her expression cold as snow. "I am Archmage."

"As am I," Stal replied. "That makes us equals."

A shockwave hit his chest and threw him back against the

wall. The air left his lungs in a rush. He wheezed when he inhaled again.

Air pushed against him and forced him to the wall like a hand against his throat. The woman in white crept closer. "I have no equal."

"And soon, you will have no allies, if you don't listen to reason!" He clawed at the invisible forces that held him and grimaced. Even though her grip on him was measured and controlled, the sense of her power that came with it was crushing. He dared not try to peel back the flows, though he was certain he could. If she exerted such force to simply hold him in place, what might she do if he tried to escape?

Her eyes narrowed as she considered his words. The stream of magic that held him to the wall abated, then faded to a tiny trickle that dribbled off to nothing. Stal rubbed his throat and swallowed against the tight discomfort that remained. How long did he need to hold her off? He sensed the ebb and flow of Gates opening and closing, but the mages in the chapter house came and went as they pleased. How was he to know if Sera had already escaped?

"This is my home," Stal said, his words measured and patient. "I have no information here. If you wish to know more about where the Collective's mages have gone, the only place we might learn is in the chapter house." He dreaded the idea of letting Envesi in before he had a chance to warn his mages, but he assumed she would invade the chapter house regardless. If he escorted her in, perhaps they could avoid bloodshed.

"Take me," Envesi ordered without an ounce of hesitation.

Stal straightened his robes and made soothing motions with both hands. Sera had always praised his even temper in dealing with their children. He wished his patience extended to unreasonable mages, too. As it was, annoyance at Envesi's hostility and demanding nature simmered high, cooled only by the cold fear for his wife's safety that ran through his heart and mind.

"I regret that I have no news to give you yet," he said as he led her from the house. The Kaith estate was beautiful and the iron-nut trees in the courtyard were especially pleasant this time of year, with their fragrant flowers in full bloom. He breathed deep as he stepped outside and hoped she would unconsciously mimic him. The blossoms were said to have a calming effect. He wanted her calm. "But news always travels slowly across the trade kingdoms. Hastiness runs counter to our culture, besides. The last time mages rushed to make decisions, it began a war that lasted decades."

Envesi did not reply.

The chapter house was not far from home. Stal eyed the lights in the building's windows with a hint of regret. How many could he warn? How many would flee? By now, Sera had surely escaped. Had she warned the mages in the chapter house? Or had she left them in hopes they would aid him, if there was a fight?

A mage met them at the door. "Archmage," she began, her face pinched with worry. "Is everything all right?"

Before Stal could speak, Envesi's power wrapped around him like chains, lashed his arms to his sides and drove him to his knees. A startled cry escaped before he could stop it.

"Your other chapter houses. Your outposts. Where are they?" Envesi stopped beside Stal and put a hand down as if to hold him in place. Magic weighed down on him as surely as if she'd planted a foot on his back.

The mage in the doorway lifted a hand to her mouth.

Stal gritted his teeth and lifted his head. Words proved difficult to form with Envesi's power squeezing his chest. "The rabbits?"

"Gone," the mage replied, her face grave. So the children had already escaped. Perhaps this mage had been on her way to Stal's home.

Envesi raised a brow, but she had no way of knowing the pet name he and his wife used for their children.

"The farmers?" he asked.

Picking up on the code, the mage nodded. "Where they've taken their supply, I don't know."

"The chapter houses," Envesi snapped.

The mage in the doorway raised her hands. "Peace, Master. We are not your enemies. We do not have chapter houses, but there are stations frequently used. When one is expected to be visited by part of the Collective, they request provisions be sent." The information was accurate, but the way she smoothly used it to mask the secret behind Stal's question made his shoulders slump in relief.

Envesi's eyes flashed. "Show me the outposts."

"They will be empty," Stal said.

She turned a frosty glare on him, angry colors of light whirling in her eyes. "Then it matters not if I see them."

Though her face twisted with worry, the mage at the door bowed her head. "Come inside, please."

Stal began to protest, but found his jaw clamped so firmly shut, he couldn't part his lips to speak. Indignation flared within him, but when he craned his neck to glare up at Envesi, she merely raised a brow and left him prone on the walkway.

He exhaled hard as she disappeared into the chapter house. Calm as the mage leading Envesi had seemed, Stal did not doubt everyone in the chapter house would panic before long.

When he inhaled again, he pressed his fingers into the dust and relaxed. Power shifted beneath him as the ground answered his call. The earth sang to him, a deep, thrumming melody only others who shared his affinity could hear. He savored its voice and let it hum through his veins. Trickles of pure power fed into him from each point of contact. His knees, the palms of his hand, and each fingertip fueled him. He could twist the flows from anywhere, but he needed them now to bolster himself.

Envesi's affinity had been life. Stal could still sense it within her. Detecting another's source of power was something he was especially good at, and one of the reasons he'd been chosen as

Archmage. But life—healing, as they so often preferred to call it in the north—was a dangerous affinity to face in a madwoman. She could unravel him from existence with a thought. She could do that to every mage in the chapter house, though, and he was Archmage. To protect them was his duty.

Stal pushed. A single, hard pulse of power shattered the flows of air that held him down and freed him from the woman's grasp. He thrust himself to his feet and gasped for breath. His jaw creaked as he flexed it, and his anger only grew.

Mages fighting mages had been a theme through his youth, a deep shame for all mages in the trade kingdoms. He'd spent his entire life fighting to restore the people's trust in mages and he would be swallowed by the earth itself before he let some outsider destroy everything he'd worked for.

The air crackled with power. Someone was opening a Gate— or more than one Gate, Stal thought. The power swelled, over and over.

He burst into the chapter house. Mages cowered in the classrooms he passed, their wide, fright-filled eyes on him as he stormed to the Gating parlor at the far end of the hall.

Envesi stood before the wide, crackling Gate. The woman who had greeted them at the door knelt beside her, the Archmage's clawed hand atop her head. To either side of the Gate, a handful of frightened mages cowered against the walls, though Stal sensed the power that tied them together. One of the Collective's many outposts waited on the other side of the portal, its windows dark and its grounds abandoned.

"Another," Envesi snarled. Her claws dug into the Master mage's scalp and blood stained the poor woman's snowy hair.

The Gate closed and reopened to display another empty outpost. How many had they already seen? How closely had she studied them?

"Enough," Stal barked. His mages turned to him, startled. All save the woman on the floor, that was. A twinge of shame surfaced amidst Stal's anger. She was a newer Master in the

Collective; he did not yet know her name. "I told you the outposts were empty, the Collective on the move. Is my word not good enough?"

Envesi cast a darkening scowl over her shoulder. Wordlessly, she released the mage and plunged through the Gate.

Stal swore and followed her through. The Gate's power sizzled against his skin and made every hair stand on end as he passed into the windy plains.

Against the dark of night, Envesi resembled a ghost. Her white robes billowed as she spread her hands and seized power.

"The Collective cannot be forced to answer you," he shouted above the howling wind.

Heat burst in his senses. Envesi's arms raised higher, and with the motion, fat flames surged up around the outpost.

Stal's mouth fell open. "What are you doing?"

Her eyes seared the dark as she turned back toward him, two pinpoints of blazing cold light. The familiar electric tingle of a Gate crawled over him and the air beside her split.

Cursing once more, Stal ran. He dove for the skirts of her robes and tumbled through the portal alongside her.

Envesi moved as if he didn't exist and strode forward with her arms spread. Another outpost rose before them, and again, flames rose within it.

Stal beckoned the earth under his feet. It rumbled in answer. Fissures zigzagged across the ground from the tips of his toes to the outpost ahead, and sand and dust spewed forth to suffocate the fire, but her magic was too great. Tiny, glittering specks of glass fell in showers around the burning outpost as Envesi urged her flames to grow hotter.

Deep within the earth, something else tickled Stal's augmented senses.

Water.

"Please," he whispered as he urged the ground to part. It answered.

The air split as Envesi opened another Gate.

The urge to smother the flames tore at him, warring with the need to follow. He denied it and felt his heart twist for the village beyond the outpost as he spun to follow her through a Gate again.

This time, he landed ready. Stone surged forth the moment the Gate dropped closed. It exploded from the dirt to clap shut around the rogue mage.

A single second later, cracks lanced across the slabs and the stone shattered to fall around her feet. She was untouched, unharmed, and—evidently, as she spared him not even a glance as she raised her arms—unhindered.

The presence of magic lit up on the edge of Stal's awareness.

There were mages in the outpost.

"Stop!" Stal roared. He raised a palm toward Envesi and the earth rose to answer and envelop her again.

A flicker of angry color flashed in her eyes just before the earth closed around her and blocked her out of sight.

The ground underfoot began to tremble.

A wave rolled through the soil and the ground beneath Stal's feet gave way. He fell with a shout and pitched himself forward. His chest hit the dirt and the impact chased the breath out of him. Earth heaved up beneath his feet as he seized magic and pulled. The flows resisted. She still held them. Stal closed his eyes and sawed at her control.

Powerful as Envesi was, earth was not her specialty, and the stone answered him. A startled howl burst from within the pillar of earth that trapped her as her hold over the element snapped.

The hole beneath him sealed and Stal thrust himself to his feet. The earthen pillar squeezed closer, fit itself to Envesi's form. She favored gestures; if he could trap her, perhaps it would be harder for her to work her magic.

Mages appeared at the door of the outpost.

"Flee!" Stal roared. They disappeared just as quickly, and he prayed they followed his command.

A new tremble started in the earth. The pillar shook loose and fell apart in chunks. Envesi gave her head a twitch as she was freed, and her snowy hair shed dust and soil as if it were water. "You are becoming a nuisance."

"Then kill me," he challenged. "Pull me apart like you did Arrick Ortath!"

A harsh laugh welled up in her throat. With a flick of her hand, she dismissed the last of the pillar that restrained her, and Stal winced as his hold of those flows whipped back. Too skilled to be struck, he subdued the power before it hit him, but the last of the pillar crumbled at her feet.

"Such arrogance," Envesi said. "You believe yourself his equal, but you don't even command a chapter house that sits just beyond your front door. You call yourself Archmage, and yet you cannot speak on behalf of feeble vagrants who dare claim the title of mage."

She reached for her flames. Before she could seize them, Stal wrested the flows away from her reach and scattered them on the wind. Envesi gave a soft grunt of displeasure.

"What do you gain?" she asked. "What does it benefit you to martyr yourself over antiquated practices of feeble magic?"

"Our practices exist because we must realize no one has control of our Gifts but us," Stal replied. "Even if we join you, even if we were to become free mages like you, only we can wield the power we are given. Brant has blessed us, this is why we call it a Gift. All mages deserve to choose how their power should be used. If they do not wish to use their strength to further your goals, that should be their decision, too."

"A charmingly utopian ideal," Envesi said, her tone patronizing. The air around her hissed with building energy. The scent of heat, like the air before a lightning strike, filled Stal's nostrils. He resisted the urge to hit the ground and instead spun to face the empty space before her at the precise moment the air split and she opened a Gate.

Each time one opened, they seemed hotter, more chaotic, less stable. The white-hot, crackling edges of the portal rippled as if they fought her control. Could he hope to push her until she was too tired to keep hold of her magic?

She stepped toward the Gate just as flames burst within the outpost and panicked voices rose into the night.

Stal lit after her. If she left him behind, he could do nothing.

The Gate closed on his heel and a searing shot of pain spiked up his leg. He collapsed with a curse and tumbled against the ground.

Against all he expected, the chapter house beside his home loomed above them again.

"I was curious," Envesi said. "I wondered what could drive a man to stand against someone he knows he has no hope of defeating. But you're as useless as every other who dares stand against me. Your sense of honor is misguided, Stal Kaith."

He struggled to rise. The back hem of his robe was charred and his heel blistered, burned by the raw energy that had brushed his skin. Fortunate, he thought, that he hadn't lost his leg.

Envesi's eyes flashed, luminescent, in the dark. "You do no one favors by entertaining the notion mages should be left to their own devices. Magic demands structure and control. If you cannot submit to it, then you are no longer of use." Again, she reached for fire.

Stal slammed his foot to the ground and ignored the shock of pain. The ground seized beneath him and a wave of rock surged forward to crush her.

Before it struck, she waved a hand. Instead of fighting the wave of earth, she bore down on Stal with air. But he'd escaped those flows once already, and he hacked at her hold of them and severed the threads of power before it ever touched him.

The stone crashed down around her and bounced harmlessly off a rippling shield. He hadn't even felt her form it.

Magic surged within the chapter house and a wave of heat poured from the open doors and windows. Screams sounded inside and panic clawed at Stal's heart.

"Kill me if you desire," he spat, "but leave my mages out of it. They are free to make their own decisions. Even if that means supporting you."

The heat eased, though slightly. Envesi turned a speculative eye toward him.

Behind her, a mage appeared at a window. Before Stal could address her, the Master disappeared in a swirl of white.

"Yes," the rogue Archmage mused. "Perhaps I shall."

Something pinged inside of Stal and a wave of discomfort shot down his legs, like a nerve plucked or pinched. Then again it pinched, pulled, and he rocked on his feet.

He lifted his chin and stared at her, defiant. "Killing me changes nothing. There are still those who will oppose you. Those who will see you fall."

A cold smile quirked the corners of her mouth. "On the contrary, Archmage. Only your Collective shall fall."

A deafening roar split the air as fire erupted from the chapter house, a surge of magic like nothing he'd ever thought possible. Shrieks of fear, pain, and panic flooded the air, and the twinges of pain that speared through Stal's body grew stronger.

Sharp, picking, pulling. Pangs in his neck. His arms. His head.

Envesi's snakelike eyes hardened until they gleamed like jewels in the dark.

Unraveling him, he realized.

She meant to pull him apart.

Gritting his teeth, he wound his own energies tight, envisioning a ball of string pulled so snug that nothing came loose. The pain subsided. Then the onslaught began anew, more focused, more determined.

Behind him, the air heated.

Mages appeared beside the chapter house. Already, the building groaned and creaked as flames licked up its walls and across its roof. Something cracked; embers spiraled into the air.

More than a dozen mages formed a half-circle at Envesi's back.

The woman laughed, her voice cold and harsh. "You'd be fools to attack me."

But instead of striking her, they looked at him.

"Rabbits will always return to a well-kept garden," one of the Masters called. Stal recognized her. Blood still marred her face and her hair and stained the front of her white robes.

The code was not lost on him.

At his back, reality split. The light of a well-illuminated courtyard poured from it. Stal spun, his brow furrowed. The Spiral Palace.

Suddenly, the nameless Master was beside him.

"The Collective may fall," she whispered, "but we will stand as long as we can."

With both hands, she thrust Stal through the Gate.

13

BALLADS

FORMAL DINNERS WERE RARELY ENJOYABLE AFFAIRS. FIRAL EXPECTED nothing otherwise, but she was relieved Vicamros had called for a banquet.

She hadn't spoken to any of her friends outside of the council chamber. The task of expanding the magic-nullifying barrier consumed everyone's attention and though she was a mage, Firal had not been asked to assist them. The exclusion hurt, but she couldn't be angry at them. No one seemed to know what to do with a displaced queen. She didn't know what to do with herself, left rudderless in a wild current.

Servants retrieved her long hours after nightfall and escorted her to a banquet hall remarkably similar to the one in Ilmenhith's palace. Smooth-shafted columns with unadorned capitals supported a vaulted ceiling. Streamers in the Triad's three colors hung draped between them. Two mirrored chandeliers suspended by gilded chains chased the dark away from the table, but cast double shadows of each column. An odd chill crept up Firal's spine as she passed through them.

Dozens of chairs lined the table, most of them already filled. A servant in tri-colored livery led her to her seat, a place near enough to Vicamros to lend her importance, but far enough away to make it clear she was no longer his equal.

Kytenia sat across the table, one chair nearer to the king, but the other mages were among nobles and councilors at the other end. The throne at the head of the table remained empty, as did the seats to its left and right, but she didn't have time to contemplate them.

A trumpeted fanfare announced the king's arrival and everyone around the table stood.

Firal turned her head, pleasantly surprised to see Rhyllyn take the empty place to her left. The youth flashed her a smile, then turned to watch Vicamros take his place.

He led Sera with her fingertips resting on his upturned palm, as dainty and courtly a gesture as Firal had ever seen. He seated her at the place of honor to his left before he took his place at the head of the table. Respect for her gravid state, no doubt. With a position as lofty as Sera's seemed to be, her placement wasn't a surprise, but considering she'd only just returned to Umdal a day prior, her presence was unexpected.

More surprising was that Rune took his place at Vicamros's right side. An odd place for a man who'd exchanged blows with the king only hardly any time before, but Firal bit her tongue. Had she been a queen, she might have criticized the choice. As things were now, her opinion meant nothing.

When Vicamros sat, everyone sat, and the wave of serving staff with trays of food began to flow down the table.

"I'm glad you're here," Rhyllyn whispered.

Firal smiled politely in return. "I didn't expect the mages would give you a chance to eat, to be honest." She plucked two rolls from a tray and put one on his plate.

He grinned, tore a piece from its top and popped it into his mouth. "They're keeping me busy, but we've made progress. I've learned some important things. I can't wait to tell you about them."

"I'm sure you'll have a chance. It's not like I've anything else to do. I feel a bit like a bird in a gilded cage." She filled her plate with various tidbits as servants filtered past.

Behind the throne, a lute plucked a sour note and made everyone cringe.

"Fine entertainment for us, eh, Vicamros?" Sera smirked as the musician tuned his instrument in preparation to play.

"Not the best choice I could have made, it seems." Vicamros chuckled, waiting for his taster to nod before he sampled his food.

"Perhaps Rhyllyn could play for us after he's had a bit to eat." Sera glanced his way, amusement clear in her eyes.

Firal turned to the young man beside her, curious. "You did tell me before that you can play a number of instruments. Are you skilled?"

"He's a bard," Rune said over the rim of his goblet. He leaned one elbow on the table. "Formally trained and recognized."

Rhyllyn flushed and stared at his plate. "I'm all right, I guess."

Firal smiled and touched his arm. "I'd love to hear you play sometime."

"A good idea, that," Vicamros murmured. "Let this fool strum a few notes and let the boy get a bit in his belly, then maybe he can be convinced to play."

"Of course, Majesty," Rhyllyn said, though his cheeks were so red Firal thought they might glow.

"I'm afraid it will be our last opportunity for levity for some time." Vicamros sobered. "It seems every war is preceded by a feast. Tomorrow morning, the mages we've gathered will depart in hopes of finding as many parts of Umdal's Collective as possible."

Sera's cheerful expression faltered and she turned her attention to her plate. Both Rune and Rhyllyn grew solemn, and Firal bowed her head.

She didn't know why the mages would be needed to recover

the Collective, but with Sera there and her husband absent, it wasn't difficult to piece together that something troubling had transpired. Firal had intended to ask why Sera had returned so soon. Now that seemed unwise. She liked the woman, her eager demeanor and upbeat attitude infectiously inspiring, but Firal didn't know her well, and the friendly ease between Sera and Rune still gave her an odd discomfort.

Conversation around the table went on without her. She didn't notice until someone directed a question toward Rhyllyn.

He straightened in his seat, drawing Firal's attention back to the affairs at hand. "Yes, Majesty. At least, I think it's true. It's much too early to tell, but we can try as soon as the barrier is taken care of."

"Extraordinary." Kytenia leaned forward, taking interest in the talk for the first time. Firal might have missed the beginning, but if Kytenia was interested, it had to be related to magic. "How did you discover this?"

"It was because of how the barrier's anchor reacted to him when he tried to manipulate it." Rhyllyn cupped his hands as if he held a pair of objects aloft to compare them. "There was something between them that caused them to repel each other. The two forces pushed apart, like mismatched lodestones. If he'd allowed me to help, I never would have noticed. The barrier is considerably stronger than the seal on his power, though, so that's why he couldn't conquer it and ended up being physically thrown back."

Firal raised a brow and leaned back in her chair to look past the boy's shoulders. Rune didn't notice, too occupied with nursing his drink and frowning. He didn't appear to sport any new injuries, but it was clear her lack of involvement with the mages meant she'd missed out on all sorts of excitement. A twinge of bitterness pulled at her heart.

"Were you able to determine how the seal works, then?" Kytenia asked as she reached for her cup.

"Not yet, but I have an idea." Rhyllyn paused to take a drink as well. "We weren't able to do much, since Sera and the messenger needed our attention too, but observing Rune trying to manipulate energy afterward let me see the seal performing the same functions as the barrier."

"And yet you never noticed this before?" Vicamros frowned.

"I had, I suppose, I just never realized what was actually happening. See, the barrier works by reacting whenever someone reaches for power. I'm not sure how, but when it senses that, it pulls the energy flows away. Toward itself. The seal does that too, but on a smaller scale, and it's attuned to his power." Rhyllyn gave the Archmage a nervous grin, as if uncertain of his explanation. "But since it's so small, it can't disrupt his power entirely. It hinders most, but allows a small trickle of energy through."

Kytenia tapped a finger against the edge of her plate. "But if it restricts energy that way, shouldn't it keep him from using yours like he does?"

Rhyllyn shook his head. "Not at all. Like I said, it's attuned to his power. It's not designed to stop anything else. I think the Alda'anan meant to use it as a training device. Something to teach him to pace himself, or maybe exercise restraint when working with magic. Because when he pushes too hard, the seal reacts in another way, punishing him with physical pain."

Rune grunted in displeasure. "The real question isn't how it works. It's whether or not he can unravel it."

Vicamros nodded, rubbing his chin. "Can you, Rhyllyn?"

The youth hesitated. "I think it's too early to tell. Either way, I need to take care of the mage-barrier first."

"Of course, of course." The king returned to his food and the conversation shifted again.

If the seal on Rune's power could be removed, it would change everything. Level the field and bring back their chance. But Firal couldn't dare hope, not yet. She drew a long breath and willed herself to be reasonable, but in the wake of such a revelation, she already found the food no longer had any taste.

The rest of the mealtime chatter remained cordial and continued until the serving staff began to clear away empty plates. Then Vicamros clapped his hands and turned to Rhyllyn again.

"Have you had enough to eat, then, bard? Are you ready to serenade us?"

Rhyllyn smiled sheepishly, dipped a corner of his napkin into his water goblet and used it to clean his hands. "I suppose I could manage a song, if you really wish me to."

"I wouldn't ask if I didn't wish it! Minstrel, here! Let the boy borrow your lute. Perhaps he can teach you to tune it."

Laughter erupted around the table and the minstrel tucked in his chin, abashed. He met Rhyllyn halfway to hand over his instrument.

"He truly is an excellent bard, you know," Vicamros said. "There's a ballad he wrote that's become quite popular in these parts. Why don't you play that one for us?"

Rhyllyn's eyes widened. "I don't know..."

The king raised a hand to silence him. "Come on, now. Don't be bashful. I'm sure our guests are eager to hear."

Wordlessly, Rune slid from the table and retreated between the columns.

"All right," Rhyllyn murmured. He carried the lute to the tall stool the minstrel had abandoned and tuned the worn lute with nimble claws, casting a furtive glance after his brother as he began. A haunting, sorrowful melody filled the banquet hall and a hush drew over the crowd. His surprising baritone rose with the music and threatened to tear Firal's heart in two.

"A SONGBIRD SINGS AT TWILIGHT,
a cage of reeds her home.
She longs to claim her birthright,
the night sky hers to roam.

SERPENT'S BLOOD

She sings of her desire,
>*and knows not who hears her song.*
>*A serpent waits and listens,*
>*and her voice makes his heart long.*

The serpent aches to join her
>*and weave songs among the trees,*
>*but snake-shed begets scales,*
>*and not feathers underneath.*

The serpent scales the tree
>*with a wish to make his love known.*
>*He breaks her lonely prison*
>*and now freed, the bird flies home.*

Abandoned in silent midnight,
>*the serpent weeps red stones.*
>*His tears capture the starlight,*
>*and the serpent is alone.*

Of raven plumes and starlit skies,
>*he's left dreaming in the mists.*
>*Of a gift of aspen seeds,*
>*and serpent's tears in golden twists.*

Alone, the venom grows inside,
>*his heart in shadow deep,*
>*baring fangs and hatred*
>*so no one will hear him weep,*

AND AT NIGHT he dreams of starlight,
   and a gift of aspen seeds."

THE LAST STRUM faded before applause erupted, but Rhyllyn kept his head down and fiddled with the instrument's strings.

Firal drew a shuddering breath, aware of the tears in her eyes for the first time. She twisted in her chair, hoping to catch a glimpse of Rune.

She found him as a shadow beside a column, toying with a necklace between his claws. He tucked it beneath his shirt and disappeared into the dark beyond the banquet hall.

"A remarkable piece, isn't it?" Vicamros wiped his eyes, evidently as touched by the sorrowful ballad as a dozen others around the table. "A beautiful expansion on a piece of old folklore, truly. But there's one piece I've never understood. The line about aspen seeds, what does it mean?" He turned to Rhyllyn, seeking an answer.

"A tradition," Firal supplied.

Vicamros regarded her, surprised.

She swallowed hard. "In my homeland, it's tradition for a newly wedded couple to exchange a gift of seeds. Different plants bear different meanings, you see. Aspen is meant to represent strength and longevity in a bond."

"A curious choice." The king eyed Rhyllyn with new respect. "So the serpent dreams of a love that could have been."

Rhyllyn forced a smile. "Yes, Your Majesty. I suppose you could say that."

Firal left her napkin over the remnants of her meal as she stood. "A lovely ballad, Rhyllyn. Thank you for playing. If you will excuse me, I think that wine was a bit stronger than what I am used to. I believe I need a bit of air."

"Of course," Vicamros said dismissively, his attention still on Rhyllyn. "Do you have time to play another before the mages reclaim you?"

Firal slipped away before she heard his answer.

The ballad had been a surprise bordering on unpleasant. She'd learned the old folk tale about the snake and nightingale what seemed an eternity ago, nestled in the cozy underground city of Core. Even then the story of the snake whose scales separated him from love had struck close to home. She'd thought that one of the reasons for the asteriated ruby that adorned her wedding ring, but after the ring disappeared, she'd tried not to think of it—or the man who'd given it to her—again.

That Rhyllyn would combine their story with the fable made perfect sense, yet the invasion of the song into the life she'd had with Rune rankled. It was nobody's business, and certainly wasn't proper for recital in front of a gathered crowd.

She shook out her skirts as she walked and huffed beneath her breath. Thinking about it replaced her tears with anger. The force of her steps kept both palace staff and wandering nobles at bay.

Though she didn't know the layout of the palace well, it wasn't hard to find a doorway that led to the courtyards and gardens. Unlike the sprawling gardens of the palace in Ilmenhith, the Spiral Palace hosted spaces that were attractive but functional. The city crowded the palace from every direction, which meant the gardens along the sides were split by narrow cobbled streets that led to the stables and barracks hidden behind the massive, twisting structure.

Firal had tried to look at the palace once before, but against the backdrop of fast-moving clouds and brilliant blue sky, it had proven so dizzying she'd almost toppled over. She was mindful not to look up this time, at least until she found a stone bench at the mouth of the garden and settled. From there, it was easier to observe the spire.

The Spiral Palace didn't twist the way she thought it might. There were no defined corners, but it wasn't quite cylindrical, either. Now that she looked at it against the backdrop of the night sky, it reminded her of a narwhal's tusk. She'd never seen such a creature herself, but they were one of many oddities that populated the books she'd enjoyed in her youth.

The tower's twisted form was dotted with windows and balconies, some lit and creating the notion it wanted to blend into the stars, as if it could. Aside from the twisted, ridged shape, the palace also resembled a narwhal's tusk in color. Pale ivory, it almost glowed in the night sky. As tall and bright as it was, Firal imagined it would be visible from every corner of the Royal City. If she were staying there as long as she'd begun to think she might, perhaps she'd find out.

She didn't have time to contemplate that before a burst of energy in the courtyard in front of the palace made her skin rise in gooseflesh. She thought nothing of a Gate opening until a figure in soot-stained white fell through and landed hard on the stone.

Firal jumped up and half ran to help, but the mage lifted one ebony-dark hand in signal for her to stop. The Gate was still open and he looked back at it, tense and waiting. She'd only met him once, but he had a commanding presence she couldn't have forgotten. She'd wondered where Stal was during the banquet. Evidently, the war had begun without them.

Long moments dragged by. The Gate closed without anyone else following, and he slumped back onto the pavement. It wasn't relief that made him collapse, but defeat. He rested his brow against the stone, his eyes squeezed closed.

Firal knelt beside him and rested a hand on his shoulder. She didn't know whether to check him for injuries or get him to his feet. Instead, she opted for a question while guardsmen ran from the palace doors to join them. "What happened?"

Stal lifted his head, his icy eyes somber. "The Collective has been shattered. Umdal's outposts have burned."

14

A TIME FOR ACTION

FIRAL FOLLOWED ON THE HEELS OF THE MEN, BITING HER TONGUE TO keep from chastising the Archmage.

Stal could barely walk and needed the support of both guards that walked with him, but he refused to sit for even a moment so she could tend his injuries. Had he stopped to think, she was sure he would have realized he'd be able to move faster after sacrificing a minute or two for recovery.

She was inclined to let him suffer, but the healer in her wouldn't allow it. Not that she was sure she could do anything, considering the barrier over the city, but she was compelled to try. So she followed as the guards half-carried him to the banquet hall she'd just left. Stal would have to sit once he made it there. She'd help mend him then, assuming she could find a mage with an access stone among those gathered, and that she could still join power with another mage without having a stone of her own.

With so many people coming and going, most of the mages at the banquet table were indifferent to one more person clouding their senses. The guards were harder to dismiss, though, and when one person at the table caught sight of them, everyone else turned to stare as well.

Sera all but leaped from her place at the table. She flew across the room, wrapped her husband in a hug and buried her face in his sooty robes. A pang of sadness and perhaps envy hit Firal. When had she last seen Vahn? She'd lost count of the days.

Stal pulled an arm free of his support, draped it around Sera's shoulders, and kissed the top of her head. He balanced on one foot, which Firal noted with a frown. She suspected a sprain, since he could walk with assistance, but she supposed a fracture was possible. If it was a fracture, perhaps he'd been right to hurry to the banquet hall. She wouldn't be able to repair a fracture as fast, but a proper examination would let her determine how severe it was.

"The children?" Sera asked in a trembling voice.

"Scattered to the winds. They will join us here when the mages with them have rested long enough to safely open another Gate." Stal cupped her face in one hand and kissed the tip of her nose. "You know I would not have left until they were safe."

Sera nodded and hugged him again.

Stal winced when she squeezed his ribs and Firal slid close to lay a hand on Sera's shoulder. "Your husband's been injured. Let's get him settled. Archmage Kytenia and I can provide healing, if someone will work with us."

"I must speak to King Vicamros first," Stal insisted.

Sera snorted and slapped his chest. "Vicamros is right there, foolish man. You can talk while the mages tend you. I'd heal you myself, but..." She didn't need to finish. Stal and Firal both knew the use of magic was discouraged during pregnancy. The new life inside her was too delicate, too easily disrupted or damaged by the fluctuations of power. No mother would risk stillbirth for sake of reaching power when another could tend what needed it.

Stal looked as if he wanted to complain, but he allowed the guards and women to escort him to the table.

Vicamros took the man's arm and shooed the guardsmen

away. He helped Stal to the chair Rune had abandoned, then drew Sera's empty chair close beside it.

"Your appearance bears no good news," Vicamros said. He moved aside as Kytenia rounded the table with one of the Royal City's court mages and joined Firal at the Umdal Archmage's side.

Kytenia was the stronger healer and Stal's equal besides, but the court mage looked at Firal as if she expected to be led. Not allowing herself to be surprised, Firal accepted the silent offer of power the court mage extended.

Access to her Gift came rushing back when their power linked, their Gifts twisted together like coils in a rope. Firal laid her hands on the sides of Stal's neck and closed her eyes. Skin contact wasn't necessary for her to investigate his condition, but she always found it made things easier.

He relaxed and let his body accept the intrusion of her energies. It was an odd connection, unlike what she held with the court mage. It was more of a temporary link that let her probe the flow of life through his body with a sort of sixth sense. Healing was difficult for mages with other affinities, but as a natural healer, Firal found it almost as easy as breathing.

"Bruises, mostly," she concluded after a moment. "A severe sprain in his left leg and knee, as well as some scrapes. A burn of some sort. Lacerations on both knees. His palms, as well. Caught yourself on the stone, Archmage?"

"You might think that," Stal grumbled. "I was thrown more than I would like to admit."

Vicamros eased himself down into his seat. "I take it your negotiations did not go well."

"There were no negotiations. She demanded I give her the whereabouts of the rest of the Collective. I told her honestly that I did not know where they were. She asked after places they may be and refused to accept that our mages have no permanent stations."

Firal pretended not to listen as she gently snared threads of

Stal's energy and trained them on his injuries. She fed them with her own strength, coaxing bruises to fade and scraped skin to mend.

Knowing Envesi had attacked the leaders of the Grand College and the leaders of the Umdal Collective in the same day made her ill, but worse was knowing the woman had left her vigil over Elenhiise.

It felt like a wasted opportunity. If only they knew what to expect on the other side, she'd have mages help Gate her directly to Vahn and her daughter. The idea had occurred to her a dozen times, but each time, Firal had been certain Envesi was with them. Gating straight into the woman's grasp could spell certain death for any normal mage. If they could unravel the seal on Rune's power, it would change everything. He wouldn't have to risk Rhyllyn's safety, his ability to open a Gate on his own restored. Though he'd Gated them out of the throne room with the seal still in place, she knew she couldn't rely on that as certainty.

Even if he could do it again, there was a real chance that without his power, Envesi would kill him before he got that far.

Stal quietly recounted the evening's events, from Sera's departure to the moment he'd escaped and the mages who aided him failed to emerge through the Gate they'd opened. Dead, no doubt, swallowed by the ruins of the burning chapter house.

Vicamros nodded, absorbing everything without comment. In his silence, Firal felt her anger grow anew.

No one told her Sera's presence had been because Envesi had been to see them. Had they, she would have seized the opportunity to send Rune and Rhyllyn to rescue her husband and daughter. They couldn't stand against Envesi, but the two of them could surely hold against Kirban's rebel mages.

"Do you want me to finish?" Kytenia asked softly.

Firal started. Anger stirred power in mages, but rarely for the better. Stal had said nothing, too occupied with conversation to pay attention to the way her energies bubbled over and thrust against his, draining more of his reserves than necessary to heal the damage done.

She swallowed hard, released the flows and withdrew her magic. "I think it's all in order now, but please do check my work." She kept her tone light and pleasant, like that of a proud student asking a teacher to confirm a job was well done.

Kytenia took her place in the link with the court mage and inspected Stal's condition.

Shrinking back, Firal cast a furtive glance at the other nearby mages. Only one seemed to have paid her any mind. Even the mage she'd linked with was otherwise occupied in conversation. The sharp, judging weight of Sera's gaze made her want to squirm.

"I should go," Firal murmured to Kytenia.

"Wait a moment, if you would," Sera said. Her voice was bright and cheery, betraying none of the hard calculation Firal saw in her eyes. "Rune went to his room with complaints of bruising and muscle spasms after the barrier threw him. He might appreciate a healer. Perhaps we should see to his injuries before we retire. Stal and I both have access stones, so we can assist you. We can inform him of these new developments, as well."

"Please do," Vicamros said, rubbing his eyes. "He is to be among the mages that will sweep the southern continent to find the surviving pieces of the Collective, which must be done before we can push back against this woman's forces. He will need to know what they may face. And be in proper condition to face it, too."

Firal fought a grimace. After this evening, tending Rune's injuries in his private quarters was the last thing she wanted to do. There was little room to object, though, and she knew it. Until something was done about Envesi, Firal had little ground to challenge Vicamros. Though if the self-appointed Archmage had already turned against him, perhaps that had changed. Overturning Envesi's rule of the island meant putting Firal back on the throne. Tragic as the attacks on the Grand College and Umdal were, they had the potential to be the best thing that had happened for her since this whole disaster began. Vicamros needed an ally to rule Elenhiise, for sake of the Triad's prosperity.

That ally was her.

Garnering her strength with that knowledge, Firal did not protest when Sera beckoned her. She fell in step behind the two Umdal mages and the servant that led them. Before she could leave the room, Kytenia grabbed hold of her hand, and Firal paused.

"Do you need my help?" Gentle and supportive, Kytenia would be her friend to the last.

Firal mustered a smile. "I'll be fine. I know you'll be up all night working on that barrier puzzle. Just worry about that." She tried not to think of her ulterior motive, though it danced across her mind. The sooner the barrier was taken care of, the sooner Rhyllyn and the rest of the mages could start trying to unravel the seal on Rune's power.

Kytenia gave her hand a squeeze. "Just call if you need me." She let go and gave Firal one last meaningful look before she retreated to the cluster of mages gathered near Vicamros to receive further instruction for the night.

Though the servant led them through the service passages to save time, they still walked far enough to make Firal's legs ache. Sera said nothing, but she did lean on her husband for support and her pace slowed with time.

"How much longer until your little one arrives?" Firal trailed her hand along the wall as they turned into another narrow passage. She would have liked to have someone to lean on, herself.

"Twenty-two days, according to the midwives," Sera replied with a hint of pride.

"Not that she's counting, as you can see." Stal chuckled.

Firal chuckled too, recalling those days too well. "Longer than I expected, if I'm to be truthful."

"Yes, this one has grown fast." Sera grinned over her shoulder. "That's why I am sure it's a boy this time."

A boy. What Firal would have done for a son. "You're blessed to have so many. I hoped for more, but Lumia is my only."

Sera made a soft, sympathetic sound in her throat. "My mother bore the same struggle. Like me, she wished for a large family, but ended up with only me and Garam. And the two of us many years apart, at that."

"One of many ways our Gifts are blessings," Stal said. "You're young yet, Queen Firal. There's still time for that."

Assuming she was reunited with her husband, that was. Firal smiled politely and said nothing more.

At first glance, the door the servant stopped at appeared no different than any of the dozens they'd passed on the way up. Then the man bowed and left them, and Firal caught the small details carved into the ivory stone around the doorway. Flowers and patterns graced the stone, so faint it was less a relief and almost more of an etching. A glance over her shoulder showed the door behind them bore a different pattern.

She much preferred the halls of her own palace in Ilmenhith, where there were only a handful of rooms off each hall and the halls themselves were decorated in different colors. The palace here twisted on itself in a writhing mass of confusion, as hard to navigate as the ruins outside Kirban Temple.

Giving her head a twitch of a shake, she reminded herself why they were there and straightened as Stal knocked.

Long silence crawled on.

Stal knocked again, harder. "Ruali!"

Firal leaned closer to Sera. "What does that mean?"

Sera raised a brow and whispered back. "Rune. It's his name in Umdalan. The school is named after the region. I've always thought it funny. There he is Ruali Dreamhunter and here he is

Rune Kaim-Ennen. No matter where he is, his name is a mixture of tongues."

"I suppose it fits him," Firal said. "He's always been a curious blend."

Just when Stal raised his fist to pound on the door, it opened. Rune rubbed one of his eyes with the side of his hand and glowered. He wore no shirt and Firal's eyes were drawn downward like a magnet. She'd not seen him in any state of undress since their life together ended. His body was as chiseled as she remembered, but the slim silver ring through his left nipple was new.

She turned red from head to toe.

"Seems you're not dead yet," Rune remarked, giving Stal a once-over as if the news was disappointing. "Let me get a shirt."

Sera planted both hands on his chest and shoved him back. "How am I supposed to see what we can do about your injuries if I can't see them? Go lie down, lizard."

He staggered back a step before he caught himself and braced against her shoves. "I was lying down. What happened?"

"A great deal in a short time, I'm afraid," Stal said. "I apologize. I know you need your rest. Vicamros told us he means for you to leave tomorrow. We thought it best you know what's happened before then." He motioned for Rune to make way and Firal was surprised when he did.

"Of course," Rune sighed, pacing back. "But why is she here?"

The edge in his tone made Firal's blood run cold. Every time she felt herself soften toward him, he grew icy again. Did he truly hate her so much? If he did, she had no one to blame but herself. She'd said the words first, brandished them as a weapon instead of the defense her feelings were. He hadn't repeated them back to her, but she didn't know what to think. His behavior ran hot and cold, one minute tempting her to fall into his arms again, and the next making her wonder if he had any feeling left at all.

Right now, it was the latter.

"The chapter house in Gand has been destroyed. The witch burned it. You will need to Gate in from somewhere else, but I can assist with that." Stal spread his hands in a gesture that fell short of a shrug. "The Collective is scattered beyond the trade kingdoms. You will find none of them there. I expect there will be some in Nura, but beyond that, I couldn't tell you. But you won't be looking alone. The witch will be there, too."

Rune sighed. "So we start in Nura."

"Are you really going without a fight?" Sera asked.

"I never said that. I have somewhere else I'd rather be." Rune climbed onto the bed and turned face down in the pillows. "That's not a fight I'm picking tonight, though."

He'd prefer to stay holed up in his mansion with his whiskey, Firal was sure. She stifled the thought and bit her tongue to keep it still. No matter how frustrating he was, riling him was never wise.

"In honesty, friend, I don't think you will find any members of the Collective. Not you and not anyone else." Stal paced across the room and rubbed his hands together. "If they wish to be hidden, you would sooner find a viper in the trees."

"I know," Rune murmured. "But you try telling Vicamros his plan is useless. He feels like his hands are tied in this."

"In many ways, he's right." Sera climbed on the bed, straddled Rune's middle and ran her hands over his back. "So many bruises! Did the mages beat you with sticks after you fell?"

He ignored the question. "Right now, Cam's just filling his time and hoping for a miracle." One violet eye opened, its slit center narrowing as it fell on Firal. "He's not the only one."

Firal fought back a shudder.

"So, ignoring Vicamros and his defensive strategy, what are our options?" Stal paused beside the table and tilted a half-emptied bottle of whiskey with one fingertip.

"Realistically?" Rune shifted to make himself more comfortable and grimaced when Sera probed a particularly sore spot in his back. "There's only one option. Always has been. We kill her, simple as that."

"Easy to say," Firal muttered. "Less easy to do."

Rune lifted his head and glared. "I told you what I needed. I told Kytenia. If you'd been a shade faster, that escapade in the throne room would have turned out different."

Sera slapped one of his bruises, yielding an angry grunt. "How dare you speak to her that way? The situation she's in is not her fault."

"Maybe not, but she could have handled it a lot better." He winced and settled back into the pillows.

Firal couldn't deny that. Had she allowed herself time to listen to him before issuing orders in the first place, everything would have gone better.

"That doesn't answer my question," Stal said. "I asked for options. Saying to kill her without saying how isn't helpful."

Rune scoffed. "With a dagger, with a guillotine, with poison, does it matter? The problem isn't killing her, the problem is getting close enough to do it. I asked them for enough mages to lend me power to stand up against her, but it's probably best that didn't happen."

"How can you say that?" Firal cried. "Better that the entire island is in her grasp now?"

"Better that we didn't try," he replied dryly. "Even if there had been enough mages nearby, it's the same problem I have with Rhyllyn. Pulling power from others slows me down. Pulling from that many would be even slower. How many would die before I could do anything?"

Stal muttered something under his breath. Firal didn't understand it, but Sera gave him a dirty look.

"So you think it's hopeless, then." Firal blinked hard to keep from crying. After everything, he made it sound as if he was eager to wash his hands of it and be done. She didn't expect him to be happy, but she had expected more compassion. He'd been the one to seek her in her room, comfort her and tell her not to give up. How terrible he was at following his own advice.

"Nothing is hopeless," Sera said, jabbing a fist into another bruise and earning another grunt. "It never is."

"But you have to admit our chances of success are slim," Rune muttered.

Stal shrugged. "Be that as it may, we have to think of something. I doubt even the barrier over the Royal City would hold that witch at bay for long."

"I'm finding a lot of people asking me to do something and not offering much help." Rune squirmed beneath Sera in effort to reposition himself. Unable to move, he reached back and pinched one of her thighs.

She squealed, grabbed a fistful of his hair and yanked his head back. Rune hissed and Sera cackled. "Oh, what's the matter? I thought you liked it rough."

Flushing, Firal turned away.

"We will have one more opportunity to speak before Vicamros sends you south." Stal made his way back toward the door, wearied. "Now that you know, I trust we will both spend the night thinking of how we will address the situation. I will be in our rooms when you are done tending him, Sera."

Firal strode after him. "Archmage?"

Stal raised a brow. "You are more than welcome to call me by name. You are a queen, are you not?"

Was she a queen? She no longer knew. "Thank you. Before you go, I just wanted to ask if... if there was anything I could do to help. With the Collective, or with anything, really."

He smiled, a broad, warm expression that made his entire being seem instantly softer. "You are a kind spirit, Queen Firal. You've already aided me, and I thank you for the healing. I am sure I will need your assistance again before all this is resolved, but right now, I'm too tired to think. We will have plenty of opportunities to speak after I rest."

She tried to smile back, but a low, gratified groan behind her made her grimace instead.

Amused, Stal tilted his head. "Does it bother you that much?" He lowered his voice.

Firal pitched hers to match. "Doesn't it bother you? The way they act together?"

Stal glanced to the bed, where Sera held a pillow over Rune's head in effort to smother him. He writhed beneath her, unable to escape. "Why would it?"

Firal frowned and rubbed her arms. She didn't know how to answer that.

"We cannot understand because we've never faced war the way they have." Stal rested a hand on her shoulder. "I am an aristocrat and a mage, as are you. We've been sheltered from the hardships they've faced. When you cower in pits of mud together, uncertain whether or not you will survive, it creates a closeness no one else can understand. But if your question is whether or not I doubt my wife's fidelity, I don't. And neither should you."

Fire lit her cheeks and Firal turned away. "I didn't mean to imply anything ill. I like Sera, I wouldn't think she—"

"I didn't mean Sera," he said with a chuckle. "You need not apologize to me."

The heat in her face grew further and Firal ducked her head. All things considered, it wasn't appropriate for her to think anything of Rune. Their connection was long severed.

"You tend to your duties. Sera will link with you to give you access to your Gift. So long as she doesn't try to use hers, and you don't try to pull power through her instead of the stone, the child will be perfectly safe. I am going upstairs to see how I can help the mages," Stal said, lifting his voice so his wife could hear.

"Be careful," Sera called back. She'd settled back to work, apparently giving up the attempt to kill her patient. Instead she punished him by digging her thumbs deep into his back, making him grimace and claw at the pillow now beneath his face.

Firal sighed. "I'll tend to him. You should go with your husband. I'm sure he'll need your help."

Sera studied her for a moment, then shrugged and slid off the bed. "You're probably right. We can't leave any of them alone or they blow holes in the walls the moment you turn away." She rested her fingertips on her belly as she moved toward the door.

Rune exhaled in evident relief and Firal pursed her lips.

Sera touched Firal's arm and offered a slight smile. "I will see that no one bothers him tonight," she offered in low tones. "He will need his rest before they embark on this journey. Try not to rile him too much, or he'll stay up drinking instead."

"I will not," Rune snapped.

Sera shot him a glare and pulled Firal into the hallway, out of earshot. "I mean that. He won't admit to it, but everyone knows it's one of his vices. He tries to drown his feelings. It never works."

"I don't mean to be here long enough to disrupt things," Firal murmured, looking back toward Rune's bed. The knowledge she'd never be comfortable near him again was both painful and troubling. Everything seemed to crawl under her skin and nettle her raw. She couldn't feel at ease around him, yet something kept him returning to her thoughts, and not all of them were bitter. How would she be able to let go after this war was over?

Sera followed her gaze. "It was a mistake."

Startled, Firal frowned. "What?"

"Bedding him." Sera nodded toward Rune.

Firal's ears grew hot. Her own embarrassment would burn her alive before the day was out.

"I heard you talking to Stal. And I've seen the way you look at me. You don't need to think anything of the way we are."

"I wasn't going to say anything," Firal murmured.

"I didn't expect you would." Sera chuckled. "He was respectful. Kind. I think he cared. But he didn't love me. He could have, in time, but what is a learned love compared to a soul that burns like your own?"

The words settled on Firal's shoulders like a burden.

Sera turned and nodded down the hall with a smile. Her husband stood some distance away, conversing with a maidservant. "Now Stal, there is a man who understands me. We share the same fire, the same sense of duty. We connected the moment we met."

Firal snorted. "When we met, Rune tried to scare me away. I thought he meant to kill me."

"I've heard." Chuckling again, Sera leaned close to share a conspiratorial whisper. "He doesn't think he ever deserved you. With me, he saw himself as my equal. But you?" She shook her head. "To hear him talk, one would think you hung every star in the sky." She patted Firal's arm and swayed down the hallway to join her husband's conversation.

Gulping against the rising lump in her throat, Firal slid back into the room and padded toward the bed. As she walked, a gentle push of energy came Firal's direction. Sera was a powerful mage, then. Firal could only offer her power to someone she could see. She snared the offering before it could escape and tried to focus on the task ahead.

Rune lifted his head at her approach and reached for his shirt.

"Leave it off," she murmured as she settled on the edge of the bed.

Reluctant, he let it go and eased himself back into the pillows.

"Now let me see what you've done." She ran her hands over his shoulders and back. She tried to ignore the rough ridges of the scars, pale against his bronze flesh, and focused instead on probing for deeper injury with her Gift.

Firal wasn't afforded many opportunities to use her abilities in Ilmenhith's palace. She didn't like to think she'd forget anything, but it certainly didn't come as easy as it used to.

Aside from the visible bruises on his shoulder blades and the too-tight muscles in his back, he seemed the picture of health. She withdrew her energy and settled her hands on his shoulders as she let go of the link. Sera's presence faded from her senses. Firal was grateful for the privacy.

He flinched and tensed beneath her hands, and his breath grew sharp.

"You should relax." She worked her thumbs into the knots in his muscles and her fingertips traveled over the scars to seek pressure points. The ridges and hollows made her queasy. She fought to ignore the churn of her stomach. As grand as the life he'd built appeared to be, it had not been without suffering.

Instead of relaxing, Rune pulled away. "It's not that easy."

"I can't do anything about that spasm if you won't lay down." She clasped her hands in her lap.

He shook his head, paced away and turned his shirt over in his hands. "Since you've been here, since we met again, you've acted like you expect everything to be all right. That I'd answer your summons and be happy about it. Eager to please you, even. The last time I saw you, I was condemned. Sentenced to death. When I needed you, you walked away."

His words turned her stomach to ice. The lump grew in her throat again. She worried her hands.

"Now you need me." Rune halted halfway across the room and shifted on his feet as if he couldn't decide whether or not he should turn to face her. He didn't. "You pretend everything between us is fine. But those feelings don't go away, Firal. And I can't lay face down in a pile of pillows and let you touch me when not that long ago, I was sure you wanted a rope around my neck."

"I never wanted that, Rune." For all the times he'd opened up to her since their arrival in the Triad, she'd never repaid the favor. The words threatened to choke her. "All I wanted was for you to come home."

He made a quiet sound of amusement in his throat and

pulled his shirt on overhead. "Little late for that to make any difference. It's not what you want now."

"What I want now is to have our daughter back in my arms." Her voice quavered. "I've done all I can to make that happen, and I've failed at every turn. I told you before, if you can return her to me, I'll give you anything in my power to give. All you have to do is tell me what you want."

"The things I want are always what I can't have," Rune said, giving her a wry look. "I suppose I've never learned my lesson."

Firal stared back, almost daring him to ask. When she'd offered herself to him in Ilmenhith, it had been with a measure of disgust. She'd thought ill of him, shaped him to a conjured idea of a villain who never existed.

Now she was no longer sure how she felt. He made her heart flutter, but he also made her sick. As a married woman, she shouldn't so much as entertain the idea. But he had been her husband too, and for the first time, she wondered what that meant. Would returning to him be wrong? Or was it her marriage to Vahn while Rune still lived that would be called adultery? She closed her eyes to chase away the thought.

Rune jerked the ties on his shirt tight and paced to the window. "I make no promises on what will happen. Vicamros wants me to move with the army of mages headed for the southern continent tomorrow, but he still doesn't have a plan beyond finding as many stragglers as possible and sending them here. My skills would be of more use here, but I doubt he'd let me stay."

Her heart sank and her face fell. "So you mean to do nothing?"

"On the contrary, I mean to end this. But I need to speak to Rhyllyn first, to see if my ideas have merit, and he won't know until he's able to expand the mage-barrier. Until that happens, I will go where my king sends me."

"And what of your queen?" she challenged.

Rune raised one dark brow. "You were never my ruler."

"But you've made it clear you're going to Elenhiise," she said. "You're still doing what I've asked."

"Make no mistake," he replied, turning back to the window and lifting his chin. The soft luminescence of his violet eyes gleamed on the glass and she realized he was using it as a mirror. She saw no others in his room. "I'm going, but not because you asked, and not because of Vicamros."

Firal slid from the side of the bed and inched closer. "Then why?"

He squared his shoulders and lifted his chin as he smoothed the fitted cuffs of his sleeves. "Do you honestly believe for a second that my father wanted you on the throne instead of me? My whole life, he'd groomed me to take his place. I meant what I said when you had me arrested. The crown is mine. If taking it back means reclaiming Elenhiise as well, then so be it."

Hurt and anger flooded her heart. Before she could speak a word, the door flew open.

"My queen," Ordin panted, bowing his head and shoulders and holding the door to keep from collapsing for lack of breath. "King Vahnil has just arrived."

1 5

────────

TURNING POINTS

EXHAUSTED HARDLY COVERED HOW VAHN FELT. EVERYONE'S insistence he rest seemed like sound advice now, a whole day too late.

Though everything had gone smoothly since Edagan's group of mages connected with those Councilor Parthanus gathered to return to the Royal City, their noisy company offered little time for sleep. His body burned with fatigue. His head ached and his thoughts were so muddled, he wasn't sure how much longer he could stay on his feet.

Then the door creaked open, and he forgot his weariness and all the pains that went with it.

Firal ran, but Vahn met her halfway. He swept her into his arms and twirled her around, hugged her close and buried his face in her thick black hair.

"You're safe," she gasped.

Vahn wasn't sure he could agree. "When they told me you were here, I hardly believed it. I didn't imagine anything could be so easy, after everything we've been through." Tangling his hands in her curls, he tilted her head to look at her eyes. "Let me see you. Brant's roots, I can't believe how beautiful you are."

Firal glowed. She nestled her cheek into his palm and hugged

199

him tight. "I was starting to fear I'd never see you again." Her voice cracked and she swiped at her eyes with her fingertips. "What are you doing here? What's happened?"

The question chased his smile away. Vahn sobered and tucked a stray curl behind the delicate point of her ear. "I was told you'd been kidnapped. I didn't believe it, but when we sent a messenger here and she returned saying you were in the palace, I didn't believe that, either. I couldn't imagine you being so close within my reach."

She cocked her head. "A messenger? Where? When?"

He closed his eyes and forced a smile. "I'm sorry. Forgive me, I'm so tired. Sit down, I'll explain everything."

Firal took him by the hands, led him to the bed and helped him settle on its edge. The quarters Vicamros had offered him were luxurious, befitting of a visiting king, and the plush bed only made the call of sleep that much louder. She knelt before him to help him out of his boots.

There was so much to tell her, he hardly knew what to say. "Lulu is home. She's safe. She's with my mother in the palace in Ilmenhith."

Firal sat back so hard Vahn thought she might swoon with relief. He leaned forward to lay a hand on her shoulder and steady her.

"Envesi is there too. Right now, she says she means the kingdom no harm. She only wishes to have control of the temple."

"No harm?" She scoffed, her evident relief replaced with anger in the blink of an eye. "She tried to kill me! She stood right in front of the throne and tried to burn me out of existence!"

He grimaced. "Her story was somewhat different. Not that I believed her," he added hastily. "The problem is that she believes herself when she says it. I'm beginning to think she's mad, Firal."

"Then you're a little late to that conclusion," she sniffed, put his boots aside and climbed onto the bed beside him. She touched his face and he shivered at the coolness of her fingers. He'd half expected a chilly wash of power to go with it, an odd sensation that would indicate she was inspecting his physical state. It didn't come. He wasn't disappointed. He wasn't fond of it, but it was more pleasant than the prickle of passing through a Gate. He'd had enough of that for a lifetime, though he knew he'd have to suffer it many more times before this was over.

"I'm sorry," he said. "I didn't mean to upset you. Being away from home has been hard for me, that's all. Especially having spent all this time among her people and hearing the way they talk." He relaxed when her cold fingers pulled away.

She made up for it with the warmth of her body as she curled against him and clung to his arm. "The reports changed all the time. You were missing for so long, then they said you were in the temple. I was ready to send people after you. I was trying to arrange it when Envesi came to the palace. If it hadn't been for Rune, I..." She trailed off and bowed her head.

Vahn's throat constricted. "I understand he's here, as well."

"Yes," Firal sighed, nuzzling his shoulder. "For all the help that's been."

"You don't sound happy." He didn't know whether that should please him or not.

"He's difficult," she muttered. "I'm not sure if I can consider him an ally, honestly. But he did save us when Envesi attacked, so I suppose I still must thank him for that. You were right to summon him. Had you not, I suppose we all would be dead."

"But he was unwilling to help?" Vahn didn't know why he asked. Had Ran been willing to help, they would have been rescued from Alwhen within a day. He paused and leaned back to look at her. "What did you call him, a moment ago?"

Firal shrugged. "His name. Rune Kaim-Ennen is what they call him here."

He frowned. "I've heard that before. Politicians and merchants both have mentioned that name when visiting the island. The Champion of the Royal City Arena. Quite a hero in the Triad. If I had realized..."

"You couldn't have known," Firal said. "Even if I'd heard it, I don't think I would have known. I never expected he would have kept that name."

Vahn shifted, unsettled. "Kept it?"

"The name I gave him," she replied quietly. "When we married, he asked what I would call him. Which identity I would expect him to take. But they were both vestiges of a troubled life. So I gave him a new name, from the scar in his hand."

And he'd kept it, through all those years. Uneasy, Vahn pulled away. "Well, perhaps things will change now. I am to discuss matters with Vicamros in the morning, but I expect we should be able to return home afterward." He busied himself with unbuttoning his shirt, pretending getting ready to sleep had been his intent all along.

Firal blinked at him. "So soon? But we've not even begun to discuss Envesi, or how she's to be dealt with—"

"By others," Vahn said before she could finish. "While I do think she's mad, I don't think it was her intention to hurt you. At least, not when she arrived. The ugly truth is that she needs us. Both of us. And as long as we keep our heads down, we should be safe until Vicamros does whatever he pleases about her."

Her mouth fell open. "You can't be serious!"

"I am." He nearly snapped. Exhausted as he was, he barely caught himself. Cross was the last thing he wanted to be. He sucked in a deep breath and tried to sound more pleasant. "Lulu is home. You're alive. Envesi wants us to keep leading Ilmenhith, which means for now, our family is safe. I want it to be safe and whole again. I want to go home and try to forget any of this ever happened."

"We're not safe," Firal protested. "We won't be safe anywhere until she's gone. She attacked the Grand College, Vahn. She attacked the school of mages on the southern continent. Both because they didn't immediately agree with her methods. How can you think it will be different for us?"

"Because we aren't the Grand College or a school of mages." Vahn frowned at her. "At worst, we'll have to cut ties with Kirban and send the mages back to the temple. Destruction of magic, preservation of magic—whatever it is, it's mage business. Other mage organizations are the only people she's attacked. She'll leave everyone else out of it."

Her cheeks colored with the hot pink of anger. "No, she won't. It will always involve us, because I'll always be a mage. So will our daughter. That's the reason she was taken in the first place!"

He heaved a sigh. "Then we'll have to negotiate something. A trade, maybe. Your freedom and Lulu's in exchange for cutting the temple free of its ties to the crown."

"So you would have me oust Kytenia in favor of a madwoman? Or worse, turn her over to Envesi along with the rest of the mages. Why not?" She snorted and shook her head.

"I know it's not a perfect solution," Vahn said, tempering his annoyance. "But it's the best chance we have right now. Right now, she's willing to let us have the island back. As long as we leave her alone, it could be years before we face problems again. Being on her good side is not without advantages, Firal."

She drew back, her eyes narrowing, and he knew he'd made a mistake.

"Advantages," she repeated. "Why would you think that? What have you heard?"

Vahn hesitated. Letting her know he'd spoken to Envesi directly on multiple occasions would clearly be another mistake. No matter how useful the woman's expertise might be in strengthening mages and restoring their hope for a growing family, now was not the time to discuss it. Not now, and not likely soon.

"Well, she'd be less likely to want to kill us, that's for certain." He mustered a smile and rubbed his eyes. "I'm sorry. I know all of this is important, but I haven't slept in two days. I'm having trouble thinking straight. I need to rest at least a little before we meet with Vicamros in the morning."

"Of course," Firal murmured, though the way she eyed him reminded him of some cautious woodland creature instead of his wife.

Vahn stripped to his smallclothes, climbed into the bed and opened an arm in invitation. Firal crawled to meet him and rested her head on his shoulder, but she didn't remove her gown.

An odd thing, that dress. He only recalled seeing her in black once before, so many years ago it seemed like a dream. He'd danced with her, spun her across the floor and mused at how the red gores in her skirt had matched her flame-like mask.

"Just think," he said drowsily, his mind on the grand ballroom in Ilmenhith and what excuse he might find to dance with her again. "Tomorrow, perhaps we'll finally be home."

The lights in the room seemed to dim as sleep reached to take him. He wondered only fleetingly why Firal didn't douse the lamps with her magic. Then a yawn chased the thought away.

"Yes," Firal replied, a thoughtful note in her voice. "Home."

AFTER SO MANY years in the Royal City, working alongside Garam, Vicamros, Redoram, and Sera, Rune's friendship with Vahn had still been the most meaningful of his life.

There was a clear divide in his head, a rift where his life had split into two distinct halves. The edge of the rift was the minute he'd given up on returning to Elenhiise and surrendered to his new life in the Triad. He cared for the people he'd met in the new chapter, but not with the same warmth he'd felt for those he'd known in his youth.

He and Vahn had grown up together. Shared secrets the people in the Triad would never understand. His friends in the

Triad had met him as Rune, the man in a monster's body, the wild mage already experienced with war. They'd never known him as Ran, the lonely and troubled youth forced to hide his true nature with illusory magic.

In spite of their long history and the close kinship they'd once shared, Rune did not go to greet Vahn. He was both relieved and grateful to know his friend had survived, and that he'd made his way to the Royal City, but on the heels of all that had happened that evening, it was simply too much.

He'd hoped to drink himself into oblivion after escaping the banquet hall. The social event before war began was bad enough, but for Vicamros to insist Rhyllyn play that blighted ballad was more than he could bear.

Rune hated that song. He'd hated it since he'd first found the lyrics scrawled on a scrap of paper in his private library, and had regretted telling Rhyllyn of his failed marriage ever since.

Yet he still wore the rings on a strap around his neck. Still lost himself in the six-rayed star of the serpent's tear whenever it caught the light. The stone was still the most beautiful he'd ever seen, deep red and crowning twists of gold that surely wouldn't fit back on Firal's finger after so many years.

They'd both changed in their years apart. He'd been battered and scarred, and she'd regained the weight she'd lost during the difficult months in Core. That time had been hard on her. Her fingers had been too slender when he gave her that ring. She'd never looked better than when he'd first laid eyes on her again, when she stood before the throne to look down on him. And oh, how he wanted her. To see the fire in her amber eyes, to breathe the sweetness of her hair while its soft strands tickled his skin, to hear the sweet melody of her laugh.

He fought that desire with everything he had. Out of respect for her, respect for his oldest and dearest friend, out of respect for the bond they shared now. Yet he hadn't been able to smother the small flame that had always burned in his heart, and it made him question himself at the most inopportune times.

What if he'd let her touch him? Administer healing and felt their energies combine again? What if he'd held her on the balcony when she'd cried? What if, instead of fleeing when Rhyllyn began his song, he'd asked her for just one dance?

And what would have happened when none of those were enough?

So Rune had remained out of sight, hiding in his room and clinging to the bottle of whiskey on his table.

Every time he closed his eyes, he saw the joy on Firal's face over again. She left without a second thought, forgetting all they'd argued over and all he'd said to drive her away. He should have been happy that it worked, but instead he found himself clinking the rings on his necklace and studying them for the thousandth time.

The plain gold band caught on one claw and he shifted his hand, dragging it farther down his finger without ever removing it from the strap. She'd outgrown her ring, but his still fit.

It always had.

He drank.

MISSING PIECES

"So, we're finally all back together." Kytenia sighed as she took a seat at the head of the table. Relieved as she was, she couldn't bring herself to smile.

A handful of other Masters took chairs of their own, their expressions as mixed as her own feelings. Rikka and Balen sat together. They hadn't stopped smiling since their reunion. After all they'd been through, Kytenia had little doubt they'd both believed the other dead. With how standoffish Rikka had grown in her time as a Master, it was good to see someone had broken through her shell and offered friendship.

Edagan and Anaide settled together as well, but they were often inseparable in the temple, too. After Kytenia had been appointed Archmage, they'd been all that remained of the old leadership. Edagan was more agreeable, but both had tendencies to dig in their heels. Normally, Shymin was there to tilt discussions in Kytenia's favor. With her sister firmly planted on the wrong side of the divide they faced, she expected meetings to be difficult, moving forward. She had hoped the temple would never split again.

The court mages bore no desire to cluster together, it seemed, and while Temar placed herself at Kytenia's left side, Asula and

Kella had taken the first chairs they'd reached. Kytenia had been afforded enough time to know she liked them both, and wished she knew more about Neve, the other temple Master who had come with Edagan's magelings.

The thought of that group made her wince, and Kytenia pressed her fingers to her temple. "Have the magelings been afforded proper sleeping arrangements?"

"Yes," Balen replied. "King Vicamros has granted them space in the floors reserved for his own court mages. They will have everything they need, including supervision."

Kytenia nodded. "Good. Now, down to business. It's best if we go over everything that's happened since... goodness, I don't even know. After I went to Ilmenhith to meet with Rune, everything began to fall apart."

Edagan squinted at her. "With who?"

"With Ran," Rikka said. "This is precisely why we need to make sure we all understand what's going on."

Beside her, Balen nodded.

So the starting point in the story was much farther back than she'd thought. Kytenia suppressed her desire to sigh again. "Right. I'd gone to Ilmenhith when I heard Ran—he goes by Rune, now—was there. That was when Envesi attacked the temple."

"While we were in the ruins for field exercises," Edagan said with a nod toward Neve. "Balen came to warn us. Rikka and Anaide were the ones in the temple."

"And Shymin," Rikka added. Her mouth took a sour twist. Several others frowned.

"Would someone fetch me a piece of paper?" Kytenia asked. "I suspect I'm going to need to write things down."

Asula stood without a word and vanished into the hall to find a page.

"Should we wait for her?" Rikka asked.

"No, let's continue. Rikka, you were the one who came to

find me in Ilmenhith," Kytenia said. "Temar, Kella, and Asula were in the palace the whole time."

"And seized your sister when she made the mistake of revealing her loyalties," Temar grumbled.

Everyone at the table sobered.

"Never mind," Kytenia sighed. "Let's wait for that paper."

A long, awkward silence followed.

When Asula returned with a stack of fine paper and a handful of writing implements and ink bottles, everyone sat without speaking while Kytenia wrote out everything they'd discussed. Eventually, this would all go into the temple's records. Assuming they ever made it back to the temple, that was. It unsettled her to admit she was no longer certain they could reclaim it.

"Okay," she said when she finished her notes. "I wrote down everything that happened to my group since things went sour in the palace. Edagan, explain everything that happened to yours." Her eyes darted to Balen and Neve. Should she have addressed them, as well? She hated to second-guess herself, but she had put Edagan in charge of field exercises, not them. The magelings lodged in the Spiral Palace now were Edagan's students.

The Master of Earth cleared her throat and clasped her hands against the edge of the table. "Of course. As I told you when we arrived earlier, we tunneled down to Core. We warned the ruin-folk and they began to prepare evacuations of their own. We left them to prepare and used the Gate in the mines to reach the mainland."

Kytenia nodded as she scratched out a new column of notes.

"Once we arrived," Edagan continued, "I left the others and made for the Grand College, in hopes Archmage Arrick could help us reach the queen. Instead, upon reaching the college, I discovered the Archmage had been killed and your sister put in his place."

"At which point you encountered Vahn?" Kytenia asked.

"In the hallway," the older Master agreed.

"And now we're here," Balen added as conclusion.

When she finished writing and saw it all laid out on paper, Kytenia couldn't help but frown at how simple what felt like chaos truly was.

A moment passed before Temar spoke. "Now, Archmage, it seems the problem we face is determining what comes next."

"Yes." Kytenia wished that part were simple, too.

"We're fortunate this many people in leadership positions were able to escape," Anaide said. "Right now, every authority figure in the western half of Elenhiise is within the Spiral Palace."

"Almost every authority figure," Kytenia corrected. "Tobias of the ruin-folk is yet unaccounted for."

Balen tapped the edge of the table. "Was he not in the underground city when we were present, Edagan?"

The Master of Earth spread her hands in a helpless gesture. "I am uncertain, but we will know soon, one way or another. I expect it did not take long for the ruin-folk to follow us through the Gate."

"If the Gate in the mines remains open, should we consider closing it now?" Temar asked. "Queen Firal had wanted all Gates that led off-island to be closed."

"We can ask, but at this point in time, that decision will be up to King Vicamros." Kytenia knew precious little about the man, for all that the Elenhiise and the Triad were allies. He'd struck her as long-suffering and level-headed since their arrival. She only hoped that foretold a favorable outcome for the meeting to be held the following morning. "And he has requested our assistance. That should be our primary focus at this time. It would be unwise to shun such a request after seeking asylum under his roof."

Rikka nodded in agreement, but the two elder Masters both fidgeted like unhappy children. Anaide was the one who spoke.

"Is that really all we are meant to do? On Elenhiise, mages are an illustrious group, respected and—"

"And expected to serve the crown," Kytenia interjected. "Whatever Firal wants us to do, we will know tomorrow. Vahn's presence will change many things, and we would be wise to hear what he has to say before we plan too far ahead."

This time, the court mages nodded along with Rikka—and Balen joined their agreement, too. That left Neve, Edagan, and Anaide frowning at her, but they were outnumbered.

"You truly wish for us to merely sit on our hands?" Edagan asked. "Our mages remain in the temple! If there's anything we can do to free them from that woman's grasp, it's our duty as heads of our affinities to aid them."

"She never said we wouldn't aid them," Balen said. "We will. But there's little we can do tonight, either way. We need more information, and we must wait for the queen's orders."

Anaide scoffed. "Are you so cowed that you must agree with whatever your sweetheart nods along to?"

Kytenia's brows shot up. "That is out of line, Anaide."

The Master of Water gestured across the table at Balen and Rikka. "It doesn't benefit anyone to pretend we don't see it. Fraternization in the temple is discouraged for a reason. As two Masters in leadership positions, they should be able to make independent choices."

Spots of red bloomed in Rikka's cheeks and she opened her mouth to speak, but Balen spoke before she could.

"All mages are allowed to have friends, Master Anaide. The fact you think it's impossible to be companionable without romantic interest may go a long way toward explaining your reputation of being sour."

Anaide's mouth dropped open.

"That is enough," Kytenia declared, though she struggled to keep amusement off her face. She wiped a hand over her mouth and hoped she looked exasperated. "Master Rikka has been a friend of mine since we were girls. Her presence has no bearing on my reasoning, and we have no reason to think it would have bearing on his, either. If you cannot refrain from such petty and absurd accusations, you will sit out our next meeting."

The Master of Water gaped further. Neve covered her mouth and turned away, but not before Kytenia caught a hint of a smile.

She pretended not to notice. "Now that we understand how all of us have come to be here, do we agree the best thing we can do is await further orders?"

All around the table, mages nodded.

"Yes, though I admit some frustration that we've had a formal meeting and the only conclusion was that we have to wait," Temar said.

"That's not the only conclusion," Kella put in from Temar's side.

Everyone's heads turned her way.

A coy sparkle lit her eyes. "We've also concluded that some of us have no friends."

Kytenia buried her face in her hands.

17

A TIME FOR WAR

THE CALL CAME AT THE CRACK OF DAWN, WHEN RUNE'S HEAD WAS pounding and his whole body ached in silent protest of the night before.

He squeezed his eyes closed and prayed whatever messenger hammered at the door would go away.

They didn't relent, hammering away until the sound of every knuckle on the wood rattled like dice inside his head. Groaning, Rune dragged himself from the pillows to answer the summons, though he already knew what it was. Two pages waited in the hallway, as usual. One to answer questions and help him prepare, and one to carry an immediate response to the nobles to ensure they knew he was coming.

Why so many nobles insisted on early morning meetings, Rune would never know. If ever he had the chance to call council meetings of his own, they'd be held at noon and meals would be served. Meals and liquor, he decided as an afterthought, cradling his head in both hands.

He insisted on selecting his own clothes and dressing by himself, but he did allow one of the young men to stay and help him shave. Sparse as his beard was, a short stubble that barely lined his jaw, it was enough to draw the king's ire in formal court.

"His lordship may regret the drink today," the youth said, his tone patronizing enough that Rune cracked open one dim-glowing eye to look at him. "I have it on good authority you're to go to war today."

As if Rune himself didn't know. He snorted and closed his eye again. "All the more reason to want a drink. I've been to war, boy. If I don't have my liquor now, I might not have a chance again."

The young man quieted and finished his work without another word. Rune struggled not to grumble, even after he left. If he thought he could get away with it, he'd have another drink now. It would have been nice to bolster himself with liquid courage, but he did need his wits about him when they left.

Despite his aching head, Rune was among the first to take his place at the table. Garam was there, as were Stal and Vicamros, but the others were later to arrive.

Sera made her appearance with aid from Redoram. Alira arrived with Kytenia and Rikka, though Rikka stood beside the wall while the others sat. Then came councilors representing Lore, Roberian, and even one from Aldaan. Self-managing as the provinces were, they changed councilors often and Rune didn't know any of them well. A small weasel of a man slid in among them, sniffing as if he didn't approve of their presence. Rune rolled his eyes and leaned back in his chair. He had no fond memories of Lord Survas. Often, he found himself wondering why the man wouldn't just die.

One by one, the visitors paid respect to Vicamros and took their seats as directed. A woman representing the Royal City's mages joined them next, then an unfamiliar man in white robes. He had a clear sense of power about him, hidden under a cheerful smile. Rune leaned forward, his brow furrowed. The Triad's mages wore low-collared robes with sleeves that flared at the wrist, but this stranger wore the high collared, narrow-sleeved cut more popular on Elenhiise. A temple mage who'd escaped, or an emissary sent to speak on Envesi's behalf?

A handful of other nobles slid in after him and arranged themselves around the outer edges of the room. They preened as they perused the faces of those at the table. Their stances and expressions made it clear they thought their position in the Royal City gave them the right to decide how war was handled. In another time, perhaps it would have. But Vicamros II was more strict than his father, and the games the politicians played were tolerated less and less each year.

Rune almost ignored them, but a woman in white among their number stood out.

The last time he'd seen Edagan had been the morning after his father's blood had stained his claws. She'd stood with the other mages, hovering over Ilmenhith's throne like vultures when Anaide passed his sentence.

His jaw tightened and his eyes lingered on her face. "Has the king's council become an attraction for spectators? I thought the arena was entertainment enough."

Edagan raised a brow. "The streets are filled with armies preparing for deployment. What you're about to discuss is no secret." Then her eyes narrowed. "I'd heard you were here. I can't say I was surprised. You always had a penchant for ingratiating yourself with those who held power. So desperate to make up for what you could never have."

Rune snorted. "I have held and lost more power of every sort than you could ever aspire to know."

"Enough," Vicamros snapped.

Sullen, Rune slouched in his seat.

A mage slipped through the door and cleared her throat. "Presenting," she began, her voice bringing the room to silence, "Queen Firal and King Vahnil of Elenhiise."

All around the table, councilors shifted in uncertainty. Aside from Elenhiise, Vicamros did not keep allies. If a country looked favorably upon him, it would be taken into the empire. The surrounding countries monitored their borders closely; with the legion at his command, it would be impossible to turn him away. This had to be the first time the Spiral Palace had hosted visiting royalty. Without any experience, how were the councilors supposed to react when another monarch entered the room?

Rune stifled a smirk as they exchanged glances and moved in their seats. Unable to decide what to do, some started to rise, then thought better of it and sank into their chairs again.

"It's not often I get to see a whole room of councilors flustered," Sera murmured at his elbow, clearly as amused as he was.

"And people criticize my manners," he whispered back. He braced his hands against the arms of his chair and pushed himself to stand at the exact moment Vicamros rose. In a rush, all the councilors followed.

Sera covered her mouth with one hand and giggled.

They entered side by side, Firal's fingertips resting lightly on Vahn's upturned palm. Strange as it was, he looked every bit a king, from the tips of his polished black boots to the gleaming silver crown on his brow. He wore Ilmenhith's colors, blue and silver, his cape a rich navy and the inside studded with gems to resemble stars.

Beside him, Firal looked no less regal. Her ebony curls were pinned atop her head and embellished with jewels to make up for her lack of crown. But instead of Ilmenhith's colors, she was a better match for the gray-embroidered black Rune wore, again clad in the fine black silk gown he had given her the night before.

She ignored him, but Vahn met his eye. His fair brows rose and his gaze flickered between Rune and the king to his left. *Council? You?* his expression said.

Rune answered with the faintest of rueful smiles and a slight tilt of his head. *What can I say?*

"Welcome, cousins." Vicamros's voice boomed in the silence. He spread his arms in greeting and left his throne to clasp Vahn's arm with the friendliness and respect such an alliance warranted. "Your presence was unexpected, both of you, but you are always welcome here."

"We thank you," Vahn replied, equally polite. "We owe you a debt of gratitude, but when all is settled, it shall be repaid."

Vicamros kissed Firal's hand, then led them to the only chairs still empty, directly across from his throne.

Guards settled in around the room as the king returned to his place at the far side of the circular table.

The kings and queen sat and the councilors followed.

"This is who she chose after you left?" Sera whispered, emitting a tiny squeak when Stal poked her ribs.

Rune gave the Archmage a sidewise glance and mouthed a silent thank-you.

"You have my deepest thanks for offering Firal sanctuary in her time of need." Vahn remained formal, diplomatic. More interesting was Firal, who remained solemn and stared ahead without seeing who was before her.

Rune watched her and frowned.

"As allies, you are always welcome within my borders," Vicamros said. "However, it seems we are now caught in a difficult situation."

Vahn's polite smile faltered. "With all due respect, I fear it may be best if Ilmenhith avoids direct involvement in this matter. As I'm sure you know, most of our strength came from our mages. Our armies can contribute little to a mainland war, and sending the mages would leave us unprotected."

"Few of our mages are here," Kytenia said, "but as Archmage of Kirban Temple, I feel we may be better served to remain in the Triad until our services here are rendered complete. As you may have heard, Your Majesty, King Vicamros has requested our assistance in a matter of magic. I fear we would be ill-mannered to withdraw before it is complete."

A tactful refusal to submit to an order she disagreed with. Rune hadn't doubted her, but her capability as a leader still impressed him. He inclined his head slightly when Kytenia looked his way. She averted her eyes, though a touch of pink shaded her cheeks.

"Of course," Vahn said. "You have acted under Firal's orders since your arrival. I would not dream of changing them now. If Firal felt it best you assist, then you have leave to keep your mages here for as long as it takes to fulfill your obligations to Vicamros."

Stal whispered something to his wife. He caught Rune's eye as he straightened and Sera leaned close to pass on the question. "Firal is monarch, is she not? Vahnil is her consort, not truly a king?"

Rune waited to reply until Kytenia offered her thanks, letting her voice mask his whispers. "According to the gossiping maids in Ilmenhith, Elenhiise rebelled when Firal took the throne. Vahn is heir to House Tanrys, the most prestigious noble family in Ilmenhith. After they wed, Firal declared him her equal and used his family's influence to quell the uprising."

Sera grunted in displeasure. "This does not appear equal. He speaks for her. Look, she is unhappy."

Rune didn't have to look. He felt the dissatisfaction in the air, as well as the tension it created. Though Vahn and Firal sat close together, they did not touch, nor did they look at one another. It seemed their reunion hadn't been as joyful as Firal might have hoped.

Vahn spoke again. "Ilmenhith cannot be without its rulers. Though our alliance stands and we are happy to assist in whatever means possible, we must return to the island."

Rune blinked, jarred back to the conversation. "Returning to Elenhiise when Envesi has declared it her base of operations is madness. We barely escaped alive. What makes you think Firal would be so lucky a second time?"

Vahn's face darkened.

"Still your tongue," Vicamros growled. "The council has not been given leave to speak."

Anger surged in Rune before he could quell it. He stayed silent, but from the way the others looked at him, he knew his eyes betrayed it. He'd tried to learn the Alda'anan trick for controlling the glow of his eyes, the soft, constant light that fluctuated with colors to mirror his feelings. His first teacher, Filadiel, had told him he couldn't control it until he controlled his emotions. All these years later, he knew he was still a long way off.

Rune bit his tongue and lowered his eyes. "Forgive me, Your Majesty. I hold great fear for the queen's safety, that's all."

Vicamros went on as if nothing had happened. "If you wish to depart, I cannot stop you. However, I question the wisdom in returning to Ilmenhith before the problem has been dealt with."

"And how would you deal with a mage whose means you disagree with?" Vahn's eyes narrowed. "If it were so easy to solve, it would have been solved by now. In the meantime, our country will not continue to function as it is. Trade is weeks behind. Elenhiise is already impacted by this obstruction in the clockwork. The Triad will be affected before long. With winter coming, I don't expect that's a risk you can afford."

"We managed before our alliance. We can manage again if need be, until peace is regained on the island." Vicamros spoke slowly, choosing his words with care. Elenhiise had always needed the Triad more than the Triad needed Elenhiise, but both parties would suffer if their alliance were to dissolve. The accelerated trade that came with the island's location was too good to pass up, regardless of who ruled.

The next part of the conversation would be more tricky.

Vicamros laced his fingers together and rested his hands atop the table as he spoke. "I expect you will need your mages to assist you in returning to Ilmenhith. My own mages will lend them strength in whatever needs they have. Is there anything else you require of me?"

"No," Vahn said. "That should suffice."

"Very well. I shall have them prepare. Now I must ask something of you."

A number of councilors frowned. Vicamros could not act against the temple without the crown's leave. To send soldiers or mages to battle their rogue charges without approval from Ilmenhith could only be seen as hostile.

Vahn shrugged. "You may ask."

"I request that you release my champion."

Rune's head jerked up and myriad colors whirled through his eyes before he caught himself. Murmurs stirred through the spectators, though those at the table remained silent, their attention equally distributed between their king, Vahn and Firal, and Rune himself. That the king asked such a concession first, before even dealing with the placement of soldiers, marked Rune's survival as a high priority. Higher even than the continued alliance between Elenhiise and the Triad.

Whispered speculations flew in the watching crowd as a number of nobles reassessed the situation. When he'd been sent to Elenhiise in chains, Rune had been discounted. Now it seemed he was a more powerful piece on the board than any of them had realized.

Rune's eyes fell to the scar in his hand, the one that gave his name and connected him to the rune-stone game piece he always carried in his pocket. Resentment stirred in his heart. That was what he'd been his entire life. Nothing more than a marked piece for kings and queens to move about in their games.

Vicamros continued. "Rune Kaim-Ennen is a valuable part of my council and my military force. Given that he sits at this table with his head still connected to his shoulders, I assume his misdeeds in your kingdom have been dealt with."

Vahn hesitated too long, drawing more speculation. "Yes," he managed eventually, meeting Rune's eye with a cold mask of an expression. "He has served his purpose. He may return to exile."

Exile. Anger flooded Rune anew and searing crimson lit his eyes. After they'd dragged him about, shamed him and threatened him, demanded compliance and driven him to risk his life to preserve the crown, Vahn—his lifelong friend!—condemned him to renewed exile?

"No." Firal straightened as she spoke for the first time. "His service is penance enough. Your champion may return to you, Vicamros. But he is no longer an exile. If he wishes to return to Elenhiise for any reason, he will be welcome there."

Vahn's jaw tightened, a shadow in his eyes.

"A relief, to be sure," Vicamros said. "I am sure he'll be visiting your lands again soon."

The shadow escaped. "What?" Vahn blinked at the king across the circle. "For what purpose?"

Instead of replying, Vicamros turned. "Archmage Kaith, you are the one who most recently spoke with Envesi. She told you where she could be found, did she not?"

Stal's mouth twisted with displeasure. "Our conversation was brief, but she indicated she has taken Kirban Temple as her headquarters."

"So it is safe to assume that is where she could be captured."

Rune gave his head a twitch. "With all due respect, Your Majesty, I don't think she can be captured."

His words earned him an acid glare. Vicamros drew a breath to admonish him, but Firal spoke first.

"May I be frank, Vicamros?"

Vicamros held that breath a long time before he spoke. "The temple answers to you, Firal. If you have an opinion on the matter, I beg you to share it."

She nodded, a stray curl bouncing beside her ear. Rune fought the urge to tuck it back in place. "I believe your champion speaks the truth," Firal said. "I have seen that sort of power only once before, and then, a long time past. Even if we were capable of overpowering her, our mages combined could not hold her captive for long. Whatever is done, it must be a quick strike."

On the east side of the table, Lord Survas cleared his throat. "May I speak, Your Majesty?"

Rune struggled not to groan.

Vicamros granted permission with a flick of his fingers.

"I am a mage, as you know, with the blood of the Aldaanan strong in my veins," Survas began.

"So strong he adheres to the common ignorant pronunciation of Alda'anan," Sera whispered. Again, she squeaked when Stal poked her ribs.

Rune covered his mouth to hold back a bitter laugh.

Oblivious, Survas sat taller and lifted his nose with a lofty sniff. "For mages to kill other mages is absolutely frowned upon."

"Which is precisely why Envesi needs to be put down." Stal motioned toward Kytenia with an open, upturned palm. "Already two Archmages have been turned out of their schools and barely escaped with their lives. We have fared better than the leaders of the Grand College. We did not ask for this fight. She brought it to us. Are you to accuse us of being soul-blighted for destroying a murderer?"

Survas gaped. "I said nothing of the sort! Merely that—"

"That you would show her pity?" Firal challenged. "And do what, bow to her? Kneel at her monstrous feet?"

Rune twitched at the choice of words.

Beneath the table, Sera placed a reassuring hand on his thigh.

"They are right in this situation, Survas." Vicamros rested an elbow against the table and tapped his lips as he spoke. "You will find I'm much more diplomatic than my grandfather. What he couldn't do with words, he achieved with his sword. But the time for words has passed. This woman comes at my people like a rabid dog and, as Stal said, she will be put down."

The sharp-faced councilor shrank in his seat, though disgust was clear in his expression.

"How do you propose such a thing?" the woman representing the Royal City mages—Birna, Rune thought her name was—lowered her voice as she spoke. Her eyes darted to the people standing around the outer edge of the room. She would have preferred they meet in privacy, it seemed. Rune felt the same.

He drummed his claws on the table. "Isn't it obvious by now? Rhyllyn is needed here. He's the only one who can work with the barrier. He has to stay here." Rune needed him to stay. The idea of the seal on his power being unraveled was tantalizing, but he wouldn't hold his breath. "There's only one other mage in the Triad—or the southern trade kingdoms—who can deal with the kind of power she has at her disposal."

Firal met his eye and for a moment, he swore she looked sad.

Kytenia shook her head. "While it does seem she hasn't yet mastered her new abilities, going against her as you are is foolhardy."

"Right now, I'm the best chance you have," Rune snapped back. "Otherwise you'll all be cowering under the mage-barrier until Rhyllyn is old enough and capable enough to challenge her on his own. Foolhardy or not, I was already sent to Elenhiise to die. If that's what it comes to, the only difference between this and why I was dragged off in chains is I get to die a hero."

The room fell into a hush. He smirked. "Sounds like a much better way to go, I think."

"You can't possibly think you have a chance against her," Kytenia protested. "With the seal on your power—"

"Strength is only one part of this," Rune interjected. "She has less control now than I did when I left Elenhiise thirty years ago. When it comes to raw power, she does have me outmatched. But I have precision she can only dream of right now, and all it will take is getting close."

"She'll strike you down the moment she sees you," Vahn said.

Rune shook his head. "She won't."

"What makes you so sure?"

"Trust me," Rune murmured. "She won't."

Vicamros nodded, then spread his hands. "Well then, ladies and gentlemen. It seems it's time for war."

18

TRADE

"Are you certain?" Kytenia's voice came as little more than a whisper. One last invitation to change his mind.

Rune ignored it. "Better this than scouting the southern continent for weeks." Better to do something. To act and achieve. If nothing else, when all of this was over, he'd have fulfilled his obligation to Firal.

Obligation. That was a funny word to cross his mind. Not that long ago, he would have resented the idea he owed her anything. Now his duty to her seemed as tight-woven into him as his Gift itself. Perhaps it had always been there, buried beneath his resentment. The longer he'd been in her presence, the closer to the surface it had come. Now, when he thought about dying for her, it didn't seem so bad.

There was a time he wouldn't have given it a second thought. Sacrifice on her behalf had been second nature, and his responsibility, besides. He'd been her husband. For all that he still carried her in his heart, she deserved to have him act like it.

The mages stood in an arc around the archway used for Gating, awaiting the order. His party was small, but he didn't need much. Kytenia, Temar, Anaide, and two of Vicamros's mages would escort him to Ilmenhith. If all went well, they'd return, too. He worried most about Kytenia, but it was as useless to try and talk her out of it as it was for her to do the same with him.

Across from the mages, his friends waited in a line. He turned to face them with a steel resolve.

"Seems we only just did this," Garam muttered as he clasped Rune's arm and gave his shoulder a slap. "Hoped I'd never have to do it again."

Rune managed a smile. "You can only cheat death so many times. I trust our agreement still stands?"

Garam glanced farther down the row and nodded.

Rune nodded back and moved down the line.

Sera raised her hand as if to slap him. Stal caught her arm, but not before Rune flinched. Then they laughed and embraced.

Most of his farewells were swift; a handshake for Redoram, a silent embrace for Alira. None of them liked the plan the king had laid out, but they recognized they had few options.

Vicamros clasped his arm like Garam had, though his grip was tighter and his face laden with grief. "If you decide you need assistance after..." He trailed off, then set his jaw and did not finish. He didn't need to.

"It's been an honor to serve you. As it was an honor to serve your father." This time, Rune couldn't quite seem to smile. "I'd like to think that if Ilmenhith's crown had fallen to me, I'd have been a king like you. But I think we both know I would have fallen short."

Vicamros laughed aloud. "Snake-heart. They should have called you silver-tongue." He clapped him on the shoulder and then shoved him away.

Rhyllyn stared at his feet, his jaw set and his shoulders tense as he tried for all the world to remain stoic. Rune stood in front of him in silence as he unstrapped his sword belt. He wrapped it around the scabbard, then held it out. Rhyllyn's eyes went first to the jeweled hilt of the kingsword, then flashed to his brother's face.

"Don't think I'll need it again." Rune grinned. "Just promise me you'll give Redoram the chance to study it."

Rhyllyn took it and blinked hard.

Now Rune had only one more treasure.

He stood longest in front of Vahn and Firal, looking between them, unsure what to say. There was something cold and guarded in Vahn's eyes again, something Rune couldn't put a finger on. Hesitance, maybe. Or fear.

Rune couldn't blame him for that. Their friendship had been forced to change the moment Vahn promised to look after Firal. Outside the council chamber, they hadn't spoken. They'd barely exchanged words within it. And even then they weren't words of friendship or so much as conversation, merely traded snippets of information to aid Vicamros in forming his plans.

It was no wonder it made things awkward now.

"Thank you," Rune said at last, holding Vahn's gaze as his eyes sparked with surprise. "For keeping your promise."

Then he turned to Firal. Expecting no words and sharing none, he lifted the strap from around his neck and pulled it off overhead. The rings he always wore chimed sweetly together, muted when he caught them in one hand.

Firal's lips parted with the beginning of a question, but Rune shook his head. Too long he'd held on, clinging to the past while the world moved on without him. He lifted her hand, pressed the rings into her palm and folded her fingers over them. He allowed himself one moment to savor that touch, her skin blessedly warm beneath his scales.

Then he pulled away. "Open the Gate."

With her head bowed, Kytenia turned to face the archway. Power filled Rune's senses as the mages linked, drew energy through a court mage's access stone, and began the elaborate workings of what had always come so easily to him. Rune watched them work, envisioning the effort they put into it.

Kytenia led the opening this time, while the other mages going on this voyage stood back. They needed to preserve their strength if they were to open another Gate to allow their escape. Rune could only help so much without arousing suspicion.

Fragments of the air fell away to reveal the familiar Gating parlor in the palace, now devoid of mages.

"Ready?" Kytenia asked.

Still silent, Rune strode into the Gate.

Envesi's power lit up like a beacon in his senses the moment he was through. There was another presence, brighter and closer, but telling them apart was easy. One was pure energy, the kind of concentrated power he'd felt in Gate-stones and in the armillary at the Spiral Palace. The other was shadowed, sickly, with a note of chaos thrumming underneath. The nearer presence was his daughter, he assumed. He waited beside the door and tried to shut out her presence while the mages filed through the Gate behind him.

"Do you think she'll feel us coming?" Temar asked as the portal closed at her heels.

Rune didn't reply right away. The others weren't as powerful, their presence—even in a group—barely a prick at his consciousness beside the others. It was like comparing stars to the two moons. One bright and constant, the other shadowed and shifting.

"I don't think so," he murmured. "But once I start pulling power, she'll certainly feel me."

"It's not too late to turn back," Kytenia said, earning herself a glare.

"You have a job. Do it." Rune strode ahead. His eyes searched the nooks and crannies of the halls as they walked. Only days before, the palace had been bursting with life. Now he didn't see a single member of the staff. He didn't feel anything, either. Giftless people didn't put off much presence, but he could still feel their life force when they were nearby. The halls here were as dead as the catacombs beneath the ruins.

"There she is," Kytenia murmured as they neared the throne

room, the rest of the group finally close enough to feel the impression of power.

Rune nodded. "Seems she's decided the throne room is a good place for her. We'll go the long way and come in the front. Gives us more room in case you need to run."

"The queen would be sorely disappointed if we return without the child." Anaide was pale as the soldier moon, but she kept her head high. Her mouth was pinched with a look of disapproval Rune decided was permanent.

"No promises," he said. "This way."

The lamps in the service passages were long since extinguished. He drew a small stone from his pocket and passed it to Kytenia, since she was closest. "Make light." It was a minuscule task, but they couldn't do anything that risked exposure of the limitation on his power. Not yet.

Kytenia obliged, though she turned the stone between her fingertips and traced the shape etched into its surface. "What is this?"

"A rock." Rune smirked at the grumble behind his back. "And I want that back before you leave. Never know when I might need it."

She grinned. "You always were a mystery, weren't you?"

He led them unerringly through the narrow passages, down branching corridors and past shadowed doorways. For all the times Rune had used these hidden halls to escape the palace, he'd never expected to use them to get back in.

They passed the throne room and descended a narrow staircase to emerge into a small front parlor. Though the palace appeared well-maintained at first glance, the finest traces of dust on the dark, polished wood table between couches betrayed the lack of service.

Vahn had been gone for two days. In that span of time, either Envesi had sent the staff away, or they'd fled. Either way, it pointed to one cause. Whatever reason they left, the staff didn't think their king would return.

Perhaps they weren't wrong.

"Do not speak to her unless you must." Rune paused outside the doors to the throne room to be sure the mages listened. "This is between the two of us. And if she frightens you, keep your head down." His eyes settled on Anaide.

She scowled, but did not object.

Rune exhaled and opened the doors.

It was not the triumphant return he'd always imagined. He'd never been given to fancy, but the thought of returning home one day was one of few dreams he'd allowed to persist. But there was no one to line the walkway, no one to cheer him or curse his name, regardless of the reason for his return. Save one woman in white, the throne room was empty. And despite her remarkable power, she was small.

Envesi strode to the edge of the dais. That she'd been on the throne was no surprise, and that she refused to step down to meet them wasn't, either.

"Always one for a grand entrance, weren't you?" Her voice echoed in the still, lending her more presence.

"I've had few opportunities to walk these halls in my own skin. After so many years, I thought I deserved the chance to enjoy it." Rune stopped at the foot of the dais. Even with the steps, she stood a scant few inches above him. He didn't even have to lift his head to look her in the eye.

Envesi had always resented her small stature—something Firal inherited from her, he supposed—but where Firal still managed to appear regal while standing eye to eye with him, Envesi only succeeded in looking angry.

"I'll be frank," she said after a time. "I thought you were dead."

"Seems to be a common misconception. Unfortunately, I'm not that easy to kill." He would have forced a smile, but her gaze wandered to the mages behind him. He cleared his throat. "I've come with a proposition. A trade."

Her eyes snapped back to him and she snorted a laugh. "What could you possibly offer me that I don't already have?"

Rune spread his hands with a shrug. "Me."

Envesi's amusement faded.

"I understand you have my daughter," he said, turning to pace lazily in front of the dais. "And I imagine by now you've discovered the same problem I had with free mages. A connection with just one more mage and you'd be virtually unstoppable. One more person to draw through would give you every edge you need. But their power is too clean. It refuses your touch. Doesn't it?"

"An inconvenience," she agreed, though her eyes narrowed. "Impossible to say, however, if my experiences with you would be any different."

He answered with a push of energy, a silent invitation to tie her Gift with his.

Envesi's lips pursed. Her eyes darkened with thought. Linking with him when he'd been the one to seek it would put him in command of the bond. A risk, if he turned against her. And vital for keeping his secret.

"What's the matter?" He smirked, knowing it would goad her. "Afraid you'll be rejected again?"

A spark of color flashed in her eyes and she seized his offering, interlacing their energies. The world came alive in his senses, all the flows around him open to his call once again. He pulled through her on purpose, stirring the wind and making streamers and tapestries flutter, forcing her to feel their combined strength.

Then he snapped a barrier down between them, cutting her off and sheltering himself from her energy.

Her lips curled back in a wordless snarl.

"Bring me the girl," he growled. "Let me send her to Firal. She's already willing to make the trade. So long as I give her the girl, she won't return. Ilmenhith will be mine. And I'll be yours."

Envesi teetered at the edge of the dais and scowled. "You've never been what anyone would call compliant. What reason do I have to believe you'll be cooperative now?"

"Because we both know I'm not strong enough to overpower you now. We might be closely matched, but you have a lot more experience than I do."

Her scowl softened until the faintest traces of smug approval curved her lips. Then she caught it and wiped the pleasure from her face.

"Besides," he went on. The color in his eyes flickered. He let it. "This benefits both of us. You want the power to perpetuate our abilities. I want my father's throne. Right now, we're in a position to make both those things happen."

He climbed the steps and crossed to the pair of silver thrones behind her. He drew a claw over the sapphire set in the taller of the two, meant to represent a star over the ruler's head. "All it takes is giving over a child who is useless to your cause."

Envesi's jaw tightened and she eyed him, considering.

Rune curled his claws into his fist and lowered his hand. "You think Firal will fight me for it."

"I think you're weak," she said. "Especially when it comes to that woman."

"I don't think you need to worry about that anymore. She hates me. She even said as much." He allowed himself a small chuckle and bowed his head. "I suspect she always has. She was only interested in me after she knew who I was. At the first opportunity where she could free herself, she had me sentenced to death. Less than a month later, with me out of the way, she remarried."

"Yet she bore your child."

"An accident, I assure you." He frowned at her. "Your mages were the ones who swore I couldn't father children."

"But you can." She moved closer, her brow furrowed with thought. Her eyes traveled over him and a new light sparked in her eyes. "Heirs for you would be heirs of magic. A new bloodline ruling Ilmenhith, supplying my temple with unfettered mages. An interesting possibility for the island's future."

"And healthy connections with the mainland means spreading that influence," Rune said. "Every king seeks to expand their power by marrying their children off into high-born places. Vicamros owes me his life several times over. The alliance with the Triad could be reinforced with blood. The Grand College answers to that crown."

Envesi nodded slowly and touched a claw to her lips. "A much easier method of keeping them under control than using brute force. Although time consuming. I cannot wait for you to produce offspring and marry them off."

"As I said, Vicamros owes me his life. I think that, coupled with Elenhiise being his most valuable ally, will give me leverage." Rune smirked. "Not to mention how I've served on his council alongside the mages he'll likely want in charge, if you surrender control of the college now."

Puzzled, she studied him as if seeing him for the first time. "It seems you're far more cunning than I ever gave you credit."

"I was raised to rule," was all he said.

The corner of her mouth twitched and for a single moment, the look in her eyes was almost that of respect. "Wait here."

Rune sank into the throne and made himself comfortable as he watched her go. When his gaze drifted back to the handful of mages waiting before him, the disgust and loathing on their faces made him start.

Unsure who was watching, he lowered his voice to the most nettling tone he could manage. "You have a job to do. Take the girl to her mother and then you can think whatever you want of me."

Temar started to speak, but Kytenia raised her hand to keep her silent. The court Master lowered her eyes.

The second pinprick of power in Rune's senses moved. It joined Envesi's presence, the two signatures so close together they became difficult to distinguish. He closed his eyes and breathed a sigh of relief. "They're coming."

Kytenia's face softened. "Rune—"

"Take the girl and report to your mistress," he growled. "I won't discuss this again."

Crestfallen, she looked away.

They emerged onto the walkway above the throne and Rune turned to look. Envesi made her way down the stairs, a plump figure with a small shadow at her side close at the mage's heels.

Despite how many times he'd told himself he was ready for this, his pulse quickened.

"The girl's nursemaid insists on going with her," Envesi sighed and rolled her eyes as if this were a grand inconvenience.

Rune raised a brow. Nursemaid hardly fit the description of the woman beside her. Vivenne was a noblewoman, through and through. "Let her. A member of her staff in a foreign country will be a gift I'm sure Firal will welcome."

Envesi stopped at the bottom of the stairs and waved Vivenne on. "Get on with it, then. Take her to the mages."

"A moment." Rune stood. The air rippled as Envesi seized the flows around her, clearly expecting betrayal. He motioned for her to calm down. "I was told she inherited my eyes. I wanted to see. I don't expect I'll have another chance."

Envesi's jaw tightened. She didn't protest, but she didn't let go of her magic, either.

Rune crept closer. The child's presence stirred something in him. Awareness of her Gift crawled over his skin like nothing he'd ever felt, even with the Alda'anan. It whined in his head like the vibrations of a bell, resonating with his power, threatening to suck him in.

Rune beckoned Vivenne near, though he did not look her way, as if she were any other servant. He didn't need to look at her to know she glowered as deeply as Temar and the others behind him. She neared, and he sank to a crouch as she drew the girl around for him to see.

The portrait he'd seen looked nothing like her. It had depicted a waif with smooth hair and sorrowful eyes.

The girl in front of him was tiny, but far from waifish. Her cheeks were round and rosy, her limbs healthily plump. Black curls rioted around her little head and serious, thoughtful eyes gazed at him from beneath delicate brows.

His eyes. Rich, vibrant violet, as expressive as they were deep. They betrayed an awareness and intelligence he'd never seen in a child before. His heart threatened to choke him. No matter what he'd thought before, all the doubts he'd had scattered like leaves before a driving wind.

"Lulu," Rune whispered before he could stop himself. The name left his lips like the most tender caress.

Her face brightened.

He looked away. "I expected she'd be larger, given her age. All this fuss. She's only a baby."

"Wild magic does strange things," Envesi said. "I suspect you only grew at the rate you did because you weren't born with it. Even after we woke it, we kept your power controlled for so many years."

"Well, it'll make little difference in the Triad. The barrier was designed by the Alda'anan and works just as well against mages like us." He rose, straightened his spine, and leveled a commanding look with the mages. "Take her. My end of the bargain is fulfilled."

Kytenia slid forward to take the girl's hand and herd both Vivenne and the child away from the dais.

Rune returned to the throne and touched the sapphire at its top again. "I commissioned a crown while I was here. I expected to work my way to power once I returned, I just didn't think it would be this fast. Has it arrived?"

Envesi waved a hand in dismissal. "I wouldn't know. I don't have time to manage the staff."

Which explained why there wasn't any. He sighed, then turned when magic pricked at him. The mages linked and wove a Gate back to the parlor in the Royal City.

None of the mages looked back as they ushered Lulu and her self-appointed nursemaid toward the portal. The strange resonance of her Gift winked out, leaving an empty echo in his senses.

"I'll need to collect the staff from wherever they've gone." Rune turned back to Envesi as the mages filed through and the Gate closed. "There are celebrations to plan. I'll want a coronation. My father never gave me one."

She chuckled darkly at that. "You'll need a new cabinet, as well. I'm afraid most of those who were a part of the royal council are no longer present."

"As if I'd want any of them to be included," he muttered. "They were as eager to see me hang as anyone. Even those who knew who I was."

"I always intended you to rule, you know." Envesi strode closer, relaxed now that the mages were gone. "It was why I put you here. If I was to be queen, I was determined to set up an ideal monarchy. A country ruled by mages. A place where our best interests were held at heart."

"It won't be easy to build. There's a great deal of damage to repair."

"Or we can simply wipe the slate clean and start over." She looked up at him with a wistful gleam in her eyes. "It never should have happened like this. You should have been honored. Revered. Though I suppose I'm as much at fault for that as anyone."

Rune raised a brow. "It's not like you to admit error."

"I've learned." She reached up, grasped his jaw in one hand, and turned his face so she could study it. "You always were my greatest masterpiece. Countless hours of study and research. Your body meticulously crafted with perfect symmetry, your face sculpted to a perfect mathematical standard. It served me right that you always sought to ruin it." She clicked her tongue and flicked one of the silver rings in his ear.

He adjusted the jewelry with a clawed fingertip. "I'm not the only one, you know. Cross enough people and it seems they all wish to take a chunk out of you. Quite a few of them succeeded."

"Even so," Envesi murmured, turning his face to look at him again. "It seems you turned out better than I ever imagined. Beautiful, still, in all your imperfections. Now you'll sire the next generation of perfect mages. And I..." She trailed a single claw down his jaw to take hold of his collar, a glimmer in her eye. "I will bear them for you."

She dragged him down and kissed him with a forceful passion, her tongue coiling hungrily in his mouth.

Rune closed his eyes. His pulse roared like thunder in his ears. His hands beckoned her closer and she was too eager to oblige. Her body pressed close, warm and malleable, and she draped her arms around his neck as her hips tilted against his. He kissed her back and cradled her close.

A dagger slid from his sleeve and he jammed it between her ribs.

Her entire body went rigid and she sucked in a breath. A black cascade poured down the side of her white gown and for an instant, he thought she would wither and die right there.

Then she screamed, long and agonizing, and the entire palace seemed to shudder beneath the swell of her power.

A hair's breadth too low. Spitting a curse, he twisted the dagger free and pulled his hand back to strike again.

He didn't get the chance.

Her magic struck like a tsunami and flung him backwards as the air currents stirred to a hurricane. Banners whipped wildly in the howling wind, Envesi's screams of pain and blind fury tearing at him from every direction. She fell to her knees, her white-scaled hands clamped over the wound in her side. Crimson light and impossible blackness filled her eyes.

Waves of power beat against him and drove him to his knees. Rune gritted his teeth as his claws scrabbled against the cold stone. The dagger was useless now. He cast it aside and struggled to find his feet. His hair lashed his face and eyes and he blinked hard against the sting.

Snaring a flow of air, he wrapped it around himself like a shield, creating a bubble of stillness in the middle of the storm. His power was limited. He had to make it count.

Training his eyes on Envesi's kneeling form, he reached for her ties to the magic coursing around them. Finding one thread among the torrent was like trying to free a single hair from a pile of sheep's wool and already, he felt the twinge of pain that meant he was overstepping the seal's bounds.

She moved. Against all reason and plausibility, she dragged herself to her feet. Black ichor still flowed from beneath her hand, but already the stream was lessened.

Rune's heart skipped a beat and panic crashed over him.

She was healing.

"How dare you!" Envesi screamed, pitch black consuming all the color of her eyes. She took a step. "I made you! I own you! I created you for me!"

"Magic created me," he spat back. "It can never be owned and never controlled." A tendril of energy touched her wound, flowing from somewhere else. His eyes snapped to the top of the stairs and the sight of the unfamiliar mages gave him an odd sense of relief.

She was healing, but she wasn't doing it alone. The mages on the stairs were linked. They funneled power into mending their Archmage as they approached. A pack of armed men appeared behind them and pushed them aside to rush down the stairs. Ennil Tanrys was at their front.

Rune snarled. He should have known.

Desperate, he tried to catch hold of Envesi's life force. If he couldn't kill her with a dagger, magic was the next best thing.

Warning pangs pulsed in his head as he hit his limit. He gasped and dropped the thread of air that formed his shield.

Pain radiated through his body, knotted his stomach and

rang in his skull. He gripped his head in both hands and dug claws into his scalp.

Focus. He pressed the silver stud in his tongue against the roof of his mouth, grounding himself the way the Alda'anan had taught. The gale around him slipped beyond his awareness.

He caught the edge of her essence and wrapped his power around it.

Envesi's eyes widened and she went pale.

With everything in him, he tore at her existence.

Her knees buckled and again she fell. For a second, her very being seemed to waver. Then her attention turned inward, toward the unseen war of their magic, and the tide turned.

Like choking vines, tendrils of her power wrapped around his and shook his grasp loose. In an instant, her strength returned. She clamped down harder and followed his strength to its source.

Rune struggled against it, desperate to stave it off.

He couldn't.

Shadow surged through the connection, flooding his awareness, blotting out his vision and leaving him gasping for breath. Overwhelmed, he couldn't stop her from seizing control. He'd opened himself to magic in his desperation. Now she turned that connection against him and twisted his power against his will. Alone, her only chance of defeating him was to unmake him as she'd done the others.

He braced for the pain he knew had to come with his body and soul being torn apart. But it didn't come and, as she began to draw through him, he understood. She meant to make him suffer, burn him out of existence by wielding his own power against him.

Too fast she pulled, sucking flows through his body until his head spun. She hit the limit and the seal on his power lit like a wildfire within him. Pain surged through every nerve, filling him from head to talon-tipped toe.

Screaming through clenched teeth, he collapsed onto the floor.

And then it stopped.

Shuddering, his stomach heaving, Rune quivered on the cold stone.

Envesi released her hold of magic and turned him free. "You've been blocked." Her tone was oddly conversational, hovering on the verge of delighted. "Your power locked away, and you still thought to challenge me?"

He tried to open his eyes, but everything swam. He groaned and lay still, gasping for breath. The pain had ceased but its aftermath remained, his muscles spasming and his stomach trying fiercely to empty itself. The scent of blood hung heavy in his nostrils and he wasn't sure who it belonged to.

"No," she sneered, "I can't laugh at you. After all, I am the one who still fell for it."

And if the mages swarming around her now hadn't felt the start of their battle and come running, he would have succeeded. Rune bit his tongue to keep silent. He'd never expected to overpower her, but he had thought it would be enough to plant a knife in her side and prepare for the backlash. To force her to exhaust herself in killing him while she bled out.

"Do you wish me to finish it?" Ennil's voice above him came accompanied by the rasp of a sword being drawn.

Envesi made a soft, thoughtful sound. "No. He's useful yet. We'll need to retrieve the girl, as well as her parents. Put him in the dungeons. One of my mages will keep watch and ensure he doesn't recover enough to use his Gift as a means to escape."

The sword returned to its sheath and strong hands grasped Rune by the arms.

The dungeons. It seemed all of his life was to run in cycles. In spite of everything, he almost laughed.

19

OATHS

THE RINGS CLINKED TOGETHER IN THE PALM OF FIRAL'S HAND AS SHE ran a finger over the purple-red stone. It tilted so the star flashed in the light. She thought she'd never see it again. After all this time, learning Rune had it—that he'd kept it and worn it—was more painful than believing she'd lost it all those years ago.

She almost wished he'd taken it with him to his grave.

Tears filled her eyes again. She blinked hard and bowed her head. Vahn had tried to offer comfort, but she shunned his efforts. She couldn't bear to have her husband soothe her while she cried for another man.

She didn't want to cry for him. She wanted to be angry, to hate him as much as she told herself she did, to tell herself he deserved his fate and believe it. It had been easier when she thought he'd abandoned her, or maybe even died in his effort to escape. Between the rings in her hands and the tears in her eyes, she was saddled with the truth, and it chafed.

After all these years, she still loved him.

And unlike her, he'd never given up. Rune had carried their rings, the only remaining symbol of their marriage, for all those years. All without ever breathing a word. So many times Firal thought him a coward and a quitter. Now she couldn't fathom

241

what sort of courage it took to live with that kind of hope, only to swallow it when he'd discovered her wed to someone else.

Looking back, Firal saw his behavior for what it was. An effort to drive her away, make himself undesirable and eliminate himself from her life. She should have known better. He'd done it before. And both times, like a fool, she'd taken the hateful things he said at face value.

The mages in the next room stirred and exclamations of surprise filtered through the open doorway. Firal wiped her eyes and blinked until she could see the slow-gyrating armillary clearly. A Gate opened in the next room and against all reason, a surge of hope filled her chest.

"Firal," Vahn called from the doorway. He stopped when he saw she was already on her feet. She hurried to join him as the mages gathered around the Gate.

All of them seized power and braced for the possibility that whoever emerged wouldn't be friendly. The barrier would protect them from a magic assault, but it would do nothing against weapons.

As if she stepped from the wall, Anaide appeared. Her face was pinched and white, but she turned back and looked expectantly at the empty space behind her.

The next figure to emerge made Firal's tears flow anew.

"Mama!" Lulu squealed, bolting away from the rest of her escort and flinging herself into her mother's arms.

Firal fell to the floor, squeezed the girl tight and sobbed into her ebony ringlets. Lulu clung to Firal's neck and tucked her face beneath her mother's jaw.

Rocking gently, Firal rained kisses on the girl's face and head and chubby hands. She was only half aware of the Gate closing behind the last mage.

Vahn rested a hand on Firal's back and kissed the top of Lulu's head before he looked up. "Is he...?"

"They are speaking," Kytenia replied softly. "But I expect it won't be long."

Even as her heart soared, Firal felt her stomach turn sick with grief. Joy and sorrow mingled in her tears. Threading her fingers through her daughter's hair, she rested her forehead against the girl's and tried to make herself breathe.

Lulu's soft hands rested on her cheeks. The girl mumbled happy nonsense and hugged Firal again.

"What do we do now?" Vahn asked.

The whole room sobered.

"The only thing we can do," a sweet voice sighed. Its owner slid past the mages to squat beside Firal. "Wait and see if Elenhiise announces a new ruler." There was an edge of contempt in her tone.

Firal lifted her head and blinked. "Vivenne? What are you doing here?"

The plump older woman offered a strained smile. "Vahnil asked me to stay with the little one. So I will. With everything happening back home, it seems she might need friendly faces around to help her adjust here."

Vahn frowned. "Whatever he said, you shouldn't believe it."

Surprised, Vivenne looked up. "I beg your pardon?"

"We sent him," Firal said. "Someone had to get Lulu away from her. Now Envesi must be stopped. He volunteered to... to..."

No sooner than they'd stopped, the tears began anew. This time, Vahn hugged Lulu and Firal both as she cried.

"We will retire to our rooms for now," Vahn said to the mages. "Notify us the moment you hear something. Mother, please accompany us."

"Of course," Vivenne murmured.

Firal tried to pull herself together. She gulped back tears and stood with Vahn's help. She still hugged Lulu tight and the girl clung to her neck, satisfied to go anywhere her mother carried her.

The mages returned to their stations. Kytenia spoke to the

leaders among them in low tones as Vahn led his small family away.

As they slipped from the mage quarters, Firal chanced a look back at the empty archway they'd come through. She prayed in silence, but her heart already sank.

Against a foe like Envesi, how long could he last?

"NEWS HAS COME from our informants in the Grand College." Vicamros stood gazing out the window with his back toward his councilors. Rhyllyn suspected he'd chosen a private parlor instead of the council chamber for that reason. So long as there was a window to look through, he didn't have to face them.

"So soon?" Garam sounded no more hopeful than the king.

"We knew it would be swift, no matter the outcome," Vicamros said. "Envesi lives. And she is angry."

Rhyllyn bowed his head.

They'd all known it was a risk. It was one of the reasons Vicamros demanded Rhyllyn stay put. He might have bettered Rune's chances for survival, but the council had agreed with the king. Keeping Rhyllyn in reserve for defensive measures was better for everyone. If he could expand the mage-barrier to encompass the majority of the Triad—or the majority of Roberian and the most inhabited fringes of Lore, at least—they could live indefinitely within its safety.

Judging by his efforts thus far, it seemed a rather large *if*.

"What are we to do?" Soft as it was, Alira's voice seemed loud in the stillness.

Had the whole council been called, someone would have asked sooner. Rhyllyn suspected Lord Survas would have been the first to try to sweep Rune's efforts under the rug and propose some self-aggrandizing plan.

Instead, only the king's closest advisors—Garam, Alira, and

Redoram—were present. As near as Rhyllyn could figure, he'd only been included so he could hear the news.

"We stay the current course," Vicamros said. "We remain defensive. Continue to try to push the barrier outward to shield the rest of the Triad, and send mages to protect our people if necessary."

Redoram nodded in agreement. "The best thing we can do now is wait."

Garam sat back in his chair and rubbed his eyes. "And what of Elenhiise?"

Vicamros clasped his hands behind his back. "I'm afraid they're on their own for now."

"Someone should tell them." Rhyllyn stared at his brother's sword laid across his knees. He'd carried it around since it was handed to him, unsure what to do with it. He wasn't a fighter and it was more of a family heirloom, besides. It should have gone to Rune's daughter. Not him.

"We will," Vicamros promised. "You may, if you wish. But before you go, we must discuss the state of the barrier."

Rhyllyn swallowed back a sigh. "I don't know what to tell you."

Alira moved close enough to rest a hand on his shoulder. "Tell us what you've learned. We'll start there. We wish to help you as much as possible, Rhyllyn."

He wasn't sure they could help him. "I haven't made much progress. I've tried, but it's... complicated. Rune was able to redirect the energy flows from the anchor to himself, but it took a lot of time and effort. I haven't even been able to get that far. When I try to do it, it's like trying to hold onto an eel, or... or catching a plume of smoke. Whenever I grab it, there's nothing there."

Redoram made a thoughtful sound. "That's Alda'anan magic for you. He may have known some technique he learned from them and merely didn't think to pass it on. Keep at it, young man. I'm certain you'll determine what he did differently."

"And if I don't?" The words spilled out before Rhyllyn could stop them, so much heat in his voice that even Vicamros turned to look at him. "You kept me here because I was supposed to be able to do this. What if I can't? I should have gone with him. I should have done something."

"It wouldn't change anything, Rhyllyn." Alira rubbed his shoulders, trying to soothe him. "You've done what you were told. Feel no remorse for it."

Easy for her to say. He was always the good, obedient boy. Respectful to elders, prompt to do as they bid him. But never before had the alternative been so drastic.

If Rhyllyn had refused to comply, had insisted on going to Elenhiise with his brother, would Rune have been able to escape alive?

THOUGH HE WASN'T TRYING to be quiet, Rune still winced when his chains clinked and rattled. The dungeons were filled with sounds of misery, but he was of special interest. Drawing too much notice could only make things more difficult.

In all the years between his escape and his return, the jailer hadn't learned any new tricks. Rune hadn't been coherent enough to notice when they chained him in his cell, his head still muddled from the pain, but he noticed now. A different cell, ages later, but they'd chained him the same way. Little chain at his ankles, meaning he couldn't move far. The chains at his wrists were anchored in the ceiling, and just short enough that when he sank toward the floor, his knees couldn't touch the ground. He hung by his wrists for a moment, testing to see how badly the manacles bit into his hands. Then he stood.

It was designed to exhaust him, keep him too tired and distracted by pain to reach magic. It had worked before, but he'd been younger. He'd also been in poor shape when he was arrested, exhausted after combat in Core, a frantic ride across the country, action on the battlefield, and the grief that came with his father's death.

This time, he'd arrived at full strength—or as close to it as he got, these days. His go-round with Envesi had been quick, but the only taxing part had been the pain that came from straining against the seal.

Rune wrapped his hands around the upper chains and held tight. He hung in place for a second before he lifted himself. His breath deepened and his focus shifted. The movement brought warmth to his muscles, combating the dank chill of prison.

They'd taken his finery and put him in rags. From the way they'd gloated about it, Rune figured it was meant to humiliate him. That and remove whatever comfort might have come from warm, good-quality clothing. The latter was a shame, but he'd lived through worse. As unpleasant as Ilmenhith's dungeons were, they couldn't compare to the prison in the Royal City.

Both experiences had been misery, though of very different sorts. Ilmenhith's dungeon had been for torture, meant to inflict as much punishment as possible before he went to the gallows. The Royal City's prison had been somewhere to stuff him and forget him—and then beat him within an inch of his life when he refused to be forgotten.

Both had tempered him like steel. If anyone thought the threat of torture would frighten him now, they were sorely mistaken.

Rune lifted himself again and pulled up until his chin passed the point where his fists bunched in the chain. The effort brought a thin sheen of sweat to his bronze skin after the fifth repetition. He slowed down, then stopped and stood with his feet wide and his eyes closed. If he alternated between periods of mindful exercise and semi-suspended rest, he'd fare best. If his last stay was anything to judge by, the jailer would be by to beat or whip him before the night was over. When that time came, he'd be ready.

He drew his hands together before his chest in one of the

meditative positions the Alda'anan had taught him and breathed deep.

"Are you a religious man?"

Rune opened his eyes.

He hadn't heard anyone approach. Focused on his own body as he was, he hadn't sensed anything, either.

A mage in white stood outside his cell's bars, gazing at him like a curious child.

"I suppose that depends on what you mean by religious," he replied, amused. "I've heard people say I must be soul-blighted to look the way I do."

"Are you?" She raised a brow.

"Perhaps. Everyone's got a little bit of rot inside them. Some of us do a better job of pruning it than others."

The mage nodded and leaned back against the empty cell opposite his. "I thought I'd ask if you were in need of healing, but you appear to be feeling well."

Rune snorted. "As well as a man in chains can. I'd much prefer to sleep in my bed upstairs, but I don't think your Archmage would take kindly to that idea."

"You could always ask to sleep in her bed," she remarked sarcastically. "She seemed fond of that notion."

He shuddered. "Don't remind me." The vile feeling of her tongue against his would haunt him until his dying day. Which, he supposed, could be tomorrow. The sooner the better, if it meant forgetting that.

The mage shrugged.

"Did someone send you to heal me?" He held the chains, unable to do much else. He thought it unlikely she had orders, though if Envesi meant to torture him, he assumed she'd prefer a clean canvas to work on. Maybe she thought the jailer had already been to see him.

She glanced over her shoulder and then spun a ward over the two of them.

He braced himself for an attack. The jailer didn't take kindly to anyone handling his prisoners. If she meant to strike him, the ward would spare her hide.

Instead the woman moved closer to the bars. "I came of my own accord. I will follow orders to protect my life, but not all of us are so eager to follow Envesi's lead."

Rune's brow furrowed. "I know you."

"And I know you. That's why I came." She smiled. "I don't think we spoke, though. My name is Hetia. I was the last Master raised to court mage before you, you know."

He straightened. She *did* know him. Not just for the name he'd made for himself, but the life he'd had before exile. "Who told you?"

"Nobody. You weren't exactly subtle in the things you said to the queen. Some of the courtiers suspect it, but I don't think any of them have taken a close enough look at you to be sure." Hetia ducked her head. "I think your limbs put most of them off from the idea. Of you being you, I mean," she added hastily. "Not of looking. I don't mean to imply it's unpleasant."

He chuckled mirthlessly. "I'm sure looking is unpleasant." It was unpleasant enough for him to see himself.

She studied his physique and shrugged. "Not particularly. I'm rather curious, to be honest. Were the situation different, I would ask for the chance to study you. Your magic, I mean," she corrected herself, "and what it's done to you. I am sure there's a great deal to learn from examining how it works."

"You might ask Envesi," he suggested. "If you're able to work out a study time that involves a chair or somewhere decent to sleep, I'm sure I'd be glad to be studied."

Hetia laughed, then caught herself and lifted a hand to cover her mouth. "You're in good spirits for a man in your position."

Rune smirked. "Knowing one of Firal's mages is still here and alive, it feels like my chances just got a little better."

"Ah." Her face fell. "I wish I could let you out. Given the state of Envesi's temper, I think it's too early for that. She had you imprisoned because she was too injured to kill you on the spot. She's feeling better now. But give her a day or so, wait for her to be distracted and forget you're down here, and your chances of escape would be better."

"So you came to make sure I'm alive enough to make it a few more days."

She nodded. "I apologize. I wish I could do more."

"There is something you can do." He dropped his hands and let them hang. The chained manacles kept them near his shoulders, but that was still better than holding them overhead. He'd have to move more. Already the blood flow to his fingertips was poor and the uncomfortable chill of the dungeon seeped into his hands.

Hetia spread her hands and shrugged. "If it's in my power."

"Send word to the mainland. There are bound to be mages all around the capital who are still loyal to Firal and willing to help. King Vicamros would appreciate knowing I'm not dead yet. And if I die shortly, let him know that, too." It was a simple message, but important. As long as he lived, it was a message of hope. Until he died, there was still a chance he could finish his mission.

"I will do what I can." She started to release the ward, then hesitated. "I trust my assistance will not be mentioned to the jailer?"

Rune twisted in place to show his scarred back. "I've already seen what Ilmenhith's jailer can do. He got nothing he wanted out of me then and he'll get less now."

Hetia blanched, but nodded. "A handful of court mages are still alive. Most are hidden in the city, for fear of being recognized. I was new enough she wouldn't know me without the blue trim on my robes, which is why they chose me to come back to the palace. We will do what we can for you, but if the things you said to Envesi are true..."

He resisted a frown. "You heard us?"

"She told us what was said, expecting you might use some of it to try to sway us." Her face hardened. "I am sworn to serve Ilmenhith and the temple both, but my first priority is protecting the city and my fellow mages from the usurper. After my oath to protect them comes my oath to the queen. If you stand in the way of her returning to the throne, we will oppose you."

Rune tried not to laugh. "I'm no threat, believe me. We're on the same side." His amusement faded and a wistful smile curved his lips. "I swore an oath to Firal as well."

Hetia's eyes narrowed. "What did you swear to her?"

"Everything."

Her brows lifted and she regarded him thoughtfully. "So they're true, then? The rumors about you and Queen Firal?"

Rumors he'd started, when he thought she meant to kill him. If he made it out of Ilmenhith alive, he'd have to apologize for that. As he'd have to apologize for answering the question. "Yes," he said, voice low. "They are."

To his surprise, Hetia gave him a wry smile. "Hmm. Her Majesty always was a scholar. It seems she beat me to the chance to study you. And quite thoroughly, at that." She looked him over again, then released the ward. "The jailer will be along to deal with you soon and the Archmage will wish to have a turn with you after. I shall return tomorrow morning to mend your wounds and prepare you for a second round of their ministrations."

It sounded like a grim promise, but he understood. Make it through tonight, and she'd let him know tomorrow if she was able to get word to the Triad.

Rune flexed his arms to keep blood flowing. Endure one night, then he could present a plan for escape. He drew a deep breath and closed his eyes. For Firal, he could endure a hundred.

2 0

GUILT

THE MESSENGER ARRIVED AT THE CRACK OF DAWN. VICAMROS HAD grilled the man, demanded to know exactly how word from Ilmenhith had reached the Grand College.

Vahn didn't care. The fact that a message escaped at all showed a large number of mages who didn't answer to Envesi still lived, and nothing could compare to the message they'd brought.

Alive.

His friend was *alive*.

Vahn didn't know whether to laugh or weep. He could have kissed the messenger, but for the sake of everyone present when the meeting was called, he didn't.

The elation he felt was a combination of joy at knowing Rune still lived and the rekindling of hope that came with it.

Guilt had wrenched his insides since this whole affair began, since he first touched pen to paper to write the missive that dragged his once closest friend into this whirlwind of events. No; he gave his head a twitch. It had clung to him longer than that, a quiet shadow that had lurked behind some of the happiest moments of his life. Somehow, it had never struck him before now how terribly unfair it all was.

In the wake of that clear understanding, the message felt like a second chance.

The rest of the message hadn't been so inspiring. Alive but imprisoned, held under mage guard with execution believed impending.

Six pents prior, Vahn had helped save Rune from those exact circumstances. Funny how fate seemed determined he should die that way.

"We have little time to decide if we're to act." Vahn wanted nothing more than to mount a rescue, but without his soldiers or Firal's mages, he knew they were at the mercy of Vicamros and what he thought was best for the Triad.

Sensing his restless eagerness, Vicamros lifted a hand and motioned for him to settle. "We can't do anything until we know how many mages we have with us. If we can provide a large enough network to support him, we may still win this fight."

Vahn clenched his teeth and released a long, controlled breath through his nose. Growling or sighing wouldn't do. Rune might have gotten away with it, but Vahn didn't have that sort of charisma. Or that kind of connection with Vicamros.

Their chances of assembling that many mages in so little time were slim. Though Redoram and Alira had set out again that morning to retrieve more mages from Roberian and Lore, their efforts proved slow-moving. The chapter houses here— embassies, they called them—weren't like the ones on Elenhiise. They were manned by skeleton crews, inhabited by more Giftless people than mages.

Umdal's Collective could have been their saving grace, but their vagrant nature meant Stal promised nothing before he went after them. Though Stal was Umdal's Archmage, the different vagrant groups changed leaders often and he knew none of them well enough to Gate directly to the groups.

One more shortcoming of magic, Vahn supposed. As a man with no magic, he often had to remind himself the power was not a panacea.

But he had no intention of giving up without a fight. Not on Rune and not on Elenhiise, but fighting was easier when it was an even match. He hated feeling incapable, as he had since the first moment Lulu disappeared. Then again, he'd had a different task then; hunting Envesi, a woman who could break him with a thought.

This was different. This was doable. Vahn had delved into the dungeons to free his friend once before, he could do it again. He owed it to him to try.

In truth, he owed him a great deal more.

"Is that really the only option?" Vahn looked around the table. So early in the morning, the meeting was small. With three members of council out scouting for more mages, it was reduced even further. Aside from himself and Vicamros, the only full-time councilor in attendance was Garam. Sera was there to speak on behalf of Umdal, and Kytenia and Edagan represented the temple. He thought he'd seen Rikka in the hallways, but she hadn't deigned to join them. Firal had refused to leave Lulu's side and council was no place for children.

"He has a point," Rhyllyn offered. He sat hunched in a chair beside Garam, making himself small. "Everything we've discussed has been action with offense in mind."

While not a part of the council, Rhyllyn had been included because of the subject at hand. Vahn had been startled by the boy, but Firal was quick to shut down his speculation. He didn't know the situation and wouldn't pretend to, but the suggestion he was Rune's son was evidently offensive. Vahn wouldn't make that mistake again.

"I think we all agree defeating Envesi is our favored outcome, but if Ran—I'm sorry, Rune—is being held prisoner, there's no reason we can't go retrieve him." Vahn glanced at Rhyllyn, who nodded. Good. If anything he had in mind was to work, they'd need Rhyllyn's help. "If we act fast, we can open a Gate directly to him, pull him out of the dungeon, and bring him back here. If he's our best shot at killing her, there's no reason not to retrieve him."

Vicamros nodded slowly and rubbed his beard. "We couldn't risk sending anyone to somewhere Envesi might be. She'd shut us down in a heartbeat, and every mage is precious right now. But if they're certain he's in a cell, it's reasonable. Opening a Gate directly to a person, what does it entail?" He glanced to Kytenia for an answer.

"It's a precise art." She twisted a lock of auburn hair around her finger, her eyes glazed with thought. "My predecessor, Archmage Nondar, was the first to do it. We know it requires a strong familiarity with the person you're trying to reach. He succeeded in opening a Gate to someone with a slightly inaccurate impression of her once, but he never passed the intimate knowledge of its workings to anyone else before his death."

"So we need someone who knows him well to open the Gate to him. Rhyllyn?" Vicamros turned to the youth.

Rhyllyn squirmed. "I know him well enough, but I'm not skilled enough to open a Gate on my own yet. I did it once, with Alira, but it took hours to get it to work. I don't think we have hours to spare."

"Sera could do it," Garam muttered, "but she's not supposed to work with magic until the baby is born."

"You should ask Firal," Sera suggested with a smirk. "She got enough of an eyeful the other night when he answered his door. It should be enough to refresh her memory."

Vahn's cheeks heated.

"That is an inappropriate suggestion to make in front of the woman's husband," Edagan snapped.

"I'm sure Firal could do it," Vahn said dismissively, "so the question is how we get him back out. How many mages can you spare for this, Vicamros?"

Rhyllyn half rose from his chair. "I'll go."

"You will not." Vicamros pressed a finger against the tabletop as if ordering the boy to sit and scowled when he didn't. "Not only do I need you to stay here and keep working with the barrier, you just said you don't have the skill to open a Gate on your own."

"I don't need to open it on my own," Rhyllyn said. "Rune's there. He and I work together all the time. Even if he's injured, all he has to do is direct my power, not use his own."

Garam cleared his throat. "I understand your concerns, Majesty, but I think he may be the best choice. It'll be a lot easier to get one or two people into a prison than a whole legion of mages. We're talking about cramped quarters in a situation where drawing too much attention means death. The fewer people who go, the better."

"It will have to be at least two," Kytenia said. "Rhyllyn to lend power for Rune to open a Gate back here, and someone to help Rune walk." Her eyes caught Vahn's.

He nodded. She'd been the one who'd aided him with just that, all those years ago. Vahn had held one arm and Kytenia held the other as they half dragged their friend out of the dungeons to help him flee.

"That's why I'll go," Vahn said. "I'm the best option for the second. I am Ilmenhith's king. Anyone we encounter in the dungeon answers to me."

"Assuming they haven't taken to lapping at Envesi's feet in the past few days," Sera said.

Vahn tried not to think of that possibility.

Vicamros closed his eyes. "You make it hard to argue. I only have one question."

"Name it," Vahn said.

"What's your plan for if Envesi catches you? I'm at risk of losing my most valuable mage, my Champion, and my ally." Vicamros leaned back in his throne. "Rhyllyn cannot work with Firal on his own and cannot open a Gate by himself, which means you need my blessing. I will give it, if you can convince me this is all in hand. But if she gets hold of Rhyllyn, I can't guarantee even the Royal City and its barrier will keep my people safe."

Vahn stared across the table, at a loss for words. He couldn't disagree with that assessment, but he couldn't think of any words to reassure Vicamros, either. Rune's had been a suicide mission. Theirs could be the same.

"Easy," Rhyllyn said. "We kill her."

Vicamros blinked at the boy, taken aback.

"I don't think that would be so easy, Rhyllyn," Sera said softly.

Rhyllyn shook his head. "No, I don't think so. But there's no other right answer, is there?"

"You don't have the control necessary to face a mage like her." Edagan snorted. Her withered face crumpled into a scowl. "The Triad's council spent days deciding not to send you because you wouldn't stand a chance against her in a fight. What makes it different now?"

"Because we won't be fighting her," Vahn said. "We'll find another way."

"The mines."

The councilors twisted in their seats to face the door.

Ordin Straes pressed a hand to his chest and bowed, first to Vahn and then to Vicamros. But it wasn't the captain who'd spoken. It was the shorter, dark-haired man beside him.

Vicamros frowned. "Who is this?"

The man stepped forward and bowed. "Forgive me, Your Majesty. I could not help hearing the conversation. I was told to wait until council broke, but I cannot stand to waste time. My name is Tobias. I am the leader of a faction beneath King Vahnil and Queen Firal. My people are the ruin-folk, those responsible for running the island's mines." His accent was thick, like most of the island inhabitants, but his grammar was excellent. Sometimes it seemed the shorter-lived ruin-folk learned faster. Vahn supposed they had to, given their lifespans. Vicamros had learned the island's native Old Aldaanan fast, as well.

"Why are you here, Tobias?" An edge colored Vicamros's words, though his face remained neutral. "Do you not see my council discusses matters of life and death?"

"I do, Your Majesty." Tobias bowed again. "But I believe I can assist, if you will give me a moment to explain."

Vicamros looked to Vahn, seeking his opinion. It was flattering, but Vahn couldn't spare thought for that now. He nodded, and Vicamros motioned for the man to continue.

"Though we look to Firal, my people remain relatively self-governing," Tobias began, striding forward to join them at the table. The captain bowed and retreated from the council chamber as Tobias went on. "When Queen Firal was taken from Ilmenhith, my people decided it was best to retreat to the city around the mines until trouble blew over. We've never been high in the Archmage Envesi's esteem, you see."

"We encountered his people when we fled the temple," Edagan said. "They offered us hospitality in Core before we made our way to the Grand College by means of the permanent Gate in the mines."

Tobias nodded. "The Gate in Core's mines doesn't actually lead to the college, but instead to a cliff overlooking the same city. Its location is convenient to a major trade road, which makes it ideal for transporting ore and gems. It was planned that way on purpose."

"We don't have time for exposition," Vicamros growled.

"Forgive me, Your Majesty." Tobias ducked his head and cleared his throat. "The past several days, Envesi has been scouring the island in search of mages. If they do not join her cause, she strikes them down. For the first time in centuries, there are mages among my people and I must protect them as I can. We sent scouts through the Gate in the mines and they returned with a message offering sanctuary in the Triad. Core is now empty. My people are on the road between here and the province of Lore, but I came ahead when I heard my king and queen were here."

Vicamros nodded. "I am glad to grant asylum to your people. But you believe your mines offer the ability to kill a powerful mage?" Skepticism colored his tone.

"Certainly. The issue at hand is a lack of control, correct?" Tobias chanced a glance toward Rhyllyn, indicating he'd watched their meeting for as long as he'd listened. "Simply flee through the mines. Core is abandoned, not a soul left there or in the ruins above. Should Envesi try to follow, control would not be necessary. If your mage has the strength to begin a collapse, she would be buried. Mage or not, she is still flesh and blood."

"You couldn't!" Edagan cried, leaping from her chair. "I've seen the tunnels that run beneath the island. I've explored them like no other. Collapsing the mine could cause a chain reaction. Half the island could fall into the sea."

Vicamros scoffed. "This isn't the time for exaggeration."

"I am not exaggerating," the mage protested. "We traveled through the tunnels on our way to Core. Had I not the skill with earth I possess, we would have been buried. Careful, controlled digging from one tunnel to the next put us at extreme risk of collapse. More than once, sections did collapse and slow us down. Deliberately causing mine shafts to cave in would spell disaster for all of Elenhiise."

Troubled, everyone at the table turned their eyes to Vahn.

His stomach sank, but the pleading, desperate look Rhyllyn wore bolstered his resolve. "We cannot know that until we try."

Vicamros met Vahn's eyes and nodded. "Be swift, my friend. We don't know how much time we have."

Edagan fell back into her chair, so pained it seemed she might cry.

"ARE YOU MAD?" Firal shook her head, unable to believe the words that spilled from her husband's mouth.

Vahn squeezed his eyes closed, exasperated. "Can you do it or not?"

She hesitated to reply. Of course she could. She wasn't as skilled as Kytenia and her other friends who'd continued to study after her expulsion from the temple, but the court mages had assisted her learning. Leading the opening of a Gate was something she'd done dozens of times before. Opening a Gate directly to someone, however...

It had been years since Firal had tried, and her first and only attempt had ended in failure. She hadn't thought of that effort in years, but at least now she knew why it hadn't worked. She'd envisioned Rune the way she last knew him. He'd grown, changed, earned the scars that striped his back, and put on new muscle. Even the way he carried himself had changed. He'd become more precise, more comfortable, but still with a hint of animal fluidity in the way he moved.

"I can," she said at last. "But you still should have discussed this with me before—"

"We didn't have time," he interjected. "We still don't. I promise you can discuss this with the mages and Vicamros and anyone else you want, but if we're going to do this, we need to do it now."

She swallowed hard. "Very well."

Lacing his fingers with hers, Vahn pulled her toward the door.

She put her heels down and held out her other hand. "Lulu, come here."

The child looked up from where she played on the floor. She planted her hands on the floor and kept them there until she found her feet, then straightened and toddled to join them.

Firal scooped the girl into her arms, shooting Vahn a glare that challenged him to protest.

Wisely, he said nothing.

The pace he set through the palace's corridors made it hard

for her to keep up, but she clung to her daughter and did her best.

"You'll need to speak to Edagan as soon as we're gone," Vahn said, glancing over his shoulder. "I may have ruffled her feathers."

A disgruntled Edagan was the last thing she needed on top of all this. Firal heaved a sigh, then hefted Lulu onto her other hip to make walking more comfortable. "Any other surprises you'd like to drop on me before you go?"

He stopped dead in his tracks and she nearly walked into his back.

Annoyed, she glowered. "What's gotten into you?"

Vahn stared down the empty hall, then bowed his head. "I know this is difficult, coming out of the blue. I know I'm asking a lot of you. But none of this should have happened, and it's my fault. I owe it to him to fix this."

Firal's brow furrowed. "You're not making any sense."

"He should have been there. In Elenhiise. Not here, not trapped with no magic." Vahn shook his head. "He should have been with you. He should have been king. Not me."

"Don't be ridiculous, Vahn. You couldn't help that. None of us could."

"But I could," he insisted, "and I didn't."

Her pulse quickened. The weight of his words threatened to make her ill. "What are you saying?"

"He asked me to protect you. If I hadn't made that promise, I wouldn't have married you." He couldn't look her in the eye, his face etched with remorse. "But I had the chance to set it all right. For one time in my life, I made a selfish decision."

Firal drew back a half step, the ill-fitting puzzle pieces of the last few weeks slowly righting themselves in her mind. "His letter."

"I didn't mean for any of this to happen," Vahn insisted. "No one was supposed to get hurt. I did it because I loved you. I thought there was a chance you could feel the same way and I had to know."

"When we needed him, you came straight to Vicamros." Her heart wrenched. Tears pricked her eyes. "All this time, you knew where he was. Didn't you?"

Vahn shook his head. Not in disagreement, but in a silent war with himself. "I never meant for any of this to happen. All I wanted was a happy ending. But if we don't hurry, he'll never get his. We'll talk about this all you want later. Right now, he's waiting for us."

She tried to make herself walk but her feet wouldn't move. Disbelief warred with hurt and disappointment. A seething sense of betrayal welled up beneath it all. Everything they'd done, everything they'd built together had happened because she thought her husband wouldn't return.

Because she hadn't received the letter he sent, trying to tie their lives back together.

And Vahn didn't deny he'd intercepted it.

He stopped not far ahead and looked back. His face softened and for a fleeting moment, she thought she saw guilt. Too little too late, it only stirred her anger and brought more tears to her eyes.

"Please," was all he said.

She wanted to scream. Even more, she wanted to cry. Breathing deep and drawing herself up, she carried on with her heart slowly shattering in her chest.

The mages were waiting when they arrived, all of them anxious. They greeted her with curtsies, her role as queen evidently restored. Firal ignored them and instead trained her attention on the young man before them.

Rhyllyn had a calm air about him, though Rune's jeweled sword at his hip made him look even more of a child. It was too long for him, the tip of its sheath only inches from the floor, but Firal was glad to see he carried it. Their plan still sounded like madness, but she couldn't make herself think about it now. She couldn't let herself think of anything, or she wouldn't be able to do what was so desperately needed of her.

Firal slid close and wrapped a one-armed hug around the youth's shoulders. Surprised, he reciprocated, then touched a claw to Lulu's cheek.

The girl grinned at him.

"Don't worry," Rhyllyn said. "We'll be back soon."

"Are you ready, Firal?" Kytenia stood among the mages.

Firal hadn't even noticed. She kissed her daughter's head and put her down, nodding in gratitude when Rikka stepped forward from the cluster of mages to keep the girl aside.

Vahn touched her arm. Firal couldn't even bear to look at him. She turned her attention to the mages and focused her strength to one pinpoint of power. She extended it toward the group, and they joined one by one.

The knot of power grew, humming through her body, tingling to the tips of her toes. Firal exhaled, struggling to push everything out of her mind. Anger released with each breath and the ache in her chest lessened. Then she began, and the hurt washed over her anew.

She couldn't keep from feeling it when she thought of him. Surely chained, likely wounded, awaiting what must be certain death. No matter how she tried to combat it, she knew she'd put him there.

"We're ready," Kytenia said.

Firal closed her eyes. She couldn't think of the dungeon. She pushed that away, refused to let it distract her. They didn't know if he was still there. Instead she trained all her thoughts on Rune and drew an image in her head.

The vibrant, expressive violet eyes rimmed by dark eyelashes. The sarcastic twist of his mouth and his tangled brown hair. The hint of shadow that trimmed his jaw in absence of a beard, and the strong, commanding presence he held. The scars on his back. The scar in his hand. The deep drive and determination, and the silver rings in his ears.

She layered in details, creating a facsimile of everything that made Rune who he was. And last of all, she thought of his heart. The gentle reassurance of every hurt and wrong forgiven in the moment he'd pressed their rings into her hand.

The air sizzled and split before her. Sections of reality fell away to fragment into shimmering motes.

He was there.

His hands were together overhead, bound in iron and tied with rope. Black blood coursed down his bare chest and sides, so fresh it still dripped to the dank floor. He hung so limply that for an instant, Firal feared he was dead. Then he stirred, lifting his head just enough to look straight at the portal.

Rune couldn't see them from that side, but he clearly felt the power in the air. Judging by the gleam in his luminescent eyes, he was bracing for a fight.

"Go," Vahn ordered, nudging Rhyllyn's arm and then pushing ahead. He paused by the Gate and looked back at Firal, but she couldn't meet his eye.

"Come back safe," she said to Rhyllyn instead, and the boy nodded before he plunged through.

The Gate closed on their heels. Firal sank to the floor and gasped as the first sob broke free.

21

RESCUE

Sleep didn't come easy, dangling from the ceiling by iron cuffs.

No matter how Rune fought to remain calm and relaxed, there was a certain anxiety that came with lack of sleep that he wasn't so sure he could fight.

The jailer visited him not long after Hetia departed. The man spared him the whip but made up for it with threats. Making a show of it to the guards nearby, the jailer had roped Rune's manacled wrists together. He'd claimed he wanted to be ready for a flogging the next morning, and it was best with hands out of the way. Afterward, it had been quiet.

Rune knew the time by the sounds in the dark prison, and the enduring silence from the jailer's post and surrounding cells meant the small hours of the morning had passed and the sun would soon rise. It was then that exhaustion sank into his bones and turned his muscles to jelly. He'd almost succumbed to it and fallen asleep when he felt her.

"You make this more difficult than it has to be." Envesi stopped outside the bars to his cell. "Although I realize this is what our problem has always been. I intended you for such great things, but all of them depended on the idea that you could be controlled."

He dragged himself to his feet. "Free will is a terrible thing to waste."

"Yet you weren't supposed to have it, and that's one thing that's always baffled me." She slid a heavy iron key into the lock. The cell door groaned open. "Spirit is not an element. It cannot be manipulated or given shape. You were meant to be an empty vessel, nothing more. A soldier who could not question orders. We did not expect you would have cognitive function. You simply were. And then you were more."

They'd never spoken of his creation beyond a bare minimum to satisfy his curiosity. His origin had always been so unsettling that he'd never delved any deeper.

Flesh was merely a composition of elements. It was easy to alter, easy to sculpt, easy to create. Their manipulations were what brought him into existence, forged of raw elements and fused with life in the first moment they made his heart beat.

He'd often wished they never had.

"A person can't be born of nothing," Rune replied. "You must be missing something."

"So I thought, for many years," Envesi said. "I studied ceaselessly after you. Even after I was evicted from my temple and sent to the Grand College, I studied. And when my power was unbound, I began to study what happened when a person passes on. I killed them in so many ways, hoping to see some sliver of a mistake, some piece of a soul that could have its course altered like the flows."

The admission gave him chills. "And?"

"And here you are. Alive and independent. Still, despite everything I found." She reached out to draw a talon down the center of his chest. "I made more. Did you know that? Dozens more, after you. We followed the same path precisely. There was no other way to do it, once the energy carved that route. And yet not a single one lived."

She traced the path over his skin again, pressing harder. He winced at the way the scratch burned.

"They never drew breath," she continued. "Empty. Yet so much worse than corpses. They were heaps of flesh that had never been, had never known life. How can something be dead if it never lived? They were foul, wrong. And then there was you. Growing, living, radiant. You were perfect in nearly every way."

Rune chuckled darkly. "My long list of vices disagrees."

Her claws bit deep and drew blood. "Don't you see?" She scoffed. "Your vices are what make you perfect. You're... human. Everything you never should have been. A punishment for my folly, the perfect device to tear down all I'd done."

"I never wanted anything to do with your work," he spat back. "I never wanted to do anything to you. All I ever wanted was a chance to be like everyone else."

"And you'll never have it." Envesi's pale eyes gleamed like ice in moonlight. "You are power. And you will aid me now, whether you like it or not." She slid close, caressing his chest and stomach with both hands.

He shuddered.

"It was a good idea, the one you gave me." She drew her hands up his sides, studying his form. "If I cannot create more like you, then I shall birth them. You will resign yourself to the fact, or it shall not be pleasant." She dug her talons into his sides, tore gashes into the skin over his ribs and chuckled when he sucked in a hissing breath. "For you, at least."

Evidently satisfied, she patted his cheek and slid from the cell. "The jailer will be along shortly to help you adjust to the idea. I suggest you think hard between now and then." She pulled the door shut and the lock snapped with a final, resounding clang.

Rune closed his eyes and sank into his chains without a sound. The cuts in his sides and chest were not deep, but they stung and bled profusely. He couldn't heal himself, but with fortune, Hetia would visit again that evening. There was little point in hoping for aid before then.

He'd be scars upon scars before this was done, but by now Hetia may have found a way to send word to the Triad. A day or two was all he'd have to wait for Vicamros to deliberate. If he could get free by then, the king would have made up his mind. Either Rune would find the support he needed in the Royal City, or he'd be able to turn to Kytenia and—hopefully—assemble a legion of loyal mages like Hetia, scrounged from the ranks of Ilmenhith and the temple.

Working with that kind of support from the start had been his first choice, but he was not king. For better or worse, he was still at the mercy of those above him.

The air stirred. It wasn't visible, but every flow of energy rippled, moved, and began to divide along a central line. A Gate. Rune braced for Envesi's return and lifted his head to watch the unseen hole in reality.

Instead of Envesi, Vahn slid from thin air to light on the filthy, bloodstained floor of Rune's cell.

Startled, Rune grasped the chains that held his bound hands overhead and pulled himself to his feet.

When Rhyllyn slid through and the Gate closed behind him, Rune cursed.

"What are you doing here?" Rune hissed in a whisper, his eyes flashing the direction Envesi had gone only minutes before. He couldn't feel her clearly anymore, but Rhyllyn's Gift would light up the whole dungeon in her senses if she was paying attention.

"We came to rescue you," Rhyllyn said.

"I don't need to be rescued," Rune growled.

Vahn's eyes dropped to the rivulets of blood that flowed down Rune's torso. "Are you sure about that?" He drew a dagger to slice the ropes, then touched the manacles with a tentative hand. "Rhyllyn, can you do something about these?"

Rhyllyn nodded and knelt to address the manacles on Rune's feet first.

Irritated as he was, Rune didn't move. The iron grew warm against his skin as Rhyllyn warped the locks. The manacles popped open. "You need to get out of here," Rune whispered. "She was here just a minute ago. If she catches Rhyllyn—"

"I almost hope she does catch us," Vahn said. "We already decided how we'll kill her."

"Well I hope it doesn't include knives, because I can already tell you that doesn't work well." Rune lifted his feet one at a time, flexing his ankles as Rhyllyn turned his attention to the cuffs at his wrists.

"Better if we just open a Gate and get out of here," Rhyllyn muttered.

"If *you* get out of here," Rune replied. "I'm not going anywhere until my job is done. Thanks for breaking the locks and all, but now I have to figure out how to hold the rest of my plan together while the two of you leave."

Vahn peered down the dungeon's central hall, then glanced back. "What plan?"

"There's a formidable number of mages still loyal to the crown here in Ilmenhith, and even more in the temple." Rune rubbed his wrists and winced when he touched the raw places where the close-fitting iron had stripped away his scales. "If I can get in touch with them, we can organize the group I need— that I needed all along, mind you—to face her."

Rhyllyn huffed, indignant. "How is that any different than having me help you?"

"Because whoever helps me might die," Rune snapped. The glow of his eyes brightened and then faded almost to nothing. His heart constricted and his whole chest ached as he forced the words that didn't want to come. "I have nothing left, Rhyllyn. Nothing but the knowledge that what I do now will keep the people I love safe. Give me that. Please."

His brother's face fell.

"Hear me out first," Vahn said, glancing over his shoulder. He kept his voice low. "Let me tell you about our idea. We're already here, maybe we should just go ahead and see it through."

Rune looked toward the ceiling as he probed the currents of energy around them. Nothing yet. Envesi was still somewhere upstairs.

Against his better judgment, he nodded. "Make it fast."

***

"Are you certain you want to do this?" Vivenne paced after Firal, bouncing Lumia in her arms and patting the girl's back.

"It's not a matter of what I want to do, it's a matter of what I know they are going to do." Firal kept a tight rein on her tongue, unwilling to snap at the woman who was the only mother she still had in her life. Minna had been the first woman to fill a motherly role, but Minna was traversing Lore on her way to the Royal City, along with all the rest of the ruin-folk.

Firal had been surprised to find Tobias among those gathered for council. In any other situation, she might have been upset to hear any group of her people had abandoned the island. Right now, it was a blessing.

"You don't know that for certain," Vivenne protested.

"But I know Vahn and I know Rune, and I know Rhyllyn is impressionable enough to do anything he's told." Firal couldn't think of a worse trio to put together. Rune was brash enough without Vahn to egg him on, and Rhyllyn gave him the power to do anything they thought of. "Besides, if they really were just dropping in to rescue him, they'd be back by now, wouldn't they?"

Edagan had briefed Firal on the details Vahn left out shortly after their departure. It hadn't taken long, but it took longer than it should have taken them to free Rune from the dungeon and return to the Royal City with him in tow. Now, over an hour later, Firal had no doubts left.

"But Firal, you've only just gotten Lulu back. The girl needs her mother." Vivenne stopped, only her eyes following as Firal gathered her things and changed into more serviceable clothing.

"She needs safety first and foremost, Vivenne. I trust you, and she's safest here until this is resolved. I don't doubt them, but if I am still queen, I owe it to my people to do this." Leaving so soon after being reunited with her child wasn't something Firal was eager to do, but the weight of the alternative was heavy.

Assuming Edagan was correct, the regions nearest the ruins had to be evacuated. More, if possible, but the temple and its surrounding settlements were the most urgent. A true blessing, then, that the ruins and Core were already empty.

Vivenne sighed but nodded. She shifted Lulu to her hip. "I understand, but surely you don't need to go. So many mages are willing to help, why not send orders from here?"

That was harder to justify. Firal knew sense said she could remain in the Royal City, but she was duty driven. "I am still a mage, too. So long as my people have need of a mage, I should act as one. Besides, Vicamros won't lend us many of his mages, which means only so many of us are able to open Gates back to the Royal City. The more of us there are, the farther we can spread out."

Not only that, but Firal's healing affinity made her an ideal candidate for scouting out places where people could be found. She couldn't reach as far as someone like Kytenia, but she'd have better luck than Rikka or Anaide at detecting living people. And if the worst happened, having every skilled healer possible on the island was a safe precaution.

Tying her hair at the nape of her neck, Firal paused to look at herself in the mirror. The white mage robes she wore were foreign. She hadn't earned them and didn't deserve to wear them, but it was what the court mages had given her. Strangely enough, it felt right to see herself in Master white. It seemed the Royal City mages felt the same way.

"I can't afford to wait any longer." Firal moved to meet them, hugged Vivenne, and kissed Lulu's rosy cheeks. "I will not be in a dangerous position, since all we're doing is leading evacuations. If my group is threatened, we'll return. Otherwise, I won't be back until I've done all I can."

Vivenne nodded and blinked back tears as she rocked Lulu in her arms. "Be safe."

Firal smiled and nodded back.

She was among the last to join the mages in the Spiral Palace's Gating parlor. Vicamros had been gracious to lend them some of his own mages to assist in evacuation, but there were also Elenhiise mages scattered through the groups. Magelings still in colored robes, mostly, but they wore looks of determination that promised they'd be useful.

The groups were carefully organized. A strong Elenhiise mage was present to lead each party, and at least one strong Royal City mage to help return them to the Triad. Firal took her place with the group Kytenia directed her to, then studied the others.

Kytenia, Rikka, Edagan, Balen, Temar, and Anaide each headed a group. The concentration of high-ranking temple mages surprised her, seeing them all together. What surprised her more was Alira at the head of another group. A number of Elenhiise mages had been frosty toward the woman, but either that was past now, or they acknowledged the woman's history was less important than the task at hand.

"Everyone's been assigned outposts to attend, starting with the settlements nearest the ruins." Kytenia pressed a piece of paper into Firal's hand. "You're to start in Ilmenhith. The city should be safe, since it's on the coast, but we aren't sure yet."

Firal's heart sank. "Then why send me there? Kytenia, I can help—"

"Of course you can, and that's why you've got the most important job, you goose." Kytenia playfully rolled her eyes. "Your job is to gather as many loyal mages as possible and Gate them to our groups. We'll need them to help us. I've certainly never been to every village on Elenhiise, but we have mages in Ilmenhith who've traveled the whole island."

Rosy spots bloomed in Firal's cheeks. She should have known Kytenia wouldn't spare her because of her rank. "Shouldn't you send someone more powerful, then?" She smoothed her white robes, suddenly self-conscious of the color, though no one seemed to notice she wore it.

"Absolutely not. Don't forget, the mages on Elenhiise are divided again." Kytenia's face fell as she spoke. After fighting so long and so hard to reunite the island's mages, that had to be a blow. "It's our mages versus hers. Mages loyal to you against those loyal to Envesi. I have no doubt she's tried to ferret them out and deal with them, so they're probably wary of anyone claiming to represent your side. If you're the one looking for them, they've no reason not to trust us."

Sound reasoning. And with Envesi surely distracted by Rune's rescue, Firal wasn't likely to be in any danger. Unless the mission had failed at the beginning. There was always the possibility the men had been captured or killed almost as soon as they'd set foot in the dungeon.

Yet something told her that wasn't the case. Though she was far from happy with the way things transpired, there was an odd spark of something in her that she hadn't felt in far too long.

Hope.

"Everyone ready?" Kytenia called.

All around the room, mages nodded. With the Archmage's command, they lined up and worked with Royal City mages to open Gates to places on Elenhiise both familiar and foreign to Firal's eyes.

When Firal's turn came, the sight of Ilmenhith on the other side brought tears to her eyes. She led her group through the portal and drew herself up with a queenly air. Her job was among the most important, but also one of the easiest. She took a step, meaning to lead her group toward the chapter house.

Beneath their feet, the tremors began.

22

PROMISE

"Last chance to change your mind." Rune flexed his clawed hands as he peered around the corner. The throne room was still a floor away and the hall ahead was empty. He couldn't see anyone, but now and then, voices carried in the empty palace.

Envesi was up there—on the dais or near the throne, if his perception of location was right. He couldn't guess as to what she was doing, but he felt her, sure as anything. There was no sneaking up on her, but he'd done his best to better their chances. He'd seen the trick the Alda'anan used to hide their magic long before he'd known they existed, a feat practiced by the Underling queen he'd once served. Rune had never been good at it, finding it took too much concentration, but he used it now. The seal on his Gift made his power muddy and faint in the senses of others, but if he masked it correctly, he'd become invisible.

The glow vanished from his eyes as he willed every flow of energy away from himself. She'd feel Rhyllyn, but the similarity between them—both free mages, both touched by corruption— would keep her from knowing Rune was not the one she sensed; if all worked as planned, she wouldn't know there were two of them until it was too late. As it was, she seemed unconcerned by his presence.

"Let's go," Vahn whispered back.

Rune nodded. They'd gone over the plan a half dozen times as he retrieved his clothing from the chest beside the jailer's desk. The jailer himself stood down the moment Vahn appeared, but Rune had still entertained the idea of stuffing the man in a cell. Had there been more time, perhaps he would have, but they couldn't risk the delay.

They ghosted up the hallway and the stairs. Rune led the way, taking every shortcut he knew. They encountered no one on the way, and the hall that led to the throne room's doors was just as empty as the rest of the palace.

"Is this place always so creepy?" Rhyllyn asked in a whisper as they lingered just outside the doors.

Without a word, Rune dropped his guard and reached for Rhyllyn's power as his own stunted magic came rushing back.

Conversation in the throne room halted. Rune strode in with Vahn on his heels.

Envesi glowered as she rose from the throne. "What have you done?"

Not caring who the question was meant for, Rune seized the invisible threads of power that constituted her Gift.

He'd tried before and failed, but this time they were near equally matched. She pulled against his hold and her eyes widened when she realized he wouldn't budge this time.

Her surprise didn't last. She twirled her fingers in the air and hacked through the flows he held with an invisible edge. At her side, her companion drew his sword and advanced on them. Ennil Tanrys. Rune had expected no other.

Vahn drew his blade and moved between them. "Stand down," he barked, holding his sword ready.

Rune tore his eyes away. He couldn't risk distraction now. The last thread of energy snapped and he released his hold. Overpowering her still wouldn't happen. The best he could hope for was driving her to exhaustion before he or Rhyllyn gave out.

Envesi didn't give him time to think. She snapped an arm toward him and jagged pieces of ice flew from her fingertips like a dozen daggers.

He brought his hands together before him and swept the ice away with a barrier of wind. The shards spun and fell, shattered against the ground and glittered beneath his feet like broken glass.

"We've tried this before," Envesi snarled, drawing her arm back in preparation for another burst of magic. "You can't possibly expect to best me now."

"I have to try," Rune replied.

To his side, Vahn advanced on his father in a duelist's stance.

"You can't possibly think you can win," Ennil goaded.

"You'd be surprised," Vahn said. "I'm not the one who lost my balls in a training exercise!" He twirled inward, blade flashing in the light that spilled from the hole in the ceiling.

The ceiling. Rune's eyes flicked upward.

Envesi spun her hands again in the elaborate gestures she favored and flung her arm toward him in a second attack.

This time, Rune dropped to the floor to avoid the daggers of ice, one palm flat on the cold marble.

Beneath their feet, the earth began to rumble.

Their swords clashed and Vahn and Ennil both stumbled.

"Deviating!" Vahn snarled.

Rune ignored him. Of course he was deviating. Following the original plan meant putting the whole island at risk. Bringing the palace down meant only they were in danger.

Envesi staggered sideways and extended both hands to regain her balance. Scowling, she swept her claws along the floor and stepped onto an invisible platform of air.

Silently swearing, Rune abandoned his attempt to shatter the palace. Drawing through Rhyllyn, he could pull down the castle or he could shield himself against her magic. Not both.

Vahn recovered the moment the quake stopped and rushed back to combat. Fast as he was, Ennil still regained his feet before the first blow fell.

Always faster, Envesi drew power into herself again. Her eyes darkened, betraying her intent.

Instead of dodging, Rune moved to meet the streak of power the moment it left her fingertips. Crackling power shot up his arm, the current flowing through him like electricity. His heart pounded off-rhythm and time slowed as magic flooded his senses and stood his hair on end.

Then he spun, and the magic shot from his claws on his other hand, missing Envesi by only a hair.

The Archmage's mouth fell open and Rune smirked. *Thanks for the trick, little brother.*

Her surprise was short-lived. Quick to compensate, she fired again, lightning bolts sparking from both hands.

Dancing backwards, Rune caught them where they converged, but this was hotter, faster, and he gasped as the searing power shot through him. It moved too fast for him to aim and the magic exploded against a column, shattered the stone and brought a chunk of the balcony down with it.

Envesi's eyes flared.

"Pull back!" Rune barked. He couldn't stay that lucky.

Vahn grunted in response, twisting away from his father's blade to run for the hall.

"Coward!" Envesi flexed her arms outward. White-hot energy drew into seething balls in either of her hands. "I'm not finished with you!"

Rune threw a shield between them as she hurled the magic toward him. It hit the barrier and burst in an explosion of white flame, the heat enough to make his eyes water.

"You think you can challenge me and live?" the Archmage screeched.

Reinforcing the shield, Rune turned and ran.

He closed his eyes, envisioning the destination, willing the path to open.

Reality split and when his eyes snapped open, a wall of pure black filled the hallway.

Vahn stopped dead in his tracks, Rhyllyn at his side.

"Go!" Rune roared.

Grimacing, Vahn dove through and disappeared.

Rhyllyn turned back, anxious. Then he met Rune's eyes and nodded. He stepped backwards through the portal and their link severed. All the weight of the Gate's power came down on Rune alone.

Pain exploded in his head and chest as the seal on his magic reacted to the raw might of the portal, making stars burst in his field of vision. Then cold black enveloped him, and he hit the ground hard.

The Gate closed.

"Where are we?" Rhyllyn asked. His eyes made two blue pinpoints in the dark. They faded whenever Rune looked directly at them. The stars in his vision were brighter.

Rune groaned, sat up and pressed both hands to his head.

Farther ahead, Vahn choked back an oath as he collided with something.

"Oh, hold on." The rasp of metal followed Rhyllyn's voice and a moment later, all three of them squinted against the flare of a mage-light.

Rhyllyn held Rune's sword aloft, the ruby in its pommel infused with magic and illuminating the room.

Years of dust coated the floor and surfaces, but the must of dried herbs still lingered. The room was roughly furnished with makeshift counters along the walls, tables and two rudimentary chairs in the middle of the room, and a narrow bed in the far corner.

It was all so unchanged it made Rune's heart ache.

Vahn studied the single room, crowded with the three of them in it, his brow furrowed. "What is this place?"

"Home." Rune winced against the throbbing in his skull as he pushed himself to his feet. "Or it was, once."

"This is in Core?" Vahn looked toward the lone doorway with a frown.

"Not far off the central column. The mines are at the bottom." Rune tried to ignore the room. "It was the only place I could think of that I was sure would be the same as I remembered it. I thought about the waterwheel or the river, but I don't know what the market looks like now."

"Better not to risk it," Rhyllyn said softly.

Vahn worried his lower lip with his teeth. "I guess we should head toward the Gate down there, then. I've never been here. Lead the way, would you?"

The door resisted when Rune tried to open it. Wood crackled and rusted hinges shrieked as it came loose. The main hallway on the other side was just as he recalled. Wide, dark, and empty. Even when Core had been fully populated, the halls were never crowded. There were thousands of cave-houses lining dozens of halls branching from the central column. Maybe enough for every one of the Underlings to have their own.

Ruin-folk, not Underlings, he reminded himself. They'd moved on, grown into their role under Firal's rule. Funny, in a way. He'd always expected he'd be the one to help them re-integrate with the people of Ilmenhith. Glad as he was it had happened without him, it was amusing to think of his hard-earned support shifting to Firal simply because they'd been married.

"How long do you think we have before Envesi follows us?" Rhyllyn asked, his voice low against the oppressive silence of the underground.

"A few minutes to get our bearings, I hope," Vahn said.

Rune made a thoughtful sound in his throat. "As far as I know, she's never been to Core. That may have changed, but I doubt it. A Gate directly to me is her only chance of finding us." And now that he thought about it, he wasn't sure that would happen. He didn't know much about Envesi's skill, other than that she was powerful. She always had been. Even when she'd been bound by affinity, her talent with magecraft let her easily outpace him in ability.

Until he'd found a teacher.

After what she'd done to the mages of the Grand College, Rune did not doubt Envesi had killed the Alda'anan he'd been seeking. The knowledge gave him a strange sense of mingled sadness and guilt.

Thirty years ago, she'd tainted Rhyllyn in her quest to gain more strength. Rune knew what she had done. Yet even after the civil war ended, even after he was given freedom to look for the Alda'anan, he'd never once thought about trying to find Envesi and making sure she couldn't harm anyone else the same way. If he had... He shook his head, unwilling to think of it any longer.

"What's that?" Rhyllyn shielded the glowing gem on the sword's hilt with one hand, dulling the light. It made the glow at the far end of the passage appear brighter.

"Sunlight," Rune replied, amused.

Rhyllyn dismissed the mage-light and let shadow fall around them. "I thought we were underground."

Rune chuckled. "You'll see."

Air stirred behind them and a cold chill rolled down his spine as magic built in the empty corridor. Faster than he'd anticipated, a Gate cracked the flows apart.

"Run!" Rune turned back as the others moved past him, though they both stalled and looked back after a few steps. He gritted his teeth. "Now!"

"Another!" Envesi's grating voice reached his ears before the portal stabilized.

Like those he created, the Gate she'd opened was functional on both sides. He could see into the throne room on the other end. For a single, fleeting moment, he considered stepping through and continuing the fight in the palace, giving Vahn and Rhyllyn a chance to escape.

Then she stepped through the Gate and let it drop.

Envesi strode forward, but she wasn't looking at him. Instead her eyes passed him, pure fury on her face. "Another one, and I didn't know! How is this? What have you done?"

Rhyllyn and Vahn had stopped, frozen in place, unwilling to let him fight alone.

Rune had an inclination to strangle them himself.

"So young, no more than a boy! A child that carries the curse..." Her lip curled in disgust. "So it does breed true."

Fighting a flare of agitation, Rune turned and grabbed Rhyllyn by the arm. Vahn needed no more than a shove to get him moving again.

Linking with Rhyllyn as they ran, Rune paused just long enough to erect a defensive barrier behind them. "We have to get to the bottom! We'd be trapped in the lift, we'll have to run."

"Where?" Vahn outpaced them easily. Supporting the barrier slowed them down, but he stopped at the mouth of the tunnel. "Which way?" He turned back and his eyes widened.

Rune felt the shield ripple as Envesi struck it, a wash of heat pouring through after the flames were stopped. He didn't dare look back. "Down the spiral!"

Vahn disappeared around the corner.

Rhyllyn stumbled, but Rune's hand on his arm kept him on his feet. They burst out of the corridor side by side, and when Rune saw the central chasm of Core, he stopped and stared in disbelief.

Trees.

All along the river, along the waterfall that fell from the corkscrew and plummeted into the earth, trees erupted from the stone. Some clung to the sides of the spiraling column, all of them reaching toward the sky like black-scarred white arms. In their presence, the air was cool. Fresh, green leaves fluttered in a faint stirring of air.

Rune dropped the link and pushed Rhyllyn ahead. "Go with Vahn."

"But—" Rhyllyn started to protest.

"Go!" Rune barked. "I have an idea."

Rhyllyn swallowed hard, but went.

Rune turned back toward the corridor and locked eyes with Envesi. Though they ran, she advanced slowly, walking with her head held high. He'd counted on that ego and hadn't been disappointed. Regal as she tried to be, she gave him all the time he needed to prepare.

Instead of reaching for Rhyllyn's power, Rune reached for the trees. All his life, mages had drilled him with rules and precautions, warnings about what to draw from and when.

The trees answered his call. Their power flowed into him, filling his mind with a deep awareness of their presence. Dozens of trees, all linked, all growing from the same root. Their life and vibrance pulsed in his senses and he breathed deep.

Pure energy coursed through him and he used it to snare the stone of the tunnel's ceiling. Rune pulled and, drawing from the aspens, the stone shattered.

The first pull was too small. Envesi batted the falling rock away without a thought and increased her pace.

Steeling himself, Rune tried again.

Like an avalanche, the hall's ceiling came down. The ground quivered beneath his feet and Rune widened his stance, waiting for the rumble to halt.

He couldn't risk running on the slick ramp, not with that gaping chasm in the center and no rail to keep him from going over. He'd once laughed at Firal for being afraid of falling. Now the same fear gripped him and he regretted ever teasing her. He hugged the wall on his way down.

An explosion on the path behind him knocked him to the ground. Rune slid several feet before he caught himself at the bridge where the walkway and river met.

A shower of gravel and stones tumbled down the walkway behind him. They pelted his back and shoulders and stung.

He pulled himself upright with the bridge's corner post,

tightening his hold on the life force of the trees beside him. Closer than before, they formed a stronger bond, and he gathered magic into his fingertips for a new attack.

Envesi appeared on the path above, disheveled and enraged, her eyes seething red and the stone walkway trembling under each stride. "How many times must you try before you realize you cannot best me?"

She swung her arm. An arc of water poured up over the bridge and formed blocks of ice around his feet.

Gasping against the burning cold, he pulled more and aimed his fingers toward the walkway below her feet. Magic whined past the seal, skirting his own abilities as he drained the trees. Beside him, their colors shifted, the vibrant green leaves taking a golden glow.

The blast struck a shield around Envesi. Dust and gravel splashed against a sphere of clear air.

She sneered.

Then the rock split through and the earth fell out from underneath her, and she shrieked as it spilled her onto the next level of the walkway in a cascade of stone.

A startled oath echoed from below and Rune hissed as he realized his mistake. He'd dropped her to the next tier—putting her that much closer to Vahn and Rhyllyn as they fled.

Still shrieking, Envesi clawed her way out of the rubble as Rune struck the ice at his feet with magic. It shattered, freeing him, and he scrambled down the ramp.

The chasm was wide. The walkway that ringed it was a lazy spiral, each tier twenty-something feet apart. Too far to try to swing down to the next level. The pit in the center that delved farther than the sun reached would swallow him if any attempt to move faster went wrong. Running alongside the outer wall was all he could do.

The others were a full ring below, on the opposite side. Vahn paused, looking across the gap.

"Keep going!" Rune shouted, giving the trees overhead

another glance. "Don't stop. You'll know the mine shaft when you see it!"

He was halfway around the ring when Envesi freed herself from the rubble and spun to face him.

She spared no retorts this time, no soliloquy to buy him time to act. Instead she struck the ground at her feet. Wide cracks shot from the point of impact, fracturing the walkway between them and sending massive blocks tumbling into the endless pit.

Rune swore and pressed his back to the wall as a crack shot past his feet, leaving him with only inches of path to stand on.

He closed his eyes and breathed deep. "Forgive me," he whispered, and he didn't know whether he spoke to his absent teachers or the trees.

The trees shuddered as he drained them past the brink, consuming their life as power. The leaves withered, curled and browned as he spread his palms against the wall and opened all his senses.

Awareness of the pathway and the mass of tunnels surrounding them blossomed in his mind, tunnels he'd walked a hundred times and some he'd never realized were there. He followed them to a central point, nearest Envesi, and focused everything there.

Wood creaked and cracked as the aspens died, the smallest trees crumbling into dust and then nothing as he pulled the last they had to offer and the trees came unmade.

The earth rumbled, vibrated beneath his feet, and threatened to shake him from his narrow ledge.

One by one, the trees burst into shimmering motes and faded into nothing as their being was consumed. The ground shook harder in return.

Earth split and rock splintered. Tunnels collapsed and floors caved in. The cascade began, stones flowing like sand in his senses, racing downward to fill the emptiness they'd been poured into. Each passage gave way more easily, the weight of rubble above it too much to bear.

The last tree sighed and slipped from reality to nothingness, and with the last shred of its power, Rune stepped off the ledge.

The Gate opened beneath his feet and he bit off a cry as he hit the ground, transported several rings down.

Vahn blinked in surprise and rushed back to aid him.

"Rhyllyn," Rune called, his voice rough in his throat.

The boy turned back, his eyes wide.

Channeling the essence of the trees still drained him, and Rune held out his hand as he extended what was left of his energy. "Link!"

Rhyllyn met his magic and meshed with it, bolstering his strength and granting him access to pure power again.

Rune had the Gate halfway open before Rhyllyn reached him.

The manor waited on the other side. Rune stared through, startled. He'd meant to reach the Royal City, his thoughts muddled with a sense of home.

He looked at Vahn and jerked his head. "Go."

"I have to see this finished," Vahn insisted.

Rune smiled grimly. "Then I guess we die together."

Before Rhyllyn could protest, Rune reached for the sword at his hip with one hand, planted the other on the youth's chest, and shoved with all his might.

The sword came free and Rhyllyn fell backwards through the portal, releasing an agonized shout of dismay.

The Gate severed their connection and the portal's power hit Rune with a force to rival the collapsing tunnel. His knees buckled and he clung to the sword, fearful it would slide from his hand when he hit the ground.

But something kept him on his feet, and it took him a moment to realize it was Vahn's arm under his.

"C'mon," Vahn breathed, hefting him back to his feet. "We're not done yet."

23

ALL THINGS END

THE GROUND SHUDDERED UNTIL EVERY MAGE IN FIRAL'S GROUP LOST
their balance. She staggered toward Ilmenhith's chapter house
until she could lay hands against its corner and cling to the
building for support. Others crouched until the tremors passed.
Cries of surprise and fear echoed down the busy streets.

"What was that?" one of the Masters asked.

Firal watched them climb back to their feet and right their
robes. Her eyes swept north, toward the gleaming spires of the
palace that rose above the city. The other mages turned the same
direction, verifying her fear. The tremors had come from that
direction. She could feel the disruption in the flows of magic that
lay over the city.

"Whatever it is, you can expect it to get worse," Firal said as
she pushed herself off the chapter house. "We need to make sure
the palace is empty, and I'm best suited to gaining entry. Sybet,
warn the mages in the chapter house, if there are any. Meet us at
the palace when you're done. The rest of you, come."

The white-robed Master bowed her head and hurried for the
chapter house door.

Firal allowed herself to close her eyes and open her senses,
seeing with her Gift instead of her eyes. All around her, the

presence of life lit up. Ilmenhith was incandescent with its light. Her stomach turned at the sheer number of people. How were they to evacuate everyone?

"Majesty," another mage said. Kella had proven herself as a court mage and worked hard among those who had escaped the palace alongside Firal. She was a welcome addition to the party. "Should we approach the palace so soon? If the plan to combat the former Archmage is already underway—"

Firal raised a hand to cut her off. "We'll need to trust that we can move around the rest of the palace without being noticed. We're no longer important to her."

A few mages exchanged doubtful looks, but they fell in step behind Firal when she began the trek toward the soaring palace.

The sight of her home wrenched her heart. If all went according to plan, the palace could be ruined, or worse. Tightness bound her throat and she worked to loosen the constriction. For the safety of her people, her family, it had to be a risk she was willing to take.

The palace gates were closed, but at the sight of a team of mages in white progressing up the street, a guard atop the wall waved to the gatekeeper. The portcullis groaned and clanked as it began its slow ascent.

"Your Majesty!" a guard exclaimed as Firal's face became clear. He ducked under the portcullis and knelt before her on the street.

Firal spread her hands to signal for the other mages to halt. "Rise. Gather my men and have them collect everyone still within the palace. Everyone is to gather in the courtyard. Not a soul left behind."

"Everyone?" the guard repeated. "But, Majesty—"

"That is an order from your queen," she snapped.

The guard shut his jaw, nodded, and hastened back into the courtyard.

Firal turned toward her team. "Six of you are to remain in the courtyard. Prepare to open a Gate and hold it firm. When Sybet rejoins you, she is to help with the Gate. The rest of you, fan out and comb the palace." She paused to explore with her Gift again. The presence of the mages in front of her burned bright, but elsewhere, glimmers of life tickled her awareness. A low sense of dread drew together in the pit of her belly.

She tamped it down and continued her orders. "You, east. You, west. If you encounter guards or soldiers, repeat the orders I just gave. Do not let anyone else assist you. Everyone else is to head for the courtyard immediately. Open the Gate when at least fifty have gathered, unless those tremors begin again. If more mages arrive, they are to wait here for my command. Do you understand?"

Every head bobbed in confirmation.

Firal nodded back. "I will return."

No one said anything else as she spun toward the palace and marched toward the door. Her slippers whispered against the stone. The white robes that swirled around her ankles glowed in the sunlight, foreign to her eye.

Clothed in Master white and leading a team of mages in the palace. In her youth, such a situation would have been everything she ever dreamed of. It was strange to realize how much her dreams had changed.

She no more than stepped inside before a Master in blue-trimmed white stepped into her path.

"My queen," the mage gasped. She clapped a hand to her heart and bowed deeply. "We were told—"

"No time," Firal interrupted. "Join the others in the courtyard. The palace is in danger of collapse."

The mage's eyes widened, but she hurried past Firal without protest.

With her head high, Firal gripped the skirts of her robes and pressed onward.

Somehow, wearing white gave her a sense of authority she'd never experienced as queen. People had listened to her then, but perhaps only because they had no choice. She had never been confident as a leader, despite the years of practice she'd gained. But her Gift had always given her a sense of security. As a mage, she knew her strengths and weaknesses, knew her role, knew what she could achieve. She had always intended to be a Master mage. The throne had robbed her of the chance. In the face of everything she suffered now, a new idea sprang to mind.

If Ilmenhith was destroyed, perhaps that chance would rise again.

A tingle of magic rose in the throne room ahead and Firal stalled at the door. Then the magic winked out, and with it, the most powerful presence disappeared. She dared not think what that could mean. Instead, she thrust the doors open and strode inside.

Pieces of the balcony and ceiling lay scattered in ruin across the throne room. Charred marks marred the walls and ceiling in places, and glass still peppered the floor from what Firal could only assume was her encounter with Envesi days before. Her stomach heaved.

"You," a voice snarled from above.

Firal turned toward what remained of the walkway that ringed the throne room. Ennil glowered down at her, his face a twisted mask of hatred and rage. A handful of mages in white clustered behind him, but a flick of his hand sent them scattering. They looked as if they'd just reached the top of the stairs when she arrived, rumpled and harried, and none of them looked happy to see her. Was she supposed to collect the mages who answered to Envesi, too? Firal did not want to leave them behind, but she did not know how she could trust them to help with evacuation.

"All of this happened because of you." Ennil descended the damaged staircase with the flat of his sword against his shoulder.

"I'm not responsible for my mother's actions," she replied levelly, "just my own. We must empty the palace. The island is in grave danger."

He went on as if he hadn't heard. "You've sullied everything you touched. The kingdom, House Tanrys, my son." His head twitched in disgust. "The mages wanted you because they thought you'd be easy to control. We never should have listened to them."

"This is hardly the time to discuss your issues with me." Firal retreated a step, though she hardly knew why. Ennil was always hard, often cold, but she had never feared him. Why did uneasiness worm its way into her belly now? "If you will not assist with evacuation efforts, then I order you to step aside."

His lip curled in a sneer. "Looked at you. You're dressed like one of those witches now. You think you can command me?" The heel of his boot clacked against the throne room floor with a chilly sense of finality.

Firal drew herself up. "I am still your queen."

A cold laugh escaped Ennil's throat. "I have no ruler." His sword slipped from his shoulder and swung for her head.

She leaped backwards with a cry of surprise. The rush of air sent by the blade's passing made her skin rise in gooseflesh. "What are you doing?"

Ennil's expression hardened and he shifted into a combat stance. "If we're all to die, then at least I'll have the satisfaction of seeing your end."

He swung again.

Firal thrust her hand out in front of her and a burst of energy deflected the blow. The blade glanced off her shield, but he twisted like a dancer and came at her again. Panic surged in her veins and set her heart to drumming in her ears.

"I don't want to fight you!" she cried. She hardly knew *how* to fight. Her Gift was life; she was a medic, not a warrior.

Ennil dove and Firal leaped aside. His sword rasped against her skirts, too close, too dangerous. Again, she thrust her hand toward him. A pulse of air knocked him off balance, but only for a moment.

She couldn't let him regain his bearings. Instead, she

twirled close to his back as he found his footing and shoved her hand against the back of his head. Another pulse answered her call, and the shockwave that followed cast Ennil to the ground.

"I'm not your enemy," Firal insisted.

Snarling, Ennil thrust himself from the debris-strewn floor and reached for his sword again. "You're a blight on the island. You always have been. The council should have killed you in your sleep."

The impulse to run throbbed in her head and Firal wheeled to go. She made it a single step before Ennil's sword tore through the skirt of her robe and rang against the stone. Her slippers slid and she crashed to the floor. Pain shot up her arms and through her shoulders as she landed.

Ennil planted a foot on her robes, jerked his sword free and raised it overhead.

Beneath her, the earth began to tremble.

Firal clenched her teeth and seized the flows underneath her.

Jagged shards of marble shot from the floor as she tied herself to the stone and pulled. They pelted the man above her and he staggered back, shielding his face.

Her skirt freed, Firal shoved herself backwards and clambered to her feet. When he came at her again, she was ready.

He charged.

Firal swept an arm to her chest and stone surged up between them. She whirled back, her skirts flaring, and she begged the winds to follow. They hit like a gale, howling through the throne room and stirring the debris. The wind dragged Ennil back, step by step.

Fury burned in his eyes as he dropped to his knees and the winds evaporated.

"Yield," Firal ordered.

His knuckles turned white as he gripped his sword and rushed toward her.

The palace shuddered. Stones fell from the ceiling and

thundered to the floor around them. Marble shattered and spiderwebbing cracks opened across the floor.

Firal planted her feet firm and spun a new shield. His sword struck dead center and sparks shot from the blade. She curled her hand to a fist and shoved it forward. A bolt of raw power struck him in the stomach and forced him to his knees.

"Yield!" she repeated.

Ennil turned his head and spat.

The earth beneath them groaned. A low crack like popping eggshells split the air. An entire section of the ceiling broke free. Firal ducked, arms over her head as she thrust her magic out to defend them. The stone bounced off a half-sphere of power that enveloped them both.

Ennil released a startled cry and his sword clanged against something solid. Her head jerked up just as the floor fell away and a chasm opened beneath them. Fragments of stone crashed down around them as the ground split and the earthquake intensified.

The floor began to slide. Ennil dug his fingers against the jagged edges of the marble as it threatened to spill him over the edge. His sword hissed against the stone as it slid past him into the chasm.

Heart in her throat, Firal lunged forward and reached for the air. The shield above them wavered. She wasn't strong enough to seize him and hold the barrier at the same time. She could have cursed.

She leaned forward and extended her hand. "Vivenne waits for you in the Royal City. It's not too late."

Ennil glowered up at her as he clawed his way up the slipping stone. "Save your pity," he snarled. "I don't need mercy from you."

Her heart sank. "Then I hope you find it in what comes next."

"Firal!" a familiar voice called from the palace entry, somewhere behind them. Kella. Her group.

"Here!" Firal called back.

A handful of mages in white and mageling colors ran toward her. The shield above them flashed as falling stones struck it, but they didn't threaten its integrity.

Kella reached her first. "We have to go."

Firal didn't resist as Kella pulled her to her feet. The white-robed Master cast Ennil a single hateful look, then spun and hurried Firal to the door.

Smoke and dust clouded the sky over Ilmenhith. The courtyard seethed with people. A half-dozen Gates shone against the castle's outer wall, and the crowd flowed toward them like water.

"We need more Gates," Kella called above the noise.

Firal nodded once and hurried to join the others. With so many people in the courtyard, she couldn't sense if there were people anywhere else. Silently, she prayed everyone had been found.

Someone reached for her. She grasped the offered magic and bound herself to it, fed what she could offer into the opening of another Gate.

Cries of terror filled the air and the crowd moved faster. One of the mages spun to point toward the sky and Firal twisted to follow.

Somewhere far south of the capital, from what had to be the heart of the island, a blinding pillar of pure white light surged into the sky.

THE COLLAPSE

A BLAST OF PURE MAGIC IMPACTED THE WALL BESIDE RUNE'S HEAD. He stumbled a step before he found his legs. Still unsteady, he let Vahn steer him across precarious ledges where the walkway's scaffolding broke away.

"How far down do we have to go?" Vahn flinched as another blast rocked the column, adding to the tremors.

"We're going to have to catch the lift." Rune raised his voice over the roar of collapsing stone. "We'll never make it down the ramp."

"Where?" Vahn shouted back.

Rune pointed vaguely to an area some four rings down.

The barrage of magic didn't stop. The walls exploded beside them, spurring them to run.

"Why doesn't she try to unmake us?" Vahn ducked as another burst sent a shower of pebbles over their heads.

Rune hadn't considered that. It was one more fear he didn't need. "She's too far away. She can't do it unless she's right on top of us."

"Better hop to it, then, she's gain—" Vahn cut off with a shout as the floor gave way beneath their feet and they plummeted to the next ring. They hit hard. Stones slid down the slanted walkway and dragged them both down the path.

Rune clutched his sword and scrabbled against the wall and floor as they slid. His claws squealed against the stone as he sought purchase and failed. The rock battered his body, bruising deep and breaking skin. More stone joined the cascade and they picked up speed.

"No, no, no!" Vahn struggled against the rock and grabbed Rune by the ankle to drag them closer together.

Rune glanced down and the bottom dropped out of his stomach as the rock slide hit a slab of fallen walkway and veered toward the pit. Twisting sideways, he grasped his sword in both hands and jammed the blade into the gap between the slab and the cracked floor.

Sparks flew from the blade as his weight pulled it down.

Vahn screamed as he slid over the edge.

The blade caught and the force of their stop almost tore Rune's arms from their sockets. He bit his tongue to stifle a cry and gripped the hilt so hard his claws dug into his palms.

Vahn hung from his legs, threatening to pull them both over the edge. "Don't let go!"

Gritting his teeth, Rune tried to pull them up. His abused muscles protested and his strength flagged. "Swing off!"

"Are you mad?"

"Swing off or we'll both fall!" Rune snarled. Black blood made his sword's twisted hilt slick.

Vahn groaned, then moved. Still clutching Rune's legs with a death grip, he swung back and forth several times, building momentum.

Rune's hold started to slip. "Hurry up!"

The weight suddenly released. Rune dragged himself back up onto the walkway and spun to look into the chasm. Rocks still tumbled and fell. His friend was nowhere in sight. "Vahn!"

A groan below answered. "Keep moving."

No time for relief, Rune pulled his sword free and used it for support. He held his ribs with one arm as he limped past the angled slab and continued downward. He no longer knew where Envesi was and didn't dare turn to see.

The vibrations of the earth made him rock on his feet. The roar of collapsing tunnels grew almost deafening. He found Vahn sitting with his back against the wall, panting for breath.

"We're almost there." Rune offered a hand. "Come on, just a little farther before we can get out of here. We have to hurry. The mine could collapse any time."

Groaning, Vahn grasped his fingers and stood. "Listen, if we don't both make it out of here—"

"Move." Rune nudged his side, hurrying him onward.

Vahn grimaced, but moved. "If we don't both make it out of here, promise me... Promise you'll..."

For half a breath, Rune paused. "Vahn—"

"Promise me," Vahn insisted.

Rune swallowed hard. "I swear." The first words that came to mind echoed the promise he'd demanded, himself, so long ago. "Anything I can do to protect her," he repeated from memory, "anything to keep her safe, I'll do."

Vahn nodded.

"I promise," Rune finished, nodding back. "Both of them."

They stumbled down half a ring together before Rune turned toward a gaping entryway. A large metal disk surrounded by gears as tall as a man sat just inside.

"What in the..." Vahn's mouth fell open.

Rune pushed him onto the lift and grabbed the lever in the center. "Help me."

Vahn took the other side and they heaved together. The lever shifted, caught, clanked, and refused to go farther.

Rune laid his sword by his feet and they tried again.

"It's stuck," Vahn groaned through clenched teeth.

"The rocks must've hit the gears," Rune growled. He dropped to his knees and spread his palms against the cold iron floor of the lift.

Vahn stared. "What are you doing?"

"Seeing if I can find what's stuck. I may be strong enough to shift—" The lift rocked and Rune stopped short. The massive iron plate beneath their feet shuddered.

Vahn grabbed the lever to try it again. The moment his hands touched it, a crack echoed below them and the plate dropped.

The massive gears whirred out of control and the lift gained speed until it felt like a free fall.

"How do we stop it?" Vahn shouted over the whine of metal and the roar of crumbling caverns.

Rune crawled toward the lever. Progress came slower than he imagined possible—or maybe it only felt that way as the ground rushed to meet them. His sword slid toward him and he slammed a foot down on it to keep it from cutting them both.

He caught the lever just above Vahn's hands and struggled to his feet. Standing felt impossible, like the lift would drop out from underneath him at any time.

Vahn stood first.

"Ready?" Rune gripped the lever in both hands.

His companion nodded, and together, they threw it.

The lift jerked so hard it pitched them both to their knees.

Pain shot through Rune's arms as his hands hit the metal. A sharp clank vibrated the platform and made it worse. It took a moment to realize they were still moving. The lift inched downward at its normal pace.

Rune collapsed onto his side, groaning. They both laid there, gasping for breath as the lift eased to the bottom of its shaft and stopped with a clunk. The mine opened beside them, the passage littered with tools and lined with new tracks for carts.

"Almost there," Vahn groaned too as he struggled to his hands and knees.

Rune grabbed his sword and used it for support as he got up. "Where's the Gate?"

"Straight ahead and then left. Tobias said to follow the wooden tracks." Vahn planted a boot on the floor, rested a hand on his knee and took a moment to simply kneel and breathe. "We might just make it out of here."

"Not until I know she's still down here with us." Rune extended a hand and helped him up. He tried to feel her, looking for her Gift, but the ache of his battered body kept him from searching far.

Vahn grunted. "Have fun with that. I'm going home."

Rune stifled a humorless laugh. All around them, he sensed the force of the crashing rocks. The earth quivered, surrendering. "If you have a home left."

Neither one of them could run, relegated to hobbling down the mine shaft on legs as shaky as the ground beneath them.

"This must be it." Vahn turned to follow a branch in the tracks.

Rune followed at his heels, watching the rails beside his feet. It struck him as odd to see the rails here so soon after he'd recommended them. Even in a place as sheltered as Core, the advancements of the modern world had taken root so swiftly, it seemed as if the people had never been without them.

Then again, he'd been a part of it. Even when he'd walked these halls and called them home, Core's libraries had been home to books of mechanical schematics. They'd hosted the lifts and the waterwheel that powered them. Why not tracks, too?

He paused for a heartbeat, staring at the tracks. "The Alda'anan."

Vahn turned back. "What?"

"The Alda'anan built all of this. The inverted tower, the tunnels and lifts. The ruins to keep everyone out—they meant them to keep everyone else safe while they developed this, didn't they?"

"Now's not a good time to be thinking like a scholar." Vahn shook his head and put a little more energy into his step. "We're almost there."

Rune lifted his head. The Gate was there, glowing daylight at the end of the tunnel. For a single instant, he felt a wash of relief.

Then the ceiling opened up before them and a streak of white filled his vision.

Envesi jerked upright like a puppet on strings, twitching and shuddering. Around her, the tattered and dirty white robes of a Master mage swirled like cobwebs. Her eyes burned black and a wicked scowl twisted her face beyond recognition.

"You walk their halls, you know their ways. Now you speak their name." She slid forward, her snowy hair twisting around her shoulders like snakes. "Alda'anan. *Elder Ones*. People of magic. Keepers of secrets they never deigned to share. But you know their secrets, don't you? You wear their silver in your tongue."

Rune took his sword in both hands. She was breathing hard, moving slow, just as bruised and exhausted as they were. If ever there would be an even match between them, it was now.

Her eyes drifted to his sword. Her lip curled and her fingers closed on air. Ice crackled around her hand, forming a long, curving blade.

This time, at long last, he moved first.

He swept forward in one of the graceful forms he'd learned from Garam, the tip of his kingsword whistling against the stone as his blade drew up to meet her.

Envesi's sword of ice shattered and reformed in the blink of an eye. She twisted back, twirling in a sideways slash that missed him by a hair's breadth and broke her blade against the wall.

As if that were a cue, the tremors increased.

"For the love of Brant," Vahn spat, lunging forward. He struck Envesi full force, toppled her to the ground and wrestled her hands to the floor. "Go!"

Rune's eyes flashed to the gap in the ceiling, where the first pebbles began to fall through. "Vahn—"

"We're out of time! Get out of here and close the Gate!"

Rune hesitated.

"Go!" Vahn roared. He slipped a dagger from his boot.

Envesi twisted one hand from his grasp and lashed out. She knocked the dagger from his hand and raked claws across his face.

Screaming, Vahn fell back and clapped a hand over his eye as blood poured from beneath his fingers.

Rune snatched the dagger from the floor, seized Envesi's arm and dragged her sideways, away from Vahn. She writhed in his grasp. The claws of her free hand pierced his leg and dug deep.

Choking back a cry of pain, he threw her against the tracks and drove the dagger through her hand, pinning her to the wooden rails.

Envesi's shriek shook him to the bone. Raw power crackled in the air and made his skin crawl. Shuddering, he snatched his sword from the floor and turned to haul Vahn to his feet. "We're almost there."

Vahn groaned but stood, letting Rune pull him forward. He stumbled and turned his head to squint at Rune's bloodied leg through his good eye. Then he shifted, caught Rune's arm and dragged it over his shoulder to lend support.

Together, they ran.

"We have to close that Gate," Vahn panted, nodding at the portal ahead. "No chance for her or anything else to come through."

It took a dozen Master mages hours to stabilize the power from a Gate-stone in order to close a permanent Gate. With Rhyllyn, there had been a possibility, but now... Rune shook his head. "I'm not strong enough."

"You have to be," Vahn said.

"Easier said than—" Something caught his ankle and Rune went down hard. The kingsword skittered across the floor, slipped through the Gate and came to a rest in the worn grass on the other side. Talons burrowed into his flesh and dragged him back into the mine.

"Ran!" Vahn caught his arm.

"You know them. You know their secrets." Envesi pulled

harder. "Tell me, how many mages does it take? What must be done to reverse the corruption? Tell me!"

Rune wanted to curse her, but when he turned to look back at her, the words didn't come.

Tears flowed from her ice-blue eyes and left pale trails down her dirty face. She clawed his leg with both hands, her face wild with madness, her eyes lit with a single hint of hope.

She'd pursued him for that. From the palace of Ilmenhith to the bowels of the earth, chancing the collapse in hopes of finding that answer. A single shred of information, given so freely to him but denied to her by every Alda'anan she'd spoken to—a slight they'd answered for with their lives.

In spite of everything, he laughed. "You can't," he said. "The corruption can't be changed. This is it. We're monsters until the end of days."

Her hands went slack. "No."

Vahn jerked him backwards and they spilled out onto the ground on the other side of the Gate.

"No!" Envesi howled. She lashed out with everything she had left. Power poured through the portal ahead of her as she clawed her way toward the Gate.

Rune lifted himself to his elbows. His eyes darted to the clear gem embedded in the stone archway, the source of the Gate's power, then fell to the kingsword in the grass.

Vahn followed his gaze. "Wait."

Rune took the blade in both hands and leaped to his feet, ignoring the pain in his legs.

"Wait!" Vahn shouted.

With every ounce of strength left in his body, Rune drove the sword forward.

The tip struck the Gate-stone and sizzling streaks of wild magic shot forth as the indestructible kingsword cracked the gem.

Envesi's shrieks echoed in his ears as the magic surged.

Wild torrents of energy flowed up the blade and Rune bore

down on it harder. The stone shattered and all its power was unleashed. A pillar of pure white magic lanced into the sky as the Gate collapsed.

Light filled his vision. Heat and agony flooded his senses and tore a scream from his throat. Magic seared his flesh until he couldn't feel, his voice fading with the last of the air scoured from his lungs.

The chaos burned until nothing was left, and only light remained.

2 5

AWAKENING

QUIET VOICES FILTERED IN FROM SOMEWHERE. GENTLE LAUGHTER, happy tones, things he hadn't heard for too long.

A soft, red glow filled his vision and Rune stared at it for a while before he realized it was light through his eyelids. He watched it for some time before he found his eyes wouldn't open. Everything felt distant, hazy, as if he were floating.

He was not floating. Soft bedding moved against his skin when he lifted a hand to rake his fingers through his hair.

His hair, too, was soft. After the grit and dust that choked the air and clung to his sweating skin in the underground, it felt foreign. Too soft, too defined. He rolled a strand between his fingers and his brow furrowed.

His eyes opened.

The arm above his face was not his own.

He jerked his hand back, suddenly wide awake. That was not his hand, either.

Except it was. Five fingers flexed when he tried to move them. The smooth bronze flesh grew pale over his bent knuckles. He reached for it with his other hand, startled to see it looked the same.

307

Sitting bolt upright, Rune flipped the blankets off his naked body and looked down at himself.

His legs were smooth, the same tanned color as the rest of him. His eyes flashed back to his hands and, tentatively, he put them together.

He felt it. *Felt* it. The smooth surface of human flesh greeted his fingertips, marred only by the strange scar that remained in his left hand.

Laughter came closer with the sound of footsteps. Edagan swept in through the open door and stopped dead in her tracks when she saw him.

Rune met her eyes, his hands still spread before him. "Am I dead?"

Pure indignation filled the old mage's face. "Mind your tongue, boy! I'm not that old. And cover yourself, for Brant's sake!"

Suddenly self-conscious, he drew the blanket back across his hips.

"Well, that answers that," Edagan called back through the door. She turned and left as soon as she'd come.

Swallowing hard, Rune made himself look around.

He was home.

Not in the loft of the manor, but in one of the guest rooms. Late-morning sunlight filled the room, the air laden with the warm smell of baking bread. He listened to the muted sounds of people talking for a time before his eyes drifted back to his hands.

They were his hands. The scar still present in the left one convinced him of that, though the fact they were connected to the rest of him should have registered sooner. He flexed his fingers again and marveled at the way they moved before he studied the rest of his arm.

There were no marks at his elbow, no more irritated skin where scales emerged, no sign that scales had ever been. Just a light dusting of hair across the top of his forearm and skin so beautifully translucent he could see the blue veins in his wrist. He cradled his right hand with the left and traced their path with his thumb. It was warm, smooth, and his pulse throbbed faintly beneath his touch. His chest tightened until it hurt to breathe. He bowed his head and covered his mouth.

"We found you that way." Firal pushed the door until it almost closed behind her. She lingered beside it. "Not naked, but..." She shrugged and paced closer.

Rune pulled the blankets a little farther, covered a few more inches of thigh and stomach.

She sat on the edge of the bed, looking at his hands. "It was the day before yesterday. Vicamros wanted you in the Royal City, but we thought it best we have you somewhere more comfortable. Until this morning, you were so still, I... I wasn't certain you would wake up."

Her fingers stroked his forearm, sending an unreasonable thrill up his spine. Then, shuddering, Rune closed his eyes against welling tears.

Firal leaned close and wrapped her arms around him. He fell against her and buried his face in her shoulder as the quiet sobs stole his breath.

She hushed him, stroking the nape of his neck and rocking him gently until the emotion passed.

"I didn't think I'd see you again," he whispered, curling his fingers in the blankets, not daring to touch her but unable to make himself move.

"And you shouldn't have, fool man." Firal shrugged him away, though she offered a handkerchief from the pockets of her skirts. "If any of you had any sense at all, you would've come right back from that prison and left that woman be."

Rune swallowed, ignoring the handkerchief and drying his face with the heel of his palm. His cheeks were so unreasonably soft, sprinkled with a hint of prickling roughness where his sparse beard shadowed his jaw. "What about Vahn's eye?"

Her face transformed into an unreadable mask and she turned away.

A chill settled in the pit of his stomach. "What?"

"He wasn't with you," she said quietly, folding her hands in her lap. "You were alone when we found you. When the pillar of light receded."

He shook his head, his brow knit. "That can't be. He was behind me. Even then, the magic went through me, it didn't..."

"There was no one else there," Firal said. "I had just reached Lore when the light faded."

"Lore? You should have been in the Royal City, why were you in Lore?"

"I was part of the evacuation team. Lore was our landing point because so many of the island mages were familiar with it." She paused and licked her lips. "We saved as many as we could, but we had to stop eventually. There was nothing more we could do."

"Saved them?" He struggled to wrap his mind around the words.

Firal searched his eyes with an almost pitying look. "From the collapse. Edagan warned us. She insisted we try to evacuate the island. Now the ruins of Ilmenhith rest beneath the waves. Elenhiise... or most of it... is gone."

He stared back at her in silence. He'd known the ruins would be lost, the tunnels around Core so numerous there was no way the labyrinth would escape collapse. But to think of the whole island caving in...

Rune pushed the blankets back and slid to the edge of the bed.

"What are you doing?" Firal caught him by the shoulders and pushed him back.

"Going to that hill." Vahn had been right beside him, safe on the right side of the Gate. All the wild magic of the Gate-stone had channeled through Rune by means of his sword. They had to have missed something. Some indication of where he'd gone, tracks or a trail of blood or something. Perhaps Vahn had gone for help when the Gate-stone shattered. No one in their right mind would have let the man walk around with his eye bleeding. He had to be holed up in Lore somewhere, recovering.

Shoving her hands away, Rune stood and immediately lost his balance, stumbling backwards until Firal caught his arms and helped steady him.

"Stupid, stubborn man," she growled.

Rune looked down at his feet and adjusted his posture, gripping Firal's forearms for support. The textured wood felt strange against the soles of his feet, but stranger was the pressure on his heel. Muscles in his legs pulled taut. Tendons in his ankles and the backs of his knees stretched uncomfortably. There was no mistaking that he was alive now. He doubted that sort of pain existed after death.

"You need to take it slow." Firal relaxed her hold on him, then shifted back to create a little space between them and force him to stop leaning on her. "You've been through a great deal. You shouldn't be out of bed at all."

He blinked at her twice before his brow furrowed. "You're taller."

She arched one eyebrow. "You're shorter."

Startled, he looked down at himself. Both his feet were flat on the floor. He raised himself to the balls of his feet, the ache in his legs subsiding as he returned to the posture he'd had his whole life. Then he sank back, feet flat once more, and met her eye. "I'm shorter."

Firal cleared her throat. "You're also naked."

Rune pulled his hands back and teetered a moment before he found his balance on his own. "Nothing you haven't seen before." Then he paused, looking at his hands. "Though some of it's quite new to me."

She chanced a glance downward and a smile slowly cracked her features.

Unable to help himself, he laughed, and his heart swelled

when her sweet voice joined in.

Rune wiped his eyes with the side of his thumb, sighed, and studied the way the moisture glistened on his skin. "Clothes. I need them. Help me."

She spun away and caught her bottom lip with her teeth. "Of course. All your things will be upstairs, won't they?" She picked up her skirts and hurried out the door. "Rhyllyn! Come help me!"

He watched her leave, then sank onto the bed again. He pulled the blankets over his lap and stared at his feet. Aside from the times he'd bound his clawed toes and stuffed them into oversized boots as part of his youth's disguises, he'd never worn shoes. He couldn't very well head for Lore barefooted and barely able to stand.

The thought of Lore made Rune's throat tighten. His heart was broken and bursting all at once. The mix of emotion made him sick. He'd woken to a dream and a nightmare at the same time, everything he'd ever wanted at his fingertips, everything he'd known—his home, his reality, his dearest friend—torn away at the same instant. Elation and agony warred within him, sobering him.

"Rune?"

His head jerked up. Rhyllyn stood in the doorway, clean clothing folded over his arm.

"Come in." Rune beckoned him nearer, then repeated the gesture more slowly, watching the way his fingers moved. He couldn't get the last two to move independently of each other. When his smallest finger bent, his ring finger did, too. He stared at them and struggled to make them work as he knew they should.

"What's wrong?" Rhyllyn padded in and dropped the clothing on the foot of the bed.

"Is it always this hard to move a fifth finger? I've never had one before."

Rhyllyn stifled a nervous laugh. "It's the ring finger, not the little finger. The ring finger is the weak one. It does what the two beside it do."

Rune squinted and tried again. "Oh."

"Don't worry," Rhyllyn said, "you'll get used to it."

"Do you miss it?" Rune drew the shirt into his hands, rubbing his thumbs over the fine gray material. He'd always thought silk soft. He'd only ever judged by how things felt when rubbed against his face—an attempt hindered if he hadn't shaved, sparse as his beard may be—or his upper arm. Between his uncalloused fingers now, it was strangely rough.

"What, five fingers?" His brother laughed. "It might make playing my instruments a bit easier, but other than that, it doesn't make a difference. I'll let you get dressed. You should come downstairs when you can. Everyone will be happy to see you."

"Who all is here?" Rune pulled on his shirt, smoothed the front and then reached for the pants. Those were gray as well. Rhyllyn must have chosen them. Firal would have put him in colors.

"A lot of people. Garam was here, but went back to the Royal City to check on Sera. They sent word to Umdal, but it will take a few days for Stal to return." Rhyllyn shrugged. "A lot of the Kirban mages are here. Firal, of course, and... her daughter. Lulu seems to have taken a liking to me. Captain Straes is here. Alira is playing hostess and a woman named Minna is helping. She said her son is in council with Vicamros about the fate of their people."

"A lot of visitors," Rune said. "You should have put me upstairs. The manor's big, but there aren't that many guest rooms."

Rhyllyn frowned. "Take you upstairs? Do you have any idea how much you weigh? Captain Straes, Garam and I could barely get you up here. There was no way we were making it to the loft."

"Who undressed me?"

"One of the mages, I suppose. All we did was dump you in bed. They chased us out, saying they needed to be sure you weren't in need of healing. They said we'd get in the way." Rhyllyn clearly resented the suggestion. Of all his abilities, healing was one of the most developed. It made sense, Rune thought; it meshed with the boy's compassionate nature.

"Sounds like all I needed was a bit of rest. Though I could go for some food now. I'm starving." Rune's stomach growled its agreement. He turned away. "Let me get dressed, but stay close. I don't think I can walk."

"You'll get used to that, too," Rhyllyn said. He slipped into the hallway and shut the door.

Rune finished clothing himself, stood unsteadily and gave his pants a quick appraisal before he sat down again and cuffed the bottom of each pant leg. He'd had most of his pants made long enough to cover his clawed heel and just brush his toes. Now every pair made that way would be too long.

Using the bedpost for support, he stood again. "How did you ever walk on feet like this?" he called.

"I didn't know any better," Rhyllyn replied through the door. "I thought the same thing about you when I changed."

"Seems like you went in the easier direction. Just standing hurts. Makes me feel like someone's trying to pull my legs off, with how it stretches. Come here."

"Maybe the mages will have some suggestions for that. You might want to rest for a few days while you're getting used to it, though." Rhyllyn returned and offered his arm.

Rune didn't like it, but he accepted the help without complaint. He'd asked for it, after all. Complaining when it was given would have been unreasonable. "No time for that. Get me downstairs. I need to get to Lore."

"You need to get to a cobbler before anything else. Not even a street urchin like me went barefoot." Rhyllyn guided him down the hallway, murmuring instructions as they walked.

Rune stayed silent, watching his toes as he followed his

brother's directions. Land on his heel, not his toes, roll forward from there. He repeated each motion with care, struggling to retrain himself. It felt strange, and counterintuitive, besides. It made much more sense to land on his toes—though they weren't as springy as they'd been when they were elongated and clawed —and sink back from there. Walking as a normal man was clunky, noisy, and graceless. "I'm going to have to learn to dance all over again," Rune grumbled.

Rhyllyn laughed. "Oh, is that high on your list of concerns?"

"A man's allowed a few guilty pleasures." Rune paused at the top of the stairs.

Rhyllyn descended a few steps before him. "All right, here's where you will want to walk like you were trying to. Toe down, then sink down. Stop trying to put all your weight on your heel, the rest of your foot's there for a reason. You'll balance better if you use it. No, not like that, you'll roll your ankle. There, perfect. Keep doing that."

Rune had a better sense of himself by the time they made it to the floor. He straightened and let go of Rhyllyn's arm, though he appreciated that the boy stayed close with his hand hovering under Rune's elbow.

The cheerful conversation in the sitting room quieted when he came around the corner.

Rhyllyn hadn't exaggerated; the house was crowded. Every chair and couch held mages, some of them familiar, some faces he wasn't sure he'd ever seen. Ordin Straes stood beside Temar now, instead of Firal, both their expressions sober when they looked at him.

"Well, come in, boy," Edagan said. "Let them get a look at you. Goodness knows I've seen more than enough already."

Rikka giggled and turned away. Kytenia elbowed her in the ribs and stood.

"Where's Firal?" Rune skimmed the faces of those gathered before he returned his attention to the Archmage.

Former Archmage, he corrected himself. If the temple was

gone, there was nothing left for her to lead. He wasn't sure he believed that, either. Elenhiise was an island of reasonable size. It couldn't have just fallen into the sea.

"In the kitchen with Minna," Kytenia said. "They're kneading bread, I believe." She paced closer, barely looking at his new fingers and toes. She focused on his eyes instead. "Has your vision changed?"

"I don't think so." He glanced past her to study the hanging baskets at the edges of the railed room. "Or not much, at least. It's a little brighter, maybe. The light seems more intense."

She nodded. "I'm not surprised. I think your pupils were more effective as slits."

"My eyes are different?" He locked on to her face, startled. His vision focused the same. Colors looked the same. Only the brightness seemed different.

"Yes." She smiled. "Odd, they appear darker now. So much more color showed before."

Rune forced a smile in return. "I suppose I had to have one appealing quality."

Kytenia laughed and lightly slapped his chest. "Oh, hush. You've always had a face to make the ladies swoon. I would know, me and half the temple fawned over it. Would you like to sit down?"

"In the kitchen," he replied. "I need to eat. Then I need someone to open a Gate to Lore for me. I don't think I'm strong enough to manage one on my own yet."

Or maybe at all. He hadn't even stopped to think about the seal on his power. Was it gone, too? He was so weary he could barely feel the magic riding the air currents around him.

"No one is helping you go anywhere," Alira protested. "Not after the headache you gave us. You're staying here and recovering."

"Then you won't deny me food." Rune gave her a hard look

before he moved on. The hallway was easier to navigate on his own. The rail along the open wall of the sitting room provided all the help he needed.

Rhyllyn had returned to the kitchen ahead of him. He was at the counter when Rune reached the door, already back to work.

Wiping her hands on a rag, Minna turned to greet him with happy tears in her eyes. "Come, sit. Sit! Two days with naught but water poured down your throat and I'd bet you're starving. And after all you've been through!" She clicked her tongue, herded Rune to the small kitchen table and pushed him into a chair.

"It's good to see you, too, Minna. I heard all of Core had been abandoned, but I didn't believe it until I saw it myself." Rune closed his eyes and leaned against the table as weariness swept over him. Food, then a Gate to Lore. Exhausted or not, he couldn't afford to wait. Any signs he could track were at risk of vanishing under wind, rain, or the footsteps of passers-by.

"Aye, and a good thing we moved when we did." She patted his cheek, then hurried to the pantry. "Rhyllyn, be a good boy and fetch a good stout drink from the cellar."

Rhyllyn gave her a dubious frown. "I don't think he should—"

"Oh, hush. Nothing gets a weakened fellow back on his feet faster than a good shot of spirits with his supper." Minna deposited an armful of food on the table and fetched dishes to go with them. She cut slices of bread and wedges of cheese, arranged them on the plate and added slivers of fruit and a thick slab of smoked ham.

"He should have broth," Alira said from the doorway. "Nothing more."

Minna scoffed. "You want to starve the poor man?"

"I want to keep him from vomiting everywhere when you foolishly hand him a bottle." Alira scowled at Rhyllyn, fresh back from the cellar with a bottle of amber liquid in hand.

"I'm tired, not ill," Rune said around a mouthful of food. "But I wouldn't mind something else to drink, as well."

"I'll pull up some fresh water," Minna said with a smile. "Miss Firal just took the little one out to the yard for some fresh air. I'll let them know you're up and about while I'm out there."

"She knows." Firal knew he'd need something to eat, too. Rune tried not to think anything of it. After everything they'd been through, he didn't blame her for wanting to avoid him. If Elenhiise *was* destroyed—a possibility he didn't want to think about—avoiding him in future days might be harder.

"Oh. Of course." Minna's cheer never faltered. She bobbed her head in a polite near-curtsy, then hurried out the back door.

Alira huffed. "Fine. I'll give you a few minutes to eat, then we'll see you back upstairs. You're not doing anything until we've had a chance to inspect you and be sure it's safe."

Until they'd had a chance to study him and try to determine what happened, she meant. Rune shot her a knowing look.

Alira huffed again and turned to leave.

Rhyllyn glanced after her once, then put the whiskey on the table without any fuss. "Do you really intend to go to Lore after this?"

"I'd be there already if I thought I could manage," Rune said between mouthfuls of food. "But I need to get back my strength. I can hardly stand."

"I can send word to Garam, if you want. He'd probably be happy to join you out there, but I don't know how soon he could come."

Rune shook his head and uncorked the whiskey. "I can't wait." He took a swig straight from the bottle and winced at the burn. He stoppered the bottle and pushed it back across the table. "Minna was right, that'll put a fire right back in me. Put that in the pantry, would you?"

Rhyllyn picked it up. "Not the cellar?"

"Might want it when I'm back from Lore." No matter what Rune found, he didn't think it would be good.

Minna returned with a pail of fresh water and filled a cup for Rune before she rejoined Rhyllyn at the counter. The two of them chatted pleasantly about spices and cooking methods until Rune cleaned his plate.

He wiped his fingers on a napkin and levered himself up from the table. "Are you coming?"

Startled, Rhyllyn picked up a rag to clean his hands. "Yes. Give me a moment to clean up. I'll be right there."

Rune drained the last of the water from his cup. That had helped. Already he felt a shade stronger, if no less tired. This time, when he entered the parlor, the mages didn't stop to gawk.

"Gate me to Lore," he ordered none of them in particular.

Indignant, Alira turned in her chair. "Have you already forgotten what I just said?"

Kytenia was a little more gentle. "After everything that happened, I think it's best if you stay here and rest a while."

"Oh, let him go," Edagan said with a sniff. "He'll have to see it sooner or later."

The other mages looked away, abashed.

Rune hesitated. "See what?"

"Balen, help me." Edagan rose and waved a few seemingly random mages to her side. "Alira, you'll need to Gate him back here. Pick a few to go through and aid you."

Kytenia and Rikka stood without prompting.

"Fine." Alira heaved a sigh and beckoned a few others. "If that's what it takes to get him to follow orders, I suppose we'll make do."

"The closest we can get you is a point on the shore." Edagan tied herself to her mages, knotted their power together and began a Gate. "It's a fair bit closer than the college, but you'll still have to walk."

"I know some shortcuts up the cliff," Rhyllyn said as he positioned himself at Rune's side. "I'll get them up there."

Alira, Kytenia and the others gathered at Rune's back, ready to slip through the Gate behind him. The portal sizzled and hissed as it split the air and opened onto one of Lore's rocky beaches just below the cliff where the permanent Gate stood.

Rune's eyes narrowed as he watched them work. It was a good thing they'd agreed to help. He was so weakened he could hardly feel the way they worked the flows. He couldn't imagine trying to do it himself in this condition, whether or not he had Rhyllyn's assistance.

"There," Edagan said as the Gate stabilized. "Keep together. Shortcut or not, I don't expect we'll see you for several hours. If you're not back by nightfall, I'll send someone to retrieve you."

Keeping Rhyllyn's instructions for walking in mind, Rune led the way.

Pins and needles coursed over his body as he moved through the Gate. He would have shuddered, if not for the distraction of his feet on the ground.

Sand tickled between his toes. Warm and pleasant as it was, not all the terrain would be. He should have checked the spare rooms to see if any of the guest wardrobes contained shoes that might fit.

"This way," Rhyllyn said, and the group started off.

No one offered Rune any assistance until they reached one of the winding trails that cut up not up the cliff, but the hill beside it at the far end of the coastal town. Halfway up they found Rhyllyn's shortcut, a set of steep, jagged and uneven steps carved into the stone.

Already Rune's tender new skin was raw, his feet and legs both aching and burning with fatigue. Even the grass at the top of the cliff was rough and cutting enough to make him regret this trip as much as possible.

Rhyllyn trotted up the swell ahead of them. "Here," he called back. "This is where we found you."

Kytenia and Rikka each took one of Rune's arms and aided him up the hill. As they walked, he watched the ground for signs Vahn might have found the cliffside trail. When they reached the top of the hill, he stopped.

Rune stared for the span of a few heartbeats, and his pulse accelerated. He pulled away from the mages and pushed past Rhyllyn at the edge.

Before him, a wide circle surrounded the ruins of the Gate. Charred earth spread twenty paces from the column in any direction.

Staring at the heap of black stone in the center, Rune took a step.

He expected ash and soot under his blistered feet. Instead it was sun-warm, hard and glass-smooth. Its surface bore no tracks, could hold none. There were no marks showing where he'd been or where the mages walked to retrieve him, nothing to indicate how many countless spectators had climbed the cliff to see the place. And in the middle of it all stood a pillar of blackened, glossy stone, his kingsword fused into it as surely as smelted steel.

The mages lined the edge of the circle behind him, waiting in silence as he limped across the scarred earth to wrap a hand around the hilt of his sword.

Rune didn't bother trying to shift it. Instead he tried to recall where they'd been when the sword split the Gate-stone and unleashed the wild fury that could do such a thing. He turned back, looking at the ground where Vahn had lain and begged him to wait. A place near the heart of the ring, where that power had burned through him in the blink of an eye.

The mages hadn't looked for Vahn. Now Rune understood why.

His fingertips left the familiar grip of his sword's hilt as he sank to his knees, still staring at that empty space on the blackened earth.

No one could have survived something powerful enough to melt a Gate onto an indestructible kingsword.

Yet, for some reason, he had.

His hands dug at the unmoving glass, his teeth clenched and

his eyes screwed shut. Neither prevented the tears of pure defeat.

"It should have been me," Rune choked when gentle arms encircled his shoulders. "Not him. It was supposed to be me."

"You know he'd say the same of you," Kytenia whispered.

Her words offered no respite from the deep ache in his chest.

ONE LAST DUTY

DESPITE EVERYTHING, A BLUE BANNER BEARING ILMENHITH'S CREST still rose above the city. The wet cloth flapped from the peak of a tower, crooked and mostly ruined, but standing above the sea. High waves covered it when the tide came in, as they covered the rest of the city, but the symbol remained.

Firal kept her head high as the men rowed their small craft closer, though her throat was so thick she could scarcely breathe, and unshed tears pricked her eyes.

Here and there, remnants of buildings stood above the rest of the city, though the murky sea water hid most. The silt hadn't yet settled, though the men steering the vessel chatted amongst themselves about what the place might look like in years to come.

Elenhiise resembled an atoll now. The outermost edges of the island remained, including some sandy stretches near Ilmenhith's ruined harbor, but the collapse of Core had swallowed most of the rest. A dark blue ring of ocean held the underground city and the ruins that had stood above it, the water there so deep it chilled her to think of it. The temple was down there, too. And, she supposed, the body of her mother.

Sniffing, Firal turned back to watch one of the sailors climb the tower and cut the flag loose. He draped it around his neck and tucked the ends under his arms to keep it in place, then returned to the water to swim back to the boat.

As the sea had swallowed the island, the surrounding reef would eventually swallow its ruins. With time, the reef would gather sand and draw the island back to the surface. As it was, most of the land was scarcely more than ten feet underwater. Shallow enough that when the water cleared, some of the ruined buildings and landmarks would be visible from a boat like theirs, yet still deep enough to mean every person who'd left the island would never return home.

"Do you regret coming to see it?" Firal asked, watching the sailor paddle back and scale the side of the boat with the aid of a companion.

"Do you?" Rune sounded calm and unshaken. She knew without looking that his face was just as placid. He'd been that way since he'd returned from Lore. She had worried how he would react to the consequences of his actions, recalling the determination and passion she knew so well. Instead, aside from the quiet moment they'd shared in his room when he awoke, she'd seen little emotion out of him at all. Perhaps the magic had burned that out of him too, right alongside the corruption that had marred his body.

Silently chiding herself for that thought, she made herself face him. He wasn't immune to the troubles they faced. What she saw from him was simply an unexpected reaction. Resignation and acceptance instead of anger.

He met her eye and for a moment, the air between them was burdened by the silence.

He looked away. "There's your memento."

The sailor unslung the flag from around his neck and wrung the sea water out of it before he presented it to Firal.

She smiled as graciously as she could as she took it from his hands. "I suppose that's all for us to do here, isn't it? Let's go back. Thank you, everyone, for your help."

The sailors manning their vessel nodded. Some men murmured responses she didn't hear, then returned to their work. They took to the oars and navigated expertly back to the larger ship waiting just off the coast of the island's remains.

Little vessels with shallow keels dotted the waters over the island. Men and women dove to recover belongings from the ruins or hunt for things they thought they could sell. The large ship they cut toward was one of several. Scavengers had come from all directions as soon as the sea had calmed.

Rune quietly thanked the men as they pulled up alongside the ship. He guarded the bottom of the questionable rope ladder as Firal clambered to the ship's deck. Then he followed. He reached the deck behind her as she called for the mages to return them to the mainland. Waiting for their answer, she looked out across her demolished home one last time.

"I don't think I was ready to see this," she remarked softly, clutching the flag in both hands.

"I don't think we'd ever be ready," Rune replied. He'd insisted they go, sooner rather than later, and—like she had when he'd asked to see Lore—Edagan urged the mages to oblige.

She'd urged Firal to join him, too. Kytenia had voiced some frustration about the matter, but she and most of the other Elenhiise mages had chosen to stay behind. With the way her heart broke when she saw what was left of her kingdom, Firal regretted allowing herself to be pushed into it.

"You're taking it well," Firal said.

He shrugged, never looking her way. His eyes were distant, almost cold. "I have to. Nothing I can do would change it."

She quieted and gazed out at the sea. She motioned toward the water after a time. "You don't care to dive for anything?"

Rune smothered a laugh and ducked his head. "Ah, no."

Firal raised a brow. "What?"

"To be honest," he said with a chagrined smile, "I don't know how to swim."

She cocked her head to the side. "Can't you?"

"No, and this is all the more time I hope I ever spend on a ship. I'm not fond of deep water, or sailing." He gestured to the white-robed mages that appeared from the ship's hold. "Let's return to dry land, shall we?"

"Of course." Firal sighed, folded the wet flag on itself and moved to join the mages. She wanted nothing more than to take her lost kingdom's banner somewhere and hang it to dry, then sit and rest with Lulu. The girl was back at Rune's manor—the safest place for the child, it seemed—but though the morning had been mentally exhausting, the day wasn't over yet.

"I FEAR this is the last time we will meet in council as equals," Vicamros said, though there was little apology in his tone.

Firal made herself smile. The meeting was small. Aside from the two of them, only Rune, Garam, and the friendly Redoram Parthanus were in attendance. No one else was necessary. There was no business to conclude, and the three of them were only present to serve as witnesses. Or spectators, she thought glumly.

"It's hard to be anything else, when there's no longer an Elenhiise for me to rule." She managed to keep her voice level, though her heart rebelled. She wanted to cry again, but at the same time, some tiny, bitter part of herself was glad she didn't have to suffer alone. Elenhiise held two kingdoms, after all, though neither was named. Both had fallen into the sea, leaving her and the young king of Alwhen without countries to lead. She didn't know what had become of Mathen, but if he lived, he shared her fate.

"The situation is a blow to both of us, believe me." Vicamros scratched his beard and frowned at the surface of the table before him. "But all things must end, and we will find new ways to manage. House Kaith stands to become a great power in the southern trade kingdoms."

"Not as ideal as the harbor in Elenhiise, I'm sure," Firal said. "But they have a strong economy. I am sure they will be valuable allies to you."

"Yes, and I intend to speak to the mages of Umdal about establishing permanent Gates to keep our economy thriving. We'll need to import a great deal while settling the Elenhiise refugees." Vicamros cast a sidewise glance at Redoram, who nodded.

"You mean to keep them in the Triad, then?" She was relieved, but she hadn't expected anything else. Bodies were the clockwork of a kingdom. So long as they integrated well and found new ways to support themselves, there was no reason for any ruler to scorn them.

"I do. Large parts of Aldaan remain uninhabited, and therefore unused. I mean to settle a large portion of them there. The country holds good land, filled with ore-rich mountains and good terrain for vineyards and orchards. A shame to let it go to waste."

"Well, I'm sure they'll be glad for the opportunity to start a new life." Again she forced herself to smile.

"As I suppose you are to do, as well." Vicamros hesitated.

Garam cleared his throat. "May I speak, Your Majesty?"

The king granted permission with a flick of his fingers, the way he always did.

"As you've said, there's a great deal of land in Aldaan that is currently unused. With the lady's expertise, it may be in your best interest to grant her a parcel and allow her to oversee the settling of her people."

Vicamros nodded in slow consideration. "What say you, Firal? Have you any desire to take a position beneath my banner? A baroness, perhaps, with holdings of your own?"

The title would make her nobility, but barely. Still, it was more than she expected. It was a relief to be trusted, but she'd played the games of royalty long enough to know she still had to tread carefully. Vicamros owed her nothing. If she accepted his offer, she'd owe him everything.

"It would be an excellent way to aid my people in establishing a new life, as Lord Kaith said." She rubbed her hands in a feeble effort to restore warmth. She'd felt cold for days, but it was a cold of spirit, not body. As if all her fire had been drained. "But while I want what is best for my people, I know they are in your capable hands. I'm afraid I must have time to think about it, Your Majesty. My family and I have been through a great deal. Will you give me time to consider?"

"Of course." Vicamros straightened, evidently pleased by her reluctance. "It will be several weeks before the refugees are organized and dispatched to their new residencies. I will expect an answer no sooner than when the first family departs for Aldaan."

"Thank you, Your Majesty," Firal murmured. "You are most gracious."

"No matter which direction you choose to go, know that you are always welcome in the Triad." The king sat back, giving tacit dismissal.

Firal nodded, then rose.

Beside her, Rune stood as well.

Vicamros cleared his throat. "You may see her off if you wish, but don't forget your obligations today."

Rune said nothing, but bowed in response and turned to escort Firal from the council chamber. They walked the halls in silence for a time before she spoke.

"I'll return to your estate and gather my things. I appreciate your hospitality. After the way I've treated you the past several weeks, I know I haven't deserved it."

He stifled a chuckle. "If I made all my judgments based on the way people behave under duress, I'd have no friends. I have few of them, as it is."

"Well, those you do have are dedicated." Firal gave him a nervous, fleeting smile. She didn't pretend to understand why he'd offered her refuge, but she was grateful for it. That he'd survived the ordeal made things easier. Her heart was still raw with loss and troubled by unresolved anger, but there was also the blessing of relief that came from seeing him awake and aware after all was said and done. She'd come so dangerously close to losing them both.

Firal cleared her throat and went on. "I'm not thrilled by the idea of controlling a barony and entangling myself in more politics, but my choices are slim. I'll try to decide where Lulu and I are to go soon, so you can return to the life you had before all these disruptions."

Rune drew his tongue over his lips and hesitated. When he finally spoke, he stared straight ahead. "You might consider staying there. At my estate. It's a large property, a furnished house. You'll find I'm not there often. Until you decide what you want to do, you're welcome to stay."

Sweet relief filled her chest. Until that moment, Firal hadn't realized she'd hoped he would let her stay. "I don't want to be a bother."

"It'd be more of a bother to have you off tending a barony in Aldaan," Rune said. "It's hard to ensure you're safe if you're in a whole different part of the Triad."

She arched a brow. "Are you so concerned with my safety?"

His eyes fell to the patterned stone floor in front of his feet. "Even if I weren't, I did make a promise."

Her amusement faded.

"In any event," Rune continued, "you're free to make yourself comfortable at the manor. I'd accompany you, but as Vicamros said, I have obligations."

"What do you have to do?" She stopped outside the mages' parlor.

"Mage business." He shrugged. "Political matters. I'm still a part of the king's council, so my presence is expected. This should be the last thing to tend before all this is over, though. Go on. I'll be home soon."

She hoped he was.

———

CALM AND SERENE were the farthest things from what Kytenia felt, but she kept her feelings close and guarded them fiercely.

Kingdoms had risen and fallen before. Life ran in a grand cycle, events repeating themselves, like a snake biting its own tail. None knew that better than the man at her side.

Grateful as she was to have Rune along for this duty, she couldn't help feeling it was too soon for him to be involved. He'd regained control of his body beautifully, though there was a hint of discomfort in the way he walked. His shoes were ill-fitting, too large and yet too narrow, lending him an uneasy gait. She didn't know where he'd found them, but she suspected they were the first pair he'd come across when they'd returned to the manor after leaving Lore.

He'd spent the night before in private, leaving the rest of them to their own devices. Looking back, Kytenia wished she'd followed his lead. Knowing what she had to do, extra time to prepare herself for it would have been wise. Instead she'd spent the evening enjoying the company of the few mages she knew she could trust completely, pretending the day wouldn't come.

The Grand College was all but empty. The few faces she did see belonged to cleaning staff and pages rather than magelings or Masters. Magic tingled on the edge of her awareness now and then, but only fleeting impressions. Whatever mages remained in the college, they feared interlopers. For good reason, she thought; the last time a strong mage had barged into the college, Archmage Arrick died.

Kytenia looked over her shoulder as they reached their destination. The mages at her heels readied their power. Beside her, Rune nodded.

She opened the door. "Shymin Silaron."

Across the office, a figure in white stood gazing out the

window. She did not move, save the slight twist of her head to turn an ear toward them.

Unable to keep her hands from shaking, Kytenia curled them into fists at her sides. "On behalf of King Vicamros II of the Triad, I've come to take you into custody. As punishment for your crimes against the crown, as well as your crimes against the now defunct crown of Elenhiise, you are to be imprisoned in the Royal City. Have you anything to say?"

"Nothing you've not heard before," Shymin replied quietly. "I'd heard you'd sided with them. I wish I could have made you understand."

Kytenia scoffed. "Understand what? Why you'd condone the murder of Alda'anan mages?"

"Magic could have saved my mother. It could have restored our brother's health. If magic weren't such a rarity, if it weren't weakening with every passing generation, we'd save so many lives. I never thought I'd need to explain that to you." Shymin glanced back at them. Her eyes skirted Kytenia and drifted over Rune. "So it's true. There was a way to cleanse it. That was always Envesi's mistake, you know. She became so fixated on one problem that she became blind to everything else."

Rune shook his head. "Envesi was mad. That was her problem, and there was no overcoming that."

"She was," Shymin agreed. "But she was also brilliant. Her death robs us of a great deal of knowledge and skill."

"And the deaths of Arrick and the Alda'anan mages rob us of more," Kytenia said.

"I never said I agreed with her actions. Just that I agree with her belief that magic is vital." Shymin smiled sadly. "But I know I won't convince you now. You may tell your mages to stand down. I won't fight you."

Though her sister turned to face them without wielding power and held her hands spread to show she was unarmed, Kytenia bristled. Whether or not she'd fight now was unimportant. She'd *been* fighting, pushing against Kytenia and their queen, helping tear their homeland apart.

Shymin spoke of needing magic to protect their family. Kytenia didn't even know if the rest of their family was still alive. Nearly two hundred thousand refugees had been pulled from the island. It could be weeks before someone found her family among them—or didn't. The island had been destroyed because of that magic, because of the woman Shymin chose to follow.

"Take her," Kytenia ordered. "Bind her and shield her from magic until we return to the Royal City."

Mages flowed out from behind her like water and swarmed over her sister.

Even as they tied her hands behind her back, Shymin leveled a look with Kytenia that was stubborn and defiant.

The struggle between them had only just begun.

HEROES

SPARKS ERUPTED OVER THE ROYAL CITY WITH A CRACKLING BOOM, drawing gasps of delight from the crowds in the courtyard.

Despite how many people packed the space behind the palace gates, the city's streets were worse. Wild cheers echoed from beyond the walls and, as beautiful and unusual as the fireworks were, Firal was glad she'd left Lulu with Minna in the private room they'd been assigned.

She worked her way through the throng, pressing toward the open palace doors. Nobles shifted aside to let her pass. Some lifted cups and expressed gratitude. She smiled politely in return and carried on.

There had been a time when working her way through crowds of people was jarring and exhausting. Now Firal rubbed elbows with nobles, all of them drinking and carousing as if they'd had part in what the city celebrated now, and it hardly warranted a response. It was another reminder she'd grown and changed, as the world had grown and changed around her.

Past the great hall, the palace was relatively empty. Firal sighed, grateful for the space. There were a hundred vantage points in the palace that were better, including the windows in her own room. She hadn't been eager to leave the manor again, but to refuse would have been offensive. So soon on the heels of being offered refuge and a barony, she couldn't afford to offend the king.

Given she'd spent the evening alone, it seemed not everyone shared the sentiment.

Instead of returning to her room, Firal made her way to a private suite under the direction of the serving staff. She knocked and tested the doorknob when no answer came. The door swung open with a low creak.

The room on the other side was dark enough that for a moment, she thought she would wake its occupant. Then a crimson flash lit the room. The glass door to the balcony stood open, a dark silhouette on the other side.

Firal tip-toed to the doorway as a shower of golden sparks filled the sky.

Rune sat on the balcony with his elbows on his knees, watching the lights with a distant, weary look.

"You're missing your party, hero," she teased.

He started, but relaxed when he saw her. Then he gave her a half-hearted smile and settled back into position without a word.

Firal crept forward, sat beside him and settled her skirts about her legs. After a time, she stole a glance at him. The light in his eyes was so faint it vanished when she focused on it. All the feelings of concern she'd had when they'd found him beside the ruined Gate returned. "Are you all right?"

His brow furrowed. Fine lines of distress skirted the corners of his eyes. "I don't deserve this." The boom of another mortar served as punctuation. It burst in rays of blue and crackling silver. "I don't deserve any of it."

Whatever cheer she'd tried to put on faded. She focused on the last shimmering motes in the air and waited for the next burst. "Of course you do. 'A celebration of the heroes who ended the war,' Vicamros said. You're..." Her throat tightened and she blinked faster. "Well, you're the only one here to enjoy it."

Rune bowed his head.

"Besides," she said with a small sigh, "I thought this was what you always wanted? Recognition. A chance to make a difference."

He shrugged. "I thought that. But after all this time, after everything that's happened, I'm not sure I ever knew what I wanted." He traced his namesake scar with a fingertip, then cradled his hand.

She nodded toward him. "Well, you can't tell me you didn't want that."

"I'm not so sure about that, either. All this time, I..." He trailed off, shaking his head.

"What?" Firal nudged his arm.

He smiled ruefully and searched her eyes. "All this time, have I only been six feet tall?"

The question was so unexpected that she laughed. "Is that what you're upset about?"

"I'm serious!" He stretched out his legs and leaned back against his hands as he flexed his bare feet. "All my life, I've been walking on my toes. I never even thought about it because it was normal for me. All my life, I thought I was six-foot-three."

"And I'm still only tall enough to reach your chin, so I hardly think you have room to complain!" She huffed and crossed her arms.

Rune laughed, and the warm tone of it was the most comforting thing she'd heard in weeks.

"Still," he said after a moment, watching the sky. "It's going to take some getting used to. No one ever told me shoes were so uncomfortable. And you're wrong, by the way. It's not just my party. I thought you'd be downstairs with Kytenia."

Firal rolled her eyes. "Kytenia has her hands full. She'd much rather be at the college, I think, if only to avoid the dirty looks from the Royal City's mages."

He made a small sound of agreement in his throat. "I don't blame her. I've spent enough time on their bad side, myself. It was the right decision, though. I agree with Vicamros. No one could be a better Archmage for the Grand College right now, and having Kytenia in the position will be good for relations with the evacuees."

"Perhaps, but he could have waited a few days for people to begin to settle. As it is, I think your council fears a takeover. If Aldaan is all but abandoned, settling our people there means they'll have an appointed leader at some point. And that means influence in the council." She half expected it would be her, though she wasn't sure how she felt about the idea.

Rune cocked his head, eyeing her. "Our people?"

She blinked, then flushed. "Well, it is as you said. You always were better suited to rule."

"They never would have had me," he murmured, his eyes returning to his hands. "I don't think I can blame them."

"Don't say that. It wasn't your fault."

"No, but I... I understand now." He curled his fingers into a fist. "When Envesi came to you in the throne room and I saw her, I understood. When I saw what she'd done—what she'd become —all I could feel was revulsion. Then I realized that all my life, whenever people looked at me, that was what they saw. What they felt. And then I couldn't blame you for moving on. Looking back now, I don't know how you ever tolerated being near me."

"Because I loved you." The words slipped from her mouth without a thought. She blushed. "Or I think I did."

The corners of his mouth tightened. "Did you?"

Firal hesitated, unsure what to say. She hadn't meant it to sound that way, as if she was trying to erase all their history. "I'm sorry," she said at last. Apology seemed the safest route. "All I meant was... well, I don't know how I'm supposed to feel. I was so sure of it then, when we were young. I thought I understood you, but now I feel you're a stranger, and..."

"And what you loved was the idea you had of me," he finished for her.

She swallowed and nodded. "Now I look back and I realize I don't know you. I never really did."

He half smiled, studying the shape of his fingernails. "I'm not that complicated."

"Sure you are. For example, I never knew until tonight that you're self-conscious about your height."

Rune snorted. "I'm self-conscious about a lot of things. I always hated the body I was given to live in."

"Is that why you did things like this?" She brushed one of his earrings with a fingertip.

"I suppose so. And because Envesi hated it." A hint of a defiant gleam shone in his eyes. "When I was young, I thought she would fix me if I pleased her. So I did as I was told, cooperated with her studies. When I hit adolescence, I realized she couldn't do anything or she would have done it already. I started with one. Vahn had one and I was jealous. She hated it, so I added more. One at a time."

"Vahn did not have one!"

"He did." He grinned, playing with the silver rings in his ear. "He saw it on one of the guardsmen and did it himself. His father made him take it out."

"That sounds just like Ennil," Firal muttered. The thought of the man stirred the heat of anger in her chest. Silently, she willed herself to let it go. It didn't matter anymore. Ennil was dead. "Who were you jealous of that made you get that one?" She motioned toward his chest.

Rune almost groaned. "That one was stupidity." He rubbed the ring through his shirt. "A drunken bet when serving as part of the army. I had spells of service now and then, between travel. Part of my agreement with Vicamros I. I don't even remember what the bet was, I was so drunk. I just remember how much it hurt, then waking up and discovering they'd soldered it shut so it couldn't be removed."

She clapped a hand to her mouth to stifle a laugh. "That's a terrible prank."

"Garam laughed at me for weeks. Embarrassed me to death and back." He shook his head and dropped his hand. "It's been a few years and I still haven't gotten up the nerve to go have a blacksmith cut it open."

"Well if it's been years, you might as well leave it," she teased. "Your wife might appreciate it. She could clip a rope to it and use it to lead you around."

His good humor faded and Rune looked away.

Another misstep. She cursed herself as another awkward silence fell, broken only by the occasional boom of fireworks.

"Five."

Firal blinked. "What?"

He stared straight ahead, his eyes unfocused. "Sera told me she spoke to you. She thought it was important I should know. You probably noticed she's very open. She'll discuss anything. She was the first. Then there were four more."

The words wrapped the chains of an unexpected anchor around her heart.

As if sensing it, he went on. "Some of them, I thought I could learn to love. The others, I..." He hesitated there, then shook his head. He didn't need to elaborate. "I'm not proud of that, but I did it, and I'll own those actions. The point is that five times in thirty years, I tried to replace you. But I couldn't, and some part of me knew it was wrong to even try."

"But you did," she said.

He nodded. "I did."

"And yet you scorned me for moving on after a year alone." Whether or not they'd discussed the miscommunication that kept them apart, that still stung like a fistful of nettles. Balancing that against the thought of him tumbling five other women made her sick.

"What hurt wasn't that you moved on," he replied, "but that you could. That you found someone you could connect with, and that you loved him so much that you were finally able to look me in the eye and tell me you hated me."

The uncomfortable flutter in her belly turned to a low feeling of guilt. "You shouldn't have believed me when I said that," she muttered. "I've always said things I don't mean when I'm upset."

Fireworks crackled overhead in rapid bursts of color, the finale drawing wild cheers from the mass of people below.

Instead of taking in the dazzling lights, Rune bowed his head. "I believed you when you said that because I hate me, too."

The sky went dark, suddenly more oppressive than ever. Firal shivered in the night and wrapped her arms around herself.

"I had one job," he said. "One simple thing to do, and I couldn't do it. I did everything I could to bring him back to you, and I failed."

"You can't hate yourself for that. Going after you was his choice, his idea." His chance to clear his guilty conscience. Firal fought the rise of bitterness. "He was told to bring you back. He was the one who decided to ignore that order. The only one to blame is him. The only one responsible for him being gone is him!"

Rune hushed her, leaned close and wrapped his arms around her shoulders. She choked on tears and hugged him tight.

"I'm sorry," he whispered, stroking her hair and rocking her in his arms. "I'm so sorry."

Burying her face in his chest, she cried herself dry while her heart rent itself between the purest grief and the sweet fulfillment of his embrace.

2 8

CLOSURE

THE GARDENS SURROUNDING THE MANOR HAD ALWAYS BEEN something of a refuge, but it was strange to watch someone else find solace in them. Rune tucked his chin, ever so slightly, and gazed out through the diamond-paned window. Vivenne pinched dead heads from flowers with a never-ending patience. In his absence, the plantings had largely been neglected. Rhyllyn had been occupied with other things, he supposed.

"You'll have to talk to her eventually," Alira said. He'd sensed her in the doorway, but hadn't seen any reason to address her.

"I know." He'd been surprised to learn Vahn's mother had come to the estate, given that he hadn't seen her, but he supposed he shouldn't have been. The house was plenty large enough for someone to hide, and Lulu and Firal were there. The two of them had been family to Vivenne far longer than they'd been part of his life. That she'd managed to avoid coming face to face with him made him doubt she wished to speak to him, but he couldn't imagine the alternative. It was his house. Eventually, they'd have to speak.

Alira remained in the doorway, though she said nothing else. Rune allowed the silence to drag on for some time before he

341

turned his head enough to look at her from the corner of his eye. Evidently, that was what she'd been waiting for.

She strode into the parlor and spread her hands. "I've received word from Vicamros that the first of the ruin-folk have reached Aldaan. They have chosen to travel by traditional means, rather than utilizing Gates. Apparently they feel seeing the countryside will help them choose where they shall settle."

"They won't be sent to Aldaeon?" He'd assumed that was their destination. He'd traveled the long, winding roads through the mountains himself, though not in the summertime. Perhaps there was more worth seeing—or settling for—in warmer months.

"They have been told they may join the settlement there or establish their own, but they've not yet indicated which they prefer. Personally, I anticipate they'll choose to settle closer to the mountains. Mining is all they've known for as long as most of them have lived. If there is good ore to be found in Aldaan, they'll find it."

Rune made a soft sound of agreement. Even when he'd lived among them, they'd excelled at pulling quality materials from what looked like barren rock to him. The wealth they'd pulled from the depths of Core had been a useful bargaining chip in securing food, and later, securing the alliance Ilmenhith held with the Triad. "Have they established a leader yet?"

A hint of a smirk pulled at the corner of Alira's mouth. "Why, do you seek to reclaim your title?"

"No."

"I don't doubt Vicamros would let you take it. You're a closer friend to him than kings ought to keep."

"I'm useful to him," Rune said. "I don't want to make myself too useful. He'd never let me free."

Her smirk broadened into a smile. "And you're free now?"

He stared at her for a time, then lowered his eyes. The desire to look at his hands as he mulled over that question pulled at him fiercely, but he resisted. He marveled at the change on a daily basis, but never where anyone could see. "I don't know."

"Hm." Alira paced forward until she could peer out the window.

"It seems to me there's a great deal of uncertainty in this house. Someone's going to need to fix that."

"And by someone, you mean me?"

The gleam in her blue eyes was nothing short of scheming. "Well, it is your house."

And Vivenne had been kind to him in his youth. Rune frowned, but he'd spent enough time around Alira to know when he wasn't likely to change her opinion. He stalked past her and crossed to the front door.

It was better to finish things, he told himself. Better not to let it sit and fester any longer than it must. Even with Firal, communication was terse and often tense, but it existed. Even stilted conversation was better than silence. He stepped out onto the stone stairs and allowed himself a moment to savor the fresh air. Making himself stride down the path and into the garden was more of a challenge, and he stopped at the mouth of the path that led between the roses, unsure how to proceed.

In the end, he didn't have to. Vivenne looked up and grew still.

They stared at each other in silence for a time before Rune forced himself to take another step. Grit on the stone walkway crunched under his boots, the sound and sensation still foreign enough to send an odd quiver up his spine. The sound was not unpleasant, but the lack of the earth's grounding presence under his feet would always be odd.

Slowly, Vivenne stood and curled her dirt-smudged fingers into her palms.

What was he to say? He hardly knew where to begin. That he'd shattered the Gate-stone had upended everything, caused the island to collapse and robbed her of her family and home. He swallowed hard and tried to find words. "Viv—Lady Tanrys—"

Before he could do more than start, she closed the distance between them, flung her arms around him, and buried her face in his chest. "Tell me it's worth it," she moaned, her voice thick with the tears that welled in her eyes. "Please, tell me it wasn't for nothing."

Rune wrapped her in a fierce hug and squeezed his eyes closed. His throat constricted and no words escaped.

For a long time, he simply stood and held her, fighting tears of his own while she sobbed into his chest. When she quieted, he found his voice again.

"I tried," he rasped. "The whole way out, he wouldn't go without me. He said we had to close the Gate. I thought—after everything—I tried so hard, but it wasn't enough."

Vivenne nodded. "But he knew it. He knew when he decided to go after you. He made that choice. And Ennil made his." A new flood of tears turned her eyes glassy, but she sniffed hard and wiped her eyes with the heel of her palm before they could fall. "I warned him. I told him so many times, the crown would be our downfall. He never listened."

"I'm sorry." He didn't know what else to say.

She shook her head and took a step back, though she still held to him, as if he was all that kept her moored. "No, no. It wasn't you. You can't blame yourself for the follies of others, and I was a fool too, always believing when he said it would work out. Well, it hasn't, and what am I to do now? I've nowhere to go." She sniffed again and scrubbed tears from her cheeks with the cuff of her sleeve.

Rune let her go when she withdrew, for all that he felt he should do more. But smoothing her grayed hair would have been inappropriate. The only tie between them had been his friendship with Vahn, a connection that had led her to open her home to him in his tumultuous youth—a connection that, whether she admitted it or not, had led to where they stood now. "You don't have to go anywhere. You're still family to Lulu. To Firal. You can stay here for as long as you like."

"Ah, I couldn't intrude. We all deserve a chance at family, and I've had mine. It's not fair to expect to be part of yours, too."

"Aren't you?" His brows drew together. He worried it made him look stern, rather than thoughtful or sympathetic, but he couldn't manage to smooth the lines that formed between them. "Your door was always open to me, when Vahn and I were children. I see no reason mine shouldn't be open for you now."

Though her eyes still glittered, a smile broke through her tears. She reached to pat his cheek. "Look at you. You always tried to be so hard, but your father's gentle spirit is in you. You've grown to be a good man." As quick as it had come, her smile faded. "I don't think I could bear it if you weren't."

"Thank you," he murmured. "I don't know what else I can tell you."

"Just that you won't waste the gift that's been given to you," Vivenne said.

That softened the worried furrow between his brows. "That, I can do."

Before he could say more, the sound of lively hoofbeats on the lane made both of them look up. Vivenne stepped back to put a greater distance between the two of them. She straightened her dress and smoothed her hair before the horse came into view.

"Good morning, m'lord," the courier called. He fished in his satchel and produced a letter, which he displayed overhead. "Got a summons for you from the king. You've gotten popular again, haven't you?"

"Unfortunately so," Rune called back. He strode to meet the courier a safe distance away from his garden. More than once, a curious horse had nipped off tender leaves or buds.

The courier lounged against the front horn of his saddle. "Anything exciting, this time?"

"More exciting than a pending execution?" He broke the wax seal and unfolded the letter to inspect its contents.

"Well, perhaps nothing that exciting, m'lord. Can't say I was right happy to hear about that little adventure."

Rune grunted in agreement. "Just a summons for council. He expects me there by this afternoon. At this rate, I don't know why he lets me come home."

"Eh, home's good for a man's spirit. Especially with so many visitors about." The courier waved to Vivenne, who offered a polite nod in return as she resumed her work among the flowers. "Is she another relative, m'lord?"

"Might as well be." Rune folded the summons and searched his pockets, but found nothing. He opened his mouth to ask the courier to wait for his coin when Rhyllyn came bounding down the front steps.

"G'morning, Thad," Rhyllyn said as he trotted over to meet them. He flashed his brother a grin before he held up a neatly-folded letter between two clawed fingers. "I was hoping you'd have something for us today, would you mind taking this for me? I've money for the postage here."

"Tip him for mine." Rune turned his summons for Rhyllyn to see the seal.

Rhyllyn's eyes grew round. "Ooh." He produced an extra coin from his pocket and pressed it into Thad's hand with his letter. "Are we headed back to the Royal City already?"

"The summons is for me, but you're welcome to come along."

"What about her?" Rhyllyn jerked a thumb toward Vivenne. "She's been out here every morning, can I take her along and show her the palace gardens? I mean, she's been there, but it's different when you have a tour."

Rune shrugged. "I don't see why not." He stepped back from the courier's horse and gave the young man a nod. "Thank you. No reply necessary this time."

Thad touched his forehead in a quick farewell. "As you wish, m'lord. For what it's worth, I'm glad to see you alive. And, um...

different, but we'll chat about that on a day I don't have more deliveries."

"Of course," Rune said.

Rhyllyn bounded off among the roses to speak to Vivenne, and Rune allowed himself a quiet sigh. Someday, he'd have a moment's peace.

WHEN RUNE APPEARED at the door of the king's council chamber, Vicamros smiled and waved him in. "So you did receive it. I admit I never know what to expect. Half the time, when I send a summons for you, you're nowhere to be found."

"Something that may change now," Rune said as the guards admitted him to the room. "It seems I no longer have a reason to travel so often as I did."

"Indeed," Vicamros chuckled. He motioned to the empty seat at his right side. The placement alone was enough to make Rune hesitate. More than a few councilors sent envious glares his direction. But Garam sat to the king's left, and he nodded his approval. The king was not given to commanding permanent seating arrangements. More often than not, he placed guests of honor strategically, based on the needs of each individual meeting. With that in mind, Rune could only assume his placement was meant for some sort of leverage.

When he sat, he found himself staring across the table at a familiar face. Tobias nodded in greeting.

"I would have thought you'd be traveling to Aldaan with your people," Rune said as he made himself comfortable. He'd noticed many things that simply felt different since his change, but one of his favorites was how simple it was to find a comfortable position for his feet when he sat in an ordinary chair.

"I'll join them soon. King Vicamros has promised a mage to Gate me to their camp." The smile Tobias offered was polite, but strained. "There are many facets to moving a group of people. Many new concerns."

Rune tilted his head. "Such as?"

"Illness, primarily," Garam said. "We had a few minutes to speak before you arrived."

Tobias nodded gravely. "I'd never stopped to consider the possibility, but it's already presented a challenge. Many of our people have been stricken by fever."

"For which I mean to send a handful of mages who specialize in healing," Vicamros concluded. "Which is why I've called council together today. Anything involving mages tends to upend things in the Triad, and I wish to gain other perspectives before I assign any to a post where they'll be largely unattended alongside a group of new immigrants."

"Not because the immigrants aren't trusted," Redoram added in a hurry. Rune hadn't even noticed him, off to the side as he was. "More because the chain of command among mages has been disrupted, so we have no way to monitor the mages and ensure they're treating our new settlers with the respect they deserve."

Rune laced his fingers together and rested his hands against his stomach as he reclined in his chair. "So what do you want? Recommendations for which mages should be sent?" Firal sprang to mind when it came to healers, but he selfishly pushed that idea aside. The last thing he wanted was for her to go where responsibility dictated he wouldn't be able to follow. At least, not unless he surrendered to whatever position of leadership Vicamros might cram him into that would afford an extended stay in Aldaan.

"Suggestions of which mages are unlikely to stray from their new leadership would be appreciated," Vicamros said.

"Then you should send one of the Masters from Kirban Temple." Rune shrugged. "Maybe with a few Kirban magelings as attendants. I don't think any of them have a healing affinity, but helping a population adjust to illness doesn't require more than rudimentary care."

Garam's brow furrowed. "Temple mages are the best choice? How do you figure?"

"The ruin-folk answered to the crown in Ilmenhith. So did the temple. All Kirban mages who've settled in the Grand College are already familiar with the ruin-folk and their needs, speak the same dialect, and will have a better understanding of cultural norms."

"And they all know who you are," Tobias said.

Rune nodded once. "And who I answer to."

A woman on the other side of the table huffed. Gillan spoke so rarely at meetings of council that Rune was surprised to hear anything from her at all. She peered down her beaklike nose at him. "That all sounds vaguely threatening."

Vicamros shrugged and adjusted his crown with a thumb. "I'm not against using threats to gain cooperation. The whole point of having powerful people on a council is knowing whose power to leverage in difficult situations."

"Still, I question his advice." That snively voice belonged to Survas. The man never missed an opportunity to stick his nose into affairs. "Must we remind you how many times this man has been labeled a criminal?"

"I don't know." Garam stroked his chin and leaned forward to peer past Vicamros, as if to size Rune up. "At this point, that may be an advantage. He's unpredictable and dangerous."

Rune snorted a laugh and raised a hand. "Less dangerous, now that I don't have knives for fingers."

"A curiosity that makes you more remarkable still." Tobias smiled, but cleared his throat and made himself sober as he turned the conversation back toward business. "If I may, Your Highness, I believe the suggestion of temple mages would serve my people well. It would reflect well upon the crown that our unique needs and our comfort in a strange land have been taken into consideration when allocating mages."

Vicamros scanned the faces around the table. "Any objections?"

A few councilors squirmed, but no one spoke. For how full the council chamber was, opinions seemed to be in short supply.

"Then it's done. Councilor Parthanus, can I trust you to oversee the task of selecting a temple mage to serve the new settlers in Aldaan?"

Redoram bowed his head in deference. "Of course, Your Majesty."

Survas sneered at that, too.

"If there are no other concerns, then the council is dismissed," Vicamros said.

Most of those around the table stood. Redoram hurried around the table to join Tobias and together, the two disappeared while the other councilors stretched and pushed in their chairs.

Rune stayed where he was. "If this is what most council meetings are like, you can't begrudge my absence. Summoning a dozen people from across the Triad to hold a five minute meeting isn't exactly efficient."

"Now you understand why I never moved to the countryside." Garam smirked, though he rubbed his eyes.

Vicamros waved a hand as if it didn't matter. "Please. With Gates at our disposal, it's hardly an inconvenience."

Rune wasn't so sure. His Gift had proven slower to recover than the rest of him. He tried not to dwell on it, but being able to open a Gate on his own again seemed a distant dream. When Rhyllyn returned to his studies, he'd be left to rely on the mages in Roberian's embassy. Which, he reminded himself, was not all that different than it had been. The seal on his Gift had left him crippled for so long, he didn't know why he still thought of it as a temporary inconvenience.

"Either way, you're welcome to depart now," the king continued. "If I have need of you, I will summon you again."

"Of course," Rune murmured. He offered what deference was expected of him, then retreated to the hall. He hadn't gone far before the click of Garam's cane against the stone floor announced he wasn't alone.

By now, Rhyllyn would have just gotten Vivenne into the gardens. Interrupting them so soon would have been rude. With that in mind, Rune slowed enough for his friend to catch up.

"There were a few other things you missed in council," Garam said without preamble. His skill with diplomacy was impressive, but his ability to cut straight to what was important had always been more valuable. "I thought you'd appreciate hearing them."

"Depends on what they are and how much more responsibility they heap on me." Rune smirked, though mirthlessly.

"Nothing like that. More than anything, I figured you'd be amused." Judging by Garam's expression, it was bound to be entertaining. "We received a message this morning. The Collective received our request for aid and they stand prepared to assist."

Rune couldn't help but laugh.

Garam grinned, too. "Just a little late, though I suppose we should appreciate the effort."

"Just means we have to be sure never to put the Collective in charge of anything time-sensitive." The tardiness of mages was an incredible irony, considering the immediacy of the Gates at their command. Rune ran his fingers through his hair and gave his head a shake. "I suppose we should be glad the Royal City never came under siege."

"This time. It seems like every time we have a problem, the possibility comes a bit closer."

"No city's safe forever. I never would have thought a place as isolated as Ilmenhith would be in danger, but now most of it is underwater." And even having seen it himself, Rune still didn't know what he felt. The understanding that Elenhiise had ceased to be where he belonged had not been unexpected, yet it struck him harder than it should have, given how long he'd been away.

He hadn't given himself time to sort through those feelings. Eventually, he'd have to.

Garam chuckled. "You still have to give me the rest of your life story, you know. The past little bit has been more confusing than enlightening."

"That's every day with me, I'm afraid."

"I assumed as much." The old man stopped when they reached the foot of the long ramp that spiraled through the palace. "Where to from here?"

Rune motioned toward the doors. "Rhyllyn's out looking at the flowers with Lady Tanrys. He was excited to show her the native plantings. I didn't want to interrupt them too soon."

"That boy's got a gift for making friends. I don't think he's got an enemy in the world."

"I hope it stays that way. He's a good boy." Rune clapped Garam on the shoulder. "I'll go get them. Give your wife my regards."

Garam returned the gesture. "She'll want you over for a formal dinner before long. You know she'll want the whole story straight from your mouth."

"I wouldn't dream of shorting her."

The old man withdrew with a snort and waved him off.

Rune nodded a goodbye and slipped out the palace doors.

That the main entry bore no steps or grandeur still struck him as odd, thirty years after he'd first seen it, but he'd seen enough of the world to have other structures replace the Spiral Palace on his list of most unusual. The courtyard gardens were small, and it did not take long for him to find Rhyllyn and Vivenne on a bench among the sword lilies. "I thought you wanted to see the native plantings," he called.

Rhyllyn and Vivenne both grinned at him.

"Well, we did, but then she was telling me about having these in her garden. Did you know she took care of all the plantings herself?" A light of admiration shone in the boy's eyes. "Even with a full staff at her command."

"And I helped rearrange the palace gardens, if you'll recall," Vivenne added with a dignified incline of her head. "That whole first summer you and Vahnil spent together, I sat in the gardens and transplanted flowers."

Rune slid his hands into his pockets as he came to a stop. The bench was framed by spears of lilies in every color, and every color of lily had been braided into Vivenne's graying hair. She looked older than he recalled, even from their time together earlier in the day, but a hint of light had returned to her eyes. "I remember. He kept hitting me with your stakes, trying to get me to sword fight."

"A boy's sense of propriety is always lacking, I'll agree," she laughed. "But between myself and Medreal, we managed to keep you both from knocking out anyone's teeth, and I still take that as a source of pride."

Thoughts of Medreal had been few since Rune had learned of her death, and thinking of her now faded his smile. "I would have liked to see her again. I would have liked her to meet Rhyllyn."

Vivenne patted the boy's shoulder. "I'm sure she'd be proud. I wouldn't have thought you'd ever be a good influence on anyone, but you've done a good job helping raise this lad."

The praise put a rosy color in Rhyllyn's cheeks and he turned away as if to hide his embarrassment. Instead, he straightened in his seat, like a cat that had just spotted a bird.

Rune glanced over his shoulder.

Across the courtyard, Redoram stood conversing with a handful of mages in Master white. Beside them, Tobias, Garam, and Ordin stood in a cluster of their own.

"That didn't take long," Rune murmured. "Excuse me a moment."

Vivenne waved him off and turned for Rhyllyn to add another stray lily to her hair.

Tobias saw him coming and turned to open their small circle, welcoming his inclusion. "I didn't have the chance to thank you for the suggestion of the rails."

"I was surprised to see them," Rune said as he joined the group. "I didn't think you would've had the time."

"We used timber we'd already cut. Without needing the open spaces of the ruins for agriculture, after we came under control of the crown, we'd taken to planting trees. Lumber was hard to come by on Elenhiise, but expensive to import, even with the Gates." Tobias rubbed the back of his neck. "I'm not sure wood was the best choice, but I suppose they didn't need to be permanent. Being able to load supplies, the children, and the infirm into converted wagons let us evacuate Core much faster."

"I saw the trees in Core. All around the mouth of the river, on the side of the tower." And he'd destroyed them, like he'd destroyed the rest of the island. Rune lowered his eyes. "I'm glad you were able to utilize the design so quickly."

Tobias shrugged. "We had few choices. We worked day and night to get it done, but it helped. So, thank you."

Discomfort crept beneath his collar with the praise and Rune resisted the urge to scratch. He changed the subject, instead. "I thought choosing a mage would take longer, but it looks like Redoram pulled plenty of good options." Most of the mages were familiar, too. Rikka grinned at him when he looked her way, but the mages kept their voices low. He wasn't sure he wanted to hear, anyway.

"Yes. Actually, choosing was easy. We're just waiting for one last blessing." Tobias glanced to Ordin, rather than the mages.

Rune regarded the captain with a speculative frown. "Where do you figure in? I thought you were at the manor."

"I was. Like he said, they're waiting for one last blessing." Ordin's eyes traveled toward the palace doors.

Just inside, Firal stood conversing with Temar and Vicamros.

Rune's brows rose.

"The court mages were sworn to serve the royal family,"

Ordin explained in low tones. "That oath doesn't end with the dissolution of the crown."

"And what of you?" Rune asked in a murmur.

A wistful look crossed the man's face. "To be honest, I haven't known what to do with myself. I was sworn to protect Ilmenhith and its rulers. Now she rules nothing, and Ilmenhith is gone. I told myself I was staying close out of a sense of duty. But the more time I have to myself to think, the more I realize it's because I don't know what else to do."

"Not an unusual predicament," Garam said. "You're a man of honor and responsibility. The honor means the responsibility always came first. No time for anything else, eh?"

"The way it usually is," Tobias agreed. "I understand too well, myself."

Rune tilted his head. "Have you married?"

"No. And you know my mother, so you know how much grief she's given me over it, too."

Garam flashed him a grin. "Maybe there'll be time, now that you don't have a mine to oversee."

"By the Lifetree's mercy," Tobias said, and Garam and Ordin both chuckled.

The king stepped into the courtyard. Rune was the first to press a fist to his heart and bow, but the motion was mirrored quickly by the other men, while the mages—all women —curtsied.

"It seems we've reached an arrangement," Vicamros announced. "The mage Temar will be assigned to the new settlement in Aldaan. She will select two Masters and four magelings to accompany her, and together, they will establish a new mage embassy wherever they land."

Temar stepped up beside him and inclined her head to Tobias. "I am to serve your people as a whole until a leader is established over your new settlement, upon which point I will answer to them."

Rune glanced past the king, to where Firal lingered just

inside the palace. The smile she gave him was weak, uncertain, and made his stomach turn.

"I have several Masters and a handful of mages in mind already," Temar continued. "We have only to summon them from the college. I trust the Masters who accompanied me on this visit shall be happy to carry word back with them."

"Of course," Rikka said.

Vicamros motioned for all of them to move inside. "Come, then. My mages are always ready to provide Gates. Any further details can be discussed as we venture that way."

Rune craned his neck to see into the gardens, where Rhyllyn and Vivenne still sat among the lilies. When he looked back to the palace, Firal was gone.

"It's been a pleasure to speak to you again," Tobias said, stilling the uneasy thoughts that stirred in his head. "I hope we're afforded the opportunity again soon."

"Of course," Rune replied. He was sure they would be.

One by one, the mages filed inside and disappeared into the wide hall that branched off the entryway. Temar looked back at them, as if asking who would follow. Tobias joined her, but her gaze shifted to Ordin before she turned to enter the palace again.

The captain watched after her, the wistful look back in his eyes.

Rune cleared his throat. "You said you don't know what to do with yourself. I think I may have a suggestion."

Sheepish, Ordin ducked his head. "Yes," he murmured. "I think it's about time."

29

A NEW HOME

By the time the festivities and council meetings ended and life returned to normal, the mornings and evenings had grown cool and crisp and the trees surrounding the manor had taken a golden tint.

Rune breathed deep and curled his fingers against the warm porcelain of his fine teacup. It was so smooth, and the cup's foot was so unpleasant in texture it gave him goosebumps to touch it. He avoided doing that again.

Normal itself had changed. But at least he was home, no duties or responsibilities vying for his attention, no soul-deep longing sending him across the face of the world in search of help that wouldn't come. Good smells came from the kitchen, and birds sang in the woods. The softest of breezes stirred his hair, begging him to venture farther outside, but he was barefoot, and he went no farther than the front steps.

He sipped his tea.

Rhyllyn and Minna had risen before him, which gave them the time they needed for Rhyllyn to show her around the kitchen and the rest of the estate. The boy was picky about how the kitchen was managed, but he'd been relieved when Minna announced her intention to stay at the manor. Vivenne, on the other hand, had not taken long to find somewhere else to be. When the first letter from Temar arrived, the news of orphans left by the island's collapse and the illnesses that followed evacuation had been of little surprise. Ever the nurturer, Vivenne had been quick to volunteer to relocate and look after them. In some ways, Rune figured it was what she needed—a family to look after, to raise in place of what she'd lost.

Aside from Temar, the mages had been quiet. Alira was needed in the college, to act on behalf of the council and help Kytenia establish new leadership. That meant Rhyllyn would go with her. Alira wouldn't pass up the opportunity to have him educated by more college mages. And now there were temple mages, as well.

Little footsteps thumped across the parquet flooring behind him and Rune turned his head. A little round face peered out the open door, studying him with a certain look of consternation he'd already grown used to. Small as she was, she was no taller than his shoulder when he sat down on the front stairs.

He smiled, then returned his gaze to the trees.

Lulu wasn't comfortable with him. Rune wasn't comfortable with her either, truth be told. For all that he enjoyed children, he'd never been afforded many opportunities to be near them. But the dark-haired little girl was curious, and she'd grown bolder every time they crossed paths. They'd spent a week in the Royal City before returning to the quiet countryside. Now that they lived in his house, they crossed paths more often.

The toddler crept outside, gripping her skirt in both hands. She still wobbled when she walked, all pudgy and swaybacked as she was, but she was confident. She studied his face for a time before her bright violet eyes settled on the teacup in his hands. "Sip?"

Rune raised a brow and lowered his cup. "It's hot."

Undeterred, she leaned forward and blew on his drink.

"You're a determined little thing, aren't you?" He blew on it as well, then helped her cradle the cup in both hands.

"Just like her mother." Firal stepped out, scooped the cup from their hands and replaced it with a wooden one full of water. "Don't give her that. I've seen how much sugar you put in your drinks."

Lulu drew back, held the cup on her own, and drank the water without knowing what she'd missed.

"I don't put any in my whiskey." He watched the child toddle back into the house with a faint smile. It was still unreal, seeing the girl in his home and knowing she was his flesh and blood. Knowing she belonged there.

"Well, you could stand to water it down a bit," Firal said. "You drink like a fish."

Rune's smile faded. Lulu was warming up to him. Firal, on the other hand, had been cold and distant since they'd watched the fireworks from his balcony. At first he'd thought she might forgive him. She'd seemed so comfortable in his arms. The curve of her body had fit to his and reminded him too clearly what he'd missed. Then she'd pulled away without a word and they'd barely spoken since. He didn't know what to think.

"Do you think they'll be gone long?" Firal took a sip from the teacup in her hand without thinking. She grimaced at the taste.

"Alira and Rhyllyn?" He shrugged. "A few weeks, most likely. I don't think it'll take longer than that for Kytenia to establish a firm hold on the college."

"So it'll just be us for a while, huh?"

"Until you give Vicamros the answer he's waiting for." Rune didn't like to think of her moving to a barony in Aldaan, but it was likely best if she did.

Firal folded her arms close to her chest and swirled the tea in the cup. "What happens if I go?"

He frowned at the question. It was as if she'd heard his thoughts. "You become a baroness, I suppose. You'd still have to deal with seeing me in meetings of council held in the Royal City. Until Vicamros releases me from the council, that is. Or his son does. I entered service with his father and I'm starting to think I'll be trapped as advisor to a long line of Vicamroses."

She laughed softly, the sound a sweet peal well-suited to go with the birdsong of early morning. "At least we'll have Minna here to run the house. Goodness knows it's been so long since I handled household affairs that I'd probably ruin the washing, or something like that."

"Fortunately for me, most of my clothes are off with a seamstress to be hemmed." A hint of bitterness colored his voice.

Firal giggled. "That really does bother you, doesn't it?"

"It's just strange. I spent more than a century walking around on a monster's legs. I've never even owned socks." He'd had shoes, once, so he couldn't claim that. He'd owned boots he used to disguise his nature whenever he left Core. But he'd bound his feet with linen then, stuffed padding around his claws to keep them from wearing through the leather. As uncomfortable as shoes were, they were more comfortable than that.

"Well, Minna says she'll teach me how to run a household again. She even said she'll teach me to knit, so perhaps I'll make you some." Her tone was teasing, but the wicked sparkle in her eye said she meant it.

Rune stood and took his teacup from her hand. "I don't know whether to thank you or be afraid. I've never had ten toes before. I'd prefer not to lose any to strangulation."

"No promises," Firal said. "In any case, I have a favor to ask before Rhyllyn and Alira leave."

He downed the last of his drink in a few gulps. "Of me?"

"You might be needed, yes. I know Rhyllyn's been practicing, but Gates don't seem to come as easily to him as they did you."

Rune hesitated. He'd tried little since breaking the Gate-stone, but his magic felt... different. The power was still there, but it didn't answer his call easily. It still behaved as it did before, except if the seal on his Gift was still present, he couldn't feel it. It didn't react to magic or inflict pain as punishment as it had for decades. But what he could draw felt choked, like the force of a whole river reduced to the trickle through a crack in a dam.

"I'm not sure I can do that yet," he said. "I haven't regained that much strength."

Firal nodded. "I'm not surprised. Nondar told me once that when a mage passes their limit and experiences the trauma that turns their hair white, it can take weeks for them to recover full use of their magic. Most mages exposed to the kind of power you were would have been burned out of existence."

And non-mages, as well. Rune couldn't keep the last vision of Vahn from his head. He'd said to stop. Had he known what would happen?

Rune swiped a hand through his hair. No one had said anything about the white wings that had begun to appear at his temples, but he knew everyone had noticed. "I may be able to help Rhyllyn open one. Otherwise, we may have to request aid from Roberian's mage embassy. The province's capital is a half day's ride from here. Longer by carriage, but horses don't have to stick to the main roads."

"Very well. We'll do what we must. I'll ask Rhyllyn what he thinks." Firal slipped back into the house and followed the same path to the kitchen their daughter had taken.

Their daughter. Now that was a strange thought. Rune had tried not to dwell on his role in the girl's parentage. Their shared blood couldn't compensate for the years he'd been absent from her life. Vahn had been the girl's father, not him. Rune—a man raised by a father who hadn't sired him—understood that all too well.

Yet despite his best efforts to remain unattached, that blood sparked something unfamiliar in him. A deep attachment to the girl already clawed at his heart, fueled by a driving urge to protect her. He'd promised Vahn that he would protect her, protect both of them, but he didn't know how long he could use that promise as an excuse to keep close. Already he'd found Firal in his study, borrowing a pen and ink to scribe a note to someone discussing the possibility of her barony in Aldaan. Aldaan wasn't the problem; he was welcome anywhere in the Triad. But he'd laid his roots in Roberian and the thought of abandoning his estate was unpleasant.

No, that wasn't it. He corrected himself with a shake of his head and carried his empty teacup to one of the polished wood tables in the sitting room.

It was the uncertainty that got him. If he knew Firal would accept him, he would have abandoned his home in an instant. The problem was that he didn't know. Her cool demeanor likely wouldn't change, and his promise was the only reason he had to stay near.

But his presence wasn't necessary to guarantee her safety. Politics and power gave him enough leverage to ensure her protection from Roberian. They never needed to come face to face.

Yet there was the girl, her springy dark curls reminding him so much of her mother, with his eyes staring out of her cherubic face. The thought of being apart from her tore at him, but the thought of Firal's hate for him still burned.

She denied it, but he'd seen it too clearly in her eyes.

He would not push.

The morning passed in peace. Rhyllyn scoured the house for his belongings, complaining now and then when he couldn't find the shirt he wanted or misplaced a preferred instrument during packing. Minna worked, Lulu played with any number of trinkets she likely shouldn't have touched, and Firal—well, Rune didn't know what she was doing. She'd carefully avoided crossing his path again, though he could see her in the garden through the fine glass in the diamond-paned windows.

The garden suited her. Seeing her there brought back a torrent of memories. Visions of her in Core's herb garden or sitting beneath the serpent's-tongue trees filled his head.

He didn't have any of those. The grove surrounding the manor house was scattered with clusters of tall pines and full of silver maples, elms, red buds and the occasional nut tree, but he'd never seen any serpent's-tongue. He thought of planting one near enough to be seen from the house, then dismissed the idea as quickly as it came.

No serpent's-tongue. No lotus blossoms for the pond, no aspens, and no serpent's-tongue trees. Nothing that still bore her memory.

Alira sought him when it was time to go.

"With luck, Rhyllyn will be back to you within a few weeks," she said, depositing her bag on one of the low couches and tightening its straps. "And with fortune, your company will be here to look after you until then."

Rune stifled his irritation. "Considering how long you've known me, I'd think you'd know I'm an adult and can look after myself."

"Adulthood has nothing to do with it. I'm more concerned with the fact you've been through a great deal of physical strain and are still recovering. Be mindful you don't allow him to strain himself further." Alira settled her gaze on Firal and frowned sternly. "He is an important part of the king's council, and his experience with the Alda'anan and their methods will make him vital for restoration of part of the college records and curriculum."

"He will be well kept," Firal said.

Rune groaned at being reduced to a tool once again.

"Are we ready?" Rhyllyn asked.

"Oh, yes. An afternoon jaunt sounds lovely." Minna gave Lulu's arm a jiggle, drawing a sweet laugh from the girl as they joined the group.

Rhyllyn nodded and turned to Rune.

Clearing his head and focusing on what he needed his limited strength to do, Rune met and joined power with Rhyllyn as he'd done countless times before. But instead of the rush of access to pure, undiluted magic he expected, the power crashed into him like a wave, made his head spin and yielded a curse.

Rhyllyn dropped their link in a heartbeat and seized one of Rune's arms as Firal took the other.

The world blurred around him. Rune gripped Rhyllyn's shoulder for support, shook his head and pressed the heel of his palm to his forehead when the dizziness didn't cease.

"Too much, too soon," Alira said, so cold and matter-of-fact she might have been noting the weather. "Better you see that now than later, when none of us will be here to tend you."

"I'm fine," Rune spat. "I just need a moment." The spinning eased and he waved them away.

"It's all right." Rhyllyn let go of his arm. "Alira wanted me to try it on my own anyway."

Firal gave Rune a look of concern, but he ignored it. Her duties as a healer demanded she look after him. He wouldn't let himself believe she cared beyond that.

Retreating to a chair, Rune sat and held his head while Rhyllyn worked on his own.

The boy's methods were clumsy and unpracticed, but the energy around him reacted well. It flowed and meshed, slowly growing into the hissing heat of enough pure power to split the air. Rhyllyn strained, but held fast, working until the portal opened and the zigzagging light inside spilled away to leave a clear image on the other side.

Alira picked up her bags. "It's close enough to the college. We'll walk from here so you don't have to do that again."

A grassy hill Rune would never forget waited on the other end of the Gate.

"Come along," Firal sighed, ushering Lulu and Minna through the Gate behind Alira.

Rune watched, unsure he should follow.

Rhyllyn didn't give him a choice. He shoved a bag into Rune's arms and nudged him toward the Gate.

They emerged into fresh coastal air, a saltwater tang heavy on the cool ocean breeze.

"We'll send some mages along from the college to help you

go home," Alira said. "I'll give you a moment to say goodbye, Rhyllyn, then I expect you'll catch up with me."

"Yes, ma'am," the boy said. He shifted the packs hung over both shoulders, mindful not to bang them against the lute slung across his back.

Rune's eyes drifted from Alira's back to travel up the hill.

Firal held one of Lulu's hands. Minna held the other, and they helped the girl up the hillside to the strange monument that waited at the top. A small bouquet dangled from Firal's other hand, made of flowers gathered from the garden and bound with a blue silk ribbon.

"Going with them?" Rhyllyn asked.

Rune shook his head. "I don't want to intrude. I'll wait down here." He hefted the bag in his arms and held it out. "Don't keep Alira waiting, though. You know how she gets when she's frustrated. We'll be all right for a few weeks. You need the training."

Rhyllyn planted a scaly palm against the bag and pushed it back to Rune's chest. "That's for you."

"For me?" He blinked down at it.

"I wanted to make sure you got it before I left," the boy said. "Go on, open it."

Rune cleared his throat. "All right, then." He fumbled one-handed with the clasp on the bag's flap, peeled it open and slid a hand inside with no small amount of apprehension.

Soft, smooth leather greeted his fingertips and Rune wrapped his hand around the object to pull it free.

A boot. He stifled a laugh and stared in disbelief. Finely made, the pair of them, worked by a skilled hand and obviously custom made. For not only were they the exact knee-high cavalry boots popular on Elenhiise, they were green. Bold, brilliantly rich emerald green.

"I know you needed them," Rhyllyn said, hiding a grin. "Given everything that's happened, I thought... I don't know, that you might miss the color."

The color Rune had spent his whole life trying to escape, that had shaped him and his life the way a hammer and anvil shaped steel.

Rune clapped an arm around Rhyllyn's shoulders, held his brother in a warm embrace and laughed until tears rolled down his face.

30

NEW DREAMS

Autumn crept deeper into the air. Fiery hues lit the grove around the manor and chrysanthemums sprinkled through the garden offered bright bursts of color. Firal spent most of her time in the garden, as Rune expected she might. When she wasn't there, she played with Lulu in the parlor or helped Minna in the kitchen, but every evening, she closed herself in the library.

Correspondence from Vicamros came at regular intervals and she was always ready. She penned responses and sent them back, then shut herself up with Rune's books and papers and pens. She kept a volume full of notes on his desk and left it within easy reach, but he hadn't opened it. He didn't need to. He already knew what the letters said.

So Rune worked, distracting himself with things to do around the estate. He visited tenants on his lands and collected rents, sorted documents and filled ledgers with numbers, and sometimes ventured to the Royal City for council meetings in hopes they'd keep out thoughts of anything else.

Lulu interrupted him from time to time, seeking attention he was more than happy to give. The girl warmed to him with time and drove the knife of sadness into his heart a little deeper every day.

It was late in the second week after Rhyllyn's departure that an opening Gate needled at the edge of Rune's awareness, stole his attention away from the food on his plate and made him turn toward the door.

Firal felt it too. She looked up with a quiet frown. Though the timing appeared to displease her, the visit right in the middle of the evening meal, she didn't appear surprised. A bad sign.

"Something the matter, my lady?" Minna asked.

"No," Firal said as she pushed herself up from the table. "Just a guest, it seems."

Rune left the table first and made his way to the door.

It opened before he got there and Rhyllyn slipped inside.

"Back so soon?" Rune greeted him with a hug, though his eyes narrowed. Rhyllyn didn't carry a bag. He wasn't staying.

"Just for a visit," Rhyllyn said with a half smile. "We've brought news."

Rune knew Alira was with him; he felt her presence just beyond the door. But there was a second presence, too, and it bore an odd, muddied feeling.

"I smell food. Did Minna make soup? I'm starving." Rhyllyn took Rune's arm, pulled him toward the kitchen, and frowned when he resisted.

"Rhyllyn! What in the world are you doing back so soon?" Firal hurried around the corner to greet the lad, who accepted her hug with a sheepish grin.

"I'm not here for long," Rhyllyn said. "I was supposed to bring a message. Stal sent word to the Grand College this morning. Their seventh child was born and Sera is in good health. It's a boy. His name is Eben."

"That's wonderful." A genuine warmth colored Firal's voice. "Though I can't imagine having seven!"

"Well, they are mages." Rhyllyn grinned. "It's probably easier when they're all born seven or eight years apart. Anyway, I was told in no uncertain terms that this time, weapons are not a suitable gift for a newborn child."

"Then he'll get a horse or something," Rune said tersely. He pushed past them and cut toward the door again.

Firal followed and caught his arm. "What's wrong with you?"

Before Rune could reply, a ghost stepped through his door.

A small woman—shorter than Alira by half a head, and clad in green silk trimmed with tawny fur—strode to the center of the parlor. Her tall and slender ears rose above her head in twisted points. A dozen golden rings pierced either one and chains connected the loops in a cascade of jewels suspended over her head. Her gray hair was drawn into a stern bun at the nape of her neck and her mouth held a serious set, but her dark brown eyes glowed with an inner warmth.

"I remember you," Rune said, his brow furrowing. It hardly seemed possible. He'd searched the world for the Alda'anan and turned up empty-handed for so many years, he'd lost hope.

"I hoped you would, boy." She glided into the foyer and Alira closed the door behind them.

"I looked for you. I looked everywhere. I traveled the world, all the way to the Chains—"

"I know, boy. And the harder you looked, the harder I had to hide." She took his elbow and gently turned him toward the sitting room. "Come, sit. We'll speak."

Too dumbfounded to form words, Rune followed.

Firal and Alira trailed at his heels, while Rhyllyn vanished down the hall in pursuit of Minna's cooking.

"Firal," Alira said as Rune and the small woman sat, "this is Indral. I believe you may wish to hear what she has to say, too."

Wordlessly, Firal took a place beside Rune and touched his arm. He felt it, yet couldn't respond.

For thirty years, he'd scoured the face of the world in search of her or any of the other Alda'anan, desperate for the help they'd promised. Now he didn't need it, and one appeared at his doorstep within weeks. The absurdity made him want to laugh, but the frustration of decades of hardship seethed atop the swell of relief, and all he could do was let his mouth work without producing words.

"I know," Indral said again, soothing. "Believe me when I say it wasn't supposed to be this way. So many things we meant to tell you, but how could we? Every time one of us ventured from hiding, they were struck down. We could not reveal ourselves, not even to you. It was tried more than once, and each time, it failed. Our numbers were already so precious few."

"You're Medreal's sister," Firal said. "Aren't you?"

Rune's mouth fell open. He'd thought the woman familiar when they first met, all those years ago in Aldaeon. But he'd never placed her, for all that her features haunted him. He should have known.

Indral straightened and puffed up like a preening bird. "All Alda'anan are related, in a way, but yes. We shared the same parents."

Firal offered a shy smile. "You look a great deal like she did, though she had her ears docked to help her hide. It was your Gift that gave it away, though. The two of you feel just the same."

"Ah, yes. A skill most Alda'anan develop. If we could not hide our strength, we could never blend in. We tried to teach this one, but he never did learn." The old woman smirked at Rune. "It seems he won't need my teachings now, though."

"What are you doing here?" Rune asked, his tongue finally cooperating.

"I felt what happened. The surge of power and the collapse of the earth when the island fell into the sea. I feared the worst. I came in hopes of finding the boy, your brother, Rhyllyn. I was sure you were dead." A sarcastic smile twisted the corners of her mouth now, a cruel spark in her eyes. "It seems you've found a worse fate."

His mouth dried, making words that much harder. "What do you mean?"

Indral leaned back in her seat and studied him. "You're weak.

You will recover some strength in time, but it will never compare to what you had. A gift in its own right, I suppose. When you plug a lamp and add no more fuel, it can only burn so long as the oil lasts. And you, for all intents and purposes, are plugged."

"Then remove the seal on my magic. You never should have put it there to begin with."

The old mage's eyes hardened. "It was there to teach you a lesson, boy. With the war creeping closer to us, we had no choice but to leave. Your lessons were not yet complete. You didn't understand our ways, our thinking. The seal was our only way to teach you from afar. And the seal is gone, boy. It unraveled the moment you struck that stone."

Gone. The absence of pain when he worked magic made sense now, but if it wasn't the seal that prevented him from wielding his Gift to its full potential...

"Now you understand," Indral chuckled as his face fell. "You're an empty lamp. You can light the wick, but it won't stay lit. Magic will answer you for small things. But power?" She shook her head. "I'm sorry, child. Your Gift is gone."

A cold uncertainty slithered down his spine and his tongue stuck to the roof of his mouth. He needed water. There were no pitchers in the sitting room. Instead, he swallowed hard and sucked on his teeth in effort to moisten his mouth. "But without magic..."

"Without a Gift, boy. Magic will never leave you. It will nurture you as you age. But you will age, and you will die. Like a bound mage, who just brushes the might of the world. It will carry you along, extend you farther than you might reach on your own, but every pen without a well shall run out of ink eventually. Your lifeline will be long. But it will end."

Firal's hand tightened on his arm. Rune closed his eyes.

"It's not a bad end, child." Indral softened her voice to the soothing tone she'd used earlier. "Many of my elders chose it for themselves, asked others to help them burn. We who are born of magic, we do not age like others. I appear old, yes, but you cannot fathom my age. I walked the earth when the world was young, when the moons Ithi and Ileara were new in the sky. I saw the growth of the first forests, the rise of man. I am weary. But my job is not yet done."

"You said you came for Rhyllyn," Rune said. Firal reached for his hand and he laced his fingers with hers out of reflex. It granted him some comfort, yet not nearly enough. "Did you mean to cleanse his power?"

Indral sighed and her shoulders sagged. "I cannot. In truth, none of us could. Not even together, when there were more of us. The shadow that sullied your power and still colors his was beyond us. But to tell you that then would have robbed you of hope. And you had so much left to accomplish."

"How many of you are left?" Despite the easy way she perched on the couch, he knew she wouldn't stay long. So many questions brimmed on his tongue. He needed to choose from them wisely.

"I am the last." With that, Indral's face fell. Even her slender ears seemed to droop, the jeweled chains between them pulling taut. Then she recovered and sat upright once more. "We sought refuge in small groups, but she found us. We were honest with her, told her we couldn't correct the filth that marred her body and power. It was then we decided to seek you, to send someone to remove the seal we'd placed so you could finish what we could not. I felt the world change as each of my brethren died. But what could we do?" She spread her hands and gave a helpless shrug. "You know our laws. We were allowed to stay, to guide, but never to act."

And then she'd thought him dead. "What would you have done with Rhyllyn?"

"Taken him away, taught him what I could and hoped he could take your role. He is not you. He doesn't have the force of the world on his side. But he is strong, and with time, he could have stood against her."

"Does he know you can't cleanse his power?"

Indral nodded. "We discussed it when I arrived at the college and learned what had happened. He is a good child. He insisted he didn't want to change back anyway. It seems he enjoys his new form."

Rune let out a weak laugh. "He would." Rhyllyn always had been that way, seeing rainbows when anyone else only saw the rain.

"The boy and I spoke at length," she continued. "I wish to teach him the ways of the Alda'anan, as we hoped to teach you. He has agreed to travel with me for half of each year, living in the lands beyond the Chains and learning all I can offer."

"Beyond the Chains?" Firal sounded skeptical. "There's nothing past the Chains of Raeldan."

A small twinkle lit the old mage's eye. "Nothing a ship can reach, but it's there. I am sure the boy will tell you all about it when he returns."

"I'm sure," Rune said dryly as the conversation circled back to the very beginning, all her explanations falling short of the answer he wanted. "But why are you here?"

Indral lifted her chin and her mouth took a stern set once more. She folded her hands in her lap. "Because there is another. And so long as she lives and bears the burden of free magic, she will need a mentor."

Firal's hand tightened on his. Rune squeezed back.

"I am not here to take her from you," the woman said. "She is so young, so desperately in need of her parents. But she and the boy are the face of the new generation of the Alda'anan. Their children may inherit the Gift, and they must know our ways, or we will face this calamity all over again. Only this time, there will be none like you to act on our behalf."

"So you will take her from me," Firal said, blinking hard. "Not now, but you will."

"Were there more of us, we could bind her power and free her of these troubles. But I am alone, and alone, I can do nothing." Indral pressed her palms together, steepled her fingers, and shifted in her seat. "She will need guidance as she grows. So I suggest what I've suggested for the boy. When she reaches an age where she can understand, I will take half the year, every year, until she knows all I can teach her. You may come with her if you desire. But there is no other solution. Without control, she is dangerous. Without our ways, she is chaos."

Firal started to speak but Rune lifted a hand, silencing her. "Once every pent. The years between, Rhyllyn will teach her while he is here. If he cannot convey the ways of the Alda'anan by the time she's old enough to learn them, then you're not fit to teach anyone."

Indral's eyebrows shot up her forehead. She stared at him in what seemed disbelief, then a smile wreathed across her weathered face. "Fair enough, boy. I suppose you speak the truth."

Beside him, Firal slumped in relief.

"I have to," Rune said with a wry smirk. "I have silver in my tongue."

Indral slapped her leg and crowed with laughter.

Despite himself, Rune laughed too.

<hr>

THE COURIER ARRIVED the morning the first snow fell, bearing a letter sealed with the official crest Vicamros only used when dealing with matters of the crown.

Rune had spent weeks steeling himself for what was to come, but his heart still sank to his toes when he saw it. He carried the letter through the house, regretting with every step that he hadn't done more. But Firal was consumed with her own affairs. She struggled through her grief by herself and avoided him in the hallways and kitchen, only sharing his company for meals and occasional playtimes with Lulu.

She sat in the library now, using his favorite pen to write a letter to one of the many people in Aldaan she'd been corresponding with since her arrival. Rune lingered in the doorway and watched her write until she put the pen aside and sat back to rub her eyes.

He tapped the letter against the door frame and she looked up in surprise.

Rune turned the letter so she could see the seal. "Were you going to tell me?"

Firal pushed back her chair and slowly rose. "Did you read that?"

"I didn't have to." His chest constricted and he crossed his arms. "It wasn't hard to figure it out."

Rosy color blossomed in her cheeks. She bowed her head. "I'm sorry. I know we should have spoken sooner, but with everything—between the refugees and the letters from merchants, Indral's visit and everything else—I just didn't know how to bring it up. But I suppose it's time, isn't it."

Rune held out the letter. She took it from his fingertips and it felt for all the world like she took his heart with it, leaving him empty inside.

She cradled the letter to her chest. "I've spent so much time agonizing over what was the right thing to do. I never wanted to be a leader, but the world had other plans. I always hoped I made a good impression, that I did what was right for my people. And this is best. I know it's quick, and I'm sure it'll be frowned upon, but it is what's best. I'm so sure of it now."

He nodded, his brows crumpled with emotion, and stepped backwards into the hall.

Firal straightened. "What's wrong?"

"Nothing," he replied, though his voice was hoarse. "You're right. It's best for you, best for your people. They need this."

"And that upsets you?"

"No," he lied. "Vicamros was right to choose you for Aldaan."

She stared at him for a long time. "For Aldaan?"

"Elenhiise thrived beneath you. I'm sure you'll make a fine baroness, as well."

Her brow furrowed. "What in the world are you talking about?"

"I've seen the correspondence, Firal. I've seen the messages going back and forth, the names of the people you're writing to, and then Vicamros sends something with his crest? The least you could have done was told me you made your decision."

"You just said you knew! I thought…" She trailed off and her eyes widened. "You thought I was leaving?"

His heart skipped a beat.

Her shoulders bunched up and her hands curled into fists. "You did, didn't you? After all I've done, all the hours I've spent writing orders and letters and telling Tobias everything he needs to know if he's to lead—"

"Tobias!" Rune cried.

Firal threw up her hands. "What in the world did you think I was doing? Didn't you read anything I left in that logbook? I wrote to Vicamros to tell him I couldn't accept his offer. I recommended Tobias take it. This letter is to formally retract the offer of the barony, acknowledging that I've relinquished my claim on the people of Elenhiise. Vicamros is granting me citizenship of Roberian. With you, you blighted fool!"

He stared back, unable to speak.

She let out a long, hissing sigh of frustration. "Is that why you've been sulking about and avoiding me? If I'd known…"

"I haven't been avoiding you," he protested. "You've barely spoken to me, I thought—"

"That I'd just leave, after everything you've put me through? After all that's happened, everything we've done, everything we've lost, I'd walk away?"

"I wasn't going to make you choose."

"It was you," Firal said, tears filling her eyes. "It was always you."

Rune drew back a step. "But it wasn't. You don't have to lie.

If we'd come together a year ago, under different circumstances, it wouldn't have been me. You wouldn't have left him for me. I never would have expected you to."

"Which is why it was you." She moved closer. "Because you made it my choice. You've never taken that from me, never pushed me to do anything. It was always my choice. When you asked me to be healer in Core, when you asked me to marry you. Vahn took that from me."

Tears tumbled over her lashes and he reached out to brush them away before he could stop himself. Her face was so soft, so warm. Cradling her face in his hands, Rune drew the pads of his thumbs over her cheeks.

"He had your letter," Firal choked. "He knew you lived. And he knew I would have gone back to you if I'd had the chance then. So he hid it from me, hid that he ever knew until the morning he left to try and save you. And it hurts, because I loved him. But everything we had was built on a foundation of control."

Rune wrapped his arms around her. "I'm sorry," he faltered. It was the only thing that seemed right to say.

"Just tell me I've not made a mistake," she moaned, hugging him tight and gulping against sobs. "Tell me you'll forgive me, that you can learn to love me again."

"Oh, Firal." He kissed the top of her head and squeezed his eyes closed. "I never stopped."

"Well, that's likely best," Minna chimed in from behind them. She stood in the hall with a bundle of linens in her arms. "According to our laws, the two of you are still married."

Firal choked back a laugh and hid her burning face in his chest.

***

THERE WAS no ceremony to reunite them, no celebration shared with family—just long winter nights filled with cautious conversation to mend what had been left in tatters. After all that had transpired, the last thing Rune wanted to do was rush. When spring came and new leaves covered the trees, they simply donned their old rings again, Firal's tempered larger, Rune's cut smaller, the scars on their hearts all that remained to show they'd ever been apart.

Sunlight spilled across the room and drew Rune from the depths of sleep. He opened one eye and nestled closer to the warm body that shared his bed. He buried his face in her ebony hair, breathed deep, and cradled her close. His breath escaped as a long and quiet sigh.

"Hmm?" Firal curved her back against his form and stroked his smooth forearm with gentle fingertips.

"I thought I was waking from a dream," he murmured.

"Was it a bad dream?" She turned her head to look at him and caressed his face with one hand.

He studied the way the light fell across her face and reached to tuck a curl behind her ear, pausing when the sunlight glittered on the slim golden band that adorned his finger. "No," he said.

The warmth in her eyes was matched by her smile and her tender touch. The feeling was contagious, and he smiled too as he traced the shape of her brows.

He leaned forward, pressed a tender kiss to her lips and felt his heart swell. "It wasn't a dream at all."

GLOSSARY

Affinity – One's natural inclination in magic. There are five major affinities: Earth, water, fire, wind, and life. These provide the primary source of power a mage can draw from and manipulate. While there are smaller subcategories affinities may fall into, granting specific talents in narrow fields, they are generally related to one of the five and, as result, only the five major affinities are recognized.

Aldaan – One of three provinces in the Triad.

Aldaanan *or* **Alda'anan** – A faction of free mages.

Alira – (*uh-LEER-ah*) – Former Master of the House of Fire, now part of the Triad's council. Rhyllyn's adoptive mother.

Alwhen – (*OWL-when*) – The capital of the eastern half of Elenhiise island, a region known as the Giftless Lands.

Anaide – (*uh-NAYD*) – Master of the House of Water.

Archmage – The leader of Kirban Temple, generally recognized as the leader of all mages.

Arrick Ortath – Headmaster and Archmage of the Grand College of Lore.

Balen – (*BAY-len*) – Master of the House of Fire.

Core – An underground city beneath the ruins, home of the Underlings.

Daemon – (*DAY-mun*) – Rune's previous name.

Davan - An officer among the Underlings. Was left in charge after Daemon's disappearance.

Edagan – (*ED-ah-gan*) – Master of the House of Earth.

Eldani – (*ell-DAN-ee*) – The only inhabitants of Ithilear who are known to be Gifted. Eldani are long-lived, due to their magic, and differ from humans only in their pointed ears. Diluted bloodlines are recognized by the reduced point of an Eldani's ear, which directly corresponds with their prowess as a mage.

Elenhiise – (*ELL-en-heese*) – A small island in the middle of the Lantaaran sea, generally used as a waypoint in trade between the region's northern and southern continents. The island is ruled by two factions, the Gifted Eldani and Giftless men.

Ennil – (*in-ill*) – Full name Ennil Tanrys. Former Captain of the Guard of Ilmenhith. Vahn's father.

Envesi – (*in-VESS-see*) – The former Archmage of Kirban Temple. Corrupted by her own power after granting herself free magic.

Eyrion Tolmarni – (*EAR-ee-on toll-MAR-nee*) – Previous Headmaster of the Grand College of Lore.

Filadiel – (*fil-LAD-ee-ell*) – Leader of the Aldaanan mages.

Firal – (*fur-ALL*) – Queen of Ilmenhith and the Eldani half of Elenhiise Island. Former green-rank mageling of Kirban Temple.

Flows – The natural ebb and flow of magic, which mages are able to seize and manipulate.

Garam – Full name Garam Kaith. Former Captain of the Royal City Guard, now part of the Triad's council. Sera's brother.

Gift – The ability to use magic.

House – A subsection of mages, ruled by a particular affinity. Mages within the House of Healing, Fire, etc. may take classes together, but their education is overseen by the Master of their House.

Ileara – (*ill-ee-ARE-ah*) – The second moon. The smaller of the two, Ileara is known as The Mother and is stationary in the sky. As it is only visible in the far western regions of the known world, such as the Westkings and the Chains of Raeldan, some residents of Elenhiise and the other eastern regions do not believe Ileara exists.

Ilmenhith – (*ill-men-HITH*) – The capital of the western half of Elenhiise island, which is under Eldani control.

Ithi – (*ith-EE*) – The first moon. The larger of the two, Ithi is known as The Soldier and circles Ithilear once per day. The thirteen months of the year are framed around Ithi's phases; its cycle is 28 days.

Ithilear – (*ith-ILL-ee-arr*) – The world. The name is derived from the two moons, Ithi and Ileara. In folklore, the moons are lovers. Ithi ventures forth to patrol and protect their child, Ithilear, while Ileara remains in one place to provide a stable home.

Kifel – (*kiff-EL*) – Full name Kifelethelas Penedhionn. The former Eldani king and ruler of the western half of Elenhiise island.

Kirban Temple – (*KER-ban*) – Founded by Archmage Envesi, Kirban Temple is the only school of magecraft on Elenhiise Island. A prestigious college sponsored by the Eldani crown and located near the southern edge of the ruins.

Kytenia – (*kit-teen-yah*) – Archmage of Kirban Temple and Firal's best friend.

Lore - One of three provinces in the Triad.

Lumia – (*loo-MEE-ah*) – Former Queen of the Underlings.

Lulu – Firal and Rune's daughter.

Mageling – A mage in training. Magelings are divided into five ranks before they graduate to Master and wear robes in corresponding colors. The five ranks are gray, lavender, yellow, green, and blue.

Marreli – (*mah-RELL-ee*) – A gray-rank mageling at Kirban Temple. Was one of Firal's friends.

Master – A mage recognized as skilled enough to wield magic without supervision. Masters outside the temple act as healers and scholars, and are in charge of scouting Gifted children to send for training. Masters who remain within the temple are generally teachers. Master mages are the only mages allowed to wear white. Court Masters and Masters of an affinity mark their eyes with black ink to distinguish their rank.

Medreal – (*mee-dree-al*) – Queen Firal's stewardess.

Melora – (*mel-LOR-ah*) – Deceased Master of the House of Wind.

Minna - An Underling woman who befriended Firal.

Nondar – (*non-DAR*) – Previously the Master of the House of Healing, later Archmage of Kirban Temple. Nondar was one of few recognized half-Eldani Masters and is unparalleled as a medic.

Ordin Straes – (*ore-DEN strays*) – Captain of Ilmenhith's guard.

Ran – Full name Lomithrandel. Another name for Rune.

Redoram – (*RED-or-AM*) – Full name Redoram Parthanus. Councilor in the Triad's Royal City.

Relythes – (*rell-uh-THEEZ*) – The Giftless King, ruler of Alwhen and the eastern half of Elenhiise island.

Rhyllyn – (*rill-in*) – Rune's adoptive brother. Like Rune, his physical body has been corrupted by wild magic, a change brought about by Envesi.

Ria – A gryphon messenger and amateur cartographer. Rune's friend. Now deceased.

Rikka – (*RIK-kuh*) – Master of the House of Wind in Kirban Temple. One of Firal's friends.

Roberian – One of three provinces in the Triad.

Royal City – The capital of the Triad.

Ruins – A sprawling labyrinth in the center of the island. The ruins fall entirely on Eldani lands.

Rune - A free mage whose physical body is corrupted by his tainted magic. Previously the leader of the Underling faction on Elenhiise, now a soldier under King Vicamros II and part of the Triad's council.

Sera – Full name Sera Kaith. A mage in the Royal City and a scout for the guard. Garam's sister.

Shymin – (*SHY-min*) – Master of the House of Healing in Kirban Temple. One of Firal's friends and Kytenia's elder sister.

Stal – Archmage of the Umdal Collective. Sera's husband.

Temar – (*tim-MAR*) – Leader of Ilmenhith's court mages.

Tobias – Current leader of the Underlings.

Tren – Full name Tren Achos. Was Lumia's general.

Triad – An empire in the north, composed of three provinces—Aldaan, Lore, and Roberian—and ruled by King Vicamros II.

Underlings – Giftless people driven into the ruins by war, rumored to be monsters and believed to be legend.

Vahn – Full name Vahnil Tanrys. King of Elenhiise and husband to Firal.

Vicamros II – (*vi-CAM-rows*) – King of the Triad.

Vivenne – (*viv-INN*) – Full name Vivenne Tanrys. Vahn's mother. Ennil's wife.